Ever since Rosy Hope got her first job on a local newspaper, people had been asking her, 'So when will you make it to Fleet Street?'

Well now she had – or thereabouts.

Rosy had spent the day in the terrifying purgatory that was a casual shift in the news-room of the *Daily Dispatch*. The news editor and his battle-hardened henchmen knew how to make dog meat of aspiring young reporters like her. They had had enough practice.

At any moment, she just KNEW she was on the point of being dispatched to any one of a dozen unpleasant towns to talk to grieving relatives and friends after accidents, murders, fires and freak storms. Every time she passed the news-desk and felt some man there noticing her, she was convinced it could only be a matter of time before she was flung out into the vast traumatised hinterland to find someone called Evans in Ebbw Vale or a sad Patel in Bradford, and she would miss her appointment with Anthony Sword.

But then, when she began to think there was a chance she might be able to make it after all, came the ache of another kind of uncertainty... why on earth did the famous gossip columnist want to see her anyway?

Deborah Lawrenson is 33, married and lives in Kent. She worked as a staff reporter on Nigel Dempster's column at the *Daily Mail* for three years and as his deputy editor on the *Mail on Sunday* for two years. She is a Cambridge graduate and has also worked for *Woman's Journal* as editor of the London section and occasional feature writer.

Hot Gossip

Deborah Lawrenson

HOT
GOSSIP

Mandarin

To Nigel, Adam, Janet, Helen and Alan,
with much affection
– they know what a
ludicrous invention this story is.

A Mandarin Paperback
HOT GOSSIP

First published in Great Britain 1994
This edition published 1996
by Mandarin Paperbacks
an imprint of Reed International Books Ltd
Michelin House, 81 Fulham Road, London SW3 6RB
and Auckland, Melbourne, Singapore and Toronto

ISBN 0 7493 2400 7

Phototypeset by Intype, London
Printed and bound by
Cox & Wyman Ltd, Reading, UK

1 3 5 7 9 10 8 6 4 2

1 | *The Gossip Columnist*

Anthony Sword went to all the best places in London. Wherever he turned up – and on any one evening he could take his pick of champagne cocktails, first-night parties and at least four tempting dinners – people danced around him hoping to catch his eye.

There were times when it seemed as if few people in London had a good word to say about Anthony Sword, yet still they whined and whispered in his ear. There were even fewer people about whom Anthony Sword ever had a pleasant word, but then that, of course, was what made his gossip column in the *Daily Dispatch* such compulsive reading.

Some people clamoured, embarrassingly, to talk to him, but his keenest followers knew, from years of assiduous observation, that that was not the way forward. They played a game of skill and cunning with the man – or so they thought.

'Have you SEEN the Sword column this morning?' the Earl of Trent would squeal at one of his titled clients.

'I never read it on principle, my dear. And you can't BELIEVE what he said about Minda on Monday,' Lady X would shriek back.

'Oh, I CAN, darling, she got me to tell him. . . .'

*

Anthony Sword revelled in his reputation as the country's premier mischief-maker, the champion of the common chatterer. His column was one of the reasons – and Sword would claim it was the only reason – that nearly two million people bought the mid-market *Daily Dispatch* every morning and passed it on to another eager four point six million over their ABCI muesli and wholemeal breakfasts.

For if the popularity of Anthony Sword's column was anything to go by, the so-called classless society could not imagine a more barren existence than being consigned to the Society-less classes. And even if Sword himself occasionally found the activities of his rich and famous subjects less than compelling, a lull in his breathless reportage of the Princess of Wales' new circle of friends, say, or the Earl of Trent's serial disasters would prompt disgruntled calls to the newspaper from friends and enemies and all those who felt they were missing out.

Most people thought that Sword survived as a gossip columnist – when even this generic name seemed impossibly redolent of bygones such as Cassandra and William Hickey – because he had become a British institution, providing vicarious pleasure in parties and partings, pride before falls, and all the dramatic minutiae of social life in much the same way as a well-loved soap opera.

There were even some who would still argue that Anthony Sword was a merciless satirist, although his send-ups of the rich at play had been sustained so accurately and for so long, that it seemed now that Sword had become a satire of himself, in the same way as Dame Barbara Cartland was a satire of an elderly pink-and-powdered romantic novelist or the National Theatre bunker on the South Bank was a satire of a terrible building. By now even the most dedicated revisionists had given up hope that Sword might throw off his cloak of artifice and announce some Marxist sympathy to their advantage.

Simply, he was what people chose to make of him; his success was based on a pact of mutual wish-fulfilment.

In fact, Anthony Sword was a man whose time had come. Worthier newspapers sneered at him but this was largely a self-protective measure before they repeated his juiciest scoops. Pages were loaded daily with the names of characters that for years had been the staples of his column, that he had built up and given identities which could be summoned up instantly by one pithy parenthesis. Even the *Independent* newspaper, a publication which Sword privately held in the greatest esteem for its inspiring food pages on a Saturday, had defied its own ban and begun to sprout articles about the Royal Family and their special friends.

Amid all this, it was Anthony Sword's opinion that was sought first on any television or radio programme where social pontification was required, his pronouncement on any character or custom which was generally taken as the last word, and no article on the Season was complete without a contemptuous quote from him.

His name was spoken with equal measures of disdain and awe, yet his tales were received every morning at the country's most imposing addresses.

His stories went with others on their commuter trains from Orpington and Guildford, Beaconsfield and Audley End, and even, days later, after his Secrets had spread a little light of inside knowledge into even the dingiest of lives, his stories could still perk up the lot of those dropping vegetable peelings on to the paper,

3

say, or reaching for the last soggy morsel from their fish and chip wrapping. There was something, Anthony Sword felt, that was profoundly democratic about that, and perhaps it was the part that pleased him most.

At the top of the Sword's Secrets page was the largest picture by-line in the newspaper. It showed Sword wearing his characteristic piratical grin: his fleshy lips smacking in anticipation through the dark round beard, his uneven nose, his bull neck set straight on shoulders that hinted at a massive unseen bulk, and his eyes flashing with alert contempt. Those eyes, it was said, drew out confidences like cork eased from vintage claret – reverently, oh-so carefully, wiggled a fraction, then yanked to the point of no return.

It was the picture of an unmarried man in the prime of life; a bon vivant, elegant but excessive and uncontainable; a masticating menace, huge in appetite, in friendship and in enmity. It was exactly what Sword wanted, the expression intimating the perfect degree of confidence and world-weariness.

And what Sword wanted, he usually got.

For twenty-odd years, Anthony Sword had blabbed about other people's business. It had made him as famous and as wealthy as those he wrote about.

What was clear to everyone who read the column, and even to those who were in a position to find the rotund inquisitor on their social round, was that Anthony Sword was a man of distinction.

He was elegant and charming, far more so – when he was being nice – than the uninitiated ever expected.

He was a gourmet and connoisseur of fine wines. Indeed, he had once earned a crust as a restaurant critic.

He let it be known that he was a passionate lover of

4

the opera, and that he read poetry with a particular devotion to Keats at his most lush and overblown.

He lived, alone, in a Gothic folly on a private road of spitting gravel in Highgate.

He was a member of Boodles and the Beefsteak, the RAC and the Poodlefakers, but he was not a dedicated club man. To belong was enough.

Beyond that, not much was known publicly about Anthony Sword, which was exactly the way he wanted it. The question those who worked closest to him on the column were constantly asked was, 'So what is HE like?', and they would answer that Anthony Sword was irascible and touchy, that he could drink two bottles of claret in an afternoon, but he was also fiendishly amusing when he was in the mood, and you had to admire him, and – really – he could be very kind. But beyond the known facts about Sword, there was little they could add.

For just as Anthony Sword had taken to proclaiming, half in jest, half in operatic fury, when he was crossed by the subjects of his stories, 'Who are these people? Nobodies all until I wrote about them.... I have INVENTED them!', so Anthony Sword was a self-invented man who did not blab about himself.

On one evening each week he would take a break from his professional party round.

He would snatch his dark raincoat – the only day of the week he wore it – from the coat-stand in his office and exit purposefully from the *Daily Dispatch* building.

For, as every publicity-minded hostess in London knew, Anthony Sword never accepted invitations for Tuesdays, although his housekeeper could vouch for the fact that he was never at home on that evening.

Not even his immediate colleagues knew where he went.

They knew better than to ask.

2 | *Swigging with Sword*

On this particular Tuesday evening, the gossip columnist picked up his raincoat as usual and hurried out of the side entrance of the *Daily Dispatch*. He turned his broad back to the rush-hour traffic on the Embankment and swaggered up a sooty side street in the direction of Fleet Street.

Or rather, what used to be Fleet Street as Anthony Sword knew it.

He stopped at a discreet entrance to the Scribblers Club and descended the stairs. It was still early.

The basement bar annexe of the *Daily Dispatch* kept a gratifyingly large picture of him on the wall. It was an action shot, taken in the days when all the Street's great newspapers were represented at the bar. By reflex instinct, an off-duty sports photographer had captured the moment the table he had been standing on collapsed under the weight of his Pavarotti impersonation, a light exploded, a row of bottles blew, and a board of cheese and grapes went flying. The effect, as snapped for posterity, had been the kind of classically artistic mess found in the aftermath of the last days of Pompeii.

Sword made for what he considered 'his' corner, and

soon sat in command of a glass of Saint Emilion and a sweeping view of the room.

If it were any other night, he would have dug his bulk into the battered chesterfield under a vast, endearingly delapidated painting of nineteenth-century Bacchanalia, and held court for an hour or so before departing, claret-fuelled, in the direction of his evening engagements.

For in Anthony Sword's mind, he did not merely attend parties and events. He was the star performance.

This evening the gossip columnist was waiting – against his better judgement – for a young woman. And she would have to be quick, he fumed to himself. Tonight he had too much on his mind to be side-tracked by time-wasters.

He looked around impatiently, even though he knew it was early. The long, low room with its intimate group-ings of artfully mismatched armchairs and tables was almost empty, the soft diamond-trellis of the carpet as yet only an expectant expanse. According to his watch, a silver fob he affected, it was still only a shade past six.

Sword had plenty of time but he hated waiting. And if there was one thing worse than waiting, it was self-inflicted fretting time caused by arriving early. All right, so he hadn't asked her to come until a quarter past, but he felt it would have been an exceedingly good sign if Miss Rosy Hope had thought to have herself installed ready for him, nervously sipping a mineral water, perhaps.

She had not.

'An unexpected pleasure tonight, Mr Sword,' said a fresh-faced barman, placing a clean ashtray on his side table.

Sword waved dismissively. 'Not staying, Michael. A fleeting pleasure from the luscious clusters of the vine before passing through. '

The barman smiled. 'Anything you want, sir, you—'

'Thank you, Michael.'

And that, thought Sword, was putting a brave face on it if anything was.

This evening he was in a volcanic mood. By turns he fumed and grumbled. Anyone else who had found out what he had found out today might have been taken aback, but then he thought stoically (because in all honesty the signs had been there), 'So this is what it has come to ... and this is what I must do now.' But Anthony Sword was not anyone else.

He had reacted badly.

There had been an almighty tantrum in the office, but then again, that was practically *de rigueur* these days. For one thing, an outburst raised his creative bile to a productive level, and Anthony Sword was a pragmatic man. Over the years he had refined his natural perception and cold-bloodedness to the point where he normally got what he wanted without too many qualms about the methods involved.

He had composed a particularly vicious Sword's Swipe for the foot of tomorrow morning's page which could well provoke a writ from the Director-General of the BBC. His professional life was no less bumpy than his private life – it was just easier to confront.

Yesterday he had sacked the last useless girl.

Again the rise in his temper edged dangerously towards meltdown as he considered the gross ineptitude and general daffiness of the females inflicted on him over the past weeks. The last girl reporter who'd passed muster on the column had stayed for two years. Then

9

she'd wandered off to South America after declaring a burning need to write about real people (whatever they were) and that unless she found some she would go quite mad. In the two months since her departure, Sword had been the victim of a series of disastrous trial replacements.

First there was Melissa, who had spent all day squawking down the telephone to friends that she was 'being a journalist' and planning crowded dinner parties in Battersea.

Then there was Caroline, who couldn't possibly write about anyone, because she either knew them, or knew someone who did, which would make things, well, frightfully embarrassing.

Then there was sweet Jane, who was reduced to tears every time a haughty voice was short with her on the phone – she was sent out to cover a wedding, but her nerve failed at the steps of the Brompton Oratory and she had to be talked back on the mobile phone.

There was Miranda who brought in her yapping dog.

There was Lucinda, who had been 'terribly good at essays at Benenden' and produced three pages worth of exclamation marks on the Berkeley Dress Show.

There was Sara, the girl he had sent packing the day before. When asked to arrange a photograph of a titled fiancée with the picture desk, she had said brightly, 'No need. She's jolly keen so she's popping down right away to the Woolies photobooth at the end of her road.'

The resultant explosion caused an elderly librarian caught in the crossfire to have to lie down with palpitations.

The only girl on trial who might have found favourable judgement was Lizza, who, admittedly, had been good. So good that she swung an interview with Robert de Niro in New York, took the next flight out and was never seen again.

Sword sighed.

One thing was sure. He needed a woman – strictly in the professional sense, that is.

The column operated with a team of four: himself and two other men, one young, one middle-aged, and a presentable young woman for the stories that needed a lighter touch. That way he had all eventualities covered.

It ought to have been simple. But if one more witless deb and her hair-tossing friends come any closer to him than the Dôme in the King's Road, then he was quite certain HE would go mad and head for Guatemala. On his desk the stack of outraged letters demanding apologies had reached a record high – and that was merely from the debs' mothers.

Sword cast a fundamentalist look at the doorway, then picked up his glass and tossed back the final glug of claret.

He lay back, wearied.

She was walking towards him as he opened his eyes.

The smile was wide, but he noticed it was fixed nervously under the red lipstick. She was tall and well built. The long hair – the streaky dark blonde which rippled like a shelled walnut he had noticed across the *Dispatch*'s news-room – was neatly pulled back somehow, and she was wearing a plain black dress.

'Mr Sword? Hello, I'm Rosy Hope.'

Her voice was pleasant enough, he judged. Unremarkable Home Counties. No rough edges there, neither suspect vowels nor irritating Sloane shrill. It was as good a start as any. He motioned her to sit down.

Sword frowned at her intently for a moment, noting

11

that her eyes didn't flinch from his, and then said, 'So, Rosy Hope, what makes you think that you have what it takes to be a gossip columnist?'

3 | *The Interview*

Ever since Rosy Hope got her first job on a local news-paper, people had been asking her, 'So when will you make it to Fleet Street?'

Well now she had – or thereabouts.

Rosy had spent the day in the terrifying purgatory that was a casual shift in the news-room of the *Daily Dispatch*. The news editor and his battle-hardened henchmen knew how to make dog meat of aspiring young reporters like her. They had had enough practice.

At any moment, she just KNEW she was on the point of being dispatched to any one of a dozen unpleasant towns to talk to grieving relatives and friends after accidents, murders, fires and freak storms. Every time she passed the news-desk and felt some man there noticing her, she was convinced it could be only a matter of minutes before she was flung out into the vast trauma-tised hinterland to find someone called Evans in Ebbw Vale or a sad Patel in Bradford, and she would miss her appointment with Anthony Sword.

But then, when she began to think there was a chance she might be able to make it after all, came the ache of another kind of uncertainty ... why on earth did the famous gossip columnist want to see her anyway?

*

As it was, Rosy had an ominously undemanding afternoon, drumming up 600 words on a new medical theory which claimed that regular deep kissing was the best exercise for keeping a jawline firm. Rosy's brief was to ask six middle-aged women stars for a quote on this, a task which had called for extraterrestrial tact.

She made it down to the Scribblers Club on time by the skin of her teeth.

And there he was in front of her: the famous Anthony Sword spread on a sofa like a sultan, head tipped back and vast belly swelling the largest cream linen suit Rosy had ever seen.

She had seen him around the *Dispatch* offices, had heard the hollering which reverberated around the corridors and burst like a hurricane into the hushed tension of the news-room. She had been there long enough to hear the usual talk about him, and even to ask an old hand what Sword was really like. But this was the first time she had ventured this close.

Walking towards him, she felt a rush of nerves and forced herself to smile confidently. When he opened his eyes and looked straight at her, nothing about him put her at her ease. He stared grimly – no, rudely – and there were no pleasantries.

'So, Rosy Hope, what makes you think that you have what it takes to be a gossip columnist?' It was almost a sneer.

Wha-a-t?

At that precise moment, Rosy had no idea that she did want to be a gossip columnist.

One moment she'd been sitting in the news-room trying to look confident and capable, and the next she'd been told there was a message for her. A gossip colum-

14

nist? Was this a sick joke, or some slack-chinned old harpy's revenge? Rosy swallowed uncomfortably.

The summons had come from Anthony Sword's office, via the news-room secretary the previous afternoon. So Rosy had come – out of curiosity, she supposed – and because the request had had all the resonance of an order.

She thought fast.

She had nothing to lose.

After a little over a month of freelance foot-soldiery, she was seriously beginning to doubt that she was cut out for the news-room and the grisly raking over of the country's general domestic tragedies that her duties there seemed to entail. That and all the 'women's miscellania': red wedding dresses and the ducks' crossing over Kensington High Street.

Gripped by that sudden appalling urge she sometimes had to throw herself off a cliff edge when she was too close, or to shout out during a quiet moment in a theatre performance, Rosy very nearly blurted out something idiotic about gossip being the same as tongue-wagging and she knew quite a bit about that now after the kissing feature, but the glint in Sword's eye was not encouraging.

He was waiting for her to say something.

She took a breath and a decision. 'I've been doing regular shifts for news for the past five weeks. I've had a good amount in the paper and some of the stories I've worked on have been quite showbusiness-like.'

Sword said nothing. He seemed to be in auto-glower.

'Which I enjoy,' continued Rosy, going for broke now. The only way forward, she decided, was to treat this odd assignation as an interview. 'And I do know what I'm doing. . . . For example, I . . . er, I've written a piece today which involved persuading actresses of a certain age to talk about ki—'

'It's not getting 'em talking that's the problem,' cut in Sword. 'It's shutting 'em up.'

'Well, I . . .' Rosy could feel jitters spreading to her legs as she realised what she was doing. Anthony Sword had indicated that she should sit, but had made no conspicuous attempt to offer her a drink despite his own empty glass.

'I should know,' said Sword.

'I'm sorry?' said Rosy, feeling she was not up to this.

'Old actresses.'

'Ah, yes. Of course . . .'

He half closed his eyes, toad-like.

'How old are you, Rosy Hope?'

'Twenty-five.'

'So you say you know what you're doing? Dear God, it shouldn't be too much to ask.'

Rosy nodded slowly, and then, sounding more assured than she felt, said, 'I know what I'm doing. I did a graduate journalism course, then worked on a reputable provincial paper for two years. Towards the end of my time there I was Court Correspondent.'

'Court and Social?'

'Crime court,' said Rosy firmly. Okay, so the apple-cheeked old clerk and friendly solicitors at Bromley magistrates court were hardly the Old Bailey, but it sounded impressive enough.

'You know how to deal with old rogues then?'

'I . . . um . . . have a good idea.'

'And before that?'

'I read English at university.'

'Oxbridge?'

'London. Royal Holloway.'

'Sounds like a prison.'

'It's actually rather beautiful Victorian red brick. I liked it there,' said Rosy. Damn. Too defensive.

'I take it for granted you enjoy going to parties,' said Sword, with menace.

'Well, I—'

'I want my people OUT. OUT and ABOUT! Can't bear these idiots who want to whine into the telephone all day and delude themselves the stories will come to them. They won't.'

'I'm sure—'

'I have been OUT every night, at LEAST four functions a night for the best part of thirty years,' roared Sword, clearly cranking himself up on to some sort of hobbyhorse. 'And it has got me where I am today. I did not achieve success and social prominence by spending all day on the blower planning spag bol dinners in Battersea and skiing trips to Meribel!'

Rosy wondered what kind of person he thought she was.

'I can ... er ... let you have a CV if you'd like it,' she said, fumbling in her bag to produce the one that was still there from the ten minute once-over she'd had with the *Dispatch*'s news editor. Thank God she hadn't mucked out her bag for weeks. 'There's a number if ... well ... if you were interested, you could check with my last editor....'

Sword held out a large pudgy hand. His nails were better manicured than hers.

'The *Dispatch* is the first national you've worked for?'

'Apart from a couple of shifts on the *Post*, yes.'

'Hmm.'

Rosy studied the dark topiary of his thick hair and beard as he glanced over the sheet.

'Crime court, eh?'

'Yes.'

He fixed her with a straight-faced glare. 'We are not, of course, dealing here with the type of party-goer whose idea of a good night out is to be charged with manslaughter.'

'Er, no.'

Still he stared.

'Are you single, married, live-in, whatever?

'Single,' said Rosy, resolutely. Clearly there was no point in getting uptight about questions like that with a man like this. No, she didn't dare.

'Good,' said Sword unrepentantly.

Then he pulled out a chain from his inside breast pocket and consulted a heavy fob watch. 'I must go,' he said. 'When can you come in and show us what you can do?'

And that was it.

4 | *At Home with Rosy*

On her way home, Rosy stopped at an off-licence on Fulham Broadway and bought a bottle of special-offer champagne. The name on the label was inauspiciously unfamiliar.

'We're not exactly at the vintage Krug stage yet,' she told her flatmate Emma, 'but think of this as a foretaste of what might be.'

'Hardly,' said Emma.

'Eh?'

'I wouldn't pretend to know everything about the high life, but from what I read I'd be very surprised if you were expected to buy your own champagne,' she said archly.

Rosy giggled, then cast around for something better to drink it from than a smeared tumbler and a mug.

The upstairs flat of 24 Endymion Road, a semi-tarted up terraced street, was what the letting agent had described as 'compact', but it was quite remarkable how much mess could be accommodated given practice and determination.

Coffee cups and encrusted plates stood in decorative pairs. Disembowelled newspapers and books were piled in clumps, overflowing from tables and chairs, keeling over tipsily on to the floor. Sagging bookshelves clung to the walls like exhausted rock climbers. Coleridge and Winnie the Pooh rubbed spines with Ezra Pound and Nancy Mitford; the Metaphysicals flopped open over volumes of Romantic theory, while Madame Bovary was squeezed against James Bond rather more intimately than Monsieur Flaubert might have thought wise.

The window by the table overlooked the small, square garden. That is, it would have done if it hadn't been bricked up by Emma's eternal-student piles of books and notes for her 'Study of the Tension between Private and Public Life in Seventeenth-Century Poetry'. Or as Rosy had come to know it: 'Andrew Marvell, the Unfinished Thesis'.

Since Rosy had resigned from the *Kent Times*, left her parents' tidy home in suburbia and moved in here a couple of months ago, she had made little impression on the chaos. If anything, she was finding it surprisingly comforting. Her mother, who was a fiend for lace mats and coasters and china plant-pot holders, would have had a fit.

Rosy averted her remaining fastidious sensibilities from a selection of apple cores browning on the carpet and seized on two wine glasses on the mantelpiece. She took them out to rinse.

'What do you reckon then? Isn't it extraordinary?' called Rosy from the tiny galley of a kitchen.

'What?'

'Should I give it a go? On the Sword's Secrets column.' Rosy came back and handed over a glass of champagne. 'I mean . . . it's not exactly ME, is it?'

'Cheers,' said Emma, 'and what do you mean, should you? Of course you should. Meeting all the most eligible men in London—'

'That's a point.'

'It's wonderful! Anthony Sword . . .'

'I know, it's extraordinary, isn't it?' said Rosy for the sixteenth time.

'He's an OGRE, isn't he?' asked Emma. 'I'm itching to know what he's like!'

Hmm, thought Rosy. The 'itching' was probably nothing a good spring clean couldn't solve. The carpet was fermenting autumnally in patches. The dust mites were living on scrumpy; it made them bold.

'W-e-ll . . .'

'Go on . . .' Emma jiggled her feet under the table in mock-excitement.

'How long have you got?'

'All bottle.'

Rosy laughed.

Since their friendship had begun at university, Emma had been the one with the wild social life. They had met staggering out of a tutor's sherry party at the same time: Rosy because her system had rebelled against four sweet Bristol Creams; and Emma because she had been drinking for three days and nights with the Hooray set.

Emma never worried – unlike Rosy – that she wasn't looking her best, that her red corkscrew curls were too wild, that she wouldn't achieve enough to do herself justice, or that there were three million calories in a cheese burger and chips. Emma never seemed to do any work, and then she came out with a First. She knew how to relax, and consequently seemed to clear life's hurdles with enviable ease. Emma was always out at parties, with plenty of different men, while Rosy had a history of long, intense relationships, the latest of which had ended badly.

Rosy was learning from her, slowly.

These days she was getting so good at pretending to be confident that she often found she very nearly was. And now look where it had got her.

'So, get on with it . . . what's Sword really like? Is he a great bear in the flesh?'

'Huge. Popping out of his suit. Rather puffy in the face, or more so than he looks in his picture.'

'And he took you for a drink?'

'Not exactly.'

'Oh?'

'I didn't get a drink. He sat me opposite him down in Scribblers – it's a kind of club bar near the *Dispatch* where everyone goes – and . . . grilled me.'

'Medium, rare . . . or *saignant*?' Emma looked up grinning expectantly through her mass of sassy curls.

'Pretty rare.'

'Ouch. He was as vile as you'd expect then?'

'No,' said Rosy. 'Not vile. He was . . . dismissive, and irritable, certainly. But I dunno . . . there was something unthreatening about him, something almost TIRED.'

Emma shook her head. 'You know, Rosy, it never ceases to amaze me how you manage to convince yourself that dreadful men always have some kind of excuse for their behaviour – and you'll dream up one for them if they don't try it on themselves.'

'Don't let's go into that again.'

'Okay, okay . . . So did he ask whether you keep *Debrett* in the loo and know Lavinia Snoots-Piffle and the Wiltshire Snoots-Piffles?'

'Not at all.'

'No connections required?'

Rosy grimaced. 'All he kept saying was that he hoped I knew what I was doing, and that he wanted his people to go out to parties all the time.'

22

'Sounds good to me!'

'When you put it like that . . .'

'. . . there has to be a catch,' said Emma.

'Mmm.'

'But you *must* give it a go!'

Rosy gave an expressive shrug then smiled.

'Born to be wild, Rosy. . . .'

Rosy responded with an obscene gesture.

Emma laughed. 'What about the other people on the column?'

'Well . . . I don't know about any others, but there's an incredibly glamorous deputy editor called Jamie Raj, who seems to have half the women on the *Dispatch* in thrall.'

'Now you're talking. When do you start?'

'Monday.'

Emma whistled. 'That was quick work.'

'W-e-ll, newspapers aren't the same as other places when it comes to recruiting people, you know. They don't like to commit to giving you the job until they've seen you on trial. Imagine, though,' said Rosy, teasing now, 'you at home with your books and me out on the town as the gossip columnist.'

'Nah,' said Emma. 'If you didn't ask me along to hold your notebook and tidy up after you've been through the crowd I'd never forgive you.'

'You? Tidy—?'

'I could pick up stray heirs. . . .'

Groans.

'So how long will this trial period be?' asked Emma.

Rosy downed her glass with a flourish. 'Oh . . . knowing Anthony Sword's reputation, just the day, I expect.'

5 | *Green Sword*

When Anthony Sword opened his mouth to sing it was like a mid-ocean greeting from the QE2. He planted his feet, swelled his diaphragm and opened the throttle.

His penchant for a musical blow-out in the cool of the morning was one of the reasons he had chosen to live in the substantial Gothic folly in Highgate. It was surrounded by mature trees, shrubs and ornamental hedging which muffled the sound and allowed him to live in relative harmony with his neighbours. There had been trouble in the past, in other places.

The star gossip columnist found singing therapeutic.

Wrapped in a voluminous flowered kimono (a remnant of his brief *Mikado* phase), he let rip to an aria from *Madame Butterfly* which roared from the sound system inside the house.

He lived alone, his domestic requirements met by the unobtrusive ministrations of a trusted daily housekeeper, cleaner and gardener who had been with him for years. They would not even think of disturbing his peace before nine o'clock.

Meanwhile he could come to from his enviably deep slumbers in his own way. He knew all about that other famous gossip columnist who used to jog at dawn across Richmond park with six yapping Pekingese. Sword shuddered. That was not for him.

'Ah-aah-Ayee-OOO!' blared Sword to the dewy green outside.

From a distant lawn, a dog howled.

Next year he would be fifty.

Not old enough.

Time was, reflected Sword as he sipped lemon tea, the porcelain cup dangerously crisp in his great bear's hand, when all eminent men would breakfast on claret and beef. That was when he should have lived. He would have been a monument to meat and Mammon. If it were true that they thought copious drink a perfect start to the day, then it led one to the interesting possibility that most great events of British history were planned and carried out when the participants were roaring drunk.

That would have suited him fine.

As it was, he heaved himself up from the long oak refectory table, scratched and pitted from long years of intensive use, and lumbered across the Tuscan-tiled kitchen floor to boil more water. The kimono hung spaciously as a festive marquee from his belly.

So this was what he had come to. After the disbelief, the office tantrums, the sheer terror of it . . . Anthony Sword, arch-gossip, had unpleasant facts to face.

Stuck to the fridge was an austere notice, which began:

DAY ONE. 2oz porridge oats, skimmed milk, fruit (one piece), herbal tea (unlimited).

It was barely enough to keep a weevil alive.

Perhaps the doctors were wrong. . . .

No, for once in his life, the facts had to be faced.

25

The Harley Street quack had said he was a fine figure of a man – perhaps a drink or two less if he couldn't stop completely, cut back a little on food, and his old ticker would be right as rain.

That was when he knew it was serious.

Then Sword had climbed on to the weighing scales, and there was no point in anyone pretending. The needle swung straight round to twenty-five stones and stopped vertically opposite his nose, wobbling indignantly. Sword had a horrible feeling it wanted to go further.

No wonder his temper was short.

Anthony Sword, the rotund inquisitor, the unchallenged master of restaurant reconnaissance, had been put on a diet.

He'd known it all along. He was never going to last out until lunchtime (6oz skinned chicken, broccoli (unlimited), fruit (2 pieces). Lunchtime? His stomach was not going to last out until ten o'clock before its rumblings were picked up by some seismic monitoring instrument. There it would be, flashed on the Reuters screen: 'Earthquake registered in North London, Richter scale 8. Casualties feared as authorities try to locate source.'

It was still only 9.30. His regular black cab taking him south to the river and the *Dispatch*'s new offices would pull up outside within the hour. Sword picked at the folds of his new velvet curtains and tried to concentrate on the calming delights of interior decoration. It was better than kicking the fridge.

The Sword residence was a shrine to the art of deception.

He had long ago discovered that all things are possible with imagination, time and patience – a theory he applied not only to his house but to his entire life.

The Gothic folly with a jumble of later additions was a house of few windows, but those it had were substantial, deep set and high. Thick grey stone trapped permanent shadows. It was his fortress and his cradle.

Dramatic effects had been achieved inside, here in the drawing room with pleated calico and Petersham braid, swagging and superglue. He had bold stripes and bows, and curious lit recesses. His marbled pillars were made of drainage pipes (they made a hollow clunk if hit). He had intricate screens of Victorian collage made of old Christmas cards. He had *trompe l'oeil* bookcases in ivy green, and painted tables which looked at first glance to have food on them. There were dark oil paintings in crumbling frames and two ingenious stone urns which hid the speakers pumping operatic arias from his music system.

Throughout the house he favoured deep red and blue-green, although he was not afraid of pastel stippling, in its place.

He had sensuous flooring: wood lovingly varnished and polished; sharp cold marble; the warm russet tiles in the kitchen; silk Turkish carpets.

He had fake book spines bought by the yard and glossed with clear lacquer – he was fond of the titles on them: *Venus Observed* by I. Sawyer and more in that vein. The real books he possessed were more in the line of *The English Country House*, *The Treasure Houses of Britain* and *Doing up a Dump*.

The house was rich and eclectic and cultured, and – most people would have been astounded to discover – he had done it all himself.

Sword fidgeted with the *objets de* junk shop on a side

27

table, then tried to settle on a wooden monk's seat to read *The Times*. The seat felt shrunken beneath him. He found it impossible to concentrate, and wandered out again to the comforting shade and mature camouflage of his garden.

Outside, he seriously contemplated the nutritional value of a bed of spring flowers and the remains of an old shed.

The point was, he rationalised to a dying clump of narcissi, that Anthony Sword had become what he had become because of good food. And now, all these years later, this was what had come of bluffing his way into a restaurant. But he still smiled at the memory. And why not? There was no shame in remembering special birthdays.

At nineteen, he'd worked part-time in a grocery shop, which financed his dream – singing lessons and attendance at a little-known drama school two afternoons a week. Miss Betty LaValle of the LaValle School of Performance Arts had evaluated his squat-ish form and foreseen, at best, a career of stock parts. Swollen with disappointment, he filched a suit from the stage wardrobe and went off as a character of his own invention.

The restaurant – somewhere in Soho; long gone now – was just new enough and pretentious enough to take him at face value and make him welcome. He ate, he drank, then had an attack of remorse. That night, back in his cheap digs in Kentish Town, he wrote a florid review of the *truite aux amandes* and *crème brûlée* he had consumed. He sent it to the *Evening News*; it was printed on the Out and About pages later that same week. A letter came back with £2 for expenses and a list of restaurants he might care to visit in the near future.

Anthony Sword, the pseudonym he had chosen for

this endeavour (being more dramatic than sillier alternatives like 'Knife' or 'Fawkes'), had come into existence.

With each review, he grew in confidence. He ate in restaurants all over London. In new restaurants and in old established venues, large and small, good and bad, Anthony Sword ate FOR London. His pieces were idiosyncratic and entertaining. Soon – still starstruck – he was going to establishments where he could see the actors and actresses he admired, to see for himself whether they were really so different from those turned out by Miss Betty LaValle (they were). In a small way at first, Anthony Sword, in his assumed role, did his showing off in print.

He learned quickly that famous names caught the eye. He realised the impact of seeding his copy with pen portraits of famous husbands and wives dining out together – or, even better, with someone else.

After a year of spicing his reviews with social titbits, he wrote up a lunch at Chez Victor which contained only one passing reference to the *boeuf en croûte* but enough evidence for two high-profile divorces, and was given his own gossip column once a week.

He had barely stopped chomping since.

6 | *The* Daily Dispatch

The Sword's Secrets office occupied a majestic suite in the *Daily Dispatch*'s new high-tech building. Its picture windows held a panoramic view of the Thames and the tree-lined Embankment humming distantly below. The spring sun bounced across the river wash, and beams of light flitted nosily around the room and its celebrity-covered walls.

To Rosy, as she walked tentatively through the door, it was like crossing into Switzerland after escaping the terror régime of the news-room.

A feeling which was only possible, of course, when Anthony Sword was not there.

Haphazard piles of books and magazines stood on every desk and shelf. Slews of papers lay all around, new and white, some branded with black coffee rings, some toasted brown and brittle.

Embossed invitations were pinned to the wall next to a lengthy list of the week's parties and engagements.

The photographs on the walls were a testament to past parties and triumphs. She noted there was a special section above deputy editor Jamie Raj's desk devoted to London Society's most luscious blondes, and which celebrated his unique achievements in this field.

There were several refinements to the usual working environment. In one corner was a mini-bar fridge, on which stood empty bottles and some dirty glasses. An emergency dinner jacket was hanging on the coat-stand in a recess by the door. It had two bow ties dangling from the top pocket: one plain black, the other garish in case there was a television awards dinner to attend.

In front of the river view, shaded by a handsome potted palm, was a chaise-longue, upholstered in what had once been cream damask. Here, Rosy knew from *Dispatch* lore, Anthony Sword would recline after he returned from lunch at four o'clock to dictate rude letters, and even, occasionally, his copy. Claret stains had spread over the arm and it sagged ominously where its structure was most severely tested.

'Hello,' she said to a smiling pink and white blonde sitting at the desk nearest the door. 'I'm Rosy Hope. I, er, arranged with Mr Sword to come in for a shift today.'

'Ooh, yes,' said the girl. She looked no more than twenty, with a friendly, chubby face and a sweet voice. 'Hello. I'm Tina.'

'Hi.'

'You can put your coat on the stand here.'

'Thanks.'

Rosy unbelted her trenchcoat and smiled at the only other person in the room, a sandy-haired middle-aged man slouched in his seat. He was flipping through a copy of *Spotlight*, the theatrical directory.

'Pearson, this is Rosy,' said Tina.

The man nodded at her, and smiled painfully.

'And this is Pearson McKnight, who's been with Sword for years and years and who's got a hangover as usual,' chirped Tina.

'Cheek,' said Pearson.

'Hello,' said Rosy.

'Uh-uh,' he mumbled, returning to Actresses S–Z.

Rosy hung up her coat and smoothed down the fitted tan jacket and black skirt (black tights, black shoes) that drew attention to her voluptuousness without exacerbating it too much. At twenty-five, she fervently hoped she was in the last throes of self-loathing that is the trap and treadmill of the unhappily Rubensesque. She had read *Fat Is a Feminist Issue* and every new diet sold to the magazines. She had despaired at the string-thin models used on the fashion pages, and finally she had slimmed her most extravagant curves while grossly resenting the pressure to do so.

People told her she was attractive, but she never quite believed them.

She pulled her stomach in to counteract a flutter of nerves.

'You can go and use that desk,' said Tina, pointing at the only corner of four desks pushed together that was not subsumed by old papers and press releases. Pearson sat, staring morosely at one picture in *Spotlight*, at the side furthest from the vast single desk with a bank of telephones that could only be Sword's.

Rosy obeyed.

Ten minutes later, Rosy looked up from a press release about the Monte Carlo Rally and into the acceptable face of froth journalism. VERY acceptable.

'Well, hello . . .' he said, coming towards her and holding out his hand. It was warm and dry and firm when she shook it. 'It's Rosy, isn't it? Jamie Raj.'

The deputy editor of the column was languidly sure of himself. He was a good six feet tall, with lustrous dark curls, amazing amber eyes under straight eyebrows, full prominent lips, and golden skin. He was improbably debonair and today he was wearing a brocade waistcoat straight out of *GQ* magazine. And he was terribly well-spoken.

'Hello,' croaked Rosy.

She had heard all about Jamie Raj and his charmed life – or so rumour had it – from the other, envious, front-line foot soldiers on News. Once she had seen him across the atrium with what looked like blonde triplets, and once asking for cuttings on Patsy Kensit in the reference library. Close up, he was devastating. He was not much older than she, but he had the presence of one who had Arrived.

'You've come to us from the news-room, haven't you,' he said. It wasn't a question.

'That's right.'

'Welcome to civilisation,' he grinned.

Rosy tried to smile non-committally.

'Do you have any stories?' He leaned against her desk and looked, disconcertingly steadily, into her eyes.

'Well, I... they sent me out to find someone in Ashford the other day, only the news editor bounced me out so fast I didn't have time to find out if it was Ashford in Kent or Ashford in Middlesex. It was awful, I had to phone the reference library from the call box outside.'

Jamie laughed. 'Par for the course. I didn't mean that, actually.'

'I'm sorry?'

'I meant, have you brought in any stories? That we can write up for the column.'

'Er, not really,' admitted Rosy. 'Not that I can think of offhand.' Damn, she thought, she should have known she'd be expected to come in throwing names about.

She should have asked Emma and her smart friends. She should have had a social life of her own. What could she come up with? Offcuts from Emma's social life? Her mother's riveting campaign to become Lady Captain next year at Chislehurst Golf Club? Her father's latest Bridge night débâcle? The kissing technique revealed by one highly respected middle-aged actress?

'No friends going out with the Duke of York? Fun parties you've been to? Chums marrying titles?' Jamie pressed her.

'Um, I'm afraid not. Not ... er, recent stories, at any rate.'

This was awful. She was a failure already. A deeply SUBURBAN failure.

But Jamie just grinned. 'Thank God for that,' he said.

'Hear, hear!' added Pearson.

'What?' Rosy mumbled.

'You cannot believe,' said Jamie, raking a hand through his hair, 'what we have had to put up with since Rachel – our last girl – left. Trying out dozens of brainless nitwits for the job for months. It has been an absolute nightmare.'

'They ALL had stories about their friends,' groaned Pearson, coming to life now. 'Ridiculous puffs of rubbish about their Sloaney chums. Which they spent hours attempting to write and trying to wriggle on to the page. But try and get them to follow up a decent story, and of course, it would turn out to be about someone they couldn't POSSIBLY embarrass.'

'Nightmare,' reiterated Jamie, with feeling.

Tina came round with mugs of coffee. 'It hasn't put Sword in the best of tempers, either. He's been a right so-and-so for weeks.'

'I can imagine ...' ventured Rosy.

'Look,' said Jamie, looking vaguely apologetic, 'We wouldn't normally steal the news-room casuals, but—'

'Needs must,' said Pearson firmly.

So that was it.

'At last we've persuaded Sword to get someone in who knows what they're doing,' said Jamie.

Rosy smiled weakly. She hoped he was right.

7 | Professional Gossip

It turned out to be much less intimidating than she'd dared imagine.

Anthony Sword arrived – in a wobbling, spitting, cream-suited flurry – and went out almost immediately to see his publishers.

Various informants had rung to offer stories. 'Whispering John' had offered a tale of intrigue at the BBC which no one wanted to tackle; a smart-sounding woman who apparently never left her name had called about the Princess of Wales; and a regular named Dick had suggested a piece about the Duke of Leamington's milestone seventieth birthday.

Rosy spent the morning on the telephone interviewing a divorced heiress (who sounded lovely) and was suing for custody of the marital poodle. She bashed out the story in four concise paragraphs and wondered what to do next.

Jamie Raj sat at the desk opposite her. He was as sublimely confident on the telephone as he was face to face.

He was talking to a countess on his line, evidently a distressed countess who had fallen in love with her children's male nanny. Should she bolt from the ancestral home? Could Jamie Raj put her case compassionately if she announced her daring on the Sword's Secrets page?

'Such a bore to have to send out letters telling everyone,' said Jamie.

He was all sympathetic encouragement.

'You must do what your heart tells you, Cordelia. I've heard Nanny Roger is the most terrific boon, and the little ones adore his funny gorilla. I expect you do too. . . . Shall we come and take his picture, then?'

He leaned back luxuriously in his chair.

'Cordelia, my darling, all I can say is live a little. You deserve it. Oh yes, you do. And our man will be with you to take a few snapettes at your earliest convenience . . . this afternoon?'

A few scribbles on his notepad.

'You're an angel . . . absolutely. Can't wait. Bye.'

Jamie put down the phone softly.

'Tina? Could you get the picture desk to send someone down to Middenhurst Park for three o'clock today, please. Someone well mannered, if that's not too much to ask. Not the Beast.'

Rosy was learning what she could from the old story clippings in a file envelope marked, 'Prince of Wales: Hunting Friends, 1990-'. She was pondering the ambiguities inherent in that heading when a telephone shrilled.

It was the red telephone on Sword's vast mahogany desk by the window. Pearson roused himself from his theatrical researches and answered it.

'Rosy!' he called over, seeing her unoccupied. 'Why don't you take this.'

'Okay.'

37

Pearson smiled. 'Top Contact.'

He transferred the call and Rosy reached for her notebook.

'Hello. Can I help you?'

The voice of an older woman rasped on the end of the line: 'I haven't got a lot for you, today. What I need is a nice bit of sex and undoing, but not a nibble ... no one's nibbling much anymore. Now is it too soon to do that girl again ... oh, you know the one? I spoke to her this morning. ...'

'I'm sorry, who is—?'

'Ooh, you know the one ... the little girl who was in that film with ... that singer, the blondy man with the rainforest chap with the disc thingy in his mouth ...' said the caller, insisting, as if this would pierce the fog immediately, 'You know ...! You've written about him!'

'I'm afraid I—'

'Now ... what was her name ... Deirdre, no, Diane, Danielle! That was it, Danielle Kay. She's the one he fancies. ...'

'Sorry ... who does?'

'Well, she deserves it. It has been ever so tiring, all those episodes of *Legs Eleven* on the telly, and she was Chief Legs this season and it is hard work keeping in trim, all the more if the viewers never get to see your face to divert their attention—'

Rosy opened her mouth to plead for an explanation, but was beaten back by a loud cackle.

'I knew I had it somewhere, jotted it down on the back of my shopping list, aren't I a fool!' squawked the woman. 'Here it is, Pound of Toms ... and Danielle, hols to nice weekend. Phil Naughty, is it? Can't read me own blessed writing, no, it's an H. Haughty. Of course it is. Getting daft in me old age, eh? He told me

38

anyway. That do you? I must say the old cash credits have been drying up a bit lately, very welcome this one will be. I don't suppose you've put your rates up?'

'I'm afraid I don't—'

'No, well, every little helps I suppose, but I've not had a big one since Samantha Starr and the Civil Service mole, but we live in hope of sex, rage and sin, eh?'

'Mmm,' said Rosy, nonplussed.

'Bye then,' said her informant abruptly, and rang off.

For all the sense she made, she might as well have been speaking Chinese.

Rosy replaced her receiver. 'Who was THAT?' she asked feebly.

'Eva Coutts,' said Pearson. 'Ancient theatrical tipster – or should that be tippler? Calls at least five times a day. Any of it make sense?'

'Well . . .' It sounded like crazed rubbish, thought Rosy. 'Does it usually?'

'Oh, yes. As I said, Top Contact.'

'I see.'

'There aren't many of her kind left,' said Pearson cheerfully. 'Old actresses who pass on story tip-offs. Stuff straight from the horse's mouth. All banged to rights. Only in Eva's case, her grasp of detail seems to have entered terminal decline. Did you get any names?'

Rosy flipped over her notes.

'Well done,' said Pearson in an admiring tone. Rosy warmed to him. His avuncular manner and weathered sandy features were those of a disillusioned whelker or bait-digger: a man who had grubbed for many years in muddy waters without conspicuous success. But evidently he had been with Sword for a long time, and knew all there was to know about gossip. For all she knew, Pearson's patched tweed sports jacket and air of wishing he were somewhere else could be part of an elaborate disguise he used to go out and about. Disinterested but deadly.

This was a whole new world.

Rosy took two more calls in much the same vein from the theatrical crone. It didn't take long for her to realise that this was one of the short straws involved in being the most junior member of the team, even if it was only for the day.

Rosy was fascinated.

'Why does she do it?' she asked Pearson. 'I mean, what's in it for people like Eva to tell you all this?'

'We pay her, of course,' he replied. 'By the story – or rather for every tip that makes a story we print.'

'Which is why she rings five times a day.'

'More if we'd let her.'

'Crumbs.'

'Eva Coutts probably makes more money than I do,' said Pearson, with a laden look at Anthony Sword's intimidatingly large – currently empty – desk. 'With none of the hassle.'

8 | *Sword on the Loose*

Anthony Sword's publisher was a weasel in a charcoal suit. His hair was as slick as the edition of *Sword's Society Year* he produced annually, a glossy resumé of the column's finest hours with lively pictures. Sword had been doing it for so long, he could turn it out in his sleep. It was the easiest £50,000 of the year.

For once, though, Sword suspected it was not what John Sylvester of Mega Books had summoned him to his Regent Street suite to discuss.

He was right.

'An autobiography?' hissed Sword, incredulous at the man's gall. 'I'd heard you—'

'Good move, eh?'

Sword breathed in stertorously. His suit felt as tight over the fury in his chest as an armour breastplate. He could hardly bring himself to reply.

'No. I don't think so.'

'Think it over.'

'I have.'

'It would be fanTASTic. . . . Everyone wants to know what Anthony Sword is really like. The great revealer revealed. You've got to the stage, old mate, when you're more famous than the people you write about!'

41

The publisher pulled a tight smile. 'What do I have to do to persuade you?'

'You can't.'

Sword watched the weasel lean into his intercom. 'Annie? Pop in now with the Pichon Lalande, could you?' A moment later a girl in a velvet headband appeared with the wine and two bulbous glasses on a tray.

'You can't resist this. 1967.' Sylvester poured a sample into one glass and gazed at the rich blood colour.

'No,' said Sword, wincing at the man's lack of *savoir faire*, yet having to gather all his strength to reply. 'The answer is no. Simple as that.'

'We'd be looking at an advance of . . . not less than £50,000.'

Sword snorted.

'That's just the advance.'

Silence.

'£100,000 then.'

'My function is to reveal the private lives of others, not my own.'

Silence again.

Sylvester swirled the wine, put his long nose in the glass and took a deep sniff. 'Exquisite.'

Sword's stomach gave a great growl.

'I – will – not – be – writing – any – autobiography. Is that clear?'

'Why don't we—'

'I – do – not – write – about – myself. Stick to what you do best, packaging pretty pictures and blurb.'

'There is always the option,' said the publisher slyly, 'of producing it as unauthorised biography. Create a lucrative little stink about it.'

'Oh, pul-lease.'

Sylvester smacked his lips.

'Why do I need the publicity? I have daily newspaper exposure! I have spin-off books! I have television appearances! I have an unparalleled position in Society!' ranted Sword.

His outburst had – and this was what he had feared since this sordid little scenario first surfaced – no effect.

'So what you're saying is,' said the publisher, who, unfortunately, knew his author well enough to know at least one way to play the game, 'that you don't see your way to going along either way.'

'Correct.'

'Well, in that event – and don't say I didn't do my best to warn you – let's say "unauthorised" may very well turn out to mean what it says.'

'Bastard,' wheezed Sword.

As he passed the bottle on his way out he seized it by the neck and flung it spattering into the corner of the room.

Sword had an enormous lunch – with his own wine – alone at Langan's. When he returned to the *Daily Dispatch* in mid-afternoon he was gibbering with rage and frustration.

'Coffee!' he barked at Tina.

He lumbered over to his desk, began pulling out papers from a stack and then threw out an arm to send the lot flying.

Rosy watched, wide-eyed. Then she took her cue from the others and acted oblivious.

The quiet tic-tac of stories being tapped out on computer keyboards hardly missed a beat. Unrattled, Tina put away her copy of *Ciao!* magazine and wandered off to refill the kettle.

Sword lowered himself on to his chaise-longue and closed his eyes.

Two hours later, the columnist turned to the latest addition to his staff. 'How are you, Rosy darling? Enjoying yourself?'

She looked stricken.

'Um, fine ... thank you.'

'Here's a story for you. The Earl of Trent did a runner from Langan's after a spectacularly expensive luncheon today. When they sent a man after him and stopped him on Piccadilly, he pretended he had short-term amnesia. I want that for today's page.'

She was scrawling the details. 'Er, did he settle up ... in the end?'

'No,' said Sword. 'He said, "Who are you and why have you stopped me here?" Now ... how are you going to tackle that, Rosy Hope?'

'I'll ... well, I'll call Langan's: the manager, the *maître d'*. . . . Try to contact the Earl of Trent. And, probably as a last resort, Langan's PR people.'

'You've got twenty minutes until the page goes.'

'Okay.'

'Oh, and darling ... You should bear in mind that Brett Trent is not only an appallingly arrogant young man and a hopeless ne'er-do-well, but one of this column's best contacts.'

None of the others Sword had suffered in the last months would have managed it, let alone so competently. He didn't seriously expect this Rosy Hope to come up with the goods.

But she did.

There, on his desk within half an hour, was a print-out of three chunky paragraphs which told the tale succinctly, legally and with an admirable lightness of touch. She even had a quote from Trent saying, 'Does this count as a fashionable eating disorder?'

Sword was impressed.

While Rosy was out of the room, he turned to Jamie and Pearson. 'What do you think of her?'

'We LIKE her,' said Tina.

The others smiled in agreement.

'As usual, our secretary has gauged the mood . . .' laughed Jamie. 'Yes, she seems very able. Pleasant, not over-confident – and intelligent.'

'Very pretty,' added Pearson. 'And certainly able. She actually managed to unravel an Eva Coutts special.'

'Hell's teeth . . .' said Sword.

When Rosy came back, he asked her to come back the next day and to let him know when she could start a two-week trial on the column.

9 | *Breaking the News*

Rosy waited until *Shiny Happy People* had finished, then turned the volume down on REM, removed a pair of Emma's shoes and a pile of magazines to make space to sit down on the sofa and phoned home.

'Hi, Mum. It's me.'

'Rosy, love! How are you?'

'Fine. Great, in fact. You and Daddy?'

'Same as ever. Well, we miss you, but apart from that—'

Rosy stifled a twinge of impatience. 'I was away at college for three years, don't forget.'

'I know, but—'

'I'm only in Fulham, Mum.'

'It's not too grimy and noisy? You're eating properly – none of these faddy diets you go on? And, Rosy dear, don't go to any nasty launderettes. There's no need for that. You know you can always bring your washing home. . . .'

'What's wrong with launderettes?'

Rosy could almost hear her mother shudder. 'I've heard . . . well, there was an article in one of the Sundays, and then I heard it first hand, that the ones in town are little more than . . . seedy pick-up joints.'

'Mu-um!'

'It's true. Elizabeth Binks' daughter Briony got herself a flat in Pimlico and the next thing anyone knew, she was seeing a scaffolder who made his move in a Coin-Op. You can imagine how she felt. . . .'

'Who, Briony?'

'Elizabeth. She was quite mortified. She couldn't bring herself to play Bridge for dread of the sherry conversation. It lasted for weeks, this . . . relationship of Briony's, until – and I read between the lines here – he found someone else with his dirty laundry. Of course, he was in the building trade, you see. Made a lot of clothes grimy. . . .'

Rosy shook her head to no one but the picture of Prince Charles on the front page of the *Evening Standard*. 'It's all right. We do run to a washing machine here.'

'Well, that's a relief. If you want any help, with anything we can—'

'I know, Mum. And I'm really grateful.'

'Finances, you know . . . you don't want to get into a muddle. Your father's not a chartered accountant for nothing . . . and he'd be flattered to be asked.'

'I know.'

'But it's going well?'

'Mum, you'll never guess where I've started working.'

'You said all over the country last week on the *Daily Dispatch*. I know it's all very exciting but don't get yourself tired out, Rosy. You know you need your sleep.'

Rosy took a deep breath. 'I'm working on the gossip column, with Anthony Sword.'

'The rude fat man? Oh, Rosy. . . .'

'It's only a trial period. Two weeks.'

'Well, if it's what you want, dear. . . .'

Her mother's disapproval down the line was tangible.

'He's actually quite nice. Well, most of the time. He's been very nice to me anyway. Since I've been there, which is admittedly only a couple of days.'

'As I say . . .'

'You don't ever read the *Dispatch*, do you?'

'You know we always have the *Telegraph* – cricket for your father and announcements for me.'

Announcements, thought Rosy glumly. Any moment she's going to tell me who's getting married now, and worse, who's started sprogging.

'Honestly,' she said, getting in quickly, 'If you did read the *Dispatch*, you'd see that the Sword's Secrets column is quite innocuous and funny. I know it has this reputation for nastiness, but it's really not. As far as I can see, people are positively fighting to get their stories in it. You'd be amazed.'

'Hmm,' said her mother, in the way she always did when she wanted to say she knew better but didn't want an argument.

'Why does she always make me feel I'm doing the wrong thing? I mean, I know she really cares and every-thing, but . . . why couldn't she have just said she was pleased?' Rosy asked Emma later – much later – when Emma came in.

Rosy was stretched out bleary-eyed on the sofa watching the end of the Midnight Movie. Emma had returned from an evening at the Embargo Club with a man she'd first met at Crazy Larry's. ('That's pro-gression for you,' said Emma.)

'Because,' said Emma now, kicking off her shoes, 'she wants you safely married and producing grandchildren. All mothers are the same.'

'Even yours?' Rosy couldn't believe it. Emma's

mother had married, successively, parts of Gloucestershire, Wiltshire and Berkshire in her time, and indeed so successfully that she had featured several times in Sword's column herself.

Now there was a thought. . . . Please God, prayed Rosy, that I don't end up having to investigate the formidable Mrs Blackett-Willingdon at any time.

'Especially mine,' said Emma. 'She knows what there is to be gained.'

'You know what's really worrying me,' Rosy bleated, 'now that she's started me thinking. That I'm not up to it.'

'What, marriage?'

'Bugger marriage. No, the Sword job. I don't know stacks of smart people and all about their lives. I'm just . . . ordinary. I don't know any more about, I dunno . . . the Earl of Trent, or Lord Linley or actors and actresses than anyone else who reads the paper.'

Emma shook her head in disbelief. 'So?'

'So – what?'

'Isn't that the fun of it?' asked her flatmate.

10 | Party Time

It was party night, as always.

Anthony Sword swigged defiantly from his hip-flask. Another splash of gin and Dubonnet, and he would open his offensive on Sara Chichester's affair with an Amazonian Indian.

His eager victims buzzed and droned close by, like gnats he itched to wave away. They formed restless swarms, snatching covert glances, dropping names loudly, then darting off to dance for the newspaper photographers. Laughter and shrieks and carelessness hung in the hot, still air above the simmering party.

It seemed, to Sword, that he was standing in some warm, bright jungle. Green sprays drooped over to eavesdrop on every conversation. Spears of grass surged up between the players in his game. But he decided to reserve judgement. He could not discount the effects of the two bottles of Saint-Emilion he had consumed that afternoon to spite the world.

When he had arrived in his taxi, the outside of 12 Pelham Square looked the same as it had done for the past three decades – a constant source of annoyance to the Belgravia Society and a diplomatic affront to the embassies of Turkey, Korea and Oman which looked out on it. Its roof rotted, its frontage festered, and its pillars putrified. Number 12, the town house of the Earls of Trent, was the black tooth in the full set of sharp white stucco.

Inside, its soggy walls had sprouted a terrifying mould of rampant, waving greenery. The ballroom where Sword stood, thunderous and fascinating as a summer storm, was a teeming wildlife sanctuary. There were stuffed birds and plaster fish, and life-sized papier mâché animals which glowered through the leaves at 300 guests invited to dress 'Green Countdown'. A baboon clung gamely to the gallery and a zebra stood awkwardly by the sound system as if working up the courage to ask for a sentimental record. A cross-eyed rhinoceros (rather battered) was poised to stampede either the canapé table or a clump of fake rainforest.

As a man who chased the mode, the Earl of Trent was not only At Home – he was Concerned. It was quite the smartest party since Lally Frostrup's dolphin dinner.

The Duchess of York and a sepia Texan had come and gone.

Sword observed the gathering and ran down his options.

Immediately within range were the thrice-married Earl of Salcombe with wife number two; a clutch of pert young actresses on the scent of blue blood; the up-and-coming actress Emily Strong, daughter of a Liberal peer; and Sam Allen, the millionaire yachtsman often referred to as the Bunk Bedder.

More interesting for Sword's current purposes was the ex-Cabinet Minister Sir Philip Hawty (a Tory of the arrogant tendency and fearless pursuer of unsuitable young women).

Then there was Nan Purchase, the jut-jawed Manhattan socialite-turned-businesswoman ($100 million alimony into $200 million worth of health hydros and spin-offs).

Propped against an elephant was the popular composer Curlew Trussock with his fifth wife Darlene (formerly one Trevor Reynolds, flautist), and talking to them the Marquis and Marchioness of Weedon (joint affair with estate gardener, true but as yet unproven).

In a noisy corner there were also Lord Choldermolder (pronounced 'Chommer'), the Honourable Wills Fartheringale-Abbott (affectionately known as 'Farting-About') and an amusing nobody called Joe Smith (pronounced 'Smiff').

Sword saw them neatly ordered, every one. Old stories, new stories. In his mind, he had created them as surely as he had created himself.

He had not dressed 'Green Countdown' and he had not the remotest intention of enjoying himself. He certainly did not find the idea of drinking elderflower champagne amusing in any way and he harboured a near-pathological distrust of canapés. His light suit embellished with several large claret splatters, the rotund inquisitor stood scowling as the A- and B-lists fluttered about before him.

He raised the flask of gin and Dubonnet mixture to his fleshy lips again (Queen Mum G-and-D, that magnificent matriarch's favourite tipple) and took a sultanly swig. Then he scowled over to the doorway, and the bulge of contempt in his eyes and the thrust of those thick, moist lips through the dark beard gave him the look of a resentful cod caught in a net.

52

*

There they were, thought Sword, the preening ninnies who called themselves rivals.

If he spoke to someone, they would accost that person as soon as he had finished; if he laughed loudly, they would goggle over in anguish; and if he reached into an inside pocket for his small leather-bound notebook, a scout section would surge forward, straining to hear what was being said. 'Fools,' muttered Sword under his breath.

There was Benedict Pierce of the *Daily Post*, the man who wore his hair like a trophy. He had taken that trademark from Ross Benson's ruthlessly charming coiffure during that elegant diarist's tenure at the *Daily Express* – taken it to the limit, in fact. Benedict Pierce lounged against the door frame, mesmerising his companions with The Coiffed Wings Which Did Not Move.

Foraging among the scraps of his stories was the *Prattler* magazine's over-scented social editor, Honoria Peeke.

By her side was some foreign woman reputed to travel the world for *Ciao!* magazine with a Louis Vuitton suitcase stuffed full of dollars.

A pale youth called Sebastian Hawthorne, pedlar of college contacts between the London diary pages, twitched eagerly between them.

They would have to be shown how it was done.

Tom-tom music grew louder above the hubbub.

Sword pocketed the silver hip-flask and turned casually to a well-connected blonde who had been clinging to an accidental eye-meet all the while.

'I hear the Indian has moved into Radlett Mews with Sara C.,' he said. 'Does he miss the Amazon dreadfully?'

11 | *Rosy on Assignment*

Rosy accepted a glass of elderflower champagne and locked eyes with a lion.

She gave some devils-on-horseback a tortured look as they rode by on a tray and shifted her weight (rather more of it than she'd intended to bring with her after several evenings like this) on the pitching high heels. Observe, she reminded herself, and plan the attack. There are people who do well at parties and those who don't, and it's all a matter of confidence.

She seemed to be surrounded by animals. They were not real, and nor, on closer inspection, had they ever been, though some bore an expression of startled sociability, as if unexpected guests had crashed through the undergrowth when there were only chewed bones for supper.

Rosy searched for a friendly, if not a familiar face.

The room was full of people who might never actually have met before, yet who must have been acquainted with the most galling details of each other's lives. The Earl over there was almost certainly conversant with the affairs of the actress in the tiger's skin. The actress knew that the ex-Cabinet Minister was pursuing (among others) the teenage daughter of an author. The author

54

would have seen and fallen in love with a photograph of the sloe-eyed model, which was probably what he was telling her right at this moment over by the open window.

Rosy swayed uncomfortably. She rarely wore high heels; she was tall enough without them. These were borrowed, part of her 'Green Countdown' costume. She wished she'd had the courage not to bother.

Leaves pinned to a tight black dress would not suit every woman, but with Emma's help Rosy had positioned them cleverly, so that they accentuated the curves that were in the right place, and disguised those that weren't. That was the idea, anyway. She hoped the bronzing powder on her wide cheekbones wasn't overdoing it. Emma said it would bring out the green in her hazel eyes. Bring her out in a rash, more likely.

Anthony Sword, who saw her arrive and hesitate in the doorway, gave her a wry smile.

She smiled back valiantly.

Attached to a passing tray of broccoli dip, the Honourable Harry Someone – she recognised him from a hundred silly pictures in the *Prattler* – slid by and popped a large wink at her. He was dressed as a hunter, which only went to show, thought Rosy, how money and a privileged education could never guarantee intelligence.

'I'm doing my bit,' Harry told her excitedly. 'This could be just the night to get environmentally friendly with several concerned young women. . . . I could tell you all about it later if you like. Want a dip?'

'No thanks,' said Rosy, wondering whether that meant he knew who she was and why she was here. It probably meant she stuck out like a sore bumpkin.

55

'You look nice,' said Harry vaguely, appraising her generous proportions.

'I didn't have that much time to get ready. It's supposed to be like a tree, or something. It was all I could find in my neighbour's garden,' she babbled nervously, but the Honourable Harry was disappearing into the braying throng.

Rosy forced herself to stay calm. What was it Emma had said about London parties? That whenever she went to one, she thought: 'Flying lessons for unbelievers.' Which meant, broadly translated, that wherever you soared in the social stratosphere, you were vindicated by finding no sign of Heaven up there in the clouds.

Too right. This was hell – and Anthony Sword was over there scowling like the old devil everyone expected.

Rosy took a gulp of the elderflower champagne. The babble around her intensified. A joker let out a high-pitched monkey scream. If she could only get into one good conversation. Or overhear one even.

Perhaps she should go and talk to Nan Purchase. There she was, touching cheekbones with another thin woman. Only that morning in the *Daily Dispatch*, the skinny Manhattan millionairess had been on television plugging her latest book, *How to Re-Model Yourself*. Her new health hydro and self-awareness centre in Hertfordshire was THE place to unlock one's potential, according to several glossy magazines this month.

With a fabulously successful chain of these spas across the States, and all that publicity, surely Mrs Purchase could spare a little homespun wisdom?

Then, as Rosy was steeling herself to go over, the host disentangled himself from a mock liana and loped towards her.

The 8th Earl of Trent wore his frizzy black hair in a ponytail and a dark tracksuit streaked with dust. His noble, inbred cockroach face bore the lipstick imprints of several affectionate greetings, but he looked far less raddled in the flesh than in the photographs that always accompanied his exploits in the papers.

'Sword tells me you're Rosy!' He leaned down to peck her on both cheeks. 'We spoke on the phone the other day – glad you could come! Love the dress – very wood nymph.'

He sounded younger than the thirty-four which *Debrett* had made him when she wrote the story about his runner from Langan's. And he was very gushy.

'Hello,' said Rosy. 'I ... um ... hope that story, that I did the other day ... wasn't too.... I mean, I hope it was all right.'

The Earl smiled, showing small pointy teeth. 'My dear, I don't remember a thing.'

'I wrote that ...'

But he was laughing at her.

'Oh, I see ... yes. ...' Rosy relaxed fractionally. 'This is amazing.'

'My heritage, eh?' He gestured around. 'You should see the state of the place – upstairs is worse. I think I might keep the jungle. It covers up the most hideous mould.'

'It's a great idea for a party.'

The Earl shrugged. 'Ecological parties are the only kind to be seen at these days. No one dares to refuse in case people think they don't care.'

Rosy kept smiling.

'Sword's here already,' he said. 'Over there by the drinks.'

'Yes, I've seen him.'

'And the Beast's here too.'

'Oh, er, good.' The Beast, Rosy had discovered, was Keith Silver, the *Dispatch*'s paparazzo photographer.

'Snapping away like an endangered alligator, he is,' went on the Earl. 'He posed me on the zebra with Caro Whitely and Lulu Newsome, and then a special with Fergie, when I still had my gorilla suit on – it got rather hot, not to mention niffy, so I'm afraid I got rid of it. But don't worry, Sword's done his bit there.'

'I bet he has.'

'He's such a fuckhead. You have to admire it.'

Rosy didn't know what he expected her to say.

'Anyway, it's marvellous that he came – and you, of course. We share quite a client list these days,' said the fashionable Earl.

This year – according to the file cuttings – the Earl of Trent was a personal exercise trainer. Previously, he was into numerology, and before that – pre-title, naturally – service dog-walking in Chelsea.

'Is it true you go to work in an ermine-trimmed track-suit now?' asked Rosy. 'I read that somewhere, but somehow I couldn't believe it.'

The Earl sighed. 'I would love one, darling. But I can't decide. Fur is definitely OUT, but is it coming back? And do the aristocracy CARE?'

Rosy laughed, pretty sure he was joking.

'Now, who would you like to talk to?'

'Er, who do you reckon?' asked Rosy.

The Earl grinned with sly delight. 'Sir Philip Hawty's after Emily Strong—'

She must have looked momentarily puzzled.

'You know Emily Strong, the actress. And the Bunk Bedder had the Countess of Salcombe on board his boat at the weekend. Come on, I'll introduce you. Hawty's an old ram and he's positively dribbling to meet you already.'

Rosy couldn't believe it could be that easy.

12 | *The Rivals*

Benedict Pierce was becoming exceedingly irritated by Anthony Sword. Every day that week Sword had printed some snide jibe at the Pierce Column. 'The *Daily Post*'s tortured tortoise has finally caught up with my March scoop on the Duke of Bunster's facelift,' was that morning's sneer on the Sword's Secrets page in the *Daily Dispatch*. 'If the dreary fool had bothered to read my exclusive revelations here on Monday, he would have known why the Duke had developed the fixed smile which has led to such distressing misunderstandings.'

'Smug bastard,' spat Benedict Pierce.

The rival gossip columnist had not dressed up either. It would have ruined his shining horns of blond hair, for one thing.

One of life's frustrations for Benedict Pierce was that he was doomed to rank second behind Sword. No matter how good his stories were – and he had had some crackers in his three years as the *Post*'s man in the know since quitting the City desk – he would always be the pretender. He was David against Goliath, or as the *Dispatch*'s theatre critic once memorably sniped: Fay Wray against King Kong.

It had happened again, only that morning. He had

arrived at a television studio at 6.30a.m. to let the country know what was happening to the Princess of Wales' exercise regime at Kensington Palace during these trying times, only to be told by an earnest researcher that the incomparably rude Anthony Sword had treated them to a virtuoso aria of expletives when they'd approached him first to do the interview. 'He said it was a ∗∗∗∗∗∗∗ waste of time, Mr Pierce! What do you make of that?'

Sadly, Benedict Pierce knew only too well. The most irritating aspect of Sword was that he was invariably right. Pierce involuntarily smoothed down his dark Savile Row suit and turned away from the full malevolence of Anthony Sword's cod glare.

Here they were again, at the same party.

He was damned if he was going to use the same material as Sword. But then, he was damned if he did not.

Pierce had seen the way that Sam Allen, that brown mast of a yachtsman known as the Bunk Bedder, had caught the arm of Lizzie Salcombe as she passed. He had noted the shudders of antipathy between the Marquis and Marchioness of Weedon. And there was the ex-Cabinet Minister Sir Philip Hawty, variously known as the matinee idol of the Tory shire-ladies or as an embarrassing old roué, depending on the purveyors of his publicity.

The *Daily Post*'s columnist watched with affected disinterest as his rival's new recruit Rosy Hope stood talking earnestly to their preposterous host. Those leaves on her dress quivered faintly as if a rogue breeze had cut through the scented heaviness of the party atmosphere to her alone.

Clever girl, he thought, as well as pretty. That pretence of uncertainty – people would tell her anything.

'Benedict?'

'Honoria. Sorry, I—' With some effort, he concentrated on what the woman in front of him was saying.

Honoria Peeke was in a gentle flap.

'Would you mind awfully if we went over it again?' she asked, poised to jot in a discreet notebook. 'On the *Prattler*, one absolutely has to get things right.'

'Sorry, Honoria. What were you saying?'

The *Prattler*'s social editor exuded a great waft of gardenia scent and tapped a gold propelling pencil on the page she had opened. 'The Earl of Trent. I was asking what you knew about his . . . er, profession before he succeeded to the title. He was a dog-walker before he trained as a personal fitness coach, is that right?'

'Cocaine supplier,' said Benedict Pierce.

Around him, the other hacks were forced to take momentary refuge in their glasses of elderflower froth. They wanted to know. But none could admit they did not.

'Oh, you people, all the same!' The sultry foreign woman from *Ciao!* magazine broke the tension at last. 'I never know how anyone ever talks to you. I cannot understand. They must be mad. Crazy!'

Benedict Pierce shrugged. He called over to a passing waitress, dressed as a parakeet, for some cigarettes. His own lightly tanned, mildly beaky features were composed as he waited for a reaction to his edict. He was hoping for substantiation. It often worked.

Honoria Peeke had pursed her shiny coral lips together in an expression of distaste. The embryonic diarist Sebastian Hawthorne's eyes were telescopes while the struggle to strike an informed attitude played out on his elfin face.

The woman from *Ciao!* was not to be deflected. 'I don't know how you can say these things, and write these so terrible stories.'

'Are you planning a piece on Lord Trent?' inquired Benedict Pierce calmly, patting his pockets for the platinum cigarette lighter once given to him by a grateful polo entrepreneur.

'I am to spend the next three days with the Lord Trent. A very handsome and aristocratic man,' said *Ciao!* magazine.

Benedict Pierce honoured the young thruster Sebastian Hawthorne with a sceptical arch of a well-groomed eyebrow.

'The curse is upon him then,' said the columnist with a bright smile. 'For as we all know, the best and the bravest bare their homes for a full-colour spread in magazines like *Ciao!* only for disaster to strike. Perfect marriages end in acrimony while still smiling glossily on the front cover. Films flop and fortunes divide. But that is what comes of asking only polite questions of difficult subjects.'

He pulled out the platinum lighter and felt the heavy smoothness of wealth. He lit up, then thought of the low, cigar-shaped Jaguar XJS parked in the darkening streets below and the weekend's shooting to come.

It was amazing what a judicious weave of discretion and publicity could achieve – with benefits all round.

Benedict's methods had always owed more to PR than PC.

If Benedict Pierce was distracted at this party, it was because there were dark thoughts ticking over under those sleek tresses. His eyes were on the wealthy Manhattan socialite Nan Purchase: with her racehorse face and starved jockey's body rattling in evergreen silk Armani, she drew her teeth back and whinnied at the Earl of Trent.

The Alimony Queen, no more. Since her well-publicised and lucrative divorce from Jim Purchase, the rubber engineering billionaire, she had triumphed. Out in the cold world with only $100 million between her and oblivion, she had come good as her own woman.

Alimony. Now there was a facet of our life and times on which Benedict, with two grasping ex-wives, was an expert. Only that morning he had found his hand forced, yet again, in the direction of his bank account. If he hadn't known how much they hated each other, he might have suspected they were in it together. The two ex-Mrs Pierces, he thought, could learn a lot from Mrs Purchase. Come to that, so could he.

Which made him doubly anxious.

Benedict wondered what exactly Nan Purchase had been doing with Anthony Sword the previous night, when he had seen them leaving Mirabeau's Club. Surely it was not possible that she could be a more than usually profitable contact?

Both envy and pride motivated Benedict Pierce, and he needed to know more.

Naturally he quivered at the closeness of $100 million and the rest in the form of Nan Purchase and what it could do for him.

Then, in his mind he saw Sword and Nan Purchase together, the cash swelling between them like a great fat juicy golden gooseberry.

Benedict Pierce gritted his expensive teeth.

Sword always got what they both wanted.

13 | *The Chelsea Glower Show*

'Tarragon, thyme, parsley, rosemary, basil,' said Anthony Sword the next day to his new friend-for-a-purpose Nan Purchase. 'I grow all my own in my kitchen garden. Fresh cut herbs make all the difference.'

He and the skinny health-hydro millionairess were at the Chelsea Flower Show.

The annual horticultural event in the grounds of the Royal Hospital more than passed muster with the arbiters of the new social conscience. It was Old Green.

Exuberantly frothing flowers and foliage were pinned down into courtyard gardens, country gardens, town gardens, window boxes, wild gardens, hanging gardens. Cascades of leaves spumed from tinkling water runs and witty seats. Red-coated military pensioners shuffled around proprietorially in the sunshine. The Queen and the Duke of Edinburgh were making stately progress round the show and, heading the royal party, Her Majesty had been called upon to say, 'Hmm. How lovely,' many times.

A brass band at the entrance played 'Roll Out The Barrel'.

Having missed lunch – or rather, anything that he

would recognise as lunch – Sword lumbered along emptily.

Soon they came across the Texan model Jerry Hall dressed in eighteenth-century costume to do her bit for the National Trust. 'I jes' love your National Truss,' she cooed, monstrously eyeballed by two straining purple-faced Pensioners.

'There are Texans everywhere,' said Sword, tetchily. 'That woman Fergie must be around.'

Nan clapped her hands in rapture.

Amid the competing blusters of colour (this year haci-enda orange was popular), the inmates of Leyhill Open Prison had laid out an Edible Garden.

'Cabbages, cauliflowers, rocket, broad beans – and will you look at those zucchini climbing up the pergola?' cried Nan ecstatically. 'This is Diet Heaven. You could eat as much as you wanted of that.'

Sword grunted.

The pink shirt under his linen suit was already moist with the exertion of keeping up with the American Diet Queen's jaunty, well-exercised strides. She was a vision in acid yellow, with thin brown legs knotty as wisteria branches.

'I could just stop eating. Make m'self really miserable and get it over quickly.'

'Oh, I already did that. It's the worst. You gain twice over when you stop.'

She flashed him a this-will-kill-you smile.

'No. We discussed this in the beginning. If you are serious about this and if I'm going to help you, it has to be a long-term plan to develop a meaning inter-relationship between your body and your fuel. Now I have a glass of warm water on waking, and a little *radicchio*. . . .'

A great rumble of hunger escaped from Sword. He was finding it difficult to concentrate. He let the Marchioness of Weedon go by with her estate gardener, arm-in-arm and trailing schoolgirl giggles. The ex-Home Secretary Sir Philip Hawty dived ostentatiously behind a bank of lilies, but he need not have bothered. Sword hardly noticed him, nor the blushing young television hostess with him.

They found the Duchess of York and a friend examining a tropical island display. Phallic lilies, palms and a banana tree cuddled up to a perky rattan hut.

A large woman under a fruit salad hat hissed audibly to her companion, 'That Fergie. Left her husband and she's had twenty-three holidays so far this year, you know. Disgraceful. Have you seen the paper this morning? There's a picture in there – she was away in the jungle somewhere, and she still managed to find a party there.'

The other woman pursed her mouth purposefully and contented herself with a disapproving glare.

They moved off, muttering.

Sword guffawed.

The royal party had begun its stately progress up the tented path between a brazen flare of rhododendrons and a swank of dahlias, Her Majesty out-pinking them all in a cyclamen coat and dress. Now and then she and the Duke of Edinburgh stopped to greet a familiar worthy in the crowd, while the Prince of Wales communed, in his way, with various of his botanical acquaintances: the ornamental mugwort and the Apuan oleander.

Those who knew the ropes had staked their positions along the route.

The rival gossip columnist Benedict Pierce and his photographer were waiting eagerly in line as Sword and Nan trundled up. The men from the *Daily Post* had been cornered by an angular woman with spun-sugar hair decked out in red Versace. She was wearing so many gold chains she could have been a refugee from a bondage night at Tiffany's.

There was no mistaking Bea Goff, nor the look of anguish on Pierce's face. Bea Goff would stop at nothing to get herself featured in the social columns.

'Ah, the species Plantus Social Embarrassica,' said Sword, informatively pointing her out to Nan. 'Shrivels in shade, thrives despite overexposure to bucketfuls of shit.'

Nan giggled girlishly.

From ten feet away Benedict Pierce shot them a foul look; Sword automatically turned away and led Nan down a side path.

'Oh, I must tell you,' said Nan, making sure she moved ahead far enough to get the full benefit of his reaction. 'Bea Goff's latest. She's heard there's a book coming out and she's telling everyone she was one of Prince Philip's old flames. She's FURIOUS she's not mentioned by name.'

Sword snorted.

'You know she reads your column to see who's divorcing, then she writes them a letter which says, "Remember me?" They say she's gotten herself fixed up with at least two husbands that way.'

'Don't remind me.'

'Where DOES she get off?'

'Making a bloody nuisance of herself,' said Sword.

'So-o-o embarrassing,' said Nan, plainly enjoying every syllable.

'The words "courting" and "disaster" spring to mind.'

'Where did she come from?'

'She was found,' said Sword, 'in the aftermath of Lord Rutford's divorce, wearing Chanel and a knowing smile. Ghastly woman.'

'Do you write about her?'

'Only if I'm feeling vindictive.'

'If you can't cut her down to size, no one can,' said Nan.

Sword puffed up his chest.

He was about to reply when they came to a halt by a display of giant cacti dominated by a colossal prickly growth.

The name on its black plate was Dry Sword.

14 | *The Afternoon After*

Across town at the *Daily Dispatch*, Rosy sat deeply hungover at her computer terminal and typed with jellyfish hands:

> '... Among the wildlife at the new Earl of
> Trent's Green Countdown party was the
> Countess of Salcombe, who became entangled
> in a liana with millionaire yachtsman Sam
> Allen, 38, affectionately known as the Bunk
> Bedder.
>   "I was rather enjoying myself," she said as
> she was pulled free by concerned friends. "I
> didn't expect my husband would notice." '

It had been a long night and an even longer morning. Rosy's eyes stared, watered, then closed. She felt late nights more than most people – disastrously so, sometimes. It was yet another reason she suspected she was not cut out for this job.

Pearson sifted through the Beast's party photographs from the previous evening. As the longest-serving hack on the country's most popular page of prattle, he clearly considered himself a fine judge of these matters.

'Ah . . . the lovely Emily Strong,' he said, loosening his woollen tie to study her form. 'She did a trapeze act once. Always good value, the muscular Emily Strong.'

Rosy tried not to imagine swinging from any height at this particular moment.

'Good evening was it?' he inquired.

'Amazing,' said Rosy feebly. 'I cannot believe the things people will tell you!'

'You did have a good evening.'

'I met Sir Philip Hawty—'

Pearson sniffed. 'Home Secretary for a week. Been an old goat on the back of it ever since . . . disgusting old roué.'

'Yes, well . . .' said Rosy. 'The Earl of Trent told me Hawty was after Emily Strong.'

'What?!' Pearson turned back to his photograph of Emily, a buxom brunette with dimples. 'How I've nurtured this girl's career!' he muttered. 'From her first stumbling words on the Fringe, to her triumphant swing on the trapeze in Barnum, to now, when she stands on the brink of international success . . . and to throw herself away on a has-been!' Then he composed himself for the worst. 'Were they, er, together at the party?'

'Not exactly,' said Rosy.

'Oh?'

'He launched himself at her from behind a hippo—'

'From where . . . ?'

'Just don't ask.' Rosy clutched her head. 'Hawty sprang out at her yelling "Ambush!" as she was passing, ripped her dress half off as he grabbed her – then marched her over to me, demanding to know where the Beast was!'

Pearson let out a leaden sigh.

'The sod. That old trick,' he said.

'Sorry?'

'Hawty. Shock tactics to get noticed.'

'I don't think anyone did,' said Rosy. 'It was that kind of party. Even the Beast missed it.'

Pearson shrugged. 'There will be other times, believe me.'

'Would we run a picture like that?'

'Rosy Hope, you have a lot to learn.'

'Now, have you got anywhere with that little girl ... you know, the one I gave you the other day ... it'll come to me in a minute ... she's going on a lovely holiday ... at least, I'm sure he's going to ask her ... the one with the LEGS ... ?'

It was that Eva Coutts time again.

Rosy scored her frustration down the side of a page as the ancient theatrical tipster wittered on.

None of it made any sense.

Of all the dotty telephone informants Rosy had been introduced to on the column, Eva was the most tenacious – even accounting for the retired Navy man who tracked every movement of the Royal Yacht *Britannia*, and the woman in Hampstead who fine-toothcombed all the celebrity planning inquiries.

Neither could Eva, it seemed, be ignored.

As Pearson explained to her, 'Eva always comes up with the girls.'

'Oh?'

'There's always got to be a picture of a pretty girl on the page.'

His matter-of-factness was shocking. 'That's pretty sexist, isn't it?'

'That's the way it is,' Pearson shrugged.

Rosy didn't sense that the elder hack had any violent objections.

'It's that basic, is it?' she asked indignantly.

'Yep.'

'Every day another smiling bit of decoration? A young, willing female for male fantasies?'

'Same in every paper, Rosy.'

'Why?'

'It makes the page look better.'

'It?? Common or garden crumpet, you mean.'

'Oh, no,' said Pearson, smiling. 'Hardly that.'

'Oh?'

'In this column we deal in CLASS crumpet.'

The elder hack was grinning widely now.

'Oh, YOU!' Rosy made as if to rip her hair out.

It was only later that she realised he hadn't been kidding that much.

Piece by piece, Sword's world was falling into place. Or so Rosy felt.

The principles of straight reporting still applied in this surreal new environment, she decided. It was just that everyone she interviewed now was famous. The stories still concerned general domestic tragedies, but they were now more specialised – the Countess running off with the male nanny and the mortifying consequences of a celebrity no-show at a soirée.

As for Anthony Sword himself, he was the king of the castle. Or should that be of the contradiction?

He was a fat man who claimed loudly that he never ate these days. He screamed and shouted; the next minute all was forgotten. She was in awe of him; he called her darling.

His routine hadn't varied much since she had been

privy to it. At around 10.30 the gossip columnist would arrive in his office. He would read the papers, holding up pages and slapping them with the back of his hand as he made dismissive comments – and none more so than on Benedict Pierce's column in the *Daily Post*. He would then scream down the phone at anyone who dared protest about any of his stories in the *Dispatch* that morning. He would lunch until mid-afternoon. And then he would get other people to write his stories.

It wasn't much in the way of personal insight, she knew, but perhaps that would come when she earned his trust. For Rosy was determined on one thing: she was not going back to the news-room if she could help it.

Despite her occasional misgivings about what she was doing there at all, Rosy found herself liking Pearson and Jamie immensely. Tina, the young secretary, was always friendly and cheerful. Even the downtrodden sub-editor who took the full wrath of Sword when he came into the office to lay out the page and write the headlines every day at four o'clock turned out to have a sense of humour on the quiet. After a week, Rosy was amazed at how much she enjoyed working with them all.

She also knew she could learn a lot.

Pearson was an old-style press man – easy-going to the point of idleness. Nothing threw him. He drank, he cooked his expenses and then he would write a brilliantly funny lead story in twenty minutes flat.

And then there was Jamie.

If Anglo-Indian Jamie Rajanayagam was the rising star of society journalism, it was because, apart from his laconic intelligence and hard work, he believed in himself. He called himself Raj, and it was a suitably grand solution to the problem of pronunciation.

The telephone rang for him constantly, and there seemed to be as many friends as useful acquaintances among the callers. He had well-born blondes for breakfast, lunch and dinner. He had a formidable contacts book and an enviably nonchalant manner. He could not have been kinder to her.

Yet Rosy could not help thinking, at odd moments when she discovered that she was staring at him, that Jamie's improbably debonair appearance – his lustrous dark curls, expensive English country clothes and brocade waistcoats (with the occasional airing of his old Christ Church scarf), together with an accent plummier than the strangled call of the Shires – gave the impression that he was the product of some humorous society handbook: he had followed it to the letter, but had failed to see the joke.

That didn't stop him being appallingly attractive.

15 | *Top Contact*

'I had a lovely clinch with Sean Connery the other evening,' said the woman on her knees. She was dusting the chest of drawers in the hall.

'He was hard and dark and the colour came off him like damp earth all over that white swimsuit with a belt. And then, *quelle coincidence*, one of my girls had him too, right after the *Ten O'Clock News* on the other channel.'

Mae West gave no indication of being impressed. She had heard it all before, so she carried on licking her leg in that superior way of hers, warm in her pool of afternoon sun. That was the trouble with cats, thought Eva, no interest in anyone but themselves.

'Film (1957), it said in the *Telly Times*. Beauty on Beach . . . Eva Coutts, there I was in the credits. It was quite a shock, all that lollipop Technicolor, perms like corrugated iron, we had – hair as stiff as the director's pants. I had a small gin after. A toast to what was once.'

Eva stood up creakily and whisked the duster over the bannister rail.

'Little Lottie – what's her other name again? – she had a proper part in her doings with Sean over on ITV. Only six down in the credits and tits out before the plot

76

even got going. It's all changed since my day. But she's a good girl, Lottie. She rang me only yesterday, always keeps in touch. Hasn't forgotten all I do for her, unlike some I could mention.'

She gave her piles of swollen scrapbooks and magazines a final flick and looked around, satisfied.

A gleaming lino-tiled hall. Rubber plant released from the grimy smothering of dust. Colour of telephone (cream) uncovered from patina of inky fingerprint. That was it. Another small victory inside 2 Fairlawn Avenue, a semi-detached box with mouldering pebbledash and chipped stained glass in the door. Not the best address in the metropolis, nor even in East Sheen. But Eva Coutts had done St John's Wood, and Crouch End when times got harder, and even Paris (though that turned out not quite what she had in mind), and now she had come back to her roots. A nice respectable neighbourhood.

Besides, it was amazing what could be achieved, even from here. In the bulging red book, which barely held together now, were numbers which represented decades of dedication.

'I could ring Sean if I wanted,' said Eva , to no one in particular. 'Better not, though. He's not someone you want to go bothering for no reason.'

At least she was still working, in her way.

'Top Contact, they call me at the *Daily Dispatch*. "It's Eva," they say when I get on the blower, "Top Contact." Then they pass me on to that nice Rosy they've got there now.'

She plumped up the cushions on the sofa. Gold velveteen: very smart. It needed something plain in the sitting room with the peony wallpaper, the Japanese screen, all the pictures and posters and photographs and knick-knacks.

Eva put out a plate of coconut creams and the door-bell chimed right on cue.

It was the third Tuesday in the month, and the ladies from St Michael's who had her on their old lady list never missed a visit. Eva had not known how to react when the first church mission had turned up on the doorstep. It was a liberty, making assumptions about ladies on their own like that. But she had found herself agreeing to see them, and now she quite enjoyed the chat when one arrived.

Mrs Thompson, the one who normally came – a bulky, sensible woman in her fifties – wiped her feet thoroughly on the mat inside the door, and said, 'How have we been keeping?'

'Well,' said Eva, 'It hasn't been so bad. A few make-ups and break-ups. That Mick Jagger's been up to his old tricks again, and there's going to be trouble with Fergie and Diana.'

Mrs Thompson squealed with laughter. 'Oh, you do cheer me up, Eva. Shall we put the kettle on?'

'Unless you want something stronger,' said Eva, with-out much hope.

'You are a one,' said the church visitor. 'I'll just take my coat off. And before I forget, I've brought you a copy of *Ciao!* magazine. My Ann left it when she came on the train the other day, and I know how much you enjoy that sort of thing.'

Eva grinned.

They studied it together over the tea and biscuits in the sitting room, Eva adding all sorts of juicy tittle-tattle about the stars, her favourite topic of conversation.

'You've got a wonderful imagination,' sighed her guest.

'I got presents that big once,' said Eva, pointing at a picture of an actress hung with jewellery at a birthday party. 'Oh yes. I've had my day. Furs and champagne, the odd diamond and lobster thrown in. I was worth spending money on, as you could have seen for yourself the other teatime in the Monday film with Sean . . . whatsisname. I had all the fellas. I was married once, but I left with the dog. It had nicer habits.'

Mrs Thompson smiled indulgently. It was marvellous really, she thought, how the old girl kept her spirits up. Sitting there with false eyelashes – at her age! – and smudged clown lipstick too big for her mouth. Not to mention the dress. It looked like something the Queen wore in the Sixties. Her thoughts turned to the rich possibilities of jumble here.

Eva was in full spate.

The old ladies all loved to talk, poor dears. Even if most of it was absolute rubbish.

'Course I don't get out so much now, but I keep in touch with what's going on. And my boy visits regular, though he's always so busy these days. Amazing what you can do over the phone even when you can't face the world. Mind you, there are days now when I can't look in the mirror. So I let the dust lie there – when I get up the courage to look, the old face is ready-powdered!'

Eva cackled on: 'Best keep fond memories intact. I was the Face of 1946, you know.'

The church visitor rattled her teacup. 'Well, I must be off. You'll be all right, will you, dear?'

'I'll probably give Lottie Landor another tinkle,' said Eva absently. 'Not that I want to pester her. Never that.

You just never know when some nice young man might answer the phone and provide a "New-Romance-Has-Blossomed" story—'

'That's right, dear. I'll be off then—'

'Mind you, it's blooming hard work. This AIDS business has a lot to answer for. You can ring and talk to dozens of people and there'll be not a nibble. They're all doing it, but they can't admit anything.'

'Of course, dear. You take care now. Bye. See you next time.'

Eva closed the front door behind her and made for the telephone. Another call to that Danielle what-ever-her-name-was before she set off on her little holiday couldn't hurt. One lived in hope of sex, rage and sin and this would be a good evening for it.

16 | *At Home*

When Rosy returned home to the feral disorder of their Fulham residence she found Emma licking doughnut sugar off her fingers and penning a letter.

'Dear Mrs Jenkins,' Rosy read over her shoulder, 'I assure you I have not been trespassing in your garden. I am sorry to hear about your disappearing bluebells and leaves. Can I suggest you investigate the involvement of the black Labrador at No. 33? Yours, Rosy Hope (Ms).

'Oi!' said Rosy. 'That's forgery.'

Emma signed off with an indignant flourish, nearly knocking over a vase containing the offending bluebells.

'There. That should sort the old bat out,' she said, grinning. 'She sent us one of her Neighbourhood Watch notes.'

'OK, but . . .'

'That woman should have a campaign medal for curtain-twitching.'

'Perhaps I should recruit her as the Endymion Road operative,' said Rosy.

Emma found the envelopes next to the toaster. She de-crumbed one and addressed it firmly to moaning Ma

Jenkins in the flat downstairs. 'There. Not really a lie as it was me who did the raid.'

Rosy giggled.

'It was worth it, wasn't it?' asked Emma.

'I suppose, although I looked a bit ... amateurish for a party like that.'

'That could be your strongest suit,' said Emma. 'Now,' she settled on the sofa, hugging a Mexican cushion. 'What about the men?'

Rosy pretended she didn't know what her flatmate was on about. 'In what sense, the men?'

'Wh-a-t? You go to one of the hottest parties in London, you have *carte blanche* to go up to anyone you fancy and introduce yourself and you don't get in with the Eligibles? They're still out there, walking around freely?'

'Oh no ... was *that* what I was supposed to do?'

'So what is Sword like, really?' Emma asked as they picked over their Mean Cuisine dinners. Emma was having a rare night in. The man she'd brought home the previous night hadn't left until teatime.

'Is that all you can talk about?'

'Rosy, it's all you can talk about – you haven't done anything else but go to work and on to some event or other afterwards and then crawl home exhausted ... and not even with a decent man in tow!'

Rosy sighed.

'I'm knackered.'

Emma rolled her eyes. 'I despair.'

'Well, you should try it.'

'Try what?'

'Holding down a full-time job and a social life. Women are expected to do everything these days.

82

Super-career, super-attractive, superman panting in the wings.'

'Wh-a-t? That's so ... Eighties,' scorned Emma.

'You know what I mean. It's not that easy – or it isn't for me. And I wish you'd stop going on about it.'

They ate in silence for a moment. 'Sorry,' said Rosy. 'It's just that everyone asks that question, the whole time, wherever I go.'

'About Sword? Okay, okay, boring,' shrugged Emma.

'No, it's all right. He was awful today.'

'In what way?'

Rosy found she did want to talk about it after all.

'It's like ... to work with Sword you have to be a combination of mindreader, MI5 and the *Encyclopedia Britannica*. For example, today, he kept yelling at us that he wanted new people in the column, he's tired of all the same old faces. So we did some new people.'

'And?'

'And all he said was, "Who the fuck are these?" '

They both laughed.

'The odd thing is,' Rosy went on, 'that there's something about him that makes it less offensive than you'd think. No one seems to take it personally. He blusters – and then it's over, forgotten.'

'Even by you?' Emma smiled knowingly.

'Mostly,' said Rosy, only too well aware of how well her friend could read her sensitivities.

'Is there a Mrs Sword?'

'Not that anyone knows of.'

'What about family then?'

'Dunno. Never heard anything about any family.'

Emma considered this, then said, 'He's quite ... lonely then?'

Rosy chewed absently. This was a facet of the man she hadn't even begun to fathom.

17 | *Sword Strikes*

Anthony Sword's taxi headed north, skirting the velvety dusk which hung over Regent's Park. The warm heaviness of the late spring evening came in through the open window only to do battle with great gusts of hot air inside.

His driver was in full flood.

'I 'ad that 'Arrison Ford in my cab once. He got in with two other blokes and I KNEW it was 'im. I wanted to talk to 'im, you know, but those other blokes, they were yappin' away something chronic. Couldn't get a word in, me. But I really wanted 'im to know I knew it was 'im. So you know what I did?'

Sword was barely listening, but managed a mumble.

'As 'e got out, right . . . I was humming the theme tune from *Indiana Jones*!'

The gossip columnist gave the required grunt of acknowledgement. He continued staring out of the window as the lushly swollen black trees and luminous white mansions sped by.

Everyone wanted to talk to him, he realised – the climbers, the publicity-seekers, the plain garrulous, the odd-bods, the vengeful – but there were very few people that he had ever wanted to talk to. Could ever have talked to. Not about the things that really mattered. Would it always be like this?

The cab lurched and rolled, ground and ticked, and carried him further away.

In the wrong direction.

It was only when he reached Highgate and the solid outline of his own ornate front door that he realised the full significance of what he had done this Tuesday night.

For once in his life he had not gone.

He didn't know why he had done it. All he knew was that he might have broken free at last.

Sword took the telephone off the hook and switched off the answering machine. He ate moderately, as advised. He put on his favourite Puccini arias but his soul obstinately refused to soar.

The past days his mood had worsened.

And even when he fought against the black clouds, all he could sense was the bitter gall of decay.

Then dust and ashes.

In the end, he mooched upstairs and unlocked the door to the bare box-room. He didn't put on the light. A few cartoon clouds jiggered past outside and Sword watched, feeling utterly detached from the world, as the old drowsy numbness pulled him down.

He didn't need to put on the light. He knew exactly where the book was. His hand trembled slightly as he reached for it, under newspaper in an old trunk. As he pulled it out he felt a few more of its tattered bindings rip. Sadness tightened in his throat.

Downstairs again, he opened its large, fading bulge as carefully as he could. There were almost more loose pages now than ones still in place and the paste which had once held the pictures in had long since crumbled and lost its grip.

It didn't matter.

In fact, he thought, it was better this way. It heightened his detachment to feel it turning to dust in his hands. It was a relic from another time. A scrapbook.

A book of scraps.

The woman in the black and white photographs had clamped hair and big, slick lips. Yet she was wholesome too, the smile pure brown-bread-and-butter. Her face was well rounded in the way that was thought attractive back then, hinting at substantial softness below.

There were other photographs: loose ones of a chubby child and a dog. There was one of a house with a garden.

And there were the brown-and-white photographs from old newspapers that always made his heart clutch. His ailing strained heart.

Sword spread the ragged hoard over the floor.

In the beginning she had made him what he was, while what he had become – he recognised all too clearly – was the invention of a nineteen-year-old boy.

A change was long overdue.

Now, as he watched over the wreckage like a man in a B-movie, he shivered when he considered what he had done and how it would appear to her – then at what she could do to him in return. What havoc she could wreak while he was half in love with easeful death. . . .

Why hadn't he gone to her, this Tuesday evening? The reasons were foggy, even to him. Pure instinct, fear of change, fear that he could not change? A sudden lunge for self-determination in the face of . . . what? The diagnosis? The biography?

Overwhelmed, he put his head in his hands and allowed himself to weep, silently, over the pictures.

18 | *Restaurant Opening*

A copy of that morning's *Daily Dispatch* was open at Sword's page on one of the simple ironwork tables at Le Dingo Café in Soho. One of the stories read:

> 'Is no one safe from the attentions of ludicrous social fantasist Bea Goff, who has flung herself at every available title in London?
> 'Busy Bea's latest "confession" concerns her so-called liaison with the Duke of Edinburgh. As if the House of Windsor did not have enough on its gold plates with Kitty Litter's poisonous biography, Bea, 60-odd, is now telling alleged friends that she was the mystery woman photographed with the Duke on a yacht off Malta in 1949.
> 'My advice to the Duke is to ignore the publicity-mad harpy and any subsequent missive from her which begins, "Remember me . . .?"'

Benedict Pierce tossed his coat over it.

Soho was not Benedict's favourite place at the best of times, and today it hunkered down into its grime and rubbish bins under close, dark clouds. The distant drums of some Oriental festivity played on his snap-pishness. He preferred an area that made him feel as if he had really made something of himself in the capital, but this was where Nan Purchase was going to be, according to his tame doorman at the Lanesborough.

Le Dingo Café was situated in a dusty alley between tall buildings veined with Victorian drainpipes. It was near enough to the Groucho Club for a noisy crowd to have gathered to quaff as much Australian plonk as possible while avoiding the eager public relations ladies who had invited them to the opening lunch party.

Last month it had been Le Café, for a year before that, the Ultra New York Deli Place, and once long ago, Marchant's, the famous theatrical restaurant.

The man from the *Daily Post* stood stiffly, waiting for his arrival to be noticed. It took a while, during which time he pondered dolefully the size of his picture by-line in the paper.

Sword's new girl Rosy Hope was there already, look-ing flushed but startlingly pretty in a short summer suit. Benedict wandered over.

'Hi there! How are you getting on?'

'Fine, thank you,' smiled Rosy, greenish eyes shining.

'I see you mentioned Sir Philip Hawty and Emily Strong in the Green Countdown party piece. Any come-back?' asked Benedict casually.

'There have been several young women who wouldn't leave their names who sounded terribly upset . . .' said Rosy.

Benedict wondered how much else she might tell him.

'All grist to the mill,' he laughed, about to probe further.

A waitress butted in with a tray of canapés.

'Mmm, these are lovely,' said Rosy, accepting a prawn on a spear.

'Mmm, great,' said Benedict, doing the same. 'How's Sword?'

'Tetchy,' said Rosy.

'What's up, then?'

'Who knows? Sword never ever gives anything away about himself.'

'Even to you lot?'

'Especially to us.'

Benedict grinned. 'What's he going to do about this book then?'

'Er, what book?'

'I hear his biography's being planned. Unauthorised. He's not best pleased.'

But Rosy gave nothing away. 'I haven't been there long enough to know.'

'Sword's biggest Secret. . . .'

She shrugged and smiled sweetly.

Benedict tried another tack. 'He's been seeing quite a bit of Nan Purchase, I notice.'

Rosy proved too much of a professional to fall for that one either. It was clear she was in a different league from the other blabbermouths Sword had hired so unwisely in the last few months. A shame, thought Benedict, a great shame.

She merely said, 'Has he? I wanted to talk to her myself, the other night at Brett Trent's, but . . . I didn't manage it for one reason and another.'

He was about to press her further when an immaculate PR lady homed in.

'Lovely to see you,' trilled the PR. 'Now would you like to meet the chef, Keith? He trained with Pierre at Pierre's, then went to Marco Jeckyl-Blanc, and then to

91

Simply Bruce in Sydney – and now he's here. Everyone's terribly excited about it.' She beamed excitedly.

'Absolutely,' said Benedict, reaching out to a tray of delicacies in filo pastry. 'Would you mind if we left it a while? I'd like to get a better idea of the food first. Mmm, delicious.'

'Fabulous,' echoed Rosy with her mouth full.

First, he had work to do, and he had her in sight.

Across the room Nan Purchase was in consultation with Honoria Peeke, the *Prattler*'s woman on the spot.

Benedict made his way over.

'The way I see it, your Queen is being a little unreal in these socially challenging times,' Nan was telling the *Prattler*'s social editrix. 'If Liz could maybe just stop being so hoity-toity about divorce and regard it as the starting point of one-on-one rebirth, then her poor children wouldn't suffer so much.'

'Not,' she added briskly when she saw the smile freeze on Honoria's face, 'that it's for me to say.'

'Not at all,' said Honoria, coolly. 'Do go on.'

'Ahem,' said Benedict.

'Benedict, darling!' Honoria launched a plump velvety cheek at him with an enthusiasm which caught him off guard. 'I was about to come over, there are one or two teensy questions I wanted to ask you, to get things absolutely right.'

Nan Purchase was gracious when the introductions were made. Close up, the lines on her thin brown face had a feathery upward slant, but Benedict was surprised to receive a perfectly genuine smile.

'Mrs Purchase was telling me that even the Queen might benefit from her new treatment theories,' said Honoria with an indignant glint in her eye. 'What was it you were saying about the interpersonal relationships of our dear Royals and the use of . . . er, regression therapy, was it? Presumably they *know* who they were. They were the Kings and Queens of England!'

'I've enjoyed your book, Mrs Purchase,' said Benedict, resolutely impaling himself on Honoria's pointedness.

'Thank you.'

'Although, if you don't mind me saying, this seems a strange event for you to attend while you're over here . . . I mean in the sense that a restaurant opening is all about eating a lot. I thought it might make a little diary piece. . . .'

'As a matter of fact, you're right,' said Nan. 'Restaurant openings with everyone going free range isn't exactly my favourite. I was hoping to meet someone here – to save him from himself. The *Daily Dispatch*, you said – do you know Anthony Sword?'

Benedict smiled. 'The *Daily Post* actually – but yes, as well as anyone.'

Nan nodded, with a diplomatic half smile.

'Oh, yes!' cried Honoria, clearly loving every moment. 'Benedict is the most marvellous diary columnist. If he doesn't print the biggest stories it's because he's far too nice to upset people.'

Nan widened her eyes.

'How refreshing,' she said.

Benedict blanched. Yet he went on with the determination of a man who had learned to accept insults gracefully, if there was something in it at the end for him. 'How long are you staying in London, Mrs Purchase?' he asked.

'A couple of months.'

'You're over for the Season?'

'Sure, in a way. I don't know how long exactly I will need to be here.'

'Oh, yes?'

Benedict waited, but she went no further.

'I've long admired your photograph in the American press,' he said.

After that they covered Liz Smith's lists, Bill Blass's connections, Elizabeth Taylor's yo-yo weight, Princess Diana's bulimia and other world events.

Then he asked if he could take her out to lunch while she was here.

To his relief, Nan accepted gracefully.

The columnist knew how Nan's world turned.

If Anthony Sword could not be relied on – and he hadn't turned up at this lunch – then she would have nothing to lose by cultivating his rival.

19 | *Solar Power*

It was another miraculously warm day. The midday sun head-butted Anthony Sword through the window as he reclined on his office chaise longue.

He thought it was best to conserve his energy in these hungry times.

He had given up lunch.

He was dodging his drinking mates.

He was running on pure bile.

'You all right, Mr Sword?' Tina, his loyal plump-and-pink secretary called over.

'I'm absorbing solar power,' he snapped, eyes closed, bulk limp in his own personal greenhouse effect.

As a matter of fact, the food deprivation seemed to be concentrating his mind wonderfully on the really important things in life. Like how to regain a feeling of control.

He could start by doing for that pompadoured pest Benedict Pierce.

A game plan was beginning to form.

Sword lay back belly up, pregnant in the dusty sunshine with gestating schemes. A smile spread in the curls of his dark beard.

Under the glassy heat, he nodded off.

Some secrets were better left alone. Anthony Sword, of course, only felt this way about his own.

Other people's were fair game.

At three-thirty, he woke feeling liverish. He and Tina were still alone.

He accepted a mug of black coffee.

'Saccharin?' asked Tina.

'No. I am not an experimental rat.'

'Suit yourself.' His young secretary clicked two into her own cup.

'Where the fuck is the rest of my staff?' roared Sword.

Tina consulted the weekly invitation list and an outsize diary on her desk.

'Jamie's having lunch with the Earl of Trent. Pearson's gone to a book launch—'

'Good grief. Some work at last. Which one?'

'Er, *The Good Nude Beach Guide.*'

'That would explain it,' he said, cuttingly.

'And Rosy's at the opening of Le Dingo in Soho, a, er, restaurant.'

A sharp intake of breath from Sword. 'What about the Beast? Any chance of him justifying his vast salary and turning his hand to some work around here?'

Tina settled for an apologetic silence.

'It's strange,' he said, 'to think that the Sword's Secrets office is allegedly a place of work. You wouldn't fucking know it the way that lot behave!' He slammed his coffee down on his desk, splashing notebooks and photographs and letters.

His secretary wisely ignored the damp display and kept quiet.

'I've got Jamie Raj, fucking his way round fucking London. Pearson salivating over actresses young enough to be his granddaughters. And that girl Rosy . . . she's so bloody PRISSY about everything. . . .'

'Poor you. Have a custard cream,' offered Tina.

'I do not want a custard fucking cream!'

'There, don't upset yourself,' said Tina. 'My stars said it would be a bumpy week, but I don't think we can take any more trauma—'

'Oh, stop twittering! Get me all the cuts on Nan Purchase, ex-wife of Jim Purchase, of Purchase New Life Centers in the US. The divorce settlement, the division of assets. Also the Duchess of York since her separation, and the Princess of Wales' theatrical interests. Oh, and Tina—'

She was already going out of the door on the way to the reference library.

She turned back to face him. 'Yes?'

It was the oddest feeling.

Not for the first time since he had sat in Harley Street to be told he could not carry on in his old ways unless he wanted a privilege pass to the widest coffin in London, Sword stopped himself short. He was aware of a sinking heaviness deep inside. And the strangest ache of – what the hell was it?

Tina stared back, defiant.

'Do you still want those two days off next week to go to the whatever-it-was with your Paul?' he asked her.

'The Save-the-Elephants rally.'

'Whatever.'

'Well, yes, but if it's not possible, that's all there is to it. I don't—'

'No. You go. Take the time off. You deserve it, and I, well I've got a lot on my mind, at the moment.'

'Oh, Mr Sword. You don't have to . . . but, if you're

sure, that's really great. Thanks.' Her scrubbed face was alight with goodwill.

He waved his hand dismissively.

'Mr Sword?'

'I hope you don't mind, but when you want to be – you can be really nice. We all think that . . . underneath . . . even if . . .'

She broke off, embarrassed. Then, she gave him a spontaneous bear hug that caught him off-balance and made him gasp.

Ten minutes later, it was as well that his secretary was out of the room. Sword answered his private line and she said straight away, 'Where were you last night?'

He'd known this was coming.

Silence.

Then he said, 'I'm sorry.'

A guilt-inducing sigh from the other end of the line.

'Tuesday has always been our night. You never miss one of our nights.'

He couldn't decide if that was a statement of fact or an order. It had all the force of an order.

'Look, I'm—'

'You might have let me know. I'd got everything ready.'

'Sorry.'

'I made treacle pud special.'

His stomach lurched.

'I – I couldn't,' he said faintly. 'I'm not well.'

'Since when did that stop a boy coming home to his mother?'

20 | *Scribblers*

It was incredible, Rosy discovered, how little time it took to slip into a routine, however strange or intimidating it may have seemed at first.

Traditionally a day on the Sword's Secrets column ended down in the Scribblers Club, the basement bar annexe of the *Daily Dispatch*, and, barely more than two weeks after she had first met Anthony Sword there, Rosy felt the warm glow of being part of that tradition. Some evenings they had a glass of house champagne, but this time Rosy and Jamie Raj settled for Sauvignon and a bowl of Twiglets.

Sword, uncharacteristically, had declined to join them.

The elder hack Pearson was already on what he referred to as 'night manoeuvres'.

'Where are you off to tonight?' asked Rosy as she flopped down on the battered chesterfield sofa which was Sword's habitual vantage point. The carpet around it bore the marks of his distinctive claret accidents.

'Royal Highland Ball,' said Jamie. 'It's a rip-off of the Caledonian.'

'I see,' said Rosy, though she didn't. 'Who are you taking?'

'One of my Sophies.'

'Which one?'

'The one with the daddy who has a yacht for Cowes Week,' he said rationally. 'One has to think ahead.'

Rosy crunched a Twiglet, then stopped mid-munch. Not, she thought, the kind of *savoir-faire* which implied the requisite metropolitan sophistication. And not that the worldly Jamie Raj would ever think of her in that way, but he would certainly have a say in whether she was up to being given the job permanently.

For now, though, it was enough for Rosy to be sitting here with him, enjoying the chat and the envious looks of other women in the room.

'It would serve you right if you got there and found she had a thing about men in kilts,' she teased gently. 'Some women find thick legs and flying plaid incredibly sexy.'

'She loathes men in kilts. I checked,' said Jamie. 'Although I might discover, of course, that I harbour dark desires for wee Scottish lassies if I find one with a big enough family castle.'

'You're incorrigible.'

He raised his glass. 'I'm practical.'

'Absolutely,' said Rosy.

'And I'm teasing.'

A pause. 'I knew that.'

'What about you?' he asked. 'Did I hear Sword trying to pass off yet another of his foodie parties on to you?'

Rosy rummaged in her bag and fished out the invitation.

' "Cuban Food Festival",' she read. ' "The Tower Hotel recreates the electrifying atmosphere of Cuba. A well-known Cuban chef will present his famous Cuban Potato Nougat, an unusual dessert of Cuban root vegetable mixed with peanuts and enjoyed by Christopher Columbus—" '

'Yuk. See what you mean.'

'Wait. There's more. "As well as the chef, Cubana Airlines have transported an exciting Cuban trio to the hotel, together with a master cigar roller and a genuine ethnic Havana fritter vendor from Marianao Beach." '

'It's the high life,' said Jamie, straight-faced.

They cracked up.

'I don't know whether my waistband can take another PR trough,' she said glumly.

'Go. You never know who you might meet. You should relax more. Enjoy it.'

He was right, of course.

'What's up with Sword anyway?' Rosy embarked on another office tradition that was more fun here than anywhere else she'd worked – griping about the boss.

'He's up to something, of course.'

'What though?'

If Jamie knew, he was giving nothing away. 'We are but galley slaves in his creaking ship,' he proclaimed.

'Wha-a-t?'

'We provide the power, dearheart, but we can't see where we're going.'

'Well I can't, anyway,' attested Rosy.

'You're doing all right.'

'Am I? Really?' She had to ask.

'Sure.'

They sipped in silence for a moment.

'What does your boyfriend think of all this? You out on the town every night?' asked Jamie.

'Oh . . . I don't have one.'

'I'm surprised.'

'Oh?'

'What happened?'

Rosy was caught off guard.

'All the usual things. It, er, had been going downhill and he met someone else.'

'You'd been together a long time?'

'About two years.'

'Not easy.'

'No. I think he might have been put off by the S and D words,' said Rosy.

'S and D words?'

'Settling Down. My mum decided she'd reached the mother-of-the-bride stage in her life. She went on about it a bit.'

'And?'

Rosy grimaced. 'She went on about it. He just went.'

'But you're not ready for settling down...?'

'No.'

'There's no one else to do it instead?'

'Family, you mean? Uh-uh. Only child.' She really didn't want to talk about it.

Only ... Jamie had turned those amber eyes on her like interrogation lamps. She hesitated, then said, 'Did you ever...?'

'What?'

'Forget it. You wouldn't understand.'

'I wouldn't bet on it,' he said.

'You wouldn't. Understand, I mean. I bet you've never known what it's like to have a moment of self-doubt. It just doesn't happen to people like you—'

'Don't you believe it, Rosy.' He gave her a long, sad and, it had to be said, practised, look.

She thought, as she always did on the rare occasions when they had talked alone together, how kind he could be when he was not putting on his ladykiller act.

Jamie persisted, softly.

She surrendered.

No wonder, she thought, as she heard herself go into the most embarrassing detail.... No wonder Jamie Raj always got the story.

21 | *Sword on Air*

Anthony Sword was live on TV. To be precise (he was in one of his most prickly, finicky moods), he was LIVID on TV, being interviewed beyond endurance by live link from his Highgate garden.

'We would all be the poorer without the Royal Family. Especially me,' he snarled at the camera.

He could just imagine the rabbity twitching of the mid-morning show's blonde poppet presenter at that one. He was being relayed instantaneously to a screen in the television studio. She could see him but he couldn't see her.

She pounced on that. 'So you admit you exploit the Royal Family for your own ends?' she asserted. Sword heard the note of triumph from the studio in his earpiece.

Housewifely daytime presenters like this one never understood when he was being funny.

'On the contrary, I have great respect for Her Majesty the Queen. If anything, my many royal scoops in the *Daily Dispatch* enable her and her family to exploit us, the decent, tax-paying, newspaper-buying public,' he replied in a smooth change of tone.

A buzzing in his earpiece. Sword strained slightly to

translate it as, 'Do you not think there are more important issues in the world today than the Duchess of York's
friends and whether the Prince and Princess of Wales
spent the weekend together?'

'No,' said Sword.

He let the pause worry his interrogatrix.

'Surely the public has had enough, there have been
too many intrusive stories about the Royals,' she persisted.

'Then why did you invite me on to your programme
to speak about them?'

Even the sound recordist with the furry animal on a
stick grinned at that.

Cables snaked from the open kitchen door out to the
terrace where Sword sat facing the outside broadcast
crew. He let them come to him these days.

The terrace was still cool although the dew had gone
from the bright busy lizzies in their regiments of terra-
cotta pots. He'd had time for a satisfying morning aria
and he was in fine voice.

'Do you not—'

He decided to humour them.

'I see my position as that of moral guardian,' he interrupted portentously. 'Those who step out of line can
expect public exposure. Censure if necessary. Outrage is
a formidable leveller.'

Flummoxed silence in his ear. A friendly girl with a
clipboard standing just behind the cameraman waved
him on to continue.

He obliged.

'I,' said Sword, narrowing his piratical eyes for effect,
'have made media stars of the Royal Family. What we
must understand is that we are dealing here with a
twentieth-century monarch who prefers the solemn

105

regality of a scrambled egg on the royal knees to the hoi-polloi of a state banquet. We have an heir to the throne who chases old friends instead of glamorous young mistresses. If the public is to pay, the public must be kept happy and interested. It's as simple as that.'

Had he gone too far? He resisted the urge to chortle.

Let us see, he thought, whether anyone is out there.

It was time for some fun.

'If the Princess of Wales is having an affair with a butch ballet dancer – and I say no more than *if* – ' he glowered convincingly, making sure his meaning was clear, ' – and if the Duchess of York wants to leave for the United States and become a New Age therapist, then they are doing no less than their public duty in these dull, standardised and impoverished times, and we should salute them for it.'

The friendly girl and the OB producer exchanged a glance he knew well. It's a scoop, it said.

There was a nervous change of tack from the studio: 'Er, how do you get all your gossip?'

The most boring question in the world.

Sword gave the strained smile of a man whose bowels have been acting up.

'Like anyone else. I talk to my friends,' he said. 'Unlike most other people, I have friends in the highest places.' He stared deep and, he hoped, menacingly into the camera lens.

'Could you—?'

'I take it you do not expect me to reveal my sources on national television.'

'I understand,' twittered his interviewer from the studio, as if she were about to unearth one of the secrets of the universe, 'that you don't actually write all the stories that appear in your column yourself.'

'My dear young woman,' said Anthony Sword. 'Sometimes I wake up in the morning and have to read the paper myself to find out who I have been talking to.'

22 | *Charming Balls*

'Where I went last night,' said Emma over breakfast at the flat, 'there was a chap complaining that his boss had slept with 1,000 Spanish women, 640 Italians, 200-odd Germans, 100 Frenchwomen and 91 Turkish ladies.'

'Christ!' gasped Rosy, incredulous. Even by Emma's standards of all-night clubbing sessions this was going some. 'Hasn't he heard about AIDS?'

'Nope. It was Don Giovanni. I went to the opera with that investment analyst I met at Madeleine's party.' Emma pulled her I-got-you-there face.

Rosy giggled.

'Was he the banker with the red face and the tie over his left shoulder?'

'That's the one,' said Emma. 'He picked me up in his Porsche, showing off that he's still got one. We had drinks with investors to begin with, then drinks with investors in the interval, and ended up having drinks and talking about high-yield bonds in the American Bar at the Savoy, which they all call "The Sav".'

'Ah,' said Rosy. 'So he's a complete banker then?'

The sash window of their lamentable sitting room was open as far as it would go and Rosy sat at the table in front of it feeling the cool air fresh on her face.

Below, the forbidden garden was a square of enticing wilderness. It had been so warm lately that ancient gnarled lilacs were bursting out like purple and white fists shoving their way into the sun. A pear tree and an old apple tree were in blossom and a patch of cow parsley foamed out from the far corner. A lone wood pigeon cooed.

After a decent night's sleep and her chat with Jamie she felt as if she could take on anything.

Who could tell? She might even make it as a social columnist.

The others were lounging around chatting when Rosy arrived at what she was beginning to think of – she realised with a jolt – as 'her' desk. The television high on the wall chattered softly to itself. A rabbity-looking presenter on the mid-morning show seemed to be doing something warm and positive with vegetables.

'Post-mortem,' explained Jamie. He was foppish in a brocaded burgundy waistcoat.

'Eh?' What had she missed?

'Sword. On the telly,' he explained.

'Oh?'

'He was ever so funny,' said Tina, 'though I don't think the woman interviewing him thought so.'

'Oh dear.'

'It was hilarious,' said Tina.

Jamie switched off the television but no one showed any signs of getting down to any work. With Sword safely out of the office, there was a holiday atmosphere.

'Any messages?' he asked idly.

Tina flipped through a neat notepad. 'Jamie: please call a Lucy, a Cordelia, two Emmas and a Sarah-Jane. Pearson: can you call your wife, the Limelight Club, the

Oxted Arms, and Emily Strong's agent, who didn't sound too happy. Rosy: er . . . Eva's been on for you.'

'Thanks a lot,' sighed Rosy.

Pearson felt his way back to his desk and groaned.

'How's your head, Pearson?' laughed Jamie. 'Eventful evening?'

'Urgh. It's beginning to come back to me.'

'Ah, the wrath of grapes,' quipped Jamie. He was enviably unaffected by late nights.

'How were the Highland flings last night, Jamie?' asked Rosy.

'Good. Apart from Honoria.'

'Honoria Peeke and her social-death-defying semi-colons,' said Pearson morosely.

Jamie grinned in agreement.

'Everywhere I turned, she was there, tapping on that little book she carries, wanting names and places.'

'Hope you made some up,' said Pearson drily.

They all laughed.

Jamie winked. 'I can just imagine it! Honoria's Report: "Last night I attended a perfectly charming ball given by Lady Sylvia Moysste-Gusset for her lovely daughter Pinkie, who rides so well." '

Pearson clutched his head but still managed to take up the recitation in an affected sing-song voice: ' "Other guests included pretty Henrietta Lampshade, who was feeling a new woman by dawn (the new woman declined to comment); and the Honourable Ophelia Balls, who had a thrilling effect on all the young men present." '

They fell about.

'Didn't you work with her at the *Prattler*, Jamie?' asked Rosy.

'Don't remind me,' he shuddered. 'I thought I'd writ-

110

ten my last piece in Peeke Speak, thanks to the Incident with Lord Empson.'

'What was that?' Rosy accepted a strong coffee from Tina.

Jamie leaned nonchalantly against the chaise longue, and raked back his dark curls.

'It really wasn't my fault. One of my first pieces for the *Prattler* was about Lord Empson's son Roland's alleged talent for playing the guitar. He had a band and had wowed the fifth forms of several well-known girls' schools, among them one of Honoria's appalling goddaughters. I was set the task of making some copy of it, which I managed. But the sub-editor must have been unwell or incapable, because my highly flattering piece was given unfortunate connotations when "music-loving teenager" appeared in print as "mucus-loving teenager" and had him "sleeping out" instead of "stepping out". It was my first libel writ. Which only goes to show how sensibility to printing mistakes can often point to the truth.'

'What do you mean?' frowned Tina.

'Roland dropped out of school shortly afterwards, and started living rough. His only real talent turned out to be for glue sniffing. Of course, all that only came out after the *Prattler* had settled out of court for £40,000 libel damages. Empson's lawyers had argued successfully that my article implied that he was – well, exactly what he turned out to be.'

'That bloody woman wouldn't know a story if it stamped on her foot and shook her by the bloody hand,' said Pearson with unnecessary emphasis.

'Which is why, in the end, she is such an asset to us,' said Jamie.

'Was Benedict there?' asked Rosy.

'Oh yes, immaculate hair gleaming in the gloaming, asking everyone who might know whether Sword was involved with Nan Purchase?'

'Subtle, then,' said Rosy.

'Benedict Pierce,' said Jamie, languidly. 'I'll bet you anything that's what THAT' – he gestured up at the TV – 'was all about this morning.'

'. . . now while you're on, there's that other little girl I've been keeping my beady eye on. Have you ever heard of that girl . . . ooh, you know the one . . . pretty little thing, was in that telly series with that chap? The one, you know, you've written about her . . . it'll come to me in a minute. Ah! I can see her clear as anything. . . .'

Rosy let the telephone slip. Her pen drew knotted snakes across her notebook. If Eva Coutts didn't get on with it, she would cut her off.

'Oh, do spit it out, Eva.' The words came out more harshly than she intended.

'Well, there's a fine way to talk. After all I do for you . . . that Danielle and the Nice-Naughty story . . . a nice big cash credit for that there'll be, won't there . . . when you eventually get down to doing it, that is. Shouldn't be hard to stand up. Now where was I—?'

'We hadn't actually got as far as a name yet.'

'Always on the lookout for a bit of romance. Not that you could call me greedy, but there's always room for another cheque in the bank, eh? And there haven't been that many lately. . . .'

'Yes, Eva. But I think you'll find you only get the cash if you actually give us a story,' said Rosy wearily.

Sarcasm was wasted on the ancient theatrical tipster.

'If you'll just let me tell you . . . the one you wrote

about . . . you weren't very nice about her . . . mmm . . . ah . . .!'

Rosy sat tight.

She was barely listening when Eva said, 'By the way, tell your boss I'm having one of my little parties next week. On Tuesday evening.'

'Sorry, what . . .?'

'I'm having one of my do's. And tell him – my girls have got to earn a crust somehow. A nice bit o' sex, rage and sin, eh? Will you tell him that?'

Likely Sword would to go to that, Rosy DIDN'T think.

23 | *Doing Lunch*

If Sword had a dark secret of his own – and as far as Benedict Pierce was concerned, that had never been in question – then it was only just that he, Benedict, should be the one to reveal it.

He was working on it.

He had even taken the initiative and been to see the top man at Mega Books.

Nan Purchase couldn't have been more delighted to accept his invitation to lunch. She kept saying so, and Benedict Pierce had no reason to doubt it.

The *Post*'s gossip columnist was feeling pretty chuffed himself. He was alone at last – or nearly – with the Manhattan millionairess and her retro-Seventies' hairstyle at the Savoy Grill. And what made it really worthwhile was that she was his rival's New Best Friend.

Here they were, thought Benedict, with some degree of satisfaction, sitting at easily the fifth or sixth best table at the restaurant among captains of industry and financiers, Government ministers and newspaper editors.

Nan was flirting outrageously with an asparagus tip. Conversation had turned to the Royal Family and the

Role of Fashion in the Maintenance of the Monarchy. A nice easy start, he thought, to get her relaxed before he began to mine more precious seams of information.

The Manhattan multi-millionairess was getting into her stride.

'You gotta keep grounded,' she extrapolated. 'That is the essential component of inner contentment. . . .'

'Well, absolu—'

'You see, you have to be strong enough to be weak. I think you would know all about that.'

Nan pulled a squared-off smile.

He noticed her long, even teeth, and the determined point of her narrow chin. This was the kind of woman who probably went for six-monthly check-ups with the plastic surgeon. She was thirty-nine forever on the outside, but how old was the birth certificate? It could be anything from fifty to sixty-five. For any man interested in her, that could be better and it could be worse.

'Oh, I—' Benedict began, then stopped. He hadn't a clue what she was on about. He thought they were talking about the Princess of Wales and the language of wearing the same dress to several events, but suddenly he wasn't so sure.

But she was off again: 'To show, publicly, a pull towards past-history is to admit to present self-doubt. This in turn can negate the very validity of the public veneer that they seek to show through the media.'

Nan regarded him earnestly, apparently waiting for confirmation. He was unable to provide any.

'There has to be a platform, don't you see?' she went on.

Benedict gambled. Nan was famous for her fashion statements, wasn't she? And with two extravagant

115

bitches for ex-wives, what didn't he know about expensive clothes?

'Oh, you are so right. Those white platform shoes,' he said. 'The platforms should be a warning to us all.'

'I'm sorry?'

'That the Queen Mother and Princess Margaret wear. . . .'

One look at her closed equine features told him they were definitely at cross purposes.

He cleared his throat uneasily.

He was rescued by the impeccable choreography of one waiter bearing Nan's smoked salmon starter-as-a-main-course and another gliding up with the roast beef trolley.

Seemingly by mutual consent, they made an effort to start again when they had been served. After some persuasion, Nan accepted a Meursault spritzer.

'I'm afraid I belong to the ABC school of thought,' she said.

Benedict hoped against hope this meant she wanted to keep it simple.

'Anything But Chardonnay,' she went on. 'In the chicest circles in California, Chardonnay is practically a dirty word.'

He gagged unpleasantly. The bottle he had chosen was ludicrously expensive and he had ordered it for her. He would rather have drunk red. Or rather, he didn't quite have the confidence to carry off white with roast beef with panache.

'Er, why exactly?'

'It's been far too over-exposed. Everybody drinks it. You gotta move on, change, grow.'

Benedict concentrated hard.

He was wondering how to broach the big subject when she brought it up herself.

'I see your great rival Anthony Sword was on TV this morning.'

'So my vigilant news editor tells me,' said Benedict leadenly.

His brain raced. How would she have known Sword was on, unless the fat man had told her himself? Surely mid-morning TV was not on Nan Purchase's normal agenda.

'That was quite a line about Princess Di and the ballet dancer,' said Nan.

'Sword's flying a kite,' he shrugged, chewing.

'Flying a kite?'

'Putting up the signal to see if anyone calls to give him more. Starting the gossip and waiting for someone to come up with the goods.'

'You think so?'

'Sword's a fat ball of hot air.'

'He's on to the Duchess of York, though,' said Nan.

Benedict smiled. 'About her going to the States to work for your organisation?'

'How did you know about—?' She gave him a long, cool appraisal.

He held her flecked eyes.

'Just flying a kite,' he said.

Over coffee they agreed. He would be the first to know.

'I can't say anything until it's definite. You know how it is,' said Nan.

Benedict raised his well-manicured hands towards her.

'I'll say no more then. We'll keep in touch, then, Mrs Purchase. Close touch, I hope.'

117

'Nan, please. Call me Nan.' She dabbed the corners of her mouth and folded her napkin coquettishly.

He felt so elated he told her one of his favourite royal stories, about the young aristocrat distantly related to the Queen who had once telephoned her from a pub pay-phone to reply to an invitation.

'He got through all right but he ran out of money. Their conversation was cut off by the pips,' said Benedict, 'an experience hitherto unknown to Her Majesty.'

So what if it was cribbed from an old Nigel Dempster cutting? The great man had gone on to other things now.

24 | *Working Lunch*

The boring part about doing celebrity interviews, Rosy decided, was they were so formulaic: Me, My Suffering, My Latest Bid for Fame, Why I Hate the Media, and the Real Me.

Who on earth cared?

It was supposed to be fun. Whoever supposed that hadn't tried working for Anthony Sword lately.

He had given her four interviews to do with impossible people. To show willing, she had cancelled her lunch with a theatrical agent's assistant who was going to try and get her a word with Mel Gibson (he said), and chomped disconsolately instead at a tuna sandwich while waiting for the calls back.

She was having the greatest difficulty concentrating on the first edition of the *Evening Standard* due to the verbal explosions from the other side of the room.

For days now Sword had not gone out to lunch. And there he was again, still at his desk and peppery as a chilli grinder with sun-stroke.

He was giving hell to people who dared to call on the telephone.

It was always dangerous when he began pleasantly: 'Now would that be the Royal Windsors? And you say they have driven through the gates of Windsor Castle. Marvellous. Today, I see, I see. Now can you tell me, madam, what is so fucking extraordinary about that that my ten million readers could possibly be interested in?'

And then: 'Minky Winkworth's twenty-first? Indeed. The Orangery. Oh, super. Now, just to be clear about this. Has Minky done anything in her life apart from reach the eve of twenty-one still breathing? I see. And how is Minky related to anyone I might conceiveably want to write about, the wealthy, the powerful and the titled? Ah. Well . . . we may have a problem here then. In fact, might I suggest – and I don't want to take anything away from the occasion here – that not even the members of Minky's immediate family would be interested . . . in any way!'

Crash went the red telephone.

Rosy kept her head down.

Everyone who worked in the Sword's Secrets office had to know when to batten down the hatches.

The worst moment had been when she'd told him about Eva Coutts' invitation.

Rosy was hardly in the habit of having jokey conversations with Sword. Gossip columnists, it seemed, gossiped with everyone but their staff. Yet, he had been pleasant enough, and she had been feeling confident enough – and she'd thought that he would be amused.

'Has anyone ever actually met Eva Coutts or is she just a voice on the end of the telephone?' Rosy had begun after one particularly gruelling session with the old theatrical tipster.

Sword had frowned at her and said nothing.

'Eva Coutts is a Great Unsolved Mystery.' Pearson's voice floated over.

'Oh?' said Rosy.

'We used to try to imagine what she was like ... tipsy wig, smudged lipstick, jumble sale clothes. ...'

'So you never have met her?' Rosy was fascinated. 'After all these years of her ringing with stories?'

'Oh, we tried,' said Pearson. 'But she always managed to slip the net.'

'I see,' said Rosy, excited now.

Still Sword stared, but said nothing.

And she wanted to show him that she had what it took. If she could prove that old contacts would take her into their confidence. ...

'Well ... this could be our chance,' she said casually, turning to Sword. 'Eva says that she's having one of her little parties – and to tell you specially. She said something about having all her girls there.'

'Wh-a-t?'

'Blimey,' goggled Pearson.

'Yes,' said Rosy, sensing this was a breakthrough. 'She said Tuesday evening, we have the address. I said as kindly as I could that she shouldn't get her hopes up that you would be able to go, but ...'

Pearson thumped his barricade of *Spotlights*, shaking his head in what was clearly amazement. 'This, I can't ... after all these years. ... Eva Coutts, past-mistress of the enthralling "Actress-in-Acting-Job-Shock" story – finally out of the woodwork! I don't believe it!'

Rosy started to say she would go if they wanted, and then stopped abruptly.

Anthony Sword had gone quite white.

25 | Eva's Night

When Anthony Sword set his mind to something, he wanted results immediately. He positively prided himself on being a Type-A personality: pathologically incapable of queueing, intolerant of mistakes and hungry for instant gratification.

Very hungry.

Once he had been a masticating menace. Now he only wished he could stop thinking about food. But there again, better he thought about food, than the other problem which would not go away this Tuesday evening. . . .

Sword stood on his Highgate terrace breathing in the electric soup of the capital's night sky. Beyond the boundaries of his garden it buzzed tangerine neon. It never got dark, truly dark, over the vast city in the plain below.

And as his thoughts ranged beyond the restaurants and clubs and faded *grandes salles* down there, and to places stored thirty years in his memory which were now only dust and rubble, he pondered the universal truth he had come to know as Sword's Law: That it was always when you were down and bruised that Life's great bovver boot would lumber up and kick you where it hurt the most.

Even though he had been expecting it, the ring on the doorbell made him jump. It was the short sharp stab made by a professional at the job. Sword made his way inside the house and down the picture-lined hall, stomping along the dark red tongue of carpet.

A young man with acne stood on the doorstep holding his salvation in a plain brown box.

'How much?' hissed Sword. He kept his head down, hugging the shadows.

'Seven-fifty, mate.'

Sword fumbled urgently in his pocket and pulled out a note. 'Keep it,' he growled.

The box was handed over and the transaction was completed in seconds.

The youth smiled. 'Thanks, mate. Ey! I know you.... Aren't you that bloke—?'

'G'night,' said Sword, abruptly shutting the door. His hands trembled on the delivery. He took it into the kitchen like a long-lost friend and ripped open the box.

Then, with his bare hands he tore at the pizza, stuffing it into his mouth in a frenzy of flying black olives and pepperoni.

The madness subsided. His equilibrium restored by a full stomach, Sword knew what he had to do. He had to see for himself whether she was bluffing.

There were two cars in Sword's garage. One was the cream Bentley he used to make an entrance. The other, a nondescript blue Vauxhall, was for more discreet arrivals.

He backed out the Vauxhall.

All the way south across the city he wanted to turn back, but he forced himself on, inexorably towards East Sheen. He had to know.

He had read her threat loud and clear. But would she go through with it to punish him?

When Sword reached Fairlawn Avenue, he drove a short way past Number 2 and pulled in to the kerb under a cherry tree. He sank low in his seat and his heart thudded like a demolition ball against his ribcage.

At first he could only hear it faintly, but then, as he latched on to the familiar rhythm, it seemed to get louder. Soon it was unmistakable. From Eva Coutts' house came the thump-thump-thump of a party in progress. The tune pumping out was 'What I Did For Love'.

Sword watched.

It was less than five minutes before a black cab drew up and disgorged three giggling young women. Then two more girls tip-tapped their way on high heels down the suburban street, then another taxi load. They were all received at the door of Number 2 by a plump silhouette.

Still Sword waited. A brief hope flared that she had invited only the girls.

Then his heart sank to meet the Deep Pan Xtra Spicy (3–4 persons) in his stomach.

For coming towards him, with a jaunty spring in his step, was Sir Philip Hawty. The womanising ex-Cabinet Minister swung into the tidy front garden of the same house with not a second's hesitation nor doubt that he had come to the right place. He was followed by several captains of industry and a TV anchorman whose dimples and home-life were subjects of lively public debate.

The next half an hour was one of the longest in Anthony Sword's life. Every new arrival at the party confirmed his worst fears:

A fairy ballerina – with a beard.

A vicar and two nuns. (Surely people weren't still on that kick?)

Then a policeman appeared, his head and shoulders moving purposefully on the other side of the street beyond a line of parked cars towards the gathering. Sword's throat constricted as he saw him march up to the door of Number 2. The "policeman" was wearing fishnet tights.

There was no doubt about it. Eva Coutts was up to her old tricks.

Why the hell hadn't he come to see her last Tuesday?

Why the hell couldn't he have had a normal mother?

And then Sword physically retched.

In his misery, he invoked Sword's Law, clause two: The worst is always worse than you imagine.

For his keen new recruit Rosy Hope had come tripping around the corner, and now she was checking the house numbers.

26 | Party Games

As at all the best suburban parties, there were clusters of balloons hung from the ceiling. Hung was right, decided Rosy. The ingenious arrangements of a long sausagey balloon between two bouncy round ones had been assembled by someone with an X-rated sense of the ridiculous.

Rosy stood in the hall of 2 Fairlawn Avenue and tried to take stock of the scene inside.

For Eva Coutts – if indeed this was the theatrical tipster's house and not the setting for some hideous rite of initiation for would-be *Dispatch* hacks – a party was clearly not a 'do' without uproarious dressing-up and stripping off. Improbable numbers of pretty young women in various states of *décolletage* were sardined into the narrow hall, while a liberal sprinkling of men were, well ... doing their lurid best to be women too.

There was one chap in a tutu, one in *Come Dancing* sequins, and another had apparently come as Carmen Miranda after consecutive accidents at Sainsbury's and the cosmetics counter at Boots.

And then – Rosy turned as whoops and roars erupted behind her – there were legs everywhere as a waving conga of guests slid down the banisters and tipped over.

From her vantage point on the Welcome mat, Rosy could imagine how a Jehovah's Witness might feel to have the door opened by the drunken participants of an Ann Summers trial night.

She stood, goldfish-mouthed.

Apart from the magnolia paintwork, this was nothing like the suburbs she knew.

There was no sign of the hostess.

A man in fishnet tights (he was a policeman from the hip up) presented her with a glass of punch. He leered obscenely as he explained the heavy intermittent CRUMP! sound from the lounge followed by blasts of loud music: 'Musical bumps.'

Rosy found herself unable to reply.

Swirling around her – for by now she had tossed back the noxious drink and was at that dangerous stage of looking around in desperation for another – were eddies of conversation.

She listened, agog.

A man who might have passed for a bank manager had his pinstripe trousers not been wrapped into a turban around his head, canoodled up to a mobile phone. 'I've got a bit caught, dear,' he confided. 'Yes . . . meeting went on for far longer than anyone thought, and then we still had a few matters to iron out. Easier over a pint. Noisy? We-e-ll, it's what I always say about pubs nowadays. Still, can't be helped. Needs must, eh . . .?'

A pointy blonde with the face and hair of an Afghan hound was in high dudgeon, dragging furiously on a Marlboro: '. . . so I went upstairs and bashed on the door and said, "Come on, give someone else a chance!" And this familiar voice comes back, "Don't you know who I am?" And it *was* him. You should have seen what he came out with. I wouldn't mind, but last time he swore blondes did nothing for him. . . .'

A bearded pantomime fairy collared the boy in blue: 'I've been waving my wand for a truncheon like that.'

'You wish, sweetie,' came the reply.

A male voice well known to Rosy from a low-tech television magazine programme was setting out its requirements: 'I asked for à real redhead – you know what a premium they're at now – not a strawberry blonde. Now what do I have to do around here to . . .'

In fact, now she came to think of it, several of the young women had a familiar look about them. . . . Rosy strained to hear one in particular.

An earnest beauty in black was lamenting: 'No, it's true, there are no decent parts anymore for women . . . and those there are, there's su-u-ch competition even if you are prepared to negotiate on your back. . . .'

'On your BACK, darling? Well, no wonder then if you can't be a bit more Sharon Stone than that. . . .'

Rosy's mind swam.

'Excuse me.' Rosy approached a bored-looking girl in blue Lennon glasses who was using her fingernails to make latticework of the leaves of a rubber plant. 'Do you know if Eva Coutts is around anywhere?'

The girl turned to her pityingly.

'Upstairs. Hasn't yours turned up either?'

'I'm sorry?'

'Your intro.'

Rosy drew a blank.

'Your potential . . . you know. Your Stairway to the Stars?' The girl's sarcasm was on a par with her PVC vest – too sad to be funny.

'Oh . . . yeah. I mean, no. No show.'

'That's a good one,' said the girl, fluffing up dispirited maroon hair. 'No show; no show.'

Surely she couldn't mean—?

'Hmm,' said Rosy.

The girl went on. 'I was told – no, promised – at least an assistant director this time. There hasn't been one of these do's for so long . . . but they used to work. Mind you, so did I, one way and another.'

Apparently she did.

Under closer scrutiny, Rosy realised that it must have been some time since the 'girl' had swapped the bloom of youth for a good make-up artist.

'Other people have tried, of course. I've been to a few other places . . . but Eva's the one who always had the magic touch. Her nights were a good mix . . . and some big names.'

'U-huh.'

'Talking of which . . .' The woman became a girl again as she caught sight of someone behind Rosy. 'All's fair . . . !'

And she was gone.

Feeling slightly sick, Rosy looked around at the tangled throng. Everywhere were couples, standing, lying, gasping, laughing, writhing together. She pushed her way through to the kitchen. If this was the nightmare where the loneliness of the teenage snogging party turned into a chilling vision of the future, she wanted to be on familiar territory.

27 | *A Familiar Face*

The kitchen was a shrine to the household god Formica.

On the small table was a vast bowl of red liquid, and next to it, empty bottles of cherry brandy, Martini Rosso and supermarket sparkling wine. Rosy rinsed her glass and gulped a neat Martini. It hit the spot.

She knew where she was now. She was in a bring-a-bottle time warp circa 1985. Any moment now someone would find a Wham! tape and the front door would get kicked in.

A couple emerged from the stone larder and ran out through the open back door into the dark garden. Rosy stared after them, feeling powerless to go or stay.

And then, she saw him.

Rosy gazed, in bafflement, at her empty glass. And then again at the man coming in from outside. Sir Philip Hawty, the ex-Cabinet Minister, was less than five feet away from her at this strange ritual in East Sheen – and he was smiling at her.

'Good evening,' he said.

His urbanity in the face of compromising chaos – his arrogant certainty that he wouldn't be recognised – took her aback. The only thing in his favour was that he wasn't dressed like an extra from the Rocky Horror Show.

Rosy's legs trembled.

This was IT. What a story! What *was* the story . . .?

She cursed herself for not bringing her Instamatic.

In a panic she thought back to the Earl of Trent's Green Countdown party. She had spoken to him there, but surely Hawty wouldn't remember her. She was certain he would not.

There again, perhaps it wasn't . . . She concentrated on his face – patrician, still lean for late middle-age, watery grey eyes under ridiculously boyish grey hair. No, there was no doubt about it.

He confirmed the fact a second later by shaking the hand she had extended, ostensibly to seek sustenance for the task ahead in an open packet of Kettle Chips.

'A great pleasure to see you again, my dear,' said Sir Philip. 'Rosy, isn't it? Of the *Dispatch*?'

She felt reality slip.

'Sir Philip . . .'

He smiled widely. 'Are you having a good time?'

'I, er . . .'

'Drink?'

'I think I'd better,' said Rosy.

'So how are you getting on at the *Dispatch*?'

'Um, fine.'

Bloody hell and party chit-chat. Maybe she should just come right out with it and ask if he came here often.

It seemed he did. The senior Tory confidently opened a cupboard and pulled out a bottle of Gordon's. She accepted a stiff gin and tonic as if in a dream.

'Enjoying it?'

'Oh . . . yes. Er . . . very much.'

131

'What kind of stories d'you tackle then?'

This was weird.

'To begin with, mostly general news stories ... anything really, that happened ... anywhere,' Rosy heard herself replying as someone turned up Right Said Fred in another room in confirmation of the deep dippiness of the situation.

'Out of London?' asked the politician.

'Quite ... often.'

'That's no good. This is where you want to be, where all the important people are,' said Sir Philip, giving no indication that he was anything less than serious. The man exuded ageing devil-may-care, yet his dark suit was immaculate and his tie regimental. The tie was set dead straight, which must mean he hadn't been outside for night manoeuvres – or had he just adjusted it after ...? What did any of it mean?

Rosy was at a loss. Lucid thought was not made easier by the bearded fairy in a tutu who came in and began rummaging about the pantry.

The evening was becoming positively surreal.

Surprisingly, for a politician, Sir Philip displayed an admirable ability to stick, unfazed, to the subject in hand. 'Besides, you're a lazy lot, you journalists. Have to be led to the facts. ...' He raised his glass to drink but did not take his eyes off her for a moment.

He had to be teasing now. Rosy coughed a giggle and clasped at formica for support.

'Mind you, when you find someone whom you can trust ...' Hawty went on.

Rosy could see exactly why he was variously described as 'suave' and 'matinee idol smooth' by the Conservative press and 'embarrassing old roué' by their opposite numbers.

'That may—'

'What do you think of Anthony Sword?' he asked, suddenly changing tack.

'I've been working for the Sword's Secrets column.'

'I know,' said Sir Philip. 'You don't think I'd want to talk to you if you were on a dull old political desk, do you? Far too depressing.'

Rosy took refuge in drink.

'No – Sword's the man. Damn good stories he gets on his page, too. Best place for them. Can't recommend him too highly, myself.'

Sir Philip poured more G and Ts.

'What are you doing here?' she asked at last.

'What . . . or whom?'

'Both, really.'

Here she was at Sodom and Gomorrah with a notebook burning a hole in her bag.

The ex-Cabinet Minister leaned towards her across a three-tier vegetable rack. 'You've heard of Danielle Kay?'

Rosy tried to look worldly.

'Presenter. On the box.'

'Oh . . . yes.'

She stayed non-committal.

'You and Danielle are good friends?' she said eventually, sounding so polite it was almost apologetic.

'Not really,' replied the politician informatively. 'She's a damn good roger, that's all.'

28 | *Liberty Hall*

She appeared, stage right, at the top of the stairs. A majestic figure in draped grey, she held a tray of glasses high with one hand. Through the haze, just for a second, she was the Statue of Liberty.

'Eva?' gasped Rosy as the woman descended.

A girlish smile spread across the aged but plump powdered cheeks. The woman was sixteen going on seventy.

'Now here's a nice new face I've not seen before . . . and I'd remember lovely hair like that. Nice to see you, dear. If you'll hang on a tick, I'll find my list. . . . Legit, ads or special, was it dear?'

'What?'

'We'll have no problem fixing you up, I shouldn't think. Ooh, where is it now . . .?' The woman was fishing into the folds of her dress. 'Take this for me, will you love.' She pressed the tray at a passing vicar.

'No, I'm Rosy. We've spoken—'

'Rose . . . it'll come to me in a mo' – you weren't in *42nd Street*, were you? *Les Miz*? Although, I must say, you'll have to make a bit more effort on costume, dear. I s'pose I haven't had a do for so long, all the old traditions have fallen by the wayside. Such pretty eyes,

134

you've got. . . .' She gave up ferreting in her skirt and peered.

'Eva, I'm Rosy. Rosy Hope. On the teleph—'

'Telly? You do telly, do you? Well, we'll definitely have no trouble placing you then. Did, er, whatsername tell you where to come?'

'TelePHONE. We speak on the telephone, Eva. Every day. Sometimes as often as six or seven times.'

'Eh?'

'I work with Anthony Sword. On the *Daily Dispatch*.'

The theatrical tipster's features clouded. Then she batted false eyelashes a lesser woman might have needed the help of a punkawallah to operate, and said gamely, 'Well, this IS a surprise. I don't suppose you brought the boss?'

'Er, no.'

'I see.'

'He never goes anywhere on a Tuesday night. It's one of his . . . things.'

Eva cackled. Rosy was uncertain quite what she meant by that.

'Well, it was, dear.'

'I did tell him, but he's not easy to—'

'I know exactly what you mean, the old devil. The things I could tell you . . .' said Eva.

'I wish you would.'

'Let's say I've known him as long as anyone and he always did go his own way. Never was one for my little . . . parties.'

'I'm sure he . . .'

But Eva gestured around and grinned impishly. 'Bugger Sword. 'Scuse my French. What do you think?'

'I . . . really don't know what to say.'

'Not quite what you expected?'

'Not entirely.'

Another cackle, punctuated by whoops from the depths of the house.

'Now have you spoken to Sir Philip?' asked Eva.

Rosy nodded, feeling out of her depth.

'That's all right then. And you've got the name. . . . Oh, you know the one—'

'Danielle.'

'That's the ticket.'

'Eva? I know this is going to sound—'

'Danielle. They're off to Nice tomorrow, so you will be sure . . . Only it's not the first time I've mentioned this story, is it dear? And you haven't seemed very keen on it. . . .'

Light flickered dimly. Nice-Naughty. . . . Neece-Hawty?

'Midday Riviera Route from Heathrow,' Eva went on with alarmingly uncharacteristic precision.

Rosy made a mental note.

Meanwhile, she wanted to clear up one pressing ambiguity.

'Eva, the other girls here . . . on what basis exactly are they . . .?'

'Why, whatever they want, dear.'

'Yes, but . . .'

'It's not what you know, but who you know – that's what they say, isn't it?'

'Sure, but . . .'

'Well, now – you know all you need to know, eh? All I do is provide the introduction. What my girls do after that is up to them. How else do you think I get my stories, dear? And no one has ever said I got it wrong.'

Rosy was stunned.

The old theatrical gave her a long look.

'You really musn't be such a prude, dear.'

The music was as loud as a funfair.

'What about the police?' Rosy was mystified. All the event lacked was loud knocking on the door from the disturbance squad.

'Already here,' shrugged Eva.

Rosy smirked. 'Real police. You know, responding to complaints from the neighbours. Don't you—?'

'As I said, everyone's here. Although Sergeant Mount only seems to have made half the effort.'

Bang on cue the officer in fishnets sashayed past. 'He's a REAL policeman?' gasped Rosy.

Now she'd heard everything.

29 | Messages

Three Armagnacs after Anthony Sword decided against a wild and reckless stroll around Hampstead Heath, he bellied out of the Spaniards Inn and headed home. He found the Vauxhall under a streetlamp and crunched it into gear before he had time to change his mind.

Okay, so Eva could well do for him.

But he could still save himself from himself.

In the hallway of the Gothic folly his senses were rewarded with an intoxicating aroma of stargazer lilies and peach pot-pourri.

Along the passage in the kitchen where the ripped pizza box lay in greasy reproach he threw the car keys into an Italian salad bowl. A red light winked on the ansaphone on the dresser. He hit the button:

PEEP! 'Hi-i, Anthony, this is Nan! I know how tough it is for you right now, so I wanted to share some words of encouragement and focusing . . . you have to come through the re-personalising challenge and on to the attainable future. In fact, I thought perhaps you could find meaningful benefit at the New Life Centre at Grasslands, Hertfordshire, and I want you to be my guest for as long as you want . . . with no obligation to write about it unless you absolutely want to. . . . Could you let me know – or I may even see you before you get this, I guess. The Trussocks are having a very intimate musical soirée tonight after the preview and Darlene will be just darling in Ungaro. . . .'

PEEP! "Lo, Sword, old boy . . . John Sylvester here. Sorry you couldn't stay for the Mega Books plonk the other day. . . . Just to let you know – and of course, you were first to get the option – that the biog is going ahead. Obviously, if you feel you can't contribute that's your decision . . . but there it is. Oh, and by the way . . . no doubt your agent will call you, but I may as well be straight – we've had a bit of a think-tank about the *Sword's Year* reviews. The general feeling is that we need to come up with a more sexy product, you know? Now this is probably something we can work around, but . . . Let me know.'

PEEP! The roar of a party in progress came on the tape. There was no spoken message.

PEEP! 'Hi-i-i-again. It's Nan. Sorry I didn't get to see you earlier, but Anthony . . . think just a moment about Grasslands. A carefully monitored relaxation, rejuvenation and reducement programme. In a very exclusive atmosphere. And the other guests! Strictly between the two of us . . . you won't have to stop working. . . . Sleep on it. G'night.'

CLUNK. Peep-peep. The machine stopped and reset itself.

Sword didn't hesitate. He went to the wine cellar and stomped up with a dusty bottle.

Across town, Benedict Pierce was also glad to get home.

The opening of a shop in New Bond Street had irked him and a party celebrating the first anniversary of a lifestyle magazine for couples had profoundly depressed him. It was held in the safe-taste environment of a Conran restaurant opposite Tower Bridge. 'After She, Me, You . . . Us!' trumpeted the shiny collaged invitation card.

The Perfect Pairs theme was hammered home by poster-sized portraits of famed twosomes 'at home' on stylised studio sets: Paul Newman and Joanne Woodward; Bruce Willis and Demi Moore; Warren Beatty and Annette Bening; and (this with a nod to the home market) John Alderton and Pauline Collins.

Benedict stayed long enough to note that the woman editor wore oversized red glasses and to collect a celebratory memento of a scented honeycomb candle.

The current Pierce residence was a large-ish flat in a mansion block which lay in the curious Byzantine shadow of Westminster Cathedral. The flats were situated almost equidistant between Westminster and Victoria, leading to inevitable location limbo – although never in Benedict's mind.

The fourth-floor apartment was currently decorated by Nina Campbell. The interior designer had done everything from the walls to the soap dishes – so no one could accuse Benedict Smith of having no style. Why, he had even taken swatches of curtain material to London Contemporary Art to ensure the paintings were a perfect match.

Inside, he hung up his jacket and kicked off his brogues – but carefully so as not to snag or soil the pale carpet with any dubious detritus from the piazza outside – and flicked on his answering machine.

PEEP! 'It's . . . seven-fifteen-and-this-is-your-duty-sub-Bill-Jackson. The Editor wants to strike the headline "Every Dog Has Its Day" on the Raine Spencer story and the lawyers aren't happy about the Streisand-Agassi piece – apparently hair is a sensitive issue.... Could you pl—'

PEEP! 'Benedict, it's Catherine. I know what you said about the maintenance last time, but there's no way I can manage. I'm getting my solicitor to call yours, so this is to let you know.... I also need you to talk to Charlotte. She's determined she's not going back to St Mary's next term and all she can think about is this ludicrous idea of making a record.... Ring me, can you, if you can find time away from your social high-life.'

PEEP! 'Ben ... darling ... this is Jo-Jo. I don't suppose – you know how I hate to ask, but – I couldn't have a bit extra this month, could I? Marta and Umberto have invited me to Gloucestershire next weekend and I really need to kit out in something Eurotrash, you know ...? I'd love to talk to you, sweetie ... gone but not forgotten, darling.'

PEEP! 'Daddy, it's me, Charlie. I know Mum's going to go on about me leaving St Mary's ... but I feel, kind of like, I haven't got that long, you know ...? Like, my whole life I've been waiting around, and I'm not like that happy.... Shit – I gotta go—'

PEEP! 'Benedict, this is Bea Goff. I know you don't want to talk to me but do listen—' He punched the forward button.

PEEP! 'Benedict? This is John Sylvester from Mega Books. Sorry to call so late but I thought you might like the good news. There was an editorial meeting this afternoon – and we're more than happy to have you on the Sword project. It goes without saying, I'm delighted you came to us and I'm sure this can be expressed ... financially. Let's talk tomorrow.'

Benedict heard the machine's CLUNK in stunned silence.

Then he punched the air like a victorious sportsman.
'Yes!'

30 | *Playing Away*

The sudden flap and hiss of the electronic departures board startled Sir Philip Hawty. He looked round furtively.

His flight to Nice was now boarding.

The former Home Secretary was feeling unpleasantly jumpy. What he hated most about Heathrow was the powerlessness of being caught in its sprawling, computerised corridor tentacles, being penned in the crowded, airless lounges. For a moment there, he thought the muted clatter was the sound of a motor-drive camera lens. That was how guilty he felt.

He had checked in at the desk (no baggage, just his leather weekend bag) and now all he could do was wait, all the while pretending that he wasn't.

Tall and rangy with thinning silver hair, he boasted the smooth butterscotch complexion of the frequent traveller and not a hint of the double chin which might be expected of a man who had endured forty years of Conservative dinners with such legendary charm. He was wearing a blazer and newly acquired designer sunglasses, which may have been a mistake. The glasses were impenetrable black wraparounds. He was conscious that people were staring at him more, not less.

He tried to quell his uneasiness by reminding himself that the last time he had made this trip south he had quite enjoyed himself. The airline called it their Riviera Route and sometimes ran to *foie gras*.

But then, the woman he had taken had been discreet. This time, he thought with a frisson, he had probably gone Too Far.

Watching the flow of well-groomed young women, the airline cabin and ground staff in their soft, efficient uniforms, it occurred to him that their attraction was the perfect combination of authority and nanny care.

Not for the first time, he wondered what he was doing here, waiting for a girl who could be his daughter. No, worse. Who could be his GRANDdaughter.

Sir Philip stuck his head into a copy of *Newsweek*, angling it so he could keep a lookout over the top.

Last Call.

The departures board chuntered again and Sir Philip noted with growing irritation that he might very well be taking the flight to Nice on his own. The prospect made him feel far worse than his previous misgivings.

He was about to set off when she teetered into view.

Danielle Kay, the Lolita of television's *Legs Eleven* gameshow, had clearly dressed for a holiday in the sun. She wore a clinging black-and-white gingham ensemble consisting of a brassiere top and tight shorts, which allowed her popular gameshow legs to create a considerable stir as she arrived at Terminal Two. They were twin living sculptures, long and smooth and lithe and firm.

She had a sweet, pale heart-shaped face, and had scraped up her blondish hair so it spurted out of the top of her head like a palm tree.

She raised herself further up from gravity-defying stilettoes when she saw him and called out, in the squeaky South London voice which gave him such a strange and disconcerting thrill, 'Hi-i! Philly-pins!'

The ant-like crowds seemed to part before her. An accusing path opened straight across the bared floor from her to him.

Sir Philip slowly drew down his magazine. Out of the corner of his mouth, through thin white lips, he hissed, 'For God's sake! Check in, and I'll see you on the plane or the other end at the . . . otteldelapay—'

'You what?'

Sir Philip swivelled round nervously. In the wrap-around glasses, he felt curiously robotic. 'The Hotel de la Paix. Get a taxi.'

'Blimey,' said Danielle, her wail carrying as he picked up his leather grip and made for the departure gate. 'Don't sound too pleased to see me.'

It took less than a minute for Keith Silver, ace paparazzo photographer of the *Daily Dispatch*, to get what he came for.

Up on the balcony, he elbowed aside a couple of leathery middle-aged ladies in studded denim, separated a mother and child from a large tub of frozen yoghurt in one direction, and their pushchair in another, and upset a group of young men in frantically coloured Bermudas.

"Ere, you watch it!'

'Waa-aah!'

'Oi!'

But at precisely the right moment, he reached into the billows of his black leather trenchcoat, took out a camera with a ten-inch zoom and shot.

145

When Sir Philip Hawty and Danielle Kay had gone their separate ways, he hurried off.

At a safe distance from any unpleasantness, and where he was sure no one could overhear, he reached into his vast coat again and extracted a mobile phone. This coat was his office, he thought, as he punched out the numbers: camera, lenses, films, light meter, notebooks, address book, pens, phone.

'Allo?'

Crackle, crackle.

'Jamie. S'me. I got 'em. Tell Rosy well done. It was them, definite.'

31 | *Out to Grass*

The message Tina had taken down for him on a yellow Post-It merely read: 'Green's 1.15. A meeting you should know about.' The informant had declined to leave a name.

As the country's premier gossip columnist, Sword held anonymous callers in his own brand of contempt – his distaste was sublimated by the recognition of their occasional usefulness in keeping him ahead of the game.

And after the events – or rather the Event – of the previous night he was suffering a gargantuan lack of will and inspiration as well as a hangover.

He hailed a taxi to Mayfair. Green's, a restaurant which specialised in nursery food for a certain class of Londoner, was a long-established haunt of his. There were worse places to drown his sorrows in fine wine.

Sword was climbing the well-worn steps to fishcakes and flattery when an unwelcome voice whined gnat-like at his back.

'Should I warn our friends inside of your current violent reaction to pre-luncheon claret?'

The columnist turned to find the weasel publisher Sylvester on his tail.

'Are you looking for me?' he responded gruffly.

'Sadly not.'

'Then kindly do not detain me. I think we have said all we have to say.' Sword pushed on towards the door, trying to ignore the painful wheeze in his chest as he reached the top step too quickly.

'Have it your way, Anthony.'

The *soi-disant* Mega Books millionaire was stomach-turningly smug.

'You have as much idea as a midge on a fuckin' Venus fly-trap, Sylvester – and half the charm. Possibly less.'

Sylvester adjusted the Ray-Bans which combined with the flashy suit and slicked hair to give him the air of an embalmed City trader. 'And we once got on so well. . . .'

'My lawyers are watching.'

'Temper, temper.'

'What are you doing here anyhow?' demanded Sword. The question was automatic.

'Waiting for a . . . friend.'

'Impossible.'

The publisher grinned. 'Okay, then . . . a new author. Or should I say . . . biographer.'

The inference was all too clear.

Sword was mid-snort when a black cab ticked up to the pavement to drop off a fare.

From its depths emerged the gleaming blond horns of Benedict Pierce, an identical bumptious smile on his beaky face.

No further information was required.

Which of the two reptiles had planted the fake tip-off was irrelevant. What was important now was self-preservation.

By mid-afternoon he had decided.

*

The gravel drive up to Grasslands Hall Health Hydro (and New Life Self-Awareness Centre) cut a one-way path through pleasant if unexciting Hertfordshire hillocks tufted with trees. It crunched opulently under the wheels of Anthony Sword's 1937 Bentley, his pride and joy.

He loved this car. It had once belonged to the 5th Duke of Bunster. It was long and wide and weighty and the colour of clotted cream.

It made him feel like an aristocrat, or at the very least, a good old-fashioned tycoon.

It made him look, to the undiscerning, like a road-worthy Toad of Toad Hall.

The fine approach to the house was a fitting climax to his two-hour journey from London at a majestic speed of thirty-five miles an hour.

If he was going to ground, it might as well be in style.

Grasslands Hall was ahead now. The house, ancestral home of the Earls of Hatfield, sat elegantly on the lawns. Its light stone blushed in the sun and birds twittered liltingly right on cue.

For the first time, Sword began to think that coming here might not be such an ordeal after all.

Anything was better than waiting in town for the shit to hit.

He was greeted with professional accomplishment. The Bentley was comfortably installed in the stable block garage. His suite was welcoming – violet, green and cream, gentlemanly stripes rather than flowers and frills. It had a view of the formal garden and beyond where the grounds unfurled into distant woodland. Even the lawns and bushes looked plumped up and pampered.

149

On the desk in Sword's bedroom was the usual selection of notepapers and information sheets, menus and a welcome card which read:

> 'Grasslands Hall Health Hydro and New Life Centre.
> You have taken the first steps towards Positive Changes In Your Life.
>   Progress.
>   Transform.
>   Enjoy.'

Sword sat on the bed to assess what kind of sleep he would get. Its soft give reassured him. He flipped through some books on the bedside table: a jazzy tome entitled *Environmental Super Health* was one; another was called *Goal Commitment*; and *The Dynaband Challenge* (he expected it would be), which seemed to involve some kind of masochism with outsize elastic bands.

Round-eyed with surprise at what he had done and unable to relax, he ran down his mental checklist:

Nan Purchase had assured him his presence at Grasslands was strictly confidential – for now.

His house was in the care of his housekeeper and gardener.

The Harley Street quack not only approved of this unexpected development in the lost cause of his health but was suspiciously enthusiastic.

The hurried memo dictated to the Editor of the *Daily Dispatch* to the effect that he was bringing his sabbatical forward for urgent personal reasons had been grudgingly accepted after a shaming outburst in front of the Proprietor's bust in the foyer.

Deputy Raj had been primed on a need-to-know basis.

So far, so good.
Now he was incommunicado.

There was a holiday atmosphere in the Diary office.

Rosy's scoop had pride of place on the morning's page, above Jamie's latest about the Earl of Trent:

> 'What foreign affair is claiming former Home Secretary Sir Philip Hawty's attention? I can reveal that he has slipped off to the South of France accompanied by energetic dancer Danielle Kay, 20, star of the TV gameshow *Legs Eleven*.
>
> 'Tory-about-town Sir Philip, 62 – who has developed a keen interest in young people since separating from his second wife Mary – and the lovely Danielle took a midday flight to Nice yesterday.
>
> 'Before she left, Danielle told friends: "It's too early to tell whether anything will come of it, but I'm very happy."
>
> 'Sir Philip is not expected back until the weekend. "He is on the first leg of a private European fact-finding tour," said a Parliamentary aide.'

'How low can the Earl of Trent slump? So

energetically did the 34-year-old Earl – former Chelsea dog-walker Brett (né Kevin) Perquinze – celebrate his release from a police cell in Wandsworth after 18 hours of questioning, than he was back inside last night for dragging an attractive policewoman into Mirabeau's nightclub proclaiming loudly: "Don't come that with me, Ma'am. You're the Princess of Wales and I know your tricks!"

'Wild-eyed and dishevelled, Lord Trent attempted to perform a samba with WPC Sharon Baxter before she managed to radio for assistance.

'He is unlikely to have helped his cause with worried Trentchester trustees, who are advising him to sell his Belgravia house and part of the historic 2,000-acre estate in Sussex to meet crippling duties and "entertainment expenses".'

And best of all, for Rosy, they wanted her to stay.

'Obviously, I won't have the final say, but while Sword's on leave . . . as far as I'm concerned, the job is yours,' said Jamie, making his first pronouncement as acting editor. He was more self-confident than ever this morning – a girl at a party the previous night had told him he was far more handsome than Imran Khan.

She stuttered her thanks.

'Hey . . . we like you!' he hammed.

'Steady on . . .' teased Pearson from across the room.

'Well, I do at any rate,' said Jamie.

'Thanks.'

What she would have liked to have said, she realised with a sudden cringe of embarrassment, was: 'That means a lot to me.'

*

153

'It would have set it off nicely to have a pic of Trent down the nick giving her a right verbal, if only I could have got in there,' frowned Keith 'the Beast' Silver, critically appraising the column. 'But with security like they had, no way.'

'Surely not even you would . . .' began Rosy.

'Oh, wouldn't he,' sighed Pearson.

But the photographer was already flipping through the day's invitations, stuffing engraved cards into his leather coat like a child grabbing for crisps at a party. 'This looks all right, Antonia ffrench-Barclam's Private View. Wouldn't mind a private view of 'er, eh what Pearson?'

'No matter how long I have to accustom myself to your *modus operandi*, Keith, effective though it may be, I cannot reconcile myself to your puerile vision of the world,' replied the elder statesman of the column. 'I'll have some tea please, Tina. There's honest toil to be done here this morning.'

'Like what?'

'I am preparing to research a transatlantic TV story. . . .'

'Oh yeah?'

'Yeah,' cut in Jamie sarcastically. '*The Bold and the Beautiful* is about to start on satellite.'

They trooped off to lunch *en masse*.

Two bottles of house champagne in the subterranean Scribblers Club later, it was up into dizzying daylight for a short walk to an Italian restaurant near the old *Dispatch* building on Fleet Street. 'They know of old,' whispered Pearson, voice hoarse with intrigue, 'the dark and secret art of blank receipts . . . big stories, big expenses. . . .'

154

Jovial waiters fussed around, glad to see hard-drinking hacks back. At the other tables accountants and solicitors who now inhabited the great landmarks of old Fleet Street sipped mineral water or a single bottle of white wine between four.

They ordered two bottles of house red.

The noise rose as Jamie and Pearson tried to outdo each other with the viciousness of their character assassinations, encouraged mercilessly by Tina. The humour was deadly.

Rosy munched her salad through giggles, all the time keeping a wary eye on her white linen dress and Pearson as he paddled around in his tomato and clam sauce.

After a while Rosy felt her cheeks glowing. None of them had even begun to write a story and it was already twenty past three. Wasn't it rather irresponsible . . .? If she'd still been grafting in the news-room, or worse still on her local paper . . . But then she relaxed: none of the others seemed worried, so why should she?

The others liked her. They wanted her to stay while Anthony Sword was off on leave. She threw back a slug of Valpolicella, and tried to put to the back of her mind what had really been worrying her since she came back from Eva Coutts' party with the big story.

Here she was being paid £100 a day to go out to lunch.

So this was the Street of Shame.

And who *were* all these people they wrote about anyway?

33 | *The Male Menu-pause*

Sword's route towards Progression, Transformation and an Enjoyment which at this stage could only be mythical began in a consultation room with the resident male medical advisor.

This dapper professional had an admirably light touch with the verbs of movement. He 'popped him on the scales' and registered no flicker of shock when the needle drove smoothly through the twenty-stone mark. He 'trotted him over to the couch' and 'whisked him through' a detailed questionnaire about his lifestyle and eating habits.

The gossip columnist gave it to him straight.

'Can you do anything with me?' he asked, at the end.

'I should think so.' The medic glanced back over his notes and smiled. 'At least you spared us the "Believe-me-I-hardly-eat-anything" routine.'

'Yes, well . . .'

'It happens . . .'

Sword glared. 'I may not be your usual kind of lettuce-cruncher.'

'This happens to a lot of men your age. Too much rich food, business lunches, restaurant dinners, excessive alcohol intake.... But with a carefully regulated eating programme the appetite can be re-educated.'

So now we have it, thought Sword. The male menupause.

The medical man handed him over to a comely beauty therapist.

'De-tox, toning, thermal, Ionithermie,' announced the beauty therapist, after giving him and the notes a once-over.

'I only serve what?' said Sword, disappointed already. He could feel his stomach working up for a seismic rumble. Her Lancashire accent was as thick and juicy as an Eccles cake. At least, that is what it seemed like to him.

'Ioni-THURRmie. It's a deep-cleansing process followed by the application of electrodes—'

'Wha-a-t?'

'—very mild current to stimulate the muscles and encourage the elimination of impurities,' the therapist assured him. 'It is proven to show actual inch loss. Many of our clients swear by it if they are going to a special event.'

He pulled his fiercest grimace.

Then it was on to the New Life counsellor charged with his 'inner well-being and positive body visualisation'.

'I see perfectly well in my mirror,' grunted Sword, which did not go down well with the counsellor, an American woman with cropped hair in her late thirties, he guessed. She began a lecture during which it became clear she would regard him as something of a personal challenge.

He returned, crotchety, to his room to indulge in a long herbal bath.

An hour later he was lying on his bed dozing fitfully when an envelope was delivered containing his programme for Week 1. Apparently he was on Rapid De-Tox. A timetable detailed the food he would eat and at what time, down to the last beansprout and minute, the activities he would report for, and the treatments and therapies he would endure.

The regimentation startled him. His immediate reaction was akin to insubordination.

He set his jaw and stamped along the carpeted corridors pausing only to adjust his snarl when other inmates came into view. But then he thought, what the hell.

He was tired of making decisions. It would do him good to have someone else to order his days for a while.

Once, when he was still eating and drinking with impunity, he had evolved a code of classification which he used to notable effect when he took victims out to lunch.

A man who ordered shepherd's pie or rice pudding, for example, would be in clear need of comfort.

Someone who chose saddle of lamb would, to Sword's practised eye, be stating a need to be in the driving seat, while pig's trotters could indicate determination to confront a fear of being trampled underfoot.

Another diner who asked for grilled goat's cheese with *roquette* would be marked down as a person who followed fashion at any cost to the palate.

Sword would observe, then season the interrogation to taste.

Naturally he reserved his worst for any unfortunate who opted for prawn cocktail with pink sauce. The columnist had honed a particularly vicious line of questioning to suit this menu, turning on the presumption that his companion's tastes also ranged to peroxide blondes and Stringfellow's nightclub.

. He had used that to fine effect when he broke the story of the opera director's affair with the page three girl.

Now he gazed forlornly at the room-service tray which had arrived. His plate offered one bare rice cake and a pile of celery matchsticks. What did that say?

34 | *Nicely Done*

By the swimming pool of a modest three-star hotel in Nice, Sir Philip Hawty sipped a Pink Lady.

Beyond were the backs of the famous white travellers' palaces on the Promenade des Anglais, and beyond them the ordered beach and the winking Mediterranean.

He settled deeper into his sun lounger with his cocktail, breathed in the faint balmy scent of frying garlic and *herbes de* Provence that he knew as the essence of southern France, and clung to the sun's undemanding caress.

'Oowwh, no! I'm peelin' already!'

Danielle sat, petulant, on the concrete poolside, examining her bare breasts. Her flesh was an even langoustine pink.

The eyes of their fellow sunbathers needed little excuse to turn. Sir Philip, still wearing his black wraparounds, laughed as calmly as possible.

'Come back under the umbrella. Don't get burned.'

She undulated towards him; perfect legs, high rounded breasts, hair scraped up into that ridiculous blond fountain.

His heart leapt into his throat.

True, their sojourn had not started well that day. She

had ignored him on the plane. Cold-shouldered him childishly at the airport the other end. And then, trembling alone in the queue for taxis, had burst into tears when he approached. He had managed to console her. It hadn't been difficult. She was so eager to please him.

'It's all your fault,' she pouted, lowering herself down next to him. 'Making me take my top off.'

'You want to be a deep even brown,' he said.

'Deep and crisp and even,' she sang. 'Reminds me of when I was about fifteen and one of the girls at school said you could get a good tan if you used cooking oil. I sat in the back garden in my bikini covered in Spry Crisp 'n Dry and all that happened was I smelled like a chip when I hotted up and attracted all the flies!'

They both laughed.

'My mum thought I was mad.'

Now that made him feel old again. Only the very young talked about their parents so naturally. 'And now?' he asked.

'Oh, she still does really. Only now she's ever so proud as well.'

'She must be.'

'She videos every show, cuts out all the pieces in the paper, you know.'

Sir Philip picked up his drink again. 'Do you want one?'

'No, ta. It's my dad who gets a bit funny about it all.'

'Oh? No drinking?'

'No, the telly show. He's a postman. Walked the same round for thirty years. The family say that's where I get my legs from. He doesn't understand that I want to make something of meself. Thinks I'm flaunting it for strange men. I should find a nice steady lad, get married, you know.'

'I see. He wouldn't be thrilled, exactly, if he could see you now. . . .'

'He'd flippin' kill me!' said Danielle, matter-of-fact.

They had dinner in a small restaurant at the edge of town. There was a long zinc bar, but it was not crowded. On walls the colour of Dijon mustard hung signed photographs of local sporting heroes. The glint of the moon on the sea was just visible through the open door.

Sir Philip made short work of a steak *au poivre* and a carafe of red wine; Danielle waved bits of a *salade niçoise* around on her fork and contemplated the nature of foreign travel.

'. . . you never expect other countries to have ordinary places in them, do you, because you've only ever seen photos of the interesting bits and you think it all must be like that. . . .'

He wondered if he had ever been so inoffensive, at any time in his youth. On reflection, he thought not. He had always had a cunning approach to life.

'. . . but that doesn't mean it's not interesting. I don't mean that. In some ways it can be more interesting, seeing how people abroad live in the ordinary bits. . . .'

She was disappointed, that was obvious. He could tell she was mystified why they were not dining somewhere more appropriate to his social status. The risk of being recognised, here – unexpectedly here – would be minimal. But she did not actually say so.

It made him realise what a sweet girl she was.

He poured another glass of rough red.

Tonight, he felt, he would sleep well in his single bed.

There was no view from Sir Philip's room. It looked out over the rubbish bins at the side of the Hotel de la Paix and a dark narrow street. The establishment, at least from his end of the corridor, was not felicitously named. For most of his two nights there, he had had not a whisper of peace. He had endured rat-a-tat conversations and shouts and slamming car doors and the phut-phut-phut-brummmm of mobilettes through his tightly shut window. He tossed and turned now in the consequent airlessness.

So this was what it was like to travel on a budget.

He had a plain bed with a hard sausage of a pillow, a wardrobe, a wooden chair and a table, and an arrangement of faded dry flowers hanging on the orangey wall. If he stood up straight in the wrong place, he clunked his head on a swinging plastic light fitting in the shape of an open flower.

Lying still, he ran through the comforting constants which could often summon sleep.

Simone Signoret in *Room at the Top*, first on the list. Well, he was in France.

Marilyn Monroe standing over the subway vent in *The Seven Year Itch*.

Marilyn Monroe with both the Kennedy brothers.

Doris Day in *Pillow Talk*.

Okay, that last one was a strange one. But as he grew older, he was finding the chirpy-but-capable blonde type more and more alluring. It was the Air Hostess Syndrome again. Someone who made you feel young again and yet protective, but who would look after you all at once.

He lay still.

In a rush of affection, which he would rather not have had, he thought, I hope she is sleeping well.

And then he wondered what on earth had made her agree to come here with him and whether she had any idea what kind of man he was.

163

35 | Covent Garden

The afternoon dragged. Rosy wrote a forced couple of paragraphs on the junior minister who had just been voted Parliamentary Twit of the Year but had misheard the accolade as Wit of the Year.

'So,' said Rosy to the junior minister's private secretary on the telephone, 'you can't really talk at the moment?'

Rasp-mu-mm-croak-croak from the other end.

'Is he there?'

More rasping.

'Ah. Okay. Let me just check I've got this right. You felt it was your duty to laugh loudly whenever he made a joke—'

Rasp, croak.

'—feeble witticism, then . . . and you've now damaged your vocal chords.'

The story was hardly going to set the world alight, but for once she felt profoundly grateful.

'Emma?'

A terrible need for reassurance made her call the flat.

'Oh hi, Rosy, what's up?'

That was the best thing, thought Rosy, having people

around who instinctively knew by the tone of your voice that something might be wrong.

'Oh, you know . . .'

'What?'

'Are you doing anything later?'

'Only my older man.'

'Wha-a-t? Who's that?'

'Only Marvell, idiot. I've got all these books out I haven't read – I was going to do some work. I've been sunbathing most of the day in Bishops Park.'

'Lucky you. Couldn't you stand him up?'

Emma laughed. 'And they say it's only women who get left on the shelf.'

They agreed to meet at seven in Covent Garden.

Rosy gave Scribblers a miss and walked along the river, leaving the Embankment to cut up to the Strand just before the Savoy, and then on up Southampton Street to the rejuvenated fruit and vegetable market. The dust and brown exhaust of the day lay on the air like a heavy blanket on a hot night.

There were already plenty of tourists pounding over the cobbles in their uniform trainers and bermudas, watching the street theatre in front of the church, and sitting in the open cafés and pubs around the piazza with the office workers.

Rosy made straight for the Crusting Pipe, bypassing the crowded sunken part of the pub beneath the main arcade of shops selling health foods and teapots and embroidered silk dresses, to the overflow on street level opposite the Transport Museum which was called something else that nobody could ever remember.

They always managed to get a table there.

Sure enough, Emma was waiting, with a table, showing off her sunglow in a short black off-the-shoulder dress. Her wild red curls were held back with a saucy black bandana. Cheerily she waved off two smiling Japanese and their street map.

'Drink?' she asked.

'What the hell,' said Rosy, 'I'm still pissed from lunch.'

'What's up?'

After half a glass of white wine, Rosy told her.

'You'll think this is really stupid . . . really sub-urban . . . but it's about this party I went to the other night – or rather I'm not sure it was just a party,' she began. 'And the worst is . . . and I don't know why I did it . . . but I didn't say anything afterwards, exactly, about my doubts . . . and now it's awful because I don't know how I can. . . .'

Emma raised her palms. 'Hold on, slow down. . . . I take it you're talking about work here.'

'Which other parties have I been to lately?'

'Start at the beginning.'

After a quick look around, Rosy leaned forward. 'There's this theatrical tipster – an old actress who tele-phones in with showbiz stories, usually about who's bonking whom. She's been doing this for years, although nobody has ever met her in the flesh. Or had . . .'

'Do her stories, you know, check out?'

'She's never been wrong, apparently. Anyway, I've been the one dealing with her and to cut a long story short – she told us she was having a party . . . and I went along. To East Sheen of all places.'

'Doesn't sound promising,' admitted Emma.

'Wait a minute though. I get there to find . . . well, the only way I can describe it is like something Cynthia Payne might have organised in her heyday.'

'You mean . . .'

Rosy nodded. 'Men in uniform and fishnets, some *well-known* men, half-dressed girls . . . the works. . . .'

'Yeah, but that doesn't necessarily . . .'

'A girl – an out-of-work actress in PVC – asked me if my . . . intro . . . had turned up. And more or less spelled out the principle of making friends and influencing people to give you a break.'

'A job, as it were . . .'

'Look, I may be naive but I know what it looked like. All the rooms upstairs were heaving.'

Emma shook her head noncommittally. 'I—'

'It would explain why the people in Eva's stories are always banged to rights—'

'As it were.'

'It's not funny.'

'It's hilarious!'

Rosy rolled her eyes.

'There's nothing wrong with introduction parties,' said Emma. 'God! Everyone's going to them. There are always articles in the papers and documentaries about them. And if they lead to a bit of networking, so what?'

'With phallic balloons and musical bumps – STRIP musical bumps, as it turned out?'

'So was this . . . tipster person wearing red satin, twirling a hoop of keys and stuffing tenners down her cleavage?' laughed Emma.

'No, but I have a horrible feeling I was part of the pay-off.'

'You?'

'Em . . . I came back with a great story from it, only . . . I knew I was being set up – and I did it anyway. I wanted . . . to prove to Sword that I was good enough.'

'So?'

'I needn't have bothered. Out of the blue yesterday Sword went off on some kind of long leave. He was utterly disinterested.'

'And?'

'The others asked me the next morning, but I was so full of the Hawty business . . . I didn't say a word about the REAL story. And now I don't know how to.'

'Forget it,' advised Emma. 'They know exactly what's going on. They must do.'

Once more, Rosy felt hopelessly naive. Emma was right. Of course everyone else knew the score.

'But,' added Emma, twisting the stem of her glass, 'I am tingling for a wild and dangerous night.'

'Oh, God,' said Rosy. 'That's the last thing I need.'

'It's exactly what you need. What's on this evening, then?'

'A party. As usual.'

'What kind of party? Can I crash?'

Rosy grimaced. 'At Home with Lady Diplock.'

'Who's she?' Emma drained her wine.

'Diplock's Garages? Lord D, who started with nothing but a bag of nuts and bolts in his pocket. Thatcher's Second Gear Peer?'

'What?'

'Think about it,' said Rosy. 'All that grinding on the way uphill.'

'Oh yeah . . . Penthouse in Mayfair, is that the one?'

'Yep. Although he still calls it a pad. And loves being neighbours with Stirling Moss.'

Emma giggled. 'It is pretty spectacular. All that black and leather, with white fluffy rugs.'

'How do you know?' Rosy was puzzled. She was the one who came back with the gen on celebrity homes these days.

'It was in *Ciao!* magazine. Stacks of pictures, with Brenda, Lady D, trussed up in a different Valentino in each.

'*Ciao!*? Emma, I'm amazed that someone like you would bother to read *Ciao!*'

'Are you kidding?' said Emma. 'The photos are the thing. The words may be drivel, but the camera never lies. Did you see those bedspreads Princess Margaret has in her house on Mustique!'

The penthouse flat off Shepherd's Market was tricked out in the kind of furniture made popular by 1960s' spy thrillers. It made Lord (Alf) Diplock feel he had achieved the pinnacle of glamour he aimed for as a young blood who smoked Embassy cigarettes and had a busty girl-friend called Brenda.

The lift door opened straight into the vast cream-and-black entertaining room. Rosy and Emma tripped in and found themselves nose to nose with their host.

'Wot, no Sword? Never mind, what's yer poison?' he boomed.

Lord Diplock had a bottle of Dom Perignon in one hand and a jug of his favourite peach juice in the other.

The eminent *garagiste* was small and round, with black twinkling eyes and large pink ears. He reminded Rosy of a nursery-rhyme piglet, an impression exacer-bated by the pink frilly dress shirt he had donned for the occasion.

Rosy took in the room and its guests like the pro-fessional she felt she wasn't, yet.

Emma twanged her black number. 'I feel like Tragedy's handmaiden: the bearer, one step behind the goddess in white, of the ritual sympathetic ear,' she joked. Then, seeing Rosy pulling nervously at her dress, she squeezed Rosy's arm companionably. 'You look great, you really do. That style really shows off your waist.'

'You really think so?'

'Of course!'

Rosy smiled her gratefulness. Why, after all the practice she was getting, did she still feel nervous when she walked into a party?

To quell her jitters, she began pointing out guests to Emma.

There, on a leather swivel chair, was the thrice-married Marquis of Salcombe flirting with Wife No. 2. Over by a smoked-glass mirror was the fashionable Earl of Trent and with him, playing coyly with the silver balls of an executive toy, the party-loving young actress Lottie Landor. A television cook was lightly grilling a millionaire writer of airport thrillers. Pearson had arrived, looking as usual like a displaced country squire up in the wicked capital for a once-a-year binge. Jamie was there too, surrounded by blondes.

Between them was a motley assortment of unknown actresses and models and red-faced older men, several Tory politicians among them.

'It's not quite what I imagined,' said Emma, 'from the stories in the papers, I mean.'

'Not quite as elegant, glamorous . . .?'

'Not nearly.'

'Welcome to the B-list,' said Rosy. 'Make that B-minus. The aspiring luvvies and perspiring squires drawn from the circle of Diplock.'

Emma took it in.

'Will you write anything about this?'

Rosy shook her head. 'Absolutely not. Diplock's parties are strictly for background information.'

Across the crowd Jamie waved and set out in their direction.

Trawling in his wake was a lanky man in a scruffy suit.

'The gorgeous Jamie Raj!' breathed Emma. It stood to reason, thought Rosy, that Emma would already have met him on her social round. 'It definitely was worth coming. You know, he really does look like that cricketer . . . what's his name? . . . only younger.'

Rosy sighed. 'Imran Khan. And you'll have to do better than that. He only likes to be told he's better looking than Imran these days.'

'I'll remember that.'

'The chap chasing him is Allan Wilks.'

'Who's he?'

'A boring playwright whose moderate success was once enhanced by a Sword's Secret alluding to his apparently unstoppable virility backstage in a northern theatre. Sadly, it was a case of *coitus misinterpretus*—'

'What?'

'A short-sighted stand-in got the wrong man.'

'Oh dear,'

'No, it was fine. The publicity was far too good for him to deny it,' explained Rosy feeling like an old hand. Pearson had told that tale with particular relish over lunch.

Jamie made it over to them, the playwright in tow.

'Emma! How lovely to see you again!'

That was Jamie on a mountain, thought Rosy. She didn't know whether to be flattered he had remembered her friend's name immediately and come over, or irri-

172

tated that Emma was yet another female whose details were entered into his auto-pilot charm system.

Emma was delighted.

'Is this work or pleasure?' asked the playwright hopefully as he docked into their little group.

'Your pleasure is our work,' said Jamie, catching the reptile eye of an eminent West End producer, who was contemplating the noble Raj profile and lustrous black floppy curls with undisguised interest.

Jamie played up to it shamelessly.

'Have you met Cheryl?' persisted the playwright. A pneumatic doll materialised at his side.

'I haven't had the pleasure in the flesh, but I recognise the body,' said Jamie. 'Hello Cheryl. I believe you rather floored the Leader of the Opposition at the Pacemaker Ball the other evening.'

'He didn't put up much opposition to me,' simpered Cheryl.

'Yi-i-ck,' mouthed Emma behind her back.

Rosy raised her eyebrows to Heaven.

'Cheryl's been asked to appear on the *London Midnight* programme,' said the playwright. 'You could do a story and say she's my new girlfriend if you like.'

'What do you think I should wear?' asked Cheryl.

'As little as possible, I should think,' said Jamie. 'Ow!' He turned as a proprietorial blonde bore down on him, sticking a sharp elbow in the inexperienced Cheryl's back.

'Jamie, dah-ling! I want you to myself,' said the blonde. 'Do you want to hear a naughty story?'

'Must I?' said Jamie. 'I'd much rather take part in one.'

37 | *The Pursuit of Love*

By eleven o'clock *chez* Diplock the drinks were flowing like Super Plus Unleaded into Putney Volvos.

Lord and Lady Diplock set the rhythm: the 'Forecourt King' was playing the maracas with a cocktail shaker in time to Elvis' Golden Greats while she flailed about in silver *lamé*.

An ageing backbencher was getting tangled up trying to jive with the star of a make-up commercial. The Minister for Social Security was aquiline nose-to-nose with a *Hansard* reporter of impeccable lineage.

A few other couples had begun to sway dreamily to the music. The Earl of Salcombe and his current Countess performed a lazy shuffle for Lord D's private photographer, while flirting with other guests over each other's shoulder.

'We can't go on together, with suspicious minds,' warbled Elvis, with a pleasing ironic touch.

It was, as Lord D said to Rosy, turning into quite a do.

Nearby she could hear Pearson regaling a gaggle of young actresses with tales (only slightly embellished) of careers he had nurtured, inspirational sagas of fresh-faced hopefuls. He spoke movingly of those he had known. Of progress from the humblest of chocolate commercials to the starriest of dreams come true. And what was most moving, was that they believed in him.

Rosy threaded her way back to where Emma was chatting to a girl who said she used to be best friends at school with the Duchess of York.

'When I knew her she was plain Fergs. She was suuuch fun! Always hiding things. She kept a bottle of Malibu under the floorboards of her study at school.'

A waiter came round with more Bellinis.

Rosy decided she was rallying.

She was just debating whether to go over to the Earl of Trent and one of his groupies – 'title-chasers', Jamie called them – who seemed to be arguing nearby, when one of several interchangeable actresses called Chloë steamed up to them.

'The bloody casting couch!' wailed Chloë, without preamble. 'I'm getting my own back. I've written a play about it all. The main part is the couch itself, which I thought I could play with great experience and feeling—'

Rosy winked at Emma.

'—the paradox of pain on the softness of the cushions in the casting director's suite—'

Above the party din they heard the girl yell at Brett. 'How could you even suggest it?'

'—the feelings of rejection as a woman as well as an *artiste* that no man seems able to comprehend on that, that execution block covered in chintz—' Chloë warmed to her theme.

'You bastard!' cried Trent's friend.

'—yet still they continue to plump us up along with the cushions, then use us up, exhaust us as emotional resources—'

'That's IT,' hissed the girl furiously to the Earl of Trent who composed his features into the picture of noble innocence.

'—it's a battle of wills,' said Chloë, 'which I don't intend to take lying down.'

Trent's girl pushed past, sending Rosy's glass of champagne and peach juice flying over a racehorse trainer and one of his attractive girl grooms.

'—so put that in your column and . . . and smoke it,' Chloë ended triumphantly.

But her audience was watching the title-chaser's progress.

Like a true pro she made straight for Jamie. She put her hand on his arm to cut in on his conversation with a teenage wonderwaif model.

A clear case of lays majesté, thought Rosy and giggled to herself. She would have to stop drinking this . . . whatever it was. It tasted like fizzy tinned fruit salad.

Over on the sheepskin rugs, there was a flutter in floozyland. Nonchalant as ever, the Earl of Trent had wandered over in that devil-may-care way of his, causing hair to be tossed and laughs to tinkle louder. By the light of a phosphorescent cascade lamp, his dark eyes glittered as he began again with another willing selection of aristo-groupies.

'It must be simple, mustn't it,' said Rosy, staring over. 'Not to allow love to muddy romantic ambition.'

Emma shrugged. 'The title-chasers?'

'I mean, their one aim in life is to step out of St Margaret's, Westminster, with no need to buy the coroneted silver.'

'And gilt-edged invitations all the way. . . .'

'How does everyone else manage to fall in and out

of relationships with no more anguish than as if they were trying on new clothes?' said Rosy as Pearson shambled over.

'They're not everyone else, they're the people we write about,' he said.

Rosy frowned.

Emma managed to drag her eyes away from Jamie.

'It's not the same thing at all,' the diary old-timer went on. 'They might have been normal at some stage, before we started writing about them. But once they get on the page, they find they like it. So they have to keep their lives changing – new lovers, break-ups, marriages, divorces, success, failure – or they think we won't be interested in them anymore. They live fictional lives.'

He took a huge mouthful from a full tumbler of whisky he had procured from somewhere. 'Filthy stuff that peach juice.'

'Surely the point of a gossip column is that it should work on several different levels,' said Emma. 'It should be glamorous, humorous, aspirational, and it should also record social mores, expose hypocrisy and point up the absurdities in our society. The conflict – and the rich seam of irony – is that between the private and public lives of the subjects. . . .'

Emma was laying it on thick now, and Rosy knew who she was getting at. 'In the end, the only justification can be the pursuit of truth,' she concluded.

Rosy tried to look confident.

'The truth?' said Pearson. 'They don't let us anywhere near it.'

38 | Flat Talk

If Rosy had learned one thing in her long battle with her weight, it was that if people told you you were looking slim it was no compliment.

It meant they always thought of you as fat.

'I'm sure Jamie didn't mean it like that,' said Emma the next day at the flat. She was surrounded by battlements of books and ring files, looking her most authoritative.

Rosy refused to dignify that with a reply.

After a long lie-in and a trawl through in the bathroom cabinet for all known antidotes to Bellini poisoning, her head seemed wired to the right nerve endings again. She leant over and touched her toes experimentally. Urgh. Not quite back to normal, but she was going to have to take action. She went into the bathroom and stepped on the scales.

Nine stone twelve.

Tense muscles! Shift weight!

Nine stone thirteen.

She had to start dieting properly.

Out came the moth-eaten tracksuit from the top of the wardrobe, along with the battered running shoes. She had a tender reunion with a forgotten rugby shirt

178

and went out for a jog. Just a couple of blocks, nothing too shattering to person – or pavement, come to that.

It was her day off at last, and the sun had gone in. The weather was as leaden as her legs.

Her thoughts settled into the rhythm of her breathing. 'S-w-ord,' she panted. 'E-e-va,' she puffed. 'I-in-tros.'

After fifteen minutes, she was red-faced and spluttering. She limped home furtively, clutching an agonising stitch.

The avocado face pack had once come free with a magazine.

Normally Rosy's slightly olive skin was one of her best features, but today it showed all the ravages of hangover. 'Moisturising and soothing,' it said on the packet. Rosy tied back her thick hair and slapped on the potion.

The bride of Dracula stared back at her in the bathroom mirror. The greenish cream highlighted an alarming redness around her eyes. Her teeth looked as if they were hacked out of crumbling yellow Cotswold stone. She staggered back in genuine horror and had to crack a smile.

There was nothing to laugh about when it came off twenty minutes later. Her face was itching and blotchy. She squinted at the sachet. 'Use before Aug 89,' it said.

'So what's happening this evening?' said Emma, taking off the granny glasses she wore when she was studying. She seemed to have made good progress, judging by the amount of open books lying around the table.

'Absolutely, blissfully, nothing. Besides, I'm not going out anywhere with a face like this. Look at the blotches!' said Rosy. 'What are you up to?'

'No plans.'

Rosy tugged at the black leggings she had put on under a huge white jumper to make her legs look slimmer in comparison. She was sitting on the floor alternatively going through the lonely hearts column in *Time Out* and doing the Quick Crossword in the *Daily Dispatch*, while working her way down a litre of spring water because it was supposed to flush out impurities.

' "Unidentifiable", eight letters, F blank C blank K?' she mused aloud.

'Fuck-knows,' said Emma.

'That's nine letters. I think that K might be wrong.'

Emma pushed away a pile of dog-eared books and sat back rubbing her eyes. 'No lords a-leaping on one, not an orgy in sight? Anyone promising in *Time Out*?'

'I can't tell you the relief,' said Rosy, 'of not having to go out and eat and drink.'

'Never thought you found it a problem,' teased Emma.

'I don't,' said Rosy. 'That's the problem.'

'There are lots of consolations though.'

'Like what?' She felt in a grudging mood.

'Like Jamie Raj for one,' said Emma.

'Oh, honestly. Not you as well!'

'He is GORGEOUS.'

'If you go for that sort of thing.'

'Come on, Rosy. He's incredibly good-looking, charming, bright – in a general kind of way – '

'Don't tell me ... you've spotted a conflict between his private and public life then?' Rosy got some of her own back for the previous night.

'Dunno. I tell you what though, Rosy, I wouldn't mind finding out.'

'Huh!'

'I always thought you got on with him all right.'

'I do. I like him. You can't help but like him. That's the whole point.'

'I'm not with you.'

'As a colleague, a friend even, Jamie's great. He's fun, he knows everyone in London, you can even have a decent conversation with him. I'm not denying that. But anything else is asking for trouble. You'd never be sure of him for a moment.'

'Yes, but—'

'Jamie Raj is an operator, Emma. He knows exactly how to play it so women come running to him. I've seen him do it, the same technique over and over again. He doesn't have girlfriends, he has charisma victims,' said Rosy savagely.

'Yes, but—'

'Do you know what they call him at the *Dispatch* – and with good reason?'

'What?'

'The Asian *Provocateur.*'

Emma laughed. 'What is his background anyway – what exactly does Anglo-Indian mean?'

'In Jamie's case, being the son of a British pilot working for Air India and a beautiful Indian stewardess,' said Rosy.

'A British father . . . but, hang on, how does he get a surname like Raj then?'

'It's Raja-something unpronounceable,' said Rosy. 'Jamie shortens it. His mother married again, to some eminent maharajah type, and they both took his name. It works for Jamie. The memories-of-Empire touch goes down a treat with the nobs and snobs.'

'So his real name could be Higginbottom, for all we know? Not that anyone who saw him would care.'

'Jamie would,' said Rosy. 'Desperately.'

Emma put both elbows on her books and cupped her chin in her hands dreamily. 'I'd be willing to help him get over it . . . someone's got to do it.'

'I'm serious, Em. Jamie has hundreds of women – he does that look of his and they all come screaming.'

'Now wouldn't that be wonderful,' said Emma. 'To come screaming, with Jamie.'

In the end, under cover of darkness – Rosy's face was still inflamed – they went to the cinema. Having discounted all the films they ought to see for the sake of dinner-party conversation (the Barbican's Fellini Season or the sub-titled Gerard Depardieu), they went to the MGM in the Fulham Road to see *Jurassic Park*.

'There was a picture of Sword in *Private Eye* last week,' said Rosy as they came out, 'next to one of the dinosaurs. One of those "Could they be related? – I think we should be told" letters.'

Emma steered her firmly past the stand selling pails of aromatic popcorn. 'Someone told me I looked like a truculent Bonnie Langford when I was fourteen. He couldn't work out why I never spoke to him again.'

'I should think not. Never mind,' said Rosy kindly. 'I can't see it now.'

'Phew,' said Emma with mock-relief. 'God it must be nice to be told you look like some true star of the silver screen, someone remote and coolly classical. Or even better to be that person, like Ingrid Bergman or Lauren Bacall, beautiful and immortalised like that on celluloid.'

'Yes,' said Rosy. 'Whereas someone like me is just mortified by my cellulite.'

39 | *Healthy Options*

Anthony Sword's first days at Grasslands Hall had not been a great success.

His hunger had a life of its own, the fury of his stomach was impossible to ignore. Yet the computer-driven diet on his Total Bodycare Programme – 'incorporating 2,500 ingredient permutations' – did little to fill the void. Certainly the permutations so far of beansprouts, alfalfa and tofu shreds were doing nothing for his spiritual nourishment.

And the psycho-babble was driving him crazy.

He was pinning his hopes on the two-hour slot on his timetable for Wednesday which promised Escape Therapy.

It was all very well Nan Purchase insisting that he was her personal guest for as long as he felt up to it. At the moment, he felt so light-headed it was more a question of not being up to making any kind of resistance.

In the high-tech torture chamber known as the gymnasium there was a notice on the futuristic exercise cycles which read: 'Use Common Sense. Stop if you feel faint, dizzy or short of breath.' Sword felt all that just contemplating the ascent of such a machine.

Outside, the tennis courts, the golf practice range and the jogging trail around the grounds seemed as unattainable to him as the summit of K2, and as inhospitable.

Other inmates drifted along the deep-pile corridors and lush hush of treatment rooms like spooks in terry-towelling. He had peered into the library and the mineral bar, but found them uninviting – the silence broken only by funereal whispers and the occcasional crunch of a carrot stick.

Plainly, he was in the top security wing.

Exfoliation. Thermal wrap. De-toxification.

One by one these mysteries were unveiled to him.

At various stages he had been smothered in abrasive cream, scrubbed down by a terrifying washerwoman with a Polish accent, covered in jelly and mummified in a hot blanket.

Now he had his Ionithermie.

The comely beauty therapist who had seen him on the first day was called Michelle. She had the kind of long curly brown hair that Sword had only ever seen on a Miss England beauty contestant, large cow-pat brown eyes and the dewiest complexion he had ever seen. When she bent over him to work, she stirred soft memories of his mother long ago.

Her familiarity by now with his vast exposed body made the process bearable.

She took the measurements of his waist, hips, stomach and thighs. Then she applied one potion to his thighs and belly, then another on top of that, soothing, chirruping away with reassuring explanations.

Then she covered him in blue clay.

And as if this were not bad enough, he watched in

horror as electrodes were slapped on to him through the muck.

'Now this looks worse than it is. Won't hurt a bit,' said Michelle gaily. She retreated and turned on the current.

Quivering in wet gloop with no control over his muscles was not Sword's idea of salvation. It went on for twenty minutes, during which time he cursed the world, Nan Purchase, and Benedict Pierce for good measure – and wondered whether, out there somewhere, Amnesty International was aware of his plight.

He was amazed, however, when he had been hosed down and measured again, to discover the process had reduced his stomach by several inches and his thighs by one inch. His skin felt silky as a woman's when he slid his robe on again.

He could not tell whether his sudden elation was due to the inch loss or the simple fact that he had survived.

That evening, after the cold comfort of his twig and weed dinner, Sword braved the Mineral Bar downstairs. It was in a light, airy room which might once have been a drawing room, with windows leading out to a balustraded stone terrace. A fine Adam fireplace lent an air of silver lining to his cloudy outlook: it was the kind of room which looked as if someone at some time might have indulged in the teensiest excess.

It was not so much that he wanted company. He needed to satisfy himself that it was there if required.

The past few days had taken the edge off his need for hue and cry, but it had not blunted his curiosity completely.

Feeling reassured now that he was no longer pink and vulnerable in his towelling robe but wearing real

185

clothes again, Sword sat down and ordered a guava-and-zinc special.

Two angular women were jutting chins over a copy of *Ciao!* magazine in one corner. A man and a woman, probably husband and wife, gazed around the room as if watching for someone else to hear their stories. A large, black woman in a flowered kaftan almost filled a two-seater sofa.

As if feeling his eyes on her, she looked up and smiled, but not in an expectant way.

What the hell, thought Sword.

It happened all too rarely with him. But he felt in his beleaguered bones that this might be one of those occasions when adversity might not be its own reward.

Sometimes you needed someone to share it with.

40 | *A Letter for Jamie*

The Monday mornings when Sword would swan in bearing quails eggs and blinis, or pralines and cinnamon tea to get the creative juices flowing had gone. Without him it was now back to basics: Tina dispensing sticky canteen buns and the cup that cheered.

And a letter for Jamie.

Jamie ripped into the envelope. He emitted a full-wattage smile and a Men Only signal to Pearson.

'Not another one?' The elder hack seemed to know exactly what it was. He abandoned the *Telegraph*'s personal column and his muttered attempts to decode the Grateful Thanks to St Jude.

'Afraid so.'

'What a naughty little girl . . . show it here. . . .'

'Ah . . . ah! This is private correspondence.' Jamie swept the lighthouse beam of his smile round the office to include them all.

Since Sword had gone off leaving him in charge of the column, thought Rosy, he was impossibly smug.

'Is she . . . going into details again?' persisted Pearson, moving his chair nearer until they were in a huddle over

187

the pink sheet of writing paper. There were schoolboy sniggers and grunts.

Rosy looked at Tina quizzically.

But the secretary was making a show of ignoring the two men.

'What are you two—?' began Rosy.

A lewd snort from Pearson as he read aloud, ' "As we lay that time, our nakedness entwined on the roof, above the maddening crowd at the Henderson ball . . . I wanted to hold you against me for all time . . ."?? Jamie, you devil . . . Mummy was at that party. . . .'

'That certainly gave it an edge.'

'If Honoria knew . . .'

'Knew what? Share the joke . . .' whinged Rosy, feeling left out.

Pearson raised an eyebrow expressively. 'Jamie's love-lorn sixteen year old. Who really ought to take up writing for Mills and Boon, judging from these efforts: "your magnificent manhood . . . with every shudder of my body as I arched in rapture . . ." et cetera, et cetera.'

'It's . . . er, steamy stuff,' said Rosy, uncomfortably.

Jamie had the grace to look sheepish.

'It gets better,' went on Pearson. 'She's only Honoria Peeke's daughter. Forward for her age, don't you think?'

'Pearson!' protested Jamie.

'He loves it,' said Pearson, unabashed. 'Our deb-deflowerer, our heat-seeking missile. Roger and Out. And they all fall for it. . . .'

'Yes, well . . . I think that's enough of that now.' Jamie tore up the letter to a howl of protest from the other man. Then he flipped through the messages on his desk, selected a number and began to dial.

'By the way, Rosy,' he paused and grinned. 'I've been

meaning to mention it. Your friend Emma – she's awfully attractive, and good fun too. . . .'

'Oh, no you don't—'

But the handsome Raj, had turned his attention to one of his twenty favourite blondes and was not listening.

'Honestly,' said Rosy, crossly. She noticed that their secretary had turned blotchy pink. 'Look, I don't care . . . but you've really upset Tina.'

Tina cast her eyes down, while Pearson had the grace to show his first hint of embarrassment.

'I'm sorry, T . . . didn't think. Oh, God . . .'

'What . . .?' Rosy puzzled.

Tina couldn't look up.

Then the light dawned. 'Oh, no . . . you haven't? Not you as well, Tina?'

The silence was eloquent.

Jamie became more autocratic later, when he returned from lunch with a motor-racing contact to find Pearson had been busy doing his expenses.

He gave them to Jamie, as acting page editor, to authorise.

Jamie was unamused.

'Pearson, you may very well have entertained Princess Michael of Kent. In fact, in view of the large amounts of the Sword's Secrets budget which have allegedly gone on keeping her in champagne over the years, I very much hope that you have. But not, even I can deduce, with a late-night takeaway from the Acropolis Chop and Kebab House in Station Approach, Oxted.'

The elder hack mumbled into his tweed. Post-pub his face was ruddier than ever and the sports coat smelled faintly of Fisons fertiliser.

Then he turned on Rosy.

'And as for you, get out and get some stories! I want new people, new stories, parties, nightclubs, all-night orgies! New angles away from Sword's tired old cast lists!'

'Well, I—'

'It's no good sitting around in the office waiting for the phone to ring – I want on-the-spot eye-witness reports.'

'But I do—'

'When I first started with Sword I was at Annabel's and Tramp and Raffles every night,' said Jamie, twisting the knife. 'I want you to come in tomorrow morning with a sparkling, sexy, intriguing night-club story.'

Rosy was stunned.

'And what's more, I want no more stories about actresses no one's ever heard of!' said Jamie ominously.

When Jamie went out of the room, Rosy turned to Pearson.

'What's got into him?'

Pearson's eyes glinted devilishly.

'Have you heard what the Editor said when he heard Sword was off indefinitely and Raj here was in charge?'

Rosy shook her head.

Pearson chortled, enjoying himself now. 'The showbiz lot were all killing themselves over it down in Scribblers – and you know what they're like, they'll have told everyone in the building by now!'

'Go on – what?'

'The Editor told conference he had a nasty feeling he might as well have told Michelangelo he'd done all right so far, but the Sistine Chapel's regular painters and decorators could take over now they'd got the idea. The

190

Hand of God was in place, but there could still be a horrible mess.'

Rosy began to laugh. Then she stopped.

'Hang on a moment,' she said. 'That means us too.'

Pearson shrugged.

'But . . .'

'You know, Rosy . . . I don't think I've ever met anyone who took a fun job as seriously as you do.'

Rosy answered the call through a mouthful of biscuit. At present it seemed that chocolate Hob-nobs were the only known antidote to life and its dilemmas – and the dread certainty that the theatrical crone would soon be back on the blower.

'Hufflo.'

'Is that Anthony Sword's office?'

'It is.'

'Right. I'm ringin' abaht that bloke Sir Philip Hawty.' It was a man's voice with a strange, wavery London accent.

'Yes?'

''E's in the Oh-tel de la Pay in Nice with TV lovely Danielle Kay. It's an ex-Minister in Sun Sin Sex Trap situation.'

Rosy hated it when informants spoke in what they imagined was tabloid style. She was about to make some Sword-like retort, when she thought better of it.

'Can you give me any more details?'

She could hear him breathing hard.

'Who is this speaking?' she asked.

The line went dead.

41 | *Nice Work*

'Can you give me any more details?'

It was a young woman's voice, and she sounded friendly enough, if a little muffled.

He thought he had better not.

'Who is this speaking?' she asked again.

In the payphone of a café bar in the Rue Sainte Olaire, Sir Philip Hawty softly replaced the receiver and cleared his throat. The heat was stifling. In the dark cupboard of a booth, he felt a trickle of thrilling anxiety make its way down his back inside his polo shirt.

He took another deep breath and eased himself out as casually as he knew how.

Outside under a delphinium blue sky Danielle was in a chatty mood.

'I'd love to go to the Cannes Film Festival. All the stars and the paparazzi!'

She looked up happily from a film magazine.

'Do you want to go?' he asked indulgently.

All the paparazzi. Now that was an idea.

'It was a couple of weeks ago. Robert Redford came for two whole hours and the whole town came to a standstill. I've seen *The Great Gatsby* eight times and I still go all goosepimply when it gets to the bit where he sees Mia Farrow for the first time,' she sighed.

The Mediterranean sun had brought out the sweetest crop of freckles across her upturned nose, and her perfect body was turning the irresistible gold of his old nanny's treacle puddings. Aromatic. Tempting.

He wondered what her effect would be on his adult nursery, the House of Commons, and once more he wondered whether he would be able to go through with what he had intended. When he was with her, he felt as if he were in charge of a beautiful, trusting child.

If she wondered why he had not made a move on her, she hadn't said anything.

Odd, he thought, that she should look so ... (the word tarty came to mind, but he rejected it) ... so experienced, yet turn out to shine with such endearing naivity. How many other young women in her position would agree to a trip to the Riviera with a man like him and then just wait as polite as could be for ... what? She had said nothing about the sleeping arrangements, not even when he had made such a song and dance at reception about the necessity for single rooms.

'Are you having a good time?' he asked.

She stirred her *café au lait* and licked the froth off the spoon.

'Ooh yes.'

'I love it here. The heat. The smells. The food,' he said. He tipped his face up to the hot sun and felt his nervous excitement calm.

'Just think,' said Danielle. 'If I'd never have gone to that party at that little fat bloke's, I might never have met you and I wouldn't be here now. I mean, I never knew him or anything, he sent an invite to my agent. I only went 'cos some of the other girls were and we thought it might be a bit of a laugh. I still don't know whose do it was. Still, that's showbusiness, eh?' She gurgled happily as if she couldn't believe she was actually part of it.

'Lord Diplock. It was one of his parties. He's quite famous for them. Or should I say, infamous.'

'Strange isn't it, going to parties given by people you don't know.'

'It happens all the time,' he said.

'Do the guests all know each other?'

'They pretend to, and after a while they think they do.'

There was a pause.

'I never thought you'd remember me. I mean, it was months ago, that party. And then when you rang me, I was ever so surprised.'

'Pleasantly, I hope.'

She didn't answer that. 'It was funny you being at Eva's the other night. I didn't know you knew her.'

He hesitated. 'I hadn't seen her for a long time.'

'What about your wife?'

For the first time, he was aware she might be sharper than he had given her credit for. Perhaps she imagined it was the wife problem which was responsible for his gentlemanly conduct. If so, all well and good.

'Ex-wife. Well, soon-to-be ex.'

'Whatever.' Danielle waited for him to continue.

'She has a house in Sussex.'

'Have you got kids?'

'No.'

'You were in the Cabinet, weren't you?'

It warmed his heart that she was clearly relaxed and confident enough now with him to be able to put questions to him that she hadn't dared before.

194

She looked serious.

'I wouldn't tell anyone here that,' said Danielle. 'I found out this morning that Cabinet means "the loo" in French!' She squealed with delight.

He was caught off guard, but then couldn't help laughing with her.

'I've forgotten what you were.'

'I was Home Secretary.'

'I always think that sounds like one of those posh ways they describe housewives nowadays. How long were you that for?'

This girl was a miracle. She knew nothing. He was about to say two years, but when he opened his mouth he admitted the truth.

'Five months,' he said.

'That's not long. I've been on *Legs Eleven* for over a year and I still feel new.'

'Let's say it didn't work out.'

'Why?'

He found himself telling her the simple facts.

'It was fifteen years ago. Over various issues including the judicial system and the press . . . I was pilloried in Tory papers. In the end I resigned rather than face being forced out, and managed to hang on to my seat ever since.'

He hadn't told it straight like that to anyone, not for years.

He gazed at her with something dangerously like affection.

Danielle was rapt.

'I used to be pilloried,' she said. 'And you do have to hang on to the seat. I had a boyfriend with a Harley-Davidson and I always went on the back.'

42 | Et in *Arcadia* . . .

The opulently fleshed black woman's name was Framboise Duprée and she was from Louisiana via the old Embassy supper club and the People's Jazz Opera of Camden. She was of indeterminate age and said that her second favourite occupation in the whole world was to sing in the bath while sipping champagne. It was a necessity of life which she had no intention of foregoing, not even in the top security wing of Grasslands Hall.

She was on the same harsh regime as he was.

Or she was supposed to be.

After meeting her, Anthony Sword was enjoying a considerable upturn in optimism. Real blood seemed to be flowing through his body again.

He recognised a kindred spirit.

'So what are you in for?' he'd asked her eventually.

Rippling freely beneath a vast kaftan of tropical flowers, Framboise gave a belly laugh so magnificent it was probably a prohibited indulgence.

'False accounting,' said Framboise.

'Oh?'

'I promised I'd get slender for the Gershwin season – y'know, nice slinky Bess – and they put me on a weights and measures chart. I played along for a while. But as soon as I found out my name got printed on the programmes a month ago, I thought what the hell?'

'You stopped losing weight?'

'Flab is fab, honey. I never began.'

'So they packed you off here.'

'It was cheaper than reprinting. Hon, I is suffering for my art.'

And she gave him an outsize wink.

He was struck by the surprising blue lagoons of her bulbous eyes, almost the same colour as his.

The next evening, he had actively sought her out.

'You wanna know what my first favourite occupation in the world is?' asked Framboise, one painted brow raised wickedly.

He was delighted to find her in the Mineral Bar again, as gaudy and loud as a carnival in the room's ghostly restraint.

She was outrageously laid-back.

She made him laugh.

She didn't give a toss about what anyone thought.

And that was just what he needed.

Tonight her hair was blonde and green – she was wearing one of those wigs that celebrate artifice. He thought she was quite perfect.

'Tell me,' said Sword, settling carefully into his side of a vast eau-de-nil sofa which swelled like a balloon between their substantial bulks.

'Champagne and sex in the bathtub.'

'No singing?'

'That entirely depends,' said Framboise.

With Framboise, Sword felt the absurd thrill of consorting with a rebel faction. If she knew who he was, she had given no indication. For once, that was exactly what he wanted.

'In the bath is all right, but I do it best in the garden,' admitted Sword after a Vitamin K Soda.

'Well, that's a good place too. At least you're not too uptight to do it outdoors.'

'I prefer it, dear lady, with the light on,' said Sword slyly. 'In the morning. I'm a morning singer.'

She gave a great bassoon-toned gurgle. 'Never at night?'

'Not to my knowledge. Not sober at any rate.'

'Never felt the night air on the larynx, huh?'

'Nope,' he shrugged.

'Are you in for a treat! C'mon!'

'What, where?'

'C'mon! Don't sit starin' like a bird up a tree.' Framboise grabbed his hand and heaved him to his feet.

'I, er—'

'Honey, you may have seen life, but until you have had it in the garden at night, you have never HEARD life.'

She ignored his grumbles and led him to the French windows. The lock fell to three twists and a thump and they were out on the darkened terrace. Down stone steps and across the crunchy gravel drive, they stopped at the head of a formal sunken garden.

The silence of the night buzzed in his head.

'Now hear this and don't ever forget it,' said Framboise.

As he turned, puzzled, to look at her, she brushed past him, a soft fragrant ball of musk and chocolate and coconut and ginger. She went down into the garden in front and when she reached the centre she turned to face him.

She began to sing.

Her voice was deep mahogany, pure molasses, rich and sensuous as truffles. It made the breath solidify in his lungs, his bones melt.

> 'I loves you Porgy, don' let him take me,
> Don' let him handle me an' drive me mad.
> If you kin keep me, I wants to stay here
> With you forever, and I'd be glad."

When she had finished the song, he felt the notes drift away on the cool air.

'That was beautiful,' he said at last.

She smiled.

'Don't get any ideas,' she said. 'You can return the compliment some other night.'

They walked slowly, companionably, back to the main house, across the tangerine glow the lighted windows threw over the dull gravel. Above, the sky was black as it never was over London.

An owl hooted, followed by a shriek.

Then another shriek.

'Nightlife in the country,' said Sword, still floating in reverie. 'I could get to like this.'

A burst of laughter was followed by a very human shriek, unmistakable this time.

He turned to Framboise, frowning.

It was then that she told him how it was possible, on a strange and magical evening like this, to pass over to the Other Side.

43 | *Nice Night*

Sir Philip Hawty felt as gauche as the public schoolboy he once was when he flexed his arm and let it come gingerly to rest on Danielle's bare shoulder.

The moon grinned cheesily in the dark sky above as the silhouette of a private plane flew across it. Below the Promenade des Anglais was the sigh of the sea stroking the shore.

'Tired?' he asked.

'Not really. It's lovely here.'

Well that was as may be. He couldn't wait any longer.

'I think I might turn in. Shall we go back to the hotel?'

'Okay.'

They walked in silence.

He tried to keep his arm light on her, and she did not shrug it off. Neither did she do anything to bring him closer to her. Her scent was a cloying Eastern musk which was all wrong for her youth and prettiness.

This was it, he told himself, heart pounding, as they rounded the corner which brought them out in front of the Hotel de la Paix.

This was what he had been leading up to.

This was . . .

Nothing.

Sir Philip peered into the neon-lit darkness of the side road. He listened intently. Nothing but a sawing concerto from the cicadas in the garden round the swimming pool.

He had expected at least a photographer, if not two and a reporter. Could they be in a van parked in view of the entrance? He understood that was often the way the papers went about getting a picture like this. He looked around in mounting dismay.

All that was parked on the road was a collection of mobilettes, waiting, no doubt, for his head to hit the pillow before they roared into life.

This was not what he had planned.

The cicadas – and the coursing blood in his head – were deafening.

Damn it. He would have to try again the next evening. Surely the *Dispatch* would have got their man in place by then.

'Well, g'night then, Danielle.'

'I'm not tired,' she said softly.

'Oh. Are you going to stay up a little while, then?'

'No, I want to go to bed.'

She took his hand, and he shivered involuntarily. At all costs he must keep his head now.

'Ah, good book?'

'*The New Life Guide to the Best Sex Ever.*'

Sir Philip gulped. He craned round in the vain hope that there was a motor-drive lens poking out of a tree nearby. The dense shadows thrown by the pine trees would have been enough even for the most ham-fisted of Fleet Street's finest.

Still nothing.

'It's by this American woman who split up from her

husband,' continued Danielle. 'She seems to have a brilliant time now.'

He was thinking fast.

Perhaps the timing was wrong. Maybe they should hang around for a while longer.

'You're right. It is a bit early. We could have a drink out here. Nightcap, you know.'

'In the garden?'

'If you like.'

'How romantic,' said Danielle.

He smiled.

'What would you like?'

'No drink, ta.'

'Go on.'

'I don't need it.'

He felt blind terror at that point, a cloud over his usually controlled face which she may have misinterpreted.

'Oh, all right then,' she relented. 'Do they do Double Zombie Stingers?'

'You sit down, I'll go and order.' He motioned her to a table visible from the street through a break in the pines.

When he returned with some foul vodka concoction for her and a double Scotch for himself, she had taken off her large hoop earrings and released her hair from its clip. She looked about sixteen.

He began to ask about her rise to TV gameshow stardom, and then, in desperation, about her family and pets. They sat in the warm, fragrant garden for an hour. To his consternation, she hardly touched her drink.

'I feel nervous, all of a sudden,' she said.

So did he.

44 | *Champagne Worker*

The motto at Annabel's, the famous Berkeley Square night-club, was, 'Who you see here, what you hear here, when you leave here, let it stay here.'

The less well-known and, it has to be said, less exclusive Mirabeau's club around the corner in Bruton Lane worked on the refreshing principle that having no reporting restrictions was very good for business.

So it was that Rosy sat there deep in thought drinking Mirabeau's icy cold house champagne.

The deep coral walls of the club reminded her of one of the excavated pornographic rooms she had once seen at Herculaneum – or was it Pompeii? A mural of trailing vines wound round photographs of members past and present. Foreigners and Londoners who still had expense accounts were seated in deep recesses. On the dance floor a few well-dressed couples were dancing uneasily to a Tom Jones re-release, as if remembering their – as well as Tom's – former glories.

It was past midnight and Rosy was hard at work.

She went through the reporter's mantra.

Who, What, Where, When, Why and How.

Who – the hell are all these people?

What – am I doing here like some kind of hooker on my own?

Where – do I start?

When – can I go home?

Why – can't I loosen up?

How – can I get a story to satisfy Jamie?

This wasn't getting her anywhere.

The champagne – on the house, thanks to the Diary's free VIP membership – was having a numbing effect, but Jamie's dismissiveness, and Pearson's comment about her seriousness, still stung.

At a table near where she sat at the bar, a group of couples barked at each other about the uncertainty in the property market and the family silver they would have to flog soon.

'Sorry about that,' said Nico, Mirabeau's sleek front-of-house manager, as he rejoined her. 'A little difficulty with some non-members wanting Country and Western music.'

'Oh?'

'Fergie's Texans. Now where were we?'

Rosy smiled drily.

'I think I was droning on about how hard my job is.'

'And you make it look so easy,' he grinned, raising his glass.

'I never get enough sleep.'

Nico tutted understandingly. His dark eyes were playing games with Rosy's.

Nico wore sharp black suits with enough design oddities to signal exclusivity. He was forty-ish, half-Greek, half-Leytonstone. Attractive too, Rosy decided, if you thought strange vowels were sexy.

'It's only practice, staying out late. You should come

204

here more often, have a good time.' Nico was giving a good impression of being totally enraptured by her.

She felt too tired to play. 'But all the time I'm thinking that I ought to go and bother someone by asking if it's true their wife has run off with the antiques restorer, or whether they know their husband has been propositioning petrol pump attendants in Harlow. I mean . . . is that dignified?'

'Well . . .'

'I feel like I'm letting everyone down.' Mostly the people who once believed in me, she thought.

He didn't get it.

'Never mind,' said Rosy.

'No, say.'

'It's not exactly Pulitzer prize stuff.'

She took a deep swig of a third glass of champagne which had appeared automatically on the bar, and sighed as she helped herself to a freshly roasted brazil nut.

'You shouldn't be unhappy. I could—' began Nico.

His leg was against hers, his hands poised to settle on her shoulders. It was obvious he considered himself gold medallion standard at body language.

'I'm not normally unhappy,' said Rosy. 'It's just . . . I always thought parties were fun before.'

'You should have your face lifted into a grin or become a Buddhist,' said Nico. 'I'm told that saying Nam Myoko Renge Kyo as you come into a room gives a very alluring smile as one makes an entrance.'

'Very New Age Aware.'

Nico smiled. 'Jamie Raj tells me that you have what it takes.'

'Oh?' Suddenly she felt reinvigorated. For about a second.

'He said what made you such an asset was that you were so unashamedly ... eager.'

'How embarrassing,' said Rosy.

'Not at all. It was sweet.'

'I haven't been on the *Dispatch* long – and it's not as if it's a permanent job or anything yet. It's still rather overwhelming,' she admitted. 'Even now I sometimes wish I was still a magistrates' court reporter in the provinces, well, Bromley actually. I only got this job because Sword thought Court reporter meant Court and Social.' She trailed off, aghast that she seemed to be confiding in this stranger. What was happening to her?

'How is the great man?'

'Sword? Er, fine. I think. He's off for a while.'

'Anywhere nice?'

'I don't know. Jamie says he usually goes on cruises – you know, the ones where it's constant food all day: dinner at eight, then a banquet at midnight – anyone else's idea of hell.'

'And the column runs itself?'

'Jamie's in charge.'

Nico gave her a meaningful look. Like all the people she had met lately, he seemed to assume intimacy after a couple of drinks. 'Now that wouldn't be why you're out of sorts, would it? The Don Juan of the *Dispatch*?'

'Do me a favour.'

'You never know.'

'I'm here, on my own, because of him. All right? He wants some nightclub stories.'

'Now we're talking!'

'We are?'

'I never thought you'd ask,' said Nico.

45 | *Benedict's Theory*

Benedict Pierce had a theory about the fidelity epidemic.

Once upon a time rich men used to trade in their wives for younger models. Now they kept the same wife, and remodelled that one. It was cheaper and less trouble. Yep, as an affordable option when cash flows were tight, therapy and plastic surgery were doing great things for the sanctity of marriage.

Hardly the best news in the world for the Onlooker Column in the *Daily Post.*

The page currently being printed carried the engagement of a minor peer's daughter, a second child for one of Diana's hairdressers, a desperate quip from an MP, and a puff for a shirt-making company set up in Battersea by a friend of his secretary Lulu.

Whichever way Benedict looked at it, 'Happily married for five years' did not have the same enticing ring as 'Five-times divorced' in a gossip column story.

Time was, he thought as he walked into the scented warmth of Mirabeau's, when it was wall-to-wall eagerness down here, when a man could contemplate taking a wife any night of the week, and the only question would be, whose?

Benedict blamed the recession and Warren Beatty.

Beatty. There was a man who had stood for what Benedict Pierce believed in. A man who put real meaning into the phrase 'star-studded'. Beautiful and famous women had once queued up to blab that once they had had Warren, no one else could compare. Now, if he was serious about this marriage and fidelity stand, any woman who wanted to find out the infamous Beatty Bed Secret – that only those who had actually made it with the man himself could know what made him so special – would have to settle for getting it strictly theoretically.

Beatty married and a father. Benedict found that hard to forgive.

For old times' sake he stalked a girl in a red leather Chanel dress and greeted a few old faces. His old mate Nico seemed to be well in there with a curvaceous young woman at the bar, so he merely saluted him over her back.

Benedict worked the room with his sharp eyes for a conversation which might prove valuable – perhaps there might even be someone here to cross-question about Anthony Sword, for Lord knew, his biographical researches were hardly proceeding apace. And he made quite sure that the social pariah Bea Goff was not lurking in wait for him with any more of her ludicrous claims – everywhere he turned these days, she was there repeating her story – before he accepted an invitation to join a merchant banker and his party.

In fact, it was only when he was almost at their table and looked a little closer at the girl at the bar that Benedict saw that it was Rosy Hope who was monopolising the club manager.

The merchant banker John Renfrew, an urbane contact from his days on the City desk, greeted him enthusiastically. The bond man had greyed alarmingly, thought Benedict, though he was less paunchy than he had been during the champagne boom of the mid-Eighties.

'Benedict! I'd like you to meet my wife Lizzie—'

He shook hands with a tired-looking strawberry blonde woman.

'—and our very good friends the Pritchards, Tom and Annie.'

They greeted him enthusiastically, a balding man and a pretty brunette. She bore all the hallmarks of a second, younger wife: a huge brilliant engagement ring and an unlikely way of agreeing with her husband's every word. Benedict immediately warmed to Pritchard.

'On your own?' Renfrew asked Benedict.

'Yes. Work, you know how it is.'

The men started talking about negative equity.

'I always read your page,' said Annie Pritchard, turning to Benedict. 'Do you know Sting?'

'Well, I've met him. Why?'

'He and his wife live in the next village to us in the country.'

'Oh, yes?' Benedict gave her a practised smile. These conversations had a habit of turning out the same way. People always needed to show him that they mixed in the right circles too. The likelihood of them ending in a fabulous story was about as remote as snow in August.

'Absolutely super house, they've got. But when you see him driving around in his Land Rover, he doesn't look anything special.'

Benedict forced himself to be jolly.

'It's always the way,' he said. 'There's a famous story about a major league rock groupie who managed to sleep her way right up the scale, all the big stars. Each time she came back in the morning and told everyone

209

about her latest conquest, she'd say, "He was good, but he wasn't Mick Jagger." Then came the day she finally got to sleep with Jagger himself. Went back the next morning, spilled the beans. How was it, everyone wanted to know.' He paused for effect.

Annie was rapt.

' "Well, he was good, but he wasn't Mick Jagger!" ' flourished Benedict.

She laughed gratifyingly.

'And that,' said Renfrew, cutting in with a wink, 'is a very old story, Benedict old mate.'

'So,' said Lizzie brightly, 'What's the latest scandal?'

Benedict bit back a sharp retort.

'The scandal, as I see it, is that there's not nearly enough traditional rock star behaviour.'

'What do you mean exactly?'

'Rock stars used to trash hotel rooms, for example. And drive around in flash cars. Now they buy country manors, and Georgian furniture, and drive their collections of vintage cars – very, very carefully. Not much fun for the rest of us.'

'I see your point,' said Annie.

Lizzie looked faintly disapproving.

'But probably to the relief of mothers everywhere,' she said.

'Oh, do you think that's what it is?' said Benedict, mock-serious.

'What?' Lizzie was intent.

'That instead of corrupting teenage daughters, it's the mothers they're knocking off now?'

They laughed, although Lizzie was not as amused as Annie.

Soon it was Lizzie's turn.

'My mother lives in the same village as Lady Hawty.'

'Oh yes?' Benedict turned to her after watching a girl in a cashmere bikini and platform-soled Doc Martens go by to join the Earl of Trent who had arrived with a noisy group. There was a loud crash from somewhere behind them.

'She and Mummy are rather good friends actually.'

Ho-hum. Benedict reached for his cigarettes.

He noticed the Beast from the *Daily Dispatch* appear in Trent's slipstream, brushing down his black leather trenchcoat.

'It wasn't you who started the story about Sir Philip and that bimbo last week, was it?' said Lizzie.

'No.'

'Just as well. It's all rubbish. Mary Hawty told Mummy she's much happier now, so we think they're getting back together again.'

'Really?' said Benedict. Now that was more like it.

46 | *Hot Lips*

Rosy couldn't help but admire Benedict Pierce. Whatever else she thought of him, conditioned as she was by Sword's merciless rubbishing campaigns, she wished she had his self-assurance. He always seemed to enjoy his work.

On her way out of Mirabeau's at something past two, feeling detached by drink and vague dissatisfaction, she saw him carousing away with a group of friends, laughing and dancing as if a visit to the nightspot was a treat he had longed for all year.

How long had he been there – and how daft did he think she was propping up the bar with only Nico for company? She was almost at the stairs leading to the door where she could scuttle out when she heard her name being called.

She turned, rattled.

It was Benedict.

'Not going already?' he intercepted her. 'The evening's hardly begun!'

'I . . . er . . .' Crumbs, what now?

She accepted his offer of another glass of champagne. He was so solicitous it seemed rude to refuse.

Whatever Sword said, Benedict Pierce was a

thoroughly nice man, Rosy decided as a whole bottle of Laurent Perrier appeared on the secluded table for two where he had led her. She could hardly imagine Sword being this attentive to one of the reporters on Pierce's Onlooker column. It wasn't just that he had asked her about herself, but he was actually listening to the answers.

His light eyes which crinkled in the corners with good humour were very persuasive.

Nose to nose over the third glass, Benedict was volunteering edited highlights of his own life story. How he had never set out to become a gossip columnist – Rosy wondered if anyone ever did – but had joined a paper in Norfolk at eighteen. His years chasing fire engines in pursuit of a story (a start she could identify with) and his haul up to the nationals by working news-room night shifts as a casual. His long tenure as a City specialist on the *Post* before he had caught the new Editor's eye. And even his two marriages culminating in two children and two divorces.

The way he talked made her feel like an equal. More than that. A confidante.

'It's really important, isn't it . . . family?' said Rosy, beginning to lose focus on his slightly beaky features. He was handsome all right, she thought, if you went for the Nigel Havers look.

Benedict looked at her even more intensely. 'You don't realise how much, until it isn't there anymore.'

Oh God. Was he going to get maudlin? She sat tight.

'. . . and I don't just mean the wife and children part.'

'Hmm . . . parents?'

Suddenly he looked terribly sad.

'I'm sorry. Your parents are—' Her voice trailed off

with the realisation that she had put her unthinking foot in it again.

He obviously realised what she meant.

'No-o. Not dead as far as I know. At least I don't know. . . .'

'Oh.' Rosy opted for the least risky response.

Benedict sighed. 'I never knew my real parents. I . . . was adopted when I was only a few weeks old. I was brought up by a couple – a lovely couple – in King's Lynn. He died some years ago, but I'm still close to her. Even though . . . you know . . . I don't get up to see her as often as I should.'

Rosy warmed to him.

He was studying what looked like a rather grand signet ring on the little finger of his right hand. Somehow Rosy knew what he was going to say.

'This was all my mother left for me.'

He looked like a small boy. 'Oh, God, I'm sorry. I don't know why I'm telling you all this. It's just . . .'

'Go on,' whispered Rosy. 'She's never been in touch?'

'Not . . . exactly. Although—' The gossip columnist hesitated.

'Go on.'

Now he seemed to be wondering whether it was wise to take her further into his confidence. Rosy sipped at her champagne in silence, willing him to carry on.

'She . . . that is, someone who now claims to be my mother . . . has been – contacting me recently. Since I got the column, in fact.'

He sounded miserable.

Uncertain what to say, Rosy gazed at him sympathetically.

Abruptly he splintered the moment. 'Come on, Rosy Hope. Would you like to dance?' asked Benedict.

The soul music was pure temptation. As Rosy clung to Benedict on the tiny dance floor it was hard to decide whether it was the drink or his high-octane aftershave that was making her head spin.

They drifted on the darkened floor, other couples gliding past like phantoms.

His hand in the small of her back sent tingles up her spine as he pulled her closer still. He was barely taller than she was, and bony under his soft wool suit.

His mouth was against her ear lobe.

'You're a beautiful girl, Rosy.'

He began to kiss her neck.

'I'd love to spend more time with you.'

'Mmm.'

'You're much too good for Sword. If I ever hear that he's being a bastard to you—'

'He won't,' she mumbled.

'I couldn't possibly induce you to work for me, could I Rosy?'

She felt his lips on her cheek.

'Mmm.' What was this? She was beginning to feel unreal.

'Sword is not what he seems,' went on Benedict softly, barely whispering into her ear. 'What I want you to know is ... I'd be here for you if you needed ... anything.' One of his trademark blond horns of hair brushed her temple. She felt a surge of goodwill and gratefulness. 'Would you help me, Rosy?'

'If I could,' she replied dreamily, her head less on than over his shoulder now.

'I have to talk to someone who has known him for a long time—'

'Known who?'

215

'Sword, Rosy. Someone who has known Sword for years, someone discreet, someone who knows all about him. There . . . would be something in it for them.'

She moved her head at this, and he closed in. Benedict's kiss was expert. Rosy kissed him back – out of instinct, curiosity and champagne-induced lust.

'Do you know anyone who might . . .?'

Rosy's mind went. In the same instant as she implored herself to get a grip – 'There's . . . you could try Eva Coutts,' she heard herself say from six dance floors away.

'Who?' Benedict caressed her hair lightly.

Rosy suddenly felt very drunk – floppy as a rag doll but with a lurching heart.

They swayed interlocked for an age as Rosy clung on.

'Come back to my place,' he urged at last.

Rosy was unsure quite what Benedict expected of her, but the fat white candles he lit should have been strictly for religious experiences. The bedroom was a hymn to World of Interiors off-white, and the wrought iron candlesticks stood flaming like giant forks at a sacrifice.

As she cowered on the crisp bedcover, he appeared in the doorway with a tray of bottles.

'Essential oils,' he said, laying it down on a black table.

'Oh,' giggled Rosy, unable to stop a terrible rising hysteria. 'Does that mean you can't do it without them?'

He was naked under a thick towelling robe. His kisses pinned her down on the bed.

Then her clothes were disappearing too, and she felt a slap of warm gloop, nauseously scented, on one bare thigh. Rosy kicked out as if in a dream. And then – yet again – was crushed by the dead weight of her own lack of confidence.

Was that why she was doing this?

Unable to rationalise, she lay back, unreal as the room swirled around her.

And now she knew what all those romantic writers meant by flames of passion. These soft flames licked around them. It was so hot Rosy could swear the fire was real.

Sodom and Gomorrah, here she was.

47 | *Nice Ruse*

It was patently obvious that she did not believe a word of it.

Even Sir Philip Hawty himself had to admit that the tallness of his story was the mark of a desperate man.

'I can understand that you wanted to have a wash and brush up before, and that people do get locked in the loo sometimes,' said Danielle petulantly, 'but what I don't understand is why you had to lock the door when it was just you in the room?'

'Force of habit?' he said weakly.

'And then,' she shuddered, 'you had to go and sit there all night long.'

Hawty concentrated on the buttery curls of his breakfast croissant and wondered whether the huge bandage he had strapped round the top of his left leg was overdoing it a bit. Judging from the suspicious looks the proprietress was giving him, she certainly thought so.

She was also in the unique position of knowing for certain that there had been nothing whatsoever wrong with the lock on his bathroom door.

The bright daffodil tablecloths of the dining room at the Hotel de la Paix taunted him with their yellowness.

'The hospital, you know . . .'

'You could have thumped on the wall,' went on Danielle. 'Or if it had been me, I'd have yelled out the window for help.'

'Well, you know, I didn't want to make a FUSS,' he mumbled. 'It seemed rather . . . embarrassing, you know, grown man and all that – had my position to think of. . . .'

'An' I didn't? All revved up and ready to go, feeling like a right lemon waiting for you in my room. I mean, haven't I waited long enough as it is, eh?'

His Lolita in white stilettoes formed her bottom lip into the most delicious pout. It was all he could do to restrain himself from throwing himself at her feet and gibbering.

'I'm awfully sorry. I did try—' He gave her a wholly inadequate little boy grimace.

'Anyone would have known,' she snapped, 'that you can't use knotted bath towels to escape from four floors up and there was no point in even trying.'

Later, Sir Philip gave Danielle 2,000 francs in cash and told her to go off and buy something to cheer herself up. He exhaled a long sigh of relief when she flounced off, unduly optimistically he thought, in the direction of the designer boutiques. Still, at least it bought him some breathing space.

Outside the hotel the heat enveloped him like a wet kiss. Checking his watch, he made for the dark café in the Rue Sainte Olaire with the old-fashioned wooden telephone booth.

'Benedict Pierce, please.'

He was put through.

'It's abaht this politician bloke Sir Philip Hawty,' said

219

Sir Philip Hawty in his best cod-Cockney. 'Ullo? Is that Benedict Pierce?'

'It's too early. He's not in. You're through to the newsroom, but go on.' The voice on the end of the line sounded disappointingly bored.

Sir Philip ploughed on. ''E's in Nice, in the Sarf o' France' (he thought he should make the directions quite clear this time), 'wiv what you call that TV Lovely, Danielle Kay. Hotel de la Paix. That's P-A-I-X. Rue des Pins.'

'Not that old story again.'

'You know all abaht it already?' Sir Philip could hardly keep the glee out of his voice.

'There's been a bit in the papers. As I say, it's rather old now.'

'Goody-go – I mean. That's a shame. Photos too, I expect?' He had to ask. After all the trouble he had gone to.

'Yeah, think so.'

Well, well. Things were looking up. The photographers had merely been far more efficient than he had dared hope.

He left the café after a celebratory Fernet Branca, feeling considerably better about his prospects.

As a senior British politician, Sir Philip had an armoury of phrases to deploy at tricky moments.

'Let me make the situation absolutely clear.'

'I want to be frank with you.'

'We must try to understand what is really meant by this.'

Tried. Trusted. Reassuring.

As he knocked on the door of her room, he only hoped they would work on Danielle.

'Yeah? Who is it?' she called from the other side.

'It's me, Danielle. Can I talk to you for a moment?'

He heard her hesitate, then open the door a fraction. He pushed it open and went in to find her sitting on the bed wearing an extraordinary satin catsuit with conical breasts.

'I think we should talk,' he said, modulating his voice to something between bad-news-about-interest-rates and we-must-take-heart-in-an-eventual-upturn.

She stared at him dumbly.

'I've reconfirmed our flight back to London, Danielle. We leave tomorrow morning at ten. Just to let you know.'

Danielle nodded.

'I, er, it's time for you to let me make the situation absolutely clear, Danielle. When we return to the UK, there are people who will try to make much more of this than there ever was. As you and I both know, there never was anything for them to make anything of, nothing to make anything of, despite what they might make of it.'

God, she made him nervous. Since the evening he had paraded her back for the cameras, his compulsion to bed her had been painfully insistent. That part, at least, was real – he supposed it would add a usefully realistic touch to the charade.

'As you and I both know, whatever appearances might imply, we didn't do anything untoward, that your mother wouldn't like – or your father come to that – did we Danielle, darling?'

She chewed at a finger, the picture of vulnerability.

'Let's be utterly frank. For whatever reason, nothing happened between us, did it, Danielle?'

She gave him a long uncomfortable screw with the baby-blue eyes that drove him wild.

'Oh yes, we did,' she said. 'I don't know what it is you're up to, but I ain't going back saying nothing 'appened. I've got my pride.'

48 | Coffee Confessions

Their warm mess in Fulham had never felt so comforting. Emma had ransacked the bathroom cupboard and was having a beautification evening. Half-used potions and jars of advertising promises were scattered from mantelpiece to table.

Rosy dug herself further into the sofa where she had thrown herself when she had arrived, shaking and sheet-white, back from work at 6.30. She pulled the mug of coffee to her as if it held the answer to the universe.

'It was awful, Em.'

Emma was sympathetic.

She put the cafetière down carefully on a stack of books and took her seat for the recital.

Rosy cocked her head tentatively. 'You don't mind me going on like this?'

'Uh-uh.'

Rosy managed a smile.

'What time did you get back this morning, Rosy?'

A deep groan from the sofa. 'I've no idea.'

'Extraordinary.'

'Extraordinary – and, let's face it, idiotic. I was at Mirabeau's.'

'A life at last . . .' teased Emma.

'Don't Em. Not now. I've . . .'

'What?' Her friend could hardly wait for some reciprocal night-out gossip. 'You've what, with whom – and why are you so down?'

'I – it's a long story. I got a bit . . . fed up, and champagne fuelled – and ended up going back to Benedict Pierce's place.'

Emma knitted her eyebrows together. 'Not—?'

'The gossip columnist on the *Post*. That Benedict Pierce, yes.'

Emma was amazed. 'What, the one who's always drooling on about nothing on the TV . . . the smarmy blond one?'

'He seemed quite nice last night,' said Rosy defensively. 'Across about three bottles of Laurent Perrier.'

'Hmm,' grinned Emma.

'Actually, if you don't mind, I can't think about champagne at the moment or I'll be sick. Again.'

'So what happened? Or can't you remember?'

'I wish I couldn't. Unfortunately, it's going to become one of those hot-and-cold running memories that will haunt me to the grave.' Rosy buried her head in her hands.

'That bad, eh?'

'Worse,' mumbled Rosy from the depths.

'So you went to Mirabeau's with him?'

'He was there already. We danced – or rather, I kind of clung.'

'And he made his move?' prompted Emma eagerly.

'His . . . er . . . we were very close.'

'So you went back with him. Did you . . . um?'

Rosy hesitated, feeling red shame creep up her neck. 'I set the bed alight.'

'Now Rosy, no bragging!'

224

'No, um, I mean I did – literally. There were all these candles in huge ecclesiastical holders standing around the bed. He produced this disgusting smelling oil – and in my sudden sobering-up panic . . . I knocked one of the bloody candleholders over! I grabbed my dress and ran while he was trying to beat out the flames with an expensive-looking rug. Oh, God . . . I can't think about it after all.'

Emma crowed with laughter. 'Oh, you must! Go on!'

'And then I was sick in an ornamental tub outside on his doorstep.' Mortification threatened to engulf her again. 'I'll never be able to look him in the eye again.'

'Nah,' said Emma. 'Bet it's all in a day's work for him – I mean, without doing down your considerable charms that is.'

Rosy broadly concurred. 'That's what's making it worse.'

'Oh, Rosy, you mustn't—'

'No, you don't understand. I think I've been a complete idiot. He was so clever . . . getting me on his side. . . . I – well, I might have told him something very stupid. With him being Sword's deadly rival and all that.' Rosy cringed, holding on to her pounding head. 'That's the part I can't quite remember . . . and now I'm sure that must be why he came on to me in the first place, and what made me panic on the bed.'

But Emma was sceptical. 'Hardly likely. What could you have told him anyway that he didn't already know? Royal contacts, prize industrial secrets? Come on, Rosy – after a couple of weeks on the column?'

'Okay, Okay. You're probably right. Only—'

'Stop fretting,' sighed Emma. 'What you need is a nice safe rave, a weekend at Turnmills. Get down to Knowledge.'

'Eh?'

'My point exactly. It means nothing to you. Go out to somewhere more hip, younger. Something less ... golden oldie.'

'Thanks a lot.'

'The trouble with your nights out is that they're all so ... Des O'Connor.'

'Wha-a-t?'

'So naff and middle-aged, if you don't mind me saying. I mean, how old is Benedict Pierce?'

Rosy let her go on about it. She didn't have the energy to disagree. Nor to have to answer EARLY FORTIES.

'Reporting, writing about anything is to categorise. Whereas where it's at now is the lost tribes. When the movement can be explained to the masses, when the media move in, it's time to move on,' explained Emma scholastically.

Rosy searched the remnants of her mind for a sarcastic retort. She found what she was looking for when she raised her eyes at last and focused on the gilt dummy hanging round her flatmate's neck.

'Anyway, look at you.'

'Eh?'

'It's no worse than pretending to be younger than you are, Em.'

Later, Emma brought her another coffee and a conciliatory smile. 'How's your head?' she asked.

'Bit better.' Rosy accepted the peace offering.

'Sorry,' said Emma. 'Friends again?'

'Suppose so.'

'Rosy, Rosy ... Do we not go back so far we remember when Michael Jackson was black? When an essay crisis meant you had to write one? Heck, did we not once dance to an A-Ha hit?'

'Who?' said Rosy, acting blank.

'That lot from Norway – was it? – they sang . . . Oh, very funny.'

'It only goes to show . . .'

'Talking of men,' said Emma, changing the subject with a gleam in her eye. 'You'll never guess who called this afternoon.'

Suddenly she sounded wary.

'Mmm?' Rosy disliked that game at the best of times, and this time Emma had clearly waited to pick her moment.

Emma pushed back her corkscrew curls self-consciously. 'Your mate Jamie Raj.'

Jamie! Rosy was momentarily caught off guard. 'Jamie? Did he . . . er, what did he want?'

'Well . . .'

'He didn't ask you out, did he?' Rosy recalled his passing remark about Emma's attractiveness after the Diplock party with a stab to the stomach, unable to work out why she should mind.

'I suppose he did,' said Emma, averting her eyes. 'I mean, despite what you say about him, he is incredibly attractive.'

'When?' croaked Rosy.

'Er, tomorrow night.'

So that would explain why Emma was having a night in with her potions and lotions. She was saving her strength and gathering her forces. It seemed useless to point out that Jamie was an old party creature *par excellence*.

Emma read her friend's disapproving sniff. 'And you can't say I don't know all about him,' she shrugged, 'and want to do it anyway.'

49 | *Strange Therapy*

The girl couldn't have been more than twenty. Her unhappy face was the texture of a greasy beefburger and she was lugging a string bag filled with bricks.

Anthony Sword frowned.

'That's her shame – she has to come to terms with carrying it before she can let it go,' explained the counsellor as she led him towards his group therapy session.

Further down the corridor a group of five or six women and two men trooped across the plush peach passage, all cuddling teddy bears.

'Brideshead Syndrome?' asked Sword, dead-pan.

The counsellor took him seriously. 'The bears represent their inner child which must be nurtured and treated with respect.'

Sword bit back his laughter.

Where was Framboise? She would love that one.

As he had feared, Escape Therapy turned out to be unconnected with any liberation from Grasslands Hall. He spent an afternoon of clapping and singing and hugging in the company of other starving inmates. There was also a strange interlude with a Red Indian tom-tom which an American woman tried to convince them was a living thing.

Later – his mood dangerously dark – Sword was cheered to find Framboise ensconced in what he already thought of as their sofa in the mineral bar.

'Hey, Chuckles!' she gurgled.

'Eh?'

'You look so damn miserable.'

'Uh. Escape Therapy? Drum Therapy? Never done anything so bloody ludicrous in m'life,' he grimaced. 'And I'm still fucking starving. You?'

'Previous Life Regression Session.' Framboise made a moon face and went beatific on him.

'Reincarnation, you mean? Might help if they spoke bloody English.'

'Man, it was wild!' she gurgled. 'I said I was SURE I was Hannibal once.'

For once he couldn't work out whether she was pulling his leg. Nothing, it seemed, was too far-fetched in this place.

'Hannibal,' he said cautiously. 'Are you serious?'

Her laughter was a rich blues riff.

'Aw, hon . . .' She wiped tears from under her brimming bowl eyes. 'I had to go big. Everyone else was Cleopatra and Henry VIII!'

Sword roared.

'Yeah,' she went on, 'what I want to know is, where are all the foot soldiers and pitcher-cleaners? Why in hell was everybody, but everybody, always famous once?!'

That evening she kept her promise. She explained how to get over to the Other Side.

'The Social Wing,' said Framboise, 'is the cruise deck of Grasslands. The sequins under the towel robe.'

229

'The *foie gras* on the dry toast?' Sword latching on to the idea.

'You got it.'

'I know we heard it from the drive the other night, but where exactly—?'

'There's no access from our side of the house. You gotta go through the grounds.'

'How did you find out?'

'On one of my nightingale sorties,' she shrugged.

'Have you actually been in?' His admiration knew no bounds.

'Hon. I'm the star attraction.'

'What? You mean—?'

'I've been every night. It's a great party.'

None of Sword's professional instincts had been deprogrammed. 'Party? Who's there?'

Framboise ran down the list. 'There's quite a crowd. Darlene Trussock does the cabaret spot sometimes with me. Brenda Diplock's here this week networking. Coupla politician's wives. Fergie got in last night.'

Sword jiggled his fat legs with pleasure. 'So, tonight? When are we going?'

'WE aren't going. As such, that is.'

That confused him.

'You can't go in. Not as you are, anyhow,' said Framboise firmly.

'Why ever not?'

'Because,' said Framboise, searching his face for clues as to how he might take this next part, 'if you went, you'd shut the show down.'

'Free speech, you mean,' he said, crestfallen. 'That old imponderable – the gossips' dilemma.'

She spread her arms wide and conceded. 'That too.

In fact several of the guests are in due to trauma caused by your column.'

'Because I've written about them?'

'More because you haven't. But the reason you'd have a hard time getting in is that it's women only.'

'But, hang on. You said—'

'Correct.' Her moon face beamed.

'I don't understand.'

He couldn't decipher her expression.

'Have you noticed,' she said slyly, 'that we are about the same size? You even wear a kaftan as near as dammit the same as mine.'

He caught on immediately. That was one of the best things about being with her, he realised. Her sense of humour was a blood match with his.

He replied as straight-faced as he could manage, prolonging the joke. 'Yes, but – would they go for a BEARDED lady? A WHITE BEARDED lady?'

Framboise bared bright teeth like the Cheshire Cat.

'I got a razor. I got my wigs. To be sure, we could even get make-up,' she winked. 'I have recommended this place to several of my friends, you understand. Any of whom might turn up at any moment.'

Sword put his head back and howled with mirth, enjoying the ridiculous vision of himself flapping around as a burlesque imaginary friend with boot polish on his shaven jowls.

'Whatever else you are,' he said, slapping his hand over hers, 'and the word mad-cap springs to mind – quite deliciously mad-cap – you are wonderful therapy for a broken man!'

She sat there batting her eyelashes like a Southern Belle.

'Let's go outside!' suggested Sword. 'I feel a song coming on.'

He hadn't felt so light and free for weeks.

50 | *Benedict's Night*

Steamy rain hissed down on St Martin's Lane. The first-night audience squeezed tight and wet into the theatre foyer like a fat woman in a shower cubicle.

The lights above twinkled:

> NAIR!
> THE SIXTIES UNCOVERED: A NEW
> MUSICAL
>
> Starring: Brian Ditch, Paul Dozy, Emily Strong
> And exhuming !!! Hermann DeathBeetle and
> the Watch

Inside, Benedict Pierce found himself pressed, rather more intimately than he would have chosen, between a perspiring actor in a red bow tie and a pint-sized critic.

'Tell me, darling,' sighed the critic, 'can we honestly take any more?'

The actor yok-yokked.

'More of what, Zack?' said Benedict, immediately defensive. Okay, so his exclusive revelation that morning in the *Post* that the show's second lead singer was romancing the box office manager wasn't exactly Burton

233

and Taylor. But what did they expect? This wasn't the Sixties no matter how many comebacks the decade staged.

The critic's embittered goblin face was practically resting on Benedict's chest. 'This endless, ersatz . . . extremism about the Sixties,' he snarled. 'As if any of it meant anything, those parades of frankly rather grubby people swinging their handbags and thinking they could sing or play! I can't bear it.'

'Eng-e-land swings like a pendulum do,' chanted the actor ingratiatingly.

'Oh, please!' Zack shuddered. 'It makes me ill.'

At that moment a friendly middle-aged redhead with chipmunk cheeks was flung against them. 'Oooh, helloo, chook! 'Ow are ya? Worra lorra people! Don't turn round, Zack, lov. It's Cilla 'ere!'

The well-known face from the Sixties was required immediately elsewhere for more affectionate greetings.

'That's it. That's exactly what I've got,' diagnosed the critic morosely. 'Cillarrhoea.'

The play was the usual spoof rehash. The party afterwards was held at the Chelsea Boot in the King's Road, where the star of the show, Hermann DeathBeetle, ran a revivalist emporium under the marginally more plausible name of Viv Tudor-King.

Paparazzi photographers outside loosed off motor-drive cameras like machine-guns. Surviving tatters of Swinging London trailed in, long hair and trouser bottoms flapping. The sound of Procul Harem blared out.

The Indian summer of love was into its twenty-seventh year.

Reassembled was the usual trough-and-quaff crowd: The A-List ('60s Division) – 'Our' Cilla Black; Michael

Caine and Shakira; Ringo Starr and Barbara; Dave Clark ('of The Dave Clark Five fame'); Cliff Richard; Mary Quant – had declined gracefully in both senses.

The B-List ('60s–'70s Division) were out in force, a mass of lined tan faces and stick legs which made it hard to tell which was Bill Wyman and which the sincere imitations. Psychedelic pioneers mixed freely with One Hit Wonders wearing their original spangly platform shoes.

When Benedict arrived the place looked like a nightmare scene from *Top of the Pops circa* 1971.

As if to underline the acuteness of his judgement, the blonde one from Pan's People danced across his field of vision, just a fraction out of time.

Marooned in this bizarre collection of past triumphs – and the unending fight to keep the flame alive – Benedict found his own modest fame difficult to handle.

There wasn't nearly enough of it.

Not when you considered what Anthony Sword had managed.

All around him were old pop stars whose pitted faces were eroding like soft chalk cliffs. Chorus-liners and models-turned-actresses whined about Flissy Kendal and what they would do for A Nice Bit of Telly. The buffet featured miniature boeuf Wellingtons and choux pastries.

Benedict's lukewarm white wine tasted bitter – even more so when he caught sight of his dogged shadow Bea Goff failing to charm a one-time teen idol. She stared in his direction, and he looked away.

That did it. He was about to call it quits and go home for his first early night for some weeks when he noticed the other woman.

She was standing by a display of chisel-toed boots, got up in an early Sixties' ensemble: a coat and dress of powder blue set off with a matching feather hat. She was talking to Emily Strong, the leading actress from the show.

Benedict watched the odd pair as the older woman – much older – peered into an old-fashioned mirror compact and applied an undercoat then an overcoat of scarlet lipstick.

Then he did a double take.

No. It wasn't.

For a split second there she looked just like . . . But then the absurdity of even thinking Her Majesty might come to a place like this made him question his grip on reality. Perhaps his night with the very attractive but evidently mixed-up Rosy Hope had affected him worse than he thought. Or then again, it may just have been the prospect of having to replace the Persian silk rug and the antique appliqué counterpane after the bedroom had disappeared in smoke.

The older woman caught his eye and gave him the most un-old-lady-like wink.

He wandered over. Sometimes Benedict felt it was a badge of his desperation that he would never pass up a chance of conversation. But then he always managed to rationalise it as professionalism.

'Super show, Emily,' said Benedict.

'Thanks. I'm glad you enjoyed it.'

Surprisingly, Emily did not entreat him to write about the show, and nor did she immediately introduce her powdered companion though the two were clearly friends.

'We were just talking about new bands. Going back to the Sixties' style,' said Emily.

'I remember that nice Englebert, and Freddie and his, oh, what were they called?' mused the woman. Close up she was about the same age as the Queen, maybe older. The garish lipstick had seeped horrifically into the lines around her mouth.

'Freddie and the Dreamers?' supplied Benedict.

'The very ones.'

'You know Brett Trent reckons the mood's right for a full-scale happening in London,' laughed Emily.

Benedict shook his head.

'Ooh, it's going to be very good, so I've heard,' said the older woman, nodding enthusiastically. 'There's going to be a nice little group,' she continued, 'with that woman – ooh, you know the one, the one with the clothes, always in the papers trying to annoy her husband. . . . Diana! That's the one.'

Emily coughed and glared.

'I don't think so, Eva,' she said pointedly. 'Your sense of humour . . .! Sorry, I should have introduced you properly, only I was sure . . . This is Benedict Pierce from the *Daily Post*.'

Benedict extended his hand.

'Delighted to meet you – er?'

'Eva,' said the woman. 'Eva Coutts.'

51 | *Getting on with It*

So this was it.

Rosy went through the electronic sigh and slide of the *Daily Dispatch*'s portals and marched through the atrium garden. She filled her mind with defiant purpose.

Onwards and upwards. Wipe the slate clean. No going back. The past is a foreign country. And, even – the schoolgirl my-little-phoniness of it made her cringe –

Today is the first day of the rest of my life.

Forget the Benedict Incident.

She took the escalator up.

She felt awful.

Upstairs in the Sword's Secrets office Tina was having one of her downs on secretarial work. She informed Rosy she was compiling an alphabetical reference work on Elizabeth Taylor. This she was producing with all the high tech a great modern newspaper like the *Dispatch* could provide – a pair of scissors and a pot of glue.

'I'm up to Q for Quickie divorce and Queasy,' she told Rosy brightly.

'That's great, Tina.'

'No need to be sarcastic.'

'I'm not. Honestly,' said Rosy indignantly. 'It could be an inspiration to us all.'

Rosy steeled herself not to mention Emma to Jamie – at least not straightaway.

He was busy with the Beast anyway.

'If only I could have got in there,' frowned Keith Silver. 'But with double glazing like they had, no way. Lucky I had the bandages in the car.'

The photographer waved a bound left fist.

'I dread to think,' said Jamie, 'what you would do if someone opened a door to you. Are you sure you'd remember what polite society normally does in such circumstances?'

But the Beast was in high good humour. 'I take the rough with the smooth.'

'Keith, you are the rough with the smooth.'

The photos from the *Nair!* opening night ended up, predictably, on Rosy's desk for captioning. On the glamour and excitement scale the event had donkey-derby rating. She flipped through them half-heartedly:

The stars of the show, Emily Strong and Hermann DeathBeetle.

The raddled remains of several old pop stars.

Emily and an overblown older woman.

The Earl of Trent kissing the producer's wife.

The producer and his wife sitting in his racing green Morgan.

'And here's them getting out at their place in Notting Hill,' said the Beast triumphantly, jabbing a finger at one of the prints from behind her. 'Look, you can see, they've already started to argue.'

'You followed them home?' asked Rosy, appalled, 'And tried to break into their house?'

'Not so much followed them, exactly,' shrugged the photographer. 'I was driving home and they kept going in front of me.'

'And I suppose when they got home they asked if you'd check the back garden for intruders . . .?'

'However did you guess?' he said.

Half an hour later the office repartee turned nasty.

Pearson staggered in with a large roll of video and television magazines. He was evidently about to embark on some female talent spotting.

'Pearson, this is the third day in a row you haven't come in until gone 11.30,' said Jamie sharply.

The elder of the diary looked aggrieved.

'In my pursuit of vital research material,' he said, indicating his bundle, 'I opted to return to base on a Number 11 bus. An unwise decision, as it transpired. I waited on the Strand until three drew up in a row. You have before you the victim of a classic case of bunching.'

Jamie was stony.

'That makes a change,' said Rosy, taking Jamie's side. 'Normally, it's a classic case of lunching.'

'Oo-er!' said Pearson, narrowing his eyes at her. 'Who rattled your cage?'

The woman wouldn't stop.

'. . . Hank Marvin! And then . . . the one . . . you know, the one they always write about . . .? Ooh, I can't think straight today! Have a little sip and it goes straight to my head these days, does it you?'

The theatrical tipster was in overdrive.

Whatever Eva Coutts was on, Rosy thought, she could

240

do with some too. On her end of the telephone Rosy had got as far as *Nair!* and managed to work out Emily Strong, but now she was lost.

'The Earl of Trent was there with the producer's wife, wasn't he?' said Rosy, trying to pull the conversation round to fertile ground.

'No, no . . . the one with the HAIR! The other chap. The one that Sword has a go at – Benedict whatsisname on the paper. Benedict Pierce.'

Rosy gulped. 'Yes, but quite frankly, Eva, we're not going to write about—'

'Yes, but you see he asked me – it's ever so funny. . . .'

'What?' said Rosy, losing patience. 'You were there? At the party last night? But you never go out. . . .'

'Yes! That's what I've been saying. I was at the *NAIR!* party last night with . . . hmm – ooh, I just said her . . .'

Rosy took a deep breath. 'Emily Strong.'

'I was with Emily and he came over. As you know, I don't get out much these days, but I make an effort when I do. Got all me glad rags on. Anyway, so Emily and me have a bit o' fun. And anyway, it's going to be even better, because the other chap, you know—'

'Benedict?'

'That's the one, he seems to have swallowed it hook, line and whatsit. Only he doesn't know that I know Sword, and why I was there and all that!'

'Er, if it's not a rude question – why were you there?' asked Rosy with sinking heart, knowing she should have gone instead of slinking off home, relieved that she had not. And terrified that she had provided Benedict with Eva's name.

There was a pause from East Sheen.

'For my boy, of course,' said Eva.

Rosy hesitated.

241

And then Eva was off again. Rosy scribbled frantically on her notepad. Her brain reeled.

52 | *Lunch with Jamie*

At lunchtime, Rosy and Jamie walked up from the river to what had once been Fleet Street. The acting diary editor had pointedly excluded Pearson when he'd asked her if she wanted to join him for a drink.

'It was so exciting when I started here,' said Jamie as they passed the shiny black curves of the old *Express* building known as the Black Lubianka. 'They still had printing presses on the ground floor. When they revved them up, the whole building would start to vibrate in late afternoon and you knew that meant lunchtime was over and it was deadline time. Reporters used to call taxis out here and not stop travelling until they reached Aden or Ulan Bator.'

'You've been reading too much Evelyn Waugh,' said Rosy.

Jamie smiled. 'It's all that's left to us.'

Now the buildings were Lego-classicism and Eighties' Toytown.

They elbowed their way past clutches of accountants and solicitors, and clerks looking for a change of scene in Tie Rack and Sock Shop, and went into the Wine Press.

As soon as they had ordered at the bar Jamie said, 'You might as well get it over with.'

'Sorry?'

'I know you're bursting to tell me, so you might as well get it over with.'

Rosy felt herself flushing. Was it that obvious that her nose was put out of joint by his call to Emma? The prospect of her evening with him? Or worse, had he heard about the débâcle with Benedict? She didn't particularly want to talk about either.

Luckily, having turned to accept the drinks and pay for them, he went on, 'You should have seen your face on the phone just now – like you'd made unexpected contact with Mars.'

'All right, all right,' said Rosy, relieved that was what he meant. And anyway, she had to talk to him about the Eva Coutts business. Now would be a good time. 'I hope you're sitting comfortably—'

He gave her one of his special you-got-me smiles.

'Eva went to the *Nair!* first-night party last night,' began Rosy.

'I thought she never went out—?'

'So did I, but anyway . . . Eva went to the party – she knows the producer, who probably put her in Golddiggers of 1933 or something, and she knows Emily Strong—'

'As we know to our cost, and Pearson's delight—'

Rosy pushed on with her story. 'Eva and Emily were at the party. They saw Benedict Pierce there, and they decided to play a joke on him. They've planted this bogus story on him that . . . get this! Princess Diana is singing in a band formed by Brett Trent!'

'Bit old hat, isn't it? Remember the Business

Connection . . . Bunter Worcester, Teresa Manners . . . the aristos' rock band?'

'Vintage 1986,' grinned Rosy.

'I'm amazed Eva had the presence of mind!'

'I'll be amazed if Benedict falls for it,' said Rosy. 'Anyway, she thinks it's an absolute hoot.'

Jamie raised his brow in sympathy. 'Clearly Eva has unimagined depths.'

He looked around and then pulled a menu towards him as if that wrapped up the subject.

You'd better believe it, thought Rosy. 'Jamie, have you ever met or seen Eva?'

He shook his head. 'Never. That's always been part of her allure.' He put on a hammy OUDS voice. 'An all-powerful secret agent no one ever met. She was but a mysterious rasp at the end of the line . . . imparting information that left others to their fate. . . .'

'An old actress turned . . .' she searched for terms that would not betray her lack of worldliness, '. . . social fixer?'

'Ye-es.'

Rosy leaned forward, aware that two female office workers nearby had stopped their conversation as if mesmerised by Jamie's stage presence. She had to admit that he looked good. In the suit he wore today he could have modelled for a full-page Boss ad.

'So you know all about her – and her girls, why she does it?'

'For the money. Getting stories out of actresses is her job now.'

Rosy let herself fall closer towards him, enjoying the undisguised envy of the other women in the bar. Besides, this was important. She felt for the fine line between imparting the obvious and relaying new information as if she had known it all along.

'It's more the jobs she can get for other actresses. . . . If she can propel them forward and get producers and directors . . . interested . . . then it's Eva who is making the stories happen.'

Jamie looked at her strangely. 'Well, of course . . .'

So there it was. Rosy felt herself flushing. Of course they all knew.

On the way back to the *Daily Dispatch*, as they walked side by side and she could avoid his eyes, Rosy broached the subject of Emma.

'So,' she said, trying to keep it light, 'I hear you couldn't resist adding another Emma to your list?'

As soon as the words were out she realised how mean they sounded.

Jamie's reaction was quicksilver.

'It didn't work out with Benedict, then?'

53 | *Hell on High Heels*

People said that sudden soul-mate friendships could knock you off your feet. Anthony Sword's new-found empathy with Framboise had him climbing gamely into her shoes.

The red patent leather high-heels were hell.

Sword wobbled experimentally.

There had been astonishingly few women in Sword's life.

His mother, of whom he had long ago decided, the less said the better.

His prep school dinner lady, to whom he owed his lifelong ability to derive comfort from custard.

His old college chum Stella Winsome, now a TV cook with whom he had once entertained the idea of a marriage of convenience.

And his enduring mistress, food.

The usual assortment of failed early relationships had left him with a cynicism that his career as a chronicler of make-ups and break-ups had only reinforced. It was all far more trouble than it was worth.

But now, at Grasslands Hall, he was in the process of

BECOMING the woman in his life. Or so it looked in the cheval mirror.

Framboise clapped her hands and whooped at the transformation. Sword found it all rather American, and said so.

'Okay, okay. Come over this way,' she said, propelling him across her suite from the wardrobe. 'Now try with a little wiggle.'

'I must have taken leave of my senses,' he said, half in disbelief, half in excitement. 'Lost my marbles. Dropped a brick from my load. Somewhere out there is my trolley with no one on it.'

'What?'

'Never mind.'

'You mean, this is crazy? You're not going through with it?'

Sword grinned. 'This is so appalling, I cannot resist.'

And frankly, he might have added, once a man has been stripped, covered in blue clay and electrocuted, he knows he can survive.

He looked in the mirror.

Staring back at him were two Framboises, one with the green and blonde wig, the other with a glossy tomato one. True, when you put them side by side one was a little bulkier under the kaftan and around the jowls. But that was because – despite the belligerence which led to occasional lapses – Sword's diet and exercise regime was taking dramatic effect.

Shaving off his pirate beard had been the worst part. Without that, he had felt as exposed and pink as a peeled prawn. Under the black make-up though – expertly mixed and applied by his accomplice – he felt secure again.

Hiding behind a disguise. A whole persona, even.

He batted his false eyelashes – they were like butterflies locking in combat on his lids – as he tried to perfect her technique.

'Oh my!' he trilled, as much like her as he could make it.

He wriggled his hips awkwardly.

'Bess, I is my woman now!'

'Have mercy Lord!' she said. 'You sure you've never done anything like this before?'

'You sure this is—?'

'Sisters under the skin,' said Framboise. 'Though it's not always like this.'

Sword laughed. He took the point though.

As they left Framboise's suite, the door closed behind with an executionary clunk. There was no going back. The nervous thrill he had was the same feeling he used to get when he was about to ask the big story's big question.

He set off cautiously down the passage. His body seemed to swell with guilt and the certainty of discovery as another guest came towards them, but she merely nodded a polite acknowledgement and went by. At the bottom of the staircase, one of the reception staff also passed him unperturbed.

The clock in the deserted mineral bar struck ten as he pitched past. The lock on the French windows fell to the first blow, and they were out in the dark grounds. He had to strain for a moment to hear any voices from the Other Side. But there it was, the faint call of the wild.

His high heels sank in the turf as he made his way over.

As he approached the side window to the Other Side,

as directed by Framboise, he could see that it was almost literally that. The brightly lit room was a mirror image of the mineral bar, with a similar grand fireplace and French windows but here the walls were flame red, there was a baby grand in a recess and the place was full.

As soon as he began to climb through the side window as instructed the thought did occur to him that this could all be a ghastly practical joke. He imagined candid cameras, Jeremy Beadle and every other agent of ridicule.

What the hell.

He was mid heave up when a glass of champagne was thrust to his mouth in the same way as marathon runners are fed performance-sustaining isotonics.

'Bet you've been gasping for that!' said a dark-haired woman with a manly chin whom Sword recognised after a second as the composer's wife Darlene Trussock. She gave him a strong helping hand in.

He was aghast to notice that he left a smear of chocolatey make-up on her hand, but she didn't seem to notice.

His entrance was something of a baptism of fire. About twenty women turned to stare.

'Hey, Framboise!'

'Framboise! Over here!'

No doubt about it. Framboise was a star attraction.

'Everybody – meet... Blanche!' she announced, plucking a name for him with a bass giggle.

Sword shot her a look which said, 'Don't push it.'

But he allowed himself to be led over to a seat by a woman he recognised as one of the Duchess of York's friends. If she fell for it, he reckoned, anyone would. Sure enough, she gave him the up-and-down.

She frowned a little. 'You all right . . . Blanche?'

'Jus' fine.' His voice sounded all wrong.

'Are you being absolutely starved?'

Sword went for it in his best Scarlett O'Hara's Mammy. 'Aw, Honey. I'm fadin' on ma feet.'

The friend was all solicitude. She turned and called, 'Cordelia? Got Framboise's first aid kit?'

A pretty petite woman – a countess and friend of Jamie Raj's, the one who had been having an affair with her children's male nanny – rushed over with a fire bucket, a plate and a silver spoon.

Sword fluttered his eyelashes and peeked into the bucket.

Inside was a plastic tub. The legend on the lid read: Häagen-Dazs. Not only that, he saw, it was Triple Chocolate Overload.

He hadn't had so much fun at a party in years. What was more, the women said as much themselves.

'Better than Mirabeau's . . .' said Cordelia.

'Better than Annabel's!' said Mary Hawty, the ex-Home Secretary's wife.

'Even better than slumming it to ogle footballers at Stringfellow's!!' said Darlene Trussock.

There was a sense of camaraderie he hadn't experienced since Lady Wensleydale's ghastly Cheese Ball.

All these women he had thought he knew. . . .

He learned more about them in an hour than he had in years of party-crawling.

Sword found himself exploring the psyche of a pretty supermarket heiress whose twenty-first birthday party he had featured prominently in the *Dispatch*. She confessed she had been forcibly introduced to Grasslands by her distressed parents.

251

He hardly had to ask why.

'Body piercing addiction,' she said.

This was effectively confirmed by a sizeable bull ring through her nose and enough rings around her ears and cheeks to hang curtains on.

'How long has this been going on?' asked Sword, wondering as the words came out whether Framboise and her friends actually spoke in Gershwin song titles.

The heiress wrinkled her nose. 'The piercing? About a year. Since I started working for this record producer.'

'Do you ever take them out?'

She nodded. 'Except for this one.' She stuck out a large quivering tongue with a metal ball embedded in it.

He thought it was quite repulsive.

'Tongue pierce,' she said. 'That's a really nice one. You can play with it and no one even knows.'

Sword tried one of Framboise's gurgles. 'You don't sound like you want to give up.'

'Course not. My boyfriend, the record producer, has got a Prince Albert.'

'What's that?'

The supermarket heiress smacked her lips. 'Genital piercing. Down the cock and out the bottom.'

Sword's instinctive horror very nearly made him blow his cover.

54 | Benedict's Quest

When you wish upon a star, it makes no difference who you are. You put in your request for an interview and if there was something a star had to plug, they'd talk. If not, you could forget it.

There were few certainties in this world, Benedict thought sourly, but here was one: the best stories were always the ones no one wanted to talk about.

By this reasoning he knew he was on to some great stories, but great stories without confirmation were ships without lifeboats.

In days he'd had no luck.

He had chased up Emily Strong and Brett Trent but they were keeping unnaturally quiet about all aspects of the Princess of Wales playing in the band. All he had managed to find out from his new acquaintance Eva Coutts was that they were called Mews-X – or something like that.

Every time he'd called the Buckingham Palace press office to check on her movements he was put through to an aide of such legendary obstructiveness that he was known as the Abominable No Man.

He had discovered that Mary Hawty, the estranged wife of the ex-Home Secretary, was at the fashionable hydro Grasslands Hall, but every time he had telephoned she had been unable to take calls. Embarrassingly, the telephonist was beginning to recognise his voice.

He had had an incomprehensible writ from Sir Philip Hawty for allegedly repeating a libel after a brief follow-up to his rival's story in the *Daily Dispatch* that he had gone to Nice with the gameshow hostess Danielle Kay.

Nan Purchase had returned to Manhattan for a major fashion industry benefit. She was going to buy some new clothes.

And then there was Bea Goff, whose tenacity and outrageous claims continued to appal him. He was beginning to think only an injunction could preserve him from her harassment. Of course, if what she said were true . . .? But no, it was too horrible for words.

As Benedict hurried home to the mansion flat he cut through the piazza in front of Westminster Cathedral. He was sure he wasn't religious any more, but he stared up at the red-and-white striped campanile and wondered whether he needed some help of a higher order.

Inside, he hung up his jacket, kicked off his shoes and sat back staring at the ceiling. He couldn't face the charred bedroom.

'Lady Hawty, please.'

Benedict never gave up for long.

The operator at Grasslands Hall treated him to a short burst of the *Pastoral Symphony*.

'Hello?'

'Lady Hawty?'

'Yes. Who is this, please?'

'Good evening, Lady Hawty. I'm awfully sorry to

bother you while you are away but this is Benedict Pierce. Of the *Daily Post*.' He hesitated here, waiting to gauge her reaction.

'Yes?' Her voice was crisp, defensive.

Benedict tried to make himself sound as much of an old friend as possible. 'I hope you're well?'

'How did you find me here?' she snapped.

He never answered questions like that.

'The reason I call – and I must reassure you, Lady Hawty – is that I understand that there is a happy ending to your marital separation—'

'Oh?' The syllable was served with ice.

'I'm sure you appreciate me coming to you personally for a comment on our story that you and Sir Philip are happily reunited.'

'Not particularly.'

He persevered, pen poised for the elusive quote. 'What would you like me to take down as an official comment?'

Silence.

'I am to understand that all is well, however?'

'You seem to understand a great deal about our private affairs, Mr Pierce.'

'It's very kind of you to say so, Lady Hawty. But can I—?'

'Good-night, Mr Pierce.'

She hung up firmly.

Benedict drummed his fingers on the side of the telephone. He had a quote but he would have to bring all his experience and judgement to bear on whether it was any kind of answer. Looking at it all ways, he decided it wasn't.

He dialled again and was put through.

'I'm most awfully sorry, Lady Hawty. We must have

been cut off. While we are on the subject of your happy reunion with Sir Philip—'

'We are not,' she replied crushingly.

Again, the line clicked dead.

Benedict mulled it over. We are not. We are not what? And who exactly did she mean by 'we'?

Damn. It was infuriating when one came up against an old pro at this game. There were far too many of them about.

Later, a five-minute taxi drive took him to the Ritz Club, after which he walked on to Mirabeau's. Benedict lost £250 at roulette at the first establishment and his sense of humour at the second.

'So what's the scandal?' asked one of his first wife's ferocious friends.

He cut her dead, then had the same done to him by the TV cook, Stella Winsome, and then by a faded actress who still resented a story he'd written the previous year.

There seemed only one thing for it. Start an anti-social column.

55 | *Hawty's Decision*

'Danielle?'

'Oh, it's you. I told you, I'm not—'

'Danielle, please don't put the phone down again. We need to talk and we can't do it like this. I want to be absolutely frank with you. Please give me a chance to make the situation perfectly clear. Please. Listen to me. We must meet.'

She had wanted to go to Mirabeau's but he'd managed to dissuade her. Sir Philip Hawty was beginning to realise, sickeningly, that the attractive and pert game-show hostess Danielle Kay was nobody's fool.

The mews house in Bayswater belonged to a loyal Tory benefactor: his old mate Lord Diplock. Diplock betrayed his age and his mentality by referring to it as the Nookie-Nest, and had filled it accordingly with an alarming waterbed, two vast velvet sofas and a whirl-pool bath. The connotations were unfortunate in the circumstances, but Sir Philip had other worries.

In the bathroom mirror, his urbane face had lost its tan.

Danielle arrived promptly at eight, dressed for business in a suit. The pin-striped skirt was disconcertingly slashed to the top of one alluring thigh. The combination of uniform and soft curves put paid to Sir Philip's sang-froid straight away.

'My darling!' he started.

'I don't think so,' she replied.

'Drink. Would you like a drink? Wine, G and T . . . double Zombie Stinger?'

'Mineral water, please.'

In the kitchen he improvised with a soda stream for her and poured himself a hefty Scotch.

Back in the sitting room he found her perched stiffly on a chair wearing the kind of priggish but quietly capable expression that would surely get her a school-leaver's job at any high street bank.

He cleared his throat and began his prepared speech. 'Enoch Powell once said that for a politician to complain about the press is like a sailor complaining about the sea. Nevertheless,' said Sir Philip, 'I feel, this time, the papers have gone too far.'

'That's nice,' she said, disinterestedly, as if to deter him from going ahead with a full-scale speech. 'Now—'

'No. No, it isn't nice at all.'

'Oh, all right then. So?'

'It has been brought to my attention' – he was sounding pompous now, even to himself – 'that during our absence from this country in Nice there were several misleading and mendacious accounts in the newspapers which cast a slur on our entirely proper relationship.'

Not a flicker of reaction from Danielle.

'I realise that there will be ramifications on your career and good name too.'

'Yeah. My agent told me.'

Sir Philip put on his uttermost-seriousness voice. 'I

have asked you here tonight to inform you that I intend to sue.'

Danielle's pretty-pink pout was dangerously enticing. 'Why?' she asked.

'Why sue? Because these are appalling lies and slurs which strike to the heart of the Establishment, and the perpetrators must be brought to book.' Sir Philip paced in front of her.

'Oh, have you got someone to write it then?'

'What? No, my dear girl, brought to book, brought to justice. Exposed, hung, drawn and quartered, if possible in the High Court.'

'Lies and slurs,' mused Danielle. 'Slur on who, do you think?'

'Lies,' said Sir Philip, feeling he was on safer ground. 'We have never had an improper relationship as reported in the *Daily Dispatch* among other rags. That is a fact.'

'You say so,' said Danielle. 'But there's nobody going to believe you.'

'Now, I'm sure we can talk about this, my dear. Let me make the whole situation absolutely clear.'

'Talk to Max,' said Danielle, standing up to go.

The former Home Secretary reeled.

'Max ... not Max, the ...' Surely she hadn't engaged the infamous PR fixer?

'The only man for the job,' said Danielle.

Sir Philip couldn't believe it.

'Oh, and by the way ...' She fished in her handbag. 'My holiday snaps turned out lovely. I thought you might like a copy of this one.'

Both naked from the waist up, their twin smiles from the poolside of the Hotel de la Paix taunted him from the photograph.

She must have asked someone to take it.

The coffee came from a gummy jar marked Safeway Choice. The irony was not lost on Sir Philip Hawty as he scrapped up the last molten granules.

'Sugar?' he called to the sitting room.

'Two, ta!' Lord Diplock, self-made man and *garagiste*, reclined on his favourite leather chair in the Nookie-Nest, and enjoyed the flattering implications of having a former Home Secretary of Her Majesty's Government making free late at night with his kitchen kettle.

Sir Philip emerged with two cups.

'So let me get this right,' said Alf Diplock, pink chops wobbling with excitement. His dinner suit strained over his porky torso. 'That Danielle came here this evening as arranged but she doesn't believe you're going to sue.'

'Not quite,' said Sir Philip. 'She doesn't think anyone will believe that I've got grounds to sue.'

'Eh?'

'She says that no one will believe I took her to Nice and nothing happened.'

'She may have a point,' said Lord Diplock. 'I must admit I'm a bit confused myself. So you didn't do anything in Nice?'

'No!'

'And before?'

'No!'

'What, a lovely bit of skirt like Danielle? Always been one of my favourites, she has.' Diplock scratched his head.

'You're beginning to understand the problem then, old boy.'

'So . . . let's get this clear. You chat her up but do nothing more. You take her to the South of France, and

260

do nothing there. You come back to find the papers got on to you leaving from Heathrow together, and that you were in Nice together. And now you want to sue. Am I all right so far?' The *garagiste* was giving the nuts and bolts a sound checking.

Sir Philip nodded.

The other man whistled. 'I must say I don't know how you could contain yerself, but I s'pose you had your reasons.'

'The fact is that the newspapers clearly implied we were having some sordid affair. That was quite untrue. Therefore I take legal action.'

But Diplock had yet to catch on. Surprisingly, given his line of business and political persuasion.

'The MONEY, Alf. Plenty of cash sloshing around the libel courts, at least while juries still have their say. Everyone's out to hammer the tabloids.'

'I'm beginning to see. . . . So tonight you told Danielle that you're going to sue – because nothing happened – but she says you gave her one, and no one will believe you if you say otherwise.'

'Right.'

'And she's got a picture that says you were naked with her in a hotel in Nice.'

'Topless. By the pool,' said Sir Philip. 'That was all.'

'And what Miss Danielle's thinking is, the publicity could be just the ticket for a nice career move.'

'You've seen it all, Alf,' sighed Sir Philip.

'And Max coming in on it . . . Max Triffid, eh? The girl doesn't get him in unless she means business.'

'It wasn't quite what I had in mind,' said Sir Philip, 'but it really has turned out better than I'd hoped.'

They got out a bottle of Armagnac.

Lord Diplock grinned. 'How much better?'

'O-oh ... possibly as much as £200,000. I'm rather looking forward to it, I must say.'

'Going to court?'

'I've been feeling the cold wind of public indifference lately, hardly ever get written about. I could even settle a few old scores from the witness box. Say what you like from there – get it reported in all the papers and no comeback. Marvellous stuff, court privilege. And then,' the ex-Home Secretary paused to examine his fingernails, 'there's the matter of Lady Hawty—'

'Ah, Monica! How is the old trout?'

'Mary. Appalling. She wants to drop the divorce case. That is, I keep asking if she's seeing her solicitor and she tells me not.'

'Not what you want?'

'Certainly not. It has taken two years of unwavering bad behaviour to get this far. I'm not giving up the tantalising prospect of divorce now.'

'But if you haven't ... with Danielle?' Bafflement got the better of admiration in Lord Diplock's voice.

Sir Philip took a sip of coffee, then chased it with Armagnac.

'It's very simple. One merely has to understand women and their ludicrous romantic sentimentality.'

'Oh?'

'My dalliance – or not – with Danielle Kay is neither here nor there for Mary. But the Hotel de la Paix in Nice is where we spent our honeymoon twenty years ago.'

56 | Bathtime with Sword

'I have to admit I wondered what it would be like in the bath tub together,' said Framboise. 'But I never figured it would be like this.'

Sword stretched out under the hot bubbles and sank luxuriously. 'I wouldn't want you to think I was entirely predictable, my dear.'

'Good though, huh?'

'Marvellous. Thrilling and cleansing all at once. Could you just carry on for a while more,' he begged.

'We-e-ll, let me see . . . that sweet little Cordelia thinks she's pregnant by Roger the nanny – though she still hasn't made the final break from the Earl – which set Darlene Trussock contemplating her insides and wondering what science could do. . . . Jeez, she's forty-five if she's a day and still a man on her birth certificate. . . .'

'Did you ever have children, Framboise?'

'No. You?'

'I very much doubt it.'

They sat quietly.

'How's your water, hon?'

'Fine. Yours?'

'Getting a little cool. I already ran more hot twice. I'm gonna get out now.'

263

'Okay. I'll see you downstairs?'

'Catch you there.'

He waited until she put the telephone down.

Then Sword put down his bathroom telephone and wallowed.

Downstairs, Framboise was reading a magazine called *Pretty Big*. She also produced a tatty clutch of newspapers.

'Smuggled back from the Social Wing,' she whispered. 'I've been finding out what you've been up to since you've been in here.'

She waved a copy of the *Dispatch*.

'I'd be quite interested myself.'

'Oh, you've never stopped. Mirabeau's, first nights, book launches, charity balls, dinners, restaurant openings.'

'And I've still got my beard.' Sword pointed at the famous piratical picture by-line glowering at the top of the Sword's Secrets page.

'You're a walking miracle. But, hey – ' she was mock-serious, 'I wouldn't let them see this here, or they'll padlock your door, Houdini.'

'You guard the door,' he said. 'I'm going to read my diary.'

Since he had been at Grasslands, he discovered, he had been very busy indeed. Or rather, his larger-than-life public persona had.

He got down to reading:

> 'A tricky question of protocol is taxing those
> arranging the royal gala performance of
> Tarquin Tate's acclaimed production of *All's
> Well That Ends Well*.

'Not a word to the Prince of Wales, but millionaire *garagiste* Lord Diplock has reserved the seats beside him, but will not be bringing his wife.

'Starlet-chasing Diplock will be sharing his Maltesers with pert gameshow hostess Danielle Kay, 20. The two have become close after discovering a mutual interest in the local politics of Bayswater and have been spotted several times at meetings with Tory ex-Home Secretary Sir Philip Hawty.

'Meanwhile, Sir Alf's unaffected wife Brenda, 55, remains at the Diplock hacienda behind imposing gates on the South Circular and says: "I've told Alf not to fidget, and to tell Prince Charles to book up a holiday with that lovely Di, for Gawd's sake." '

'Utterly gorgeous young actress Emily Strong has confessed (at last) that she is attracted to older men. The muscular minx who so enchanted her many fans with her all-too-brief appearance as an Eskimo wife in the ITV sitcom *It's Cold Out Here!* tells me: "If I meet the right man, it won't matter what age he is. Right now, I'm concentrating on my career. I'll have to see what happens."

'Scrumptious brunette Emily, 24, daughter of Liberal peer Lord Strong, is currently appearing in the West End production of *Nair!* with Sixties' legend Hermann DeathBeetle.'

'How the flighty are fallen. The Earl of Trent, sieve-like confidant of a hundred chattering Chelsea pooch-owners, has finally stepped in something nasty.

'First oh-so-trendy Trent – once a professional dog-walker who succeeded to the bankrupt earldom two years ago – had a short-lived romance with actress Lottie Landor which ended in acrimony. He informed her she was no longer a member of a pseudo-Sixties' band he was managing and that he would be looking for another singer.

'Then, at the first-night party of *Nair!* – a feeble spoof Sixties' musical which opened this week – he canoodled to his cost with producer's wife Catherine Jones. As my exclusive pictures show, husband Johnny was far from amused. He has denounced Trent as "an opportunistic amateur" and has banned Catherine from going near him.

'Word around town – ridiculously being spread by the *Daily Post*'s struggling second-rate columnist – is that Trent has his eye on another eminent wife and part-time rock-chick who is eager to annoy her high-ranking husband by putting herself up as the front woman of the band. Squidgy Beehive! We think not . . .?'

Framboise chuckled, and Sword looked up.

'I have to tell you,' she said, 'it leaves me per-plexed. What in hell does it all mean?'

'As of this moment, I haven't the foggiest idea,' said Sword.

'Oh, c'mon . . .'

'Really.'

He crumpled the paper. 'Don't look at me like that, Framboise. Only the people involved know exactly what the story is – and, sometimes, the people writing it.'

'So what it says is—'

'Never the exact story. No, the skill is in the suggestion, the shorthand, the undertow. That's the game, the fun of it. You must understand, people DO the column like *The Times* crossword. It's a growing sport.'

'But who gets the clues?'

'People who are People. People who want to be People. People who NEED People,' said Sword lyrically.

Framboise roared with laughter.

'What?' he said.

'First my poor friend Blanche, and now ... Don't tell me you do Streisand too!'

The lonely hearts advertisment in *Time Out* read: 'Alluring but directionless Oxbridge graduate (m) seeks bright, compassionate lady (24–30) to put the fun back into London life. Reply Box 1633.'

In two pages of attractive professionals seeking bikers from hell, froggy ladies seeking handsome princes and semi-detached charmers seeking securely married lovers for mutually satisfying liasons (SW preferred), this was a lovelorn plea.

At least Rosy chose to read it that way. She knew exactly how he felt.

She had never done this sort of thing before, although everyone knew that *Time Out* was the best for, well, nice people doing this sort of thing.

Should she write that in the letter?

Rosy sat on the floor with cream vellum paper and her fountain pen.

She was at a low ebb.

At home for a quiet evening alone in the flat, she felt pretty directionless herself.

From work she had been to a 6p.m. press reception for Relate, the marriage guidance council, but her faith

268

in their judgement slumped when they trotted out the Princess of Wales again as the guest of honour.

Emma was out at a film première – her date with Jamie. She had gone out, looking gorgeous, with the jaunty stride of someone who knows she can always attain whatever it is she wants.

And it had begun to dawn on Rosy as the door slammed how much she minded. In the aftermath of the disaster with Benedict, she was clearly becoming the kind of mean-spirited crone whose place on the shelf seemed ever more assured.

The only message on the ansaphone was from someone she had never heard of who wanted her to come to a party to launch a new water-purifying system.

The television chuntered softly in the corner. A £10,000-a-day supermodel with a cutesy mole was burbling, 'I have fat days, I have ugly days, but I work through this and I feel I should share it.' The only alternative was a programme on the DNA genetic claw-printing of goshawks.

Rosy stared up out of the window. From long habit she never drew the curtains – she'd always loved to look up at the stars.

London. From her suburban bedroom she once used to dream about the heart of the vast city, where the news was made, where power games, and fashions, and creative endeavour were unleashed and emboldened, connections forged and played and interwoven in front of cameras, at parties, lunches, dinners, gatherings of the great and good.

Strange to think that she had a *passe-partout*.

Had it brought her what she once imagined? It had made her feel more inadequate than ever.

She had seen Heaven, as they say, and found it wasn't her kind of night-club.

The doorbell buzzed.

It startled her. No one anyone wanted to see turned up unannounced on the doorstep in London, especially at night.

She tiptoed to her bedroom window – without putting on the light – and peered down to the street outside.

The man stood in the cumulus shadow of an over-grown bush.

Rosy jiggled up the sash window. 'Who is it?'

'It's me.'

'Who's me?'

'The one you're always writing about. I want to talk to you.'

Something about his urgent, uneasy manner made her say, 'Tell you what. Give me five minutes, and I'll see you at the Slug and Lettuce. Turn right at the end of the road, okay?'

When she she reached the pub, the Earl of Trent was hunched over a half of lager. Tonight, he had gone for radical chic: the sleeping-out look. His bloodshot eyes and pale stubbled chin above a filthy dark waxed coat made him seem more than ever like a depressed cockroach.

He didn't ask if she wanted a drink.

'Sorry if this isn't up to your usual standard of venue,' said Rosy, feeling awkward and tongue-tied. It seemed to her that some unstated boundary had been crossed by his seeking her out.

The pub was noisily full and smoky. Computerised burbles from the video game machines fought for cultural supremacy over the mock-Victorian horse brasses dangling from the bar and the juke box playing tribute to Hank Marvin's 30 Glorious Years.

The fashionable Earl stared wildly.

'Didn't you trust me enough to invite me up, Rosy?'

'I, well . . . I didn't know how you found out my address.'

'You know mine. You come to my house. You know all about me, don't you? All about me!' He was chain-smoking furiously.

'Well, that's not . . .' She tailed off, weak in the face of logic. 'I came, didn't I? Are you all right? What's wrong?'

'Oh no, no you don't. I'm not telling you anything. I'm not that stupid. My whole fucking life has been in your paper these few weeks—'

She decided not to ask why he had come for her in that case. 'I'm not asking for the paper,' said Rosy.

He lit up again and raised heavy eyelids to meet her gaze.

'Brett? You haven't had some bad stuff have you?'

'It's all bad stuff – no, I'm all right there. I overdid it a bit last night, nothing serious. Tell me, Rosy, what do you do?'

'Me? I don't, really, no. I tried cannabis once or twice. I got incredibly hungry and started enjoying *Emmerdale Farm*.'

He didn't break into a smile.

She could have bitten out her tongue. What a pathetic schoolgirly comment to make.

'I thought we were friends,' he said sulkily.

'We are.'

The Earl dug into the battered Barbour he still hadn't bothered to take off, and produced a dog-eared envelope. He tipped the contents on to the wobbly round table.

'Bills,' he said. 'Have you any idea what it is to receive bills like these? Building repairs. Building maintenance. Inheritance tax. Solicitors' fees. Pay-offs to distant relatives. Loan repayments.'

He picked up a fistful of red demands and thrust them at her. 'There's even a fucking bill from the person administering the bills. And you lot, Sword, Raj, you – after all I've done for you, you kick me in the balls when it matters.'

'Brett, I—'

'And just when I could have come good . . . this,' – he retrieved a jagged tear of newspaper from another pocket – 'this rubbish frigging well puts the final boot in!'

It was the story about his women problems and the Sixties' band.

'Brett, you know as well as I do that all publicity is good publicity for a venture like that.'

'No! She'll never do it now – you'll have scared her off. And it could have worked. If you'd left well alone, it could have been the biggest coup in showbiz history!'

'I don't understand,' said Rosy.

The Earl was agonised. 'There's a rumour going round that the Princess of Wales was interested!'

58 | Benedict's Women

It was a bad day at the *Post*.

Benedict Pierce came in to find a sheaf of papers on his desk topped with a note from the readers' letters editor: 'Any interest to the Diary?'

The first letter was from a Mrs Whittleworth in Surrey and began: 'While the government crisis over the economy and industry has occupied our television screens *ad nauseam*, has any other reader noticed that MPs are again favouring single-breasted suits?'

Another, from a gentleman in Berkshire, offered the insight: 'The more I see of Madonna in your pages, the more I am convinced that her limbs are fitted back to front. Could this explain her lewd and corrupting antics?'

A Miss Thomas from Cheshire wrote in spidery writing: 'How comforting it was to read in the excellent *Daily Post* that the fine elder statesman Sir Philip Hawty has seen sense and returned to his wife of many years standing. In the years he has served this country in Parliament he has always been an upstanding member.'

How much truer than you know, Miss T., thought Benedict. He only hoped that time would prove his story likewise.

There was another letter, sealed. From the Desk of the Editor of the *Daily Post*, he read the succinct handwritten message.

> 'Dear Benedict,
>   Of late your column has been marginally less appetising than a plate of old, cold *pommes mousselines*. I trust the reference is not lost on you.
>   Nigel.'

It wasn't.

Charming. As if he – Benedict Pierce – didn't know all about the public's apparently insatiatable gluttony for gobbling up the merest crumbs from Anthony Sword's feast of gossip.

But still, after the lucky break begun by his inspired seizure of Rosy Hope, at least he was getting somewhere with his retaliatory revelations. And a useful advance cheque from Mega Books was – he had been assured – in the post.

Midday approached. Benedict sent his minions out to trawl every PR function going.

Yet again, he tried the number he had begged from Emily Strong for Eva Coutts. Yet again there was no answer.

Then he called Sir Philip Hawty's office. He was out. Lord Diplock ditto.

He rang Jamie Raj at the *Dispatch*. 'Fancy a drink, James?' For once Jamie declined, pleading a hangover after a heavy night.

Steeling himself, Benedict put a call through to the *Prattler*'s social desk to confirm that Honoria Peeke was still meeting him for lunch at 1.15.

*

Orso's may have been the 'meeja's' own Italian nosherie, but Benedict always thought that its décor had all the pizzazz of a an upmarket gents' loo. For the metaphorically-minded, the white tiles on the far wall cast a maliciously lavatorial shine on the photographs of its famous patrons.

Honoria prattled away.

The conversation, as ever, turned to Sword and his cohorts. For once, that was fine by him.

'That beastly man Silver!' said Honoria, pinching an irksome piece of fluff from her traffic-light red suit. 'I was sipping a good dry Martini at Lady Somerton's the other evening – the only people who can make them these days are the old set, the ones who don't get nervous with the gin bottle – when he came sailing through the conservatory with that dreadful motor-drive instrument of his spitting like a machine-gun. People would have minded less if he'd used the door, but he has to make an entrance. The flying glass made an frightful mess, as well as ruining two trays of the most divine canapés. The more excitable element was convinced it was terrorists at the very least.'

Benedict could imagine.

'What do you hear of the Hawtys?' he asked.

'They're back together, of course.'

'That's a relief – for them, I mean.'

'Well, I got it from your page.'

He smiled wanly.

But Honoria was off again with an interior monologue on editorial adjustments which could change the face of London life as she knew it.

'I'd like to run a regular party critique. A more critical report of functions advising where the hosts or the caterers Could Have Done Better – which would be useful pointers to those who look to us as leaders of the social scene. You know, whether smoked salmon isn't absolutely too Thatcher, or more than 1,000 guests a little too impersonal, or indeed whether short television celebrities are too much of a let down to risk in the flesh. . . . What do you think?'

She gazed round euphorically as if she had just dreamed up the idea of a Members Only enclosure.

Benedict winced. 'What about the stories behind the parties – who met whom, and what happened then? The Royals and the rotten, the aristos and the fortune hunters, the Cabinet ministers and good-time girls?'

'Disgusting,' said Honoria. 'The lowering of the the tone is precisely the kind of thing I want to warn others about.'

Needless to say, he got no tittle-tattle from her.

Nan Purchase finally answered his call.

'You're back,' said Benedict, trying to sound casual.

'Seem to be.'

'How was Manhattan?'

'Oh, you know. Still there.'

'So,' said Benedict brightly, 'What's new?'

'Apart from the faces of several old friends, not much. A dear friend has been widowed.'

'I'm sorry.'

'Don't be. She's gone Lacroix-crazy with grief and intends to dedicate her life to keeping Bloomingdale's afloat.'

Benedict laughed.

'And Patti Grossbaum has moved in on my lunch table at the Russian Tea Room, but the light angle above doesn't suit her as well as me and they've refused to change it.'

276

'Is everyone still into Hot Monogamy?'

'Monotony?'

'Monogamy, but it comes to the same,' said Benedict.

'Oh, sure. No one just has sex anymore. You have to have incredible, wonderful, amazing sex with the same person for years. At least, that's what you SAY you're into.'

'Except for Madonna,' said Benedict.

'You know I hate to bad-mouth,' said Nan, 'but you know what they say about old dogs posing as new tricks.'

He finally managed to fix a date for dinner at his home. Even down the telephone line, he could sense her squeak of excitement when he mentioned, casually, that he was hoping to have a Very Special Guest whose attendance was dependent on the utmost discretion.

59 | *Nice Spread*

Any lingering doubt that Sir Philip Hawty might have entertained that Miss Danielle Kay was not serious about going to the newspapers herself had been swept aside.

The pictures in the *Sunday People* made his eyes water.

At his Pimlico *pied à terre* a neat pile of serious broadsheets remained unread as the former Home Secretary stared at the tabloid's coverage of his trip to Nice. His leggy holiday companion had gone to town.

The photograph of them together by the pool of the Hotel de la Paix was splashed over the front page.

Across the centre spread, Danielle was naked apart from the drapery provided by a French flag the size of a hand towel. She was superimposed against a background of the Houses of Parliament – at least, he fervently hoped she had not posed like that on the Embankment for real.

In another picture she was suggestively caressing what looked – tastelessly – like the House of Commons mace.

In yet another she was a saucy French maid.

It was all too predictable.

Sir Philip shifted in his leather armchair before beginning to read. He didn't need anything too outrageous, just the usual account of the senior British politician's traditional pursuits. At first glance, it was almost tediously satisfying. He checked that he had the private number of the country's noisiest libel lawyers next to his telephone.

Five minutes later Sir Philip found himself unable to finish his breakfast. His jaw was clenched in fury. The toast and Olde English Thick Cut in his mouth had turned to bird droppings and cardboard.

The photographs might have implied that this was a clear enough case of MP-in-Naughty-French-Sex-Scandal, but the words said something entirely different.

'Lovely *Legs Eleven* girl Danielle Kay found randy ex-Home Secretary Sir Philip Hawty a real let-down in romantic Nice – he used his hotel sheets to attempt an escape from the bedroom.

'Then he spent the rest of the night cowering in the bathroom, afraid she might seduce him.

' "It was a French farce," said Danielle last night.

'The pretty 20-year-old telly gameshow hostess hoped the Tory toff would be her Mr Right after a string of broken romances. Her spirits soared when twice-married Hawty, 62, persuaded her to accompany him to the sexy South of France.

'Danielle admitted: "I knew he was special when he booked us separate rooms. He was a gent from start to finish – far too much so, in fact. It was very upsetting. I spent whole nights in tears.

'What's wrong with me? Aren't I attractive
enough for a man to want?"'

Sir Philip stopped reading in disgust when he reached
the Readers' Phone Poll. 'Tell us what you the readers
think! Would you have cheered up lovely Danielle?'
leched the header inviting votes of OUI or NON.

He could scarcely believe it. But the result was plain
to see. His scheme lay in ruins.

When the telephone rang it was Lord Diplock.

'I'll never be able to look at the House of Commons
mace again without thinking of sex aids, you old devil,'
he joked, irritatingly chirpy.

'You've seen the papers then,' said Sir Philip.

'Most entertaining of a Sunday brunch-time.'

'For you, maybe.'

'This was what you wanted.' The *garagiste* peer
asserted. 'Now the truth will out, and a nice little profit
in court, like you said.'

'The truth HAS out,' replied Sir Philip tersely. He
slung the paper away.

'I thought that was what you were counting on.'
Diplock sounded at his most confused.

'Yes, but TOO SOON. All too soon. . . .'

'Ah.'

'It's just not what one expects, that's all. From a slip
of thing—'

Lord Diplock chortled. 'I'd say England expected you
to do more—' He knew better than to go on.

An awkward silence.

Lord Diplock coughed and said, 'But you're still going
to sue?'

'There has to be something to sue about.'

'Well . . . isn't there?'

'No,' said Sir Philip, wearily. 'There is not. She's used my bloody defence, don't you see?'

'What?'

Sir Philip sighed, and tried to explain, very slowly.

'Everything Danielle Kay is quoted as saying, I was going to use in court, denying that anything untoward had ever happened between us. That I took her to the Riviera, but that we stayed in separate rooms and the one night it seemed . . . that the obvious must happen . . . I became ineluctably locked in the bathroom. The day after, we returned to London.'

His friend digested this. 'You'd have thought that flash PR man she hired could have come up with a decent story of his own,' he said.

'That PR man is evidently cleverer than we thought.'

'What about the wife? How's Monica taking it?'

'Mary. I don't know. She's not answering the telephone – hasn't for days. Which is highly unusual.'

'She might not have seen the papers.' Lord Diplock tried to be upbeat.

'Wouldn't matter if she had,' said Sir Philip gloomily. 'On a moral level, I'm horribly in the clear. And the paper didn't even bloody try to get the name of the hotel right!'

60 | Two Magpies

Sword paused midway through his jogging circuit.

He felt alive and raw with the realisation.

It was the most beautiful morning. The sky was cloudless forget-me-not, two magpies – two for joy – had swooped across his path, and he was hardly out of breath. Well, a little bit puffed perhaps. But, still, it was extraordinary. If anyone had told him a month ago that he would be skittering up hill and down dale – okay, around the flat-ish lawns of Grasslands Hall – in a sweat suit, he would have sent for an ambulance, for both of them.

And yet, as the weeks slipped by here, his belligerence was no longer his driving force. The tension released by his morning arias seemed to be kept at bay by his clumsy attempts at athleticism. Having begun in fury and scepticism, he was determined now to see this through.

He was sticking to his food programme.

He had given up drink.

He was attending work-out sessions.

He was shaving each morning – and still finding tiny obstinate patches of chocolate brown make-up under his chin.

Sword started to jog again. Much more of this, he thought wryly – and not without a certain excitement – and he would start to walk like a Chippendale.

He had even taken up swimming.

For the past few days, he had visited the pool in quiet times when there were few other residents around to share the full horror of his white whale body.

The pool was surrounded on three sides by a Japanese mural and artistic piles of large smooth stones. Meditative twangs from discordant Eastern instruments contributed to the atmosphere of peace and tranquillity.

Sword floated on his back.

Warm silk sheets of water held him in a soporific caress.

'Do you know what my husband is playing at, Mr Sword?'

The words cut into his reverie.

A woman in a flowered bathing cap had rippled up on him.

Turning over, Sword splashed, startled. It took him a moment to make out Lady Hawty's weathered English rose face.

'Eh?'

'You do look different without the beard, I grant you. But there is a ferocity about the eyes which is quite unmistakable. I noticed it first that afternoon in drum therapy,' said the ex-Home Secretary's wife.

She had caught him unawares and was calm with purpose.

'What do you know, Mr Sword?'

Now there was a question.

The very vexed question which had been preying on his mind for several days. With a sense of disconnection to his old self, he watched silver droplets of water run down the arm he had instinctively flung across his chest.

Unlike her husband, Mary Hawty always came straight to the point, Sword remembered.

Her face, ruddy-cheeked from country life, glowed with purpose as they sat mummified in towels on plastic-covered couches at the side of the pool.

'As you have noticed, Lady Hawty, I've been out of circulation lately.'

'Really? I thought you were being dazzlingly clever by coming here.'

Sword shrugged. She could make of that what she wanted. But the politico's wife was back on tack.

'Absolute publicity corrupts, Mr Sword.'

He said nothing.

But it seemed she was not necessarily referring to him. 'As you know, my husband is an addict. Without his fix of publicity, he is no one. Or so he feels. Like so many successful men of advancing years, he has found that none of them can merely dabble in power and fame, it becomes an essential.'

He shivered uncomfortably, wondering what was coming next.

She scanned his face blatantly for a reaction as she continued, 'What I cannot understand though, is his liaison with this young girl on television. He's no chaser of flibbertigibbets – and as for the photographs in the *Sunday People*, that was downright ... tacky. Appallingly though he has sometimes behaved, he has never been tacky.'

Sword did not know what to say. It seemed a world away.

'Pictures?' he asked eventually.

'Pictures,' said Mary Hawty. 'That little madam

posing in a French flag, topless, in a catsuit, and . . . perpetrating an obscene act with what was made out to be the House of Commons mace.'

'I see what you mean.'

'Do you, Mr Sword? And do you know what he means by it?'

'Er, I haven't actually seen the *Sunday People*. . . .'

It was too feeble for words.

Sword felt distinctly at a disadvantage, and cold under the heavy wet towel. He was about to move off when she opened her mouth to begin again – and then offered up an unexpected smile.

It made him recall suddenly how much fun she had been that night in the Social Wing when he'd been dressed up with Framboise.

'Do you think I'm a fool,' she asked, 'for staying with him all these years?'

Again, he was caught off guard.

'I, er . . .'

But the Tory lady was into her stride. 'I am an English wife of a certain age, Mr Sword. I stayed in the country; he stayed in town. It worked, in its way. Then . . .'

'Go on.'

It intrigued him – not as a newspaper story, but as an insight into why and how grown men and women did ever manage to stay together.

And she seemed willing to talk.

'It was I who eventually decided enough was enough. In the end, I went to a solicitor to start divorce proceedings – then went through appalling doubts wondering if I was being too hasty.'

'Hasty?' said Sword. 'After all these years of his, er . . . well-documented womanising?'

'As I say, I am an English wife of a certain age and with a certain position.'

He let her continue.

'Then, my husband seemed to want to try again, but it was too late.'

'That old story.'

'Not quite. There is a happy ending.'

'Oh?'

'I went to my solicitor to instigate divorce proceedings ... but I ... found I couldn't keep away from him.'

Sword felt hopelessly at sea. His weeks away from the *Dispatch* began to seem like months. 'Your husband ... but ...?'

'No, no, Mr Sword. Not my husband. The solicitor. I couldn't keep away from the solicitor. He was such a lamb, knew all about the problems I faced ... one thing led to another and ...'

'You and the solicitor?' Sword was smiling broadly now, and partly, he recognised, with pleasure for her.

She nodded, with a blush. 'I may want to make an announcement, when the time is right.'

'In the *Dispatch*, you mean?'

'It's practically *de rigueur* these days, Mr Sword.'

61 | *A Star Is Worn*

The public's seemingly unquenchable thirst for the detritus of fame coupled with the general tightening of belts found its logical conclusion in A Star Is Worn. The dress agency, located amid more conventional outfitters in St Christopher's Place, specialised in selling on clothes once worn by the famous.

It was the height of chic. Even Jamie Raj was wearing a dog-tooth check suit this season which had once appeared in a classic Ealing comedy encasing Terry-Thomas.

Rosy came out of the fitting room.

'Feeling Diana Rigg, darling?' said Travers Nott, the former theatrical dresser who owned the shop. He stroked the tailored finish of his goatee beard.

Rosy smiled.

'This ol' thing,' she teased, running her hands over the black leather catsuit she was trying on. 'It isn't me at all, but I couldn't resist giving it a go.'

'I don't know, darling. Slinky, dangerous – powerful.'

'Now wouldn't that be nice,' said Rosy. She sucked in her cheeks and then her stomach for the mirror.

'Special date?'

'Maybe.' She could hardly presume. She hadn't even

287

finished her reply to Directionless from *Time Out* and even if she did he probably wouldn't want to meet her anyway. No, she was here because she wasn't eating lunch, because Jamie Raj was staying in the office and he hadn't even mentioned his evening out with Emma and because Emma seemed to be avoiding her at breakfast time.

If in doubt, go shopping. . . .

Travers clicked sequins and satin and froth along a clothes rail.

'How about something less dominating . . . but still strong and sexy – a Charlotte Rampling or a Jacqueline Bisset?'

'Mmmm . . .'

'Who do you see yourself as? Who do you want to be?'

'I don't know really,' said Rosy hopelessly. 'I've been trying to work out who I am and what I want to be since I was about fourteen.'

'We've all been there, lovie. Picture yourself – what do you see?'

Rosy thought for a moment.

'In my dreams I'm Claudia Schiffer – in the mirror I'm one of Rubens' fat ladies.'

Travers laughed. 'Born out of time, eh?'

'Exactly,' conceded Rosy. 'That's exactly it. And I know what I need . . . a Marilyn from *Some Like It Hot*.'

He whistled softly. 'No offence, but perhaps not.'

'No?'

'Not unless you've got a spare $20,000 or so. Those dresses cost an absolute fortune. And you know why?'

Rosy waited for him to tell her.

'Monroe's the sex symbol of the century – and she was size 16. Real women don't want to forget that.'

She finally chose a little-known Sandie Shaw, perfect for all the retro parties.

'Should we trust Benedict Pierce?' asked Travers slyly as he handed over the bag.

Rosy's heart thumped. Don't say that EVERYONE knew. . . .

She forced herself to sound normal. 'I really wouldn't know.'

'What do you know about his private life?' persisted the glad-rag archivist.

Where was this leading? Rosy gulped. 'Only what I hear. He never stops. Stacks of women, always the same type: glossy, socially acceptable, doing nicely –' she laughed like a stumble, 'a bit like the female equivalent of credit cards, in fact. He goes to Mirabeau's a lot. Why?'

'He's been asking a lot of questions . . . about you lot. . . .' Travers trailed off portentously.

Rosy knew he was dying to tell. 'Like what?'

'Benedict spent the best part of an hour in here the other day.'

'I bet I know – Eighties' memorabilia. *Bonfire of the Vanities. Wall Street,*' predicted Rosy with an edge of nastiness to pay him back if he'd been blabbing.

'Not at all,' said Travers. He did a stagey look around although there was no one in earshot, and hissed, 'Women's clothes.'

'I wouldn't have thought so—' She stopped herself from saying anything more incriminating.

'Not for himself . . . he was asking about SWORD dressing up in women's clothes! Apparently there are rumours—'

Rosy faltered. This was something she definitely didn't want to get into.

*

Rosy got through the rest of the afternoon on an actress's new Turkish boyfriend and an interview with the TV cook Stella Winsome, an old diary stand-by. The column was done by six o'clock. Jamie was out of the door on the dot, and Pearson shambled out soon after. Neither asked her to join him for a drink, and she was relieved not to have to make excuses.

She had her own plans.

What worried Rosy was how much she wanted this.

She could feel herself shivering like a puppy under her smart clothes as she descended the steps into Scribblers. It was early, thank God, and few other *Dispatch* staffers had reached the bar yet. It seemed decades since she'd first met Anthony Sword in what were dangerously similar circumstances.

The assistant features editor was a woman with deathly white skin, tangled matt-black hair and a reputation for straight-talking. The telephone numbers that Rosy had occasionally been able to pass on to her from the Diary contacts book had proved valuable currency.

The Features Department always wanted to follow up Diary stories – after the hard part of getting the participants to talk had been done.

They ordered espressos.

'Why do you want to leave Sword then, Rosy?'

Rosy had rehearsed her speech so many times it now sounded fake. Accentuate the positive. 'Well, it was more that I heard you were looking for a new features writer and researcher . . . and that's the side I've always wanted to work on, more than wanting to leave Sword as such. I've been on the column full time now for a while, although still only on a freelance shift basis while he's been away – and I'm enjoying it. Very much.'

Was this too gabby?

She took a deep breath. 'But I'm not sure I'm the right kind of person for the job really. I know it's only been a relatively short time, but ... I've broken some good stories, made some excellent contacts ... but in the end, the way it works isn't as satisfying as I thought it would be.'

'The no by-line grouch.' The assistant features editor sounded as if she'd heard it all before.

'That, yes. Of course it's not ideal to have Sword's name on everything you write no matter how hard you've worked on it, but it's more than that.'

'Oh, yes?'

'It would be nice to write about real people again, instead of these characters that Sword has created. They're manipulative, they thrive on spurious publicity – and their stories don't mean anything. If you do ever stumble on the truth you can bet your life you can't write it.'

'So what happens if you came to features and I wanted a Society piece using all your wonderful contacts?'

'The way I feel now,' said Rosy, 'I could tear them limo from limo.'

62 | *Regal Contact*

'Anthony Sword and I go back a long way,' said the elderly woman, fiddling with her Madame Arcarty beads, 'and I can't say more than that.' She was becoming bold now.

Her companion perched on a plush velvet tip-up seat that had once seen service in the one-and-nines at the old Regal cinema, before it went over to Bingo. This one didn't seem to believe her any more than the regular visitor did. It was the second Tuesday in the month, again, and the mission from St Michael's, East Sheen (old lady division) had arrived to keep the faith with Eva Coutts.

The church visitor sat balancing her cup of tea on tan stockinged knees. Occasionally her eyes wandered round the room with its bright mementoes of a theatrical life and she tried to introduce her own topics of conversation – the weather, the meals on wheels, the jumble sale. Deadly dull and boring, thought Eva, taking matters into her own hands.

The visitor shook her head with total conviction. 'I've heard all about you, Mrs Coutts. Lovely pictures you have . . . must be a lot of dusting for you.'

This small, pale woman in a striped polyester shirtwaister wasn't the usual one who came and Eva sensed a challenge.

When Eva got going, she was not to be deflected.

'As I say, we go back a long way. Oh yes. That's because I'm Sword's best-kept secret. You know the Sword's Secrets page in the *Daily Dispatch*? Top Contact they call me when I call up. Command HQ they say it is here. And you know what the ... what's the word ... bedrock, that's it, of our long and successful professional understanding, is?'

The visitor nodded her on.

'There's one thing about Eva Coutts. She never tells a lie. You get all sorts trying to set themselves up as informers, tipsters, correspondents, and after the first couple of times they all fall into the same trap: they make the story just too good to be true. The excitement runs away with them. Not old Eva.'

'Of course you don't, Mrs Coutts.'

'I will admit, I'm getting on a bit now and the old memory's not what it was. I have got the names a bit skew-whiff now and again, but that's not the same at all.'

The visitor reached for a coconut cream.

Eva went on. 'Then I don't get out much these days.'

'No. Still, you keep occupied though, eh?'

'Oooh, I'll say.'

Eva wondered, then she decided to tell, if only because she knew she wouldn't be believed.

'I went out the other evening though. First time I'd been to a first night for years. One of my girls was in the show, up the West End, and I thought, why not? So I got me glad rags out and went. Anyhow, you know, er ... whatsisname ... writes the column in the *Daily Post*?' asked Eva.

The visitor looked blank.

'You know ... ah! It's on the tip of my tongue. Benedict Something, that's the one.'

Still a blank reception.

'Well, anyway, Benedict ... Pierce, that's it ... he does the gossip in the *Post*. I don't do for him. He looks a proper Charlie in his picture, but he turned out pleasant enough. Me and Emily played a bit of a joke on him as a matter of fact. There's little enough sex, rage and sin about these days. You've got to have a bit o' fun, haven't you!'

The visitor had to agree, although rather grudgingly, Eva felt.

'He's been ringing and ringing ever since. Can't hardly get rid of him, though I've nothing more to say. I've done my bit, and that's that.'

The visitor used the choosing of another biscuit to find a more accessible subject for conversation.

'How's your son, Mrs Coutts – that's right, one son, isn't it?'

The question hung in the air.

'Now there's a story ...' said Eva.

'See him regular, do you dear?'

Eva sniffed. 'Did.'

'Oh?'

'There's been a bit of a to-do.'

'Oh, I am sorry.'

'More tea?' Eva picked up the pot and poured.

'Well, if you need any help. ... We don't want you getting lonely, dear. And there's always the Pop-In Parlour until he comes round.'

Eva suppressed a cruel retort. 'It'll be all right. Nothing that can't be put right with a bit o' blackmail and extortion, eh?'

The other woman pursed her lips. Eva lamented the demise of humour in do-gooders.

'And I've plenty of people to chat to – always have had. Work like a demon on that phone I do. There's always someone who wants to tell you a little story. Now take that Danielle Kay . . .'

But the church visitor was an unenthusiastic audience. She scratched a speck of something off her cuff and looked at her watch.

'And there's definitely value in getting out and about, though not too often mind. Don't want to spoil the mystique, eh?' Eva cackled.

The visitor smiled and spoke, slowly and too clearly as if to an ailing patient. 'You had a lovely evening out then? Does you good to get out now and again, doesn't it!'

'I don't know that any good will come of it,' said Eva. 'But at my age you have to take your fun where you can find it. I had all the fellas once, but they've got very thin on the ground. The ones that do still take an interest are getting older too. Now when they whistle and make kissing sounds in your direction you can never be sure they're not just sucking their false teeth.'

Her visitor's wince gave a new dimension to po-faced. Eva wondered whether to tell her the story going the rounds about a neighbouring vicar and a local lolli-pop lady. But the woman's attention, such as it had been, was diverted. She was staring out, through the open French windows, into the strip of garden. Roses nodded in the breezy sunshine.

'I say . . . did you know there's a man in your garden, Mrs Coutts?'

'Things are looking up.'

'He's coming this way. Well dressed for a gardener, I must say.'

Curious but unperturbed, Eva padded to the windows. The man dusted himself down quickly as if to distress his suit as little as possible and walked brazenly towards them down the crazy-paving path.

'Well,' said Eva, patting her hair, 'this is a turn-up for the books. I've heard of social climbing, Mr Pierce, but not over my back fence.'

63 | *The Garden Plot*

In a place where people seemed to need all too little encouragement to bare their souls – even to him – Sword was all too aware of the difficulties.

The temptation was there.

So far, he had managed to get away with saying nothing about himself in group therapy – but there was no doubt about it.

He had reached the stage when he WANTED to say something, to let the mask slip.

Face it, he already had – or very nearly – to Framboise.

He wondered sometimes whether Jamie Raj had guessed – although he was certain the amiable bumbler Pearson never had in all the years they had worked together. And Rosy? Surely it would have crossed her mind that there was a reason why Eva's persistent calls were not more vigorously discouraged? But he doubted Rosy suspected any greater significance.

Then what of these people here?

All his professional powers of intuition pointed to them spilling the beans. In fact, from what he had heard via Framboise, Benedict Pierce was probably already on to him.

*

He shared a rice cake and the dilemma with the singer in a break after introductory TM.

Her face became an unhelpful blank – or there again, it could have been the effects of the meditation.

'I need your advice,' he said.

'You mean to say, you've never talked about yourself, never given an interview, never admitted anything about your private life?' said Framboise slowly.

'Not beyond the basic biography, from places I'd be remembered: RADA, then the *Evening News*.'

'RADA?'

'Well ... okay. Not exactly RADA. A drama school of sorts.'

'You were an actor?'

'Maybe I still am,' said Sword, 'in many ways.'

Surprisingly, she let that go.

'Who knows who anyone really is?' she said dreamily.

He pulled a face. 'We've both spent too long here.'

'You've got to know us, though.'

'Us?' asked Sword.

'Me and all the other women here.'

'But I know who you are already.'

She gave him a look. 'Maybe. But not what we are.'

He had to ask and this was the perfect opportunity. It had been preying on his mind for days. 'Did they know who I was, that night in the Social Wing?'

Framboise cocked her head as if evaluating his state of mind. 'I'm not going to tell you,' she said.

He wanted to be alone that evening.

The sun was a great ball caught in the branches of the trees as he mooched out into the gardens. Pockets of midges danced in the air. He didn't bother to wave

298

them away. He wanted to feel the hum of summer o'erbrimming.

Sword walked to the sunken place where Framboise sang, that time, and stood in silence. Then, when it was almost dark, he plunged on towards the hillocks, curled like sleeping giants on the horizon.

His feet made hardly a sound on the dry grass.

Much later, he felt restored. The lights of Grasslands Hall burned like a vast ship on dark seas as it came within his sights again.

He listened for the familiar party shrieks of the Social Wing, and caught a tantalising whoop on a breeze. Then the trees whispered above his head.

Sword broke free of the copse and skirted the shrubbery at the edge of the lawn, unwilling to expose himself to the wide black lawn in front of the house.

A rustle and crack of twigs made him start.

He stopped and peered around.

Nothing. It must have been further away than it sounded.

He went on, though more cautiously.

There. There it was again.

Sword stopped again, more out of curiosity than fear. He knew he had nothing to fear – it was probably a badger or a rabbit. Then he saw the light, as if from a torch.

Some badger. He held his breath and tried as soundlessly as possible to push himself further into a bush.

The dark figure turned and skittered into the copse before it reached him.

Sword exhaled and moved onwards.

He had never moved so stealthily . . . so lightly. He was intrigued. Then, at last, he could see. The torch lit up the scene well enough for him to identify the well-known figure.

What the hell was SHE doing here, in the copse?

64 | Benedict's Informant

At last, Benedict felt, he was getting somewhere.

The other old bat had made herself scarce after his unannounced arrival, and Eva Coutts had cleared the tea set and produced a bottle of Gordons.

The legendary Pierce determination was paying off. He settled himself on a gold velveteen sofa surrounded by the debris of a theatrical life and wondered how straight to be about his intent.

Eva sat, adjusting the ropes of beads which swang from her neck, her demeanour polite but expectant. The hard crimson of her lipstick was barely bent into a Mona Lisa smile.

She was waiting for him to begin.

Benedict swallowed hard. 'Emily Strong gave me your telephone number,' he said by way of explanation. 'I, er, got your address from a contact at BT who helps now and then.'

She gave no discernible reaction.

'You see, Mrs Coutts, I think we may be able to help each other. There is a project I'm working on – and as we met the other evening—'

'Project?'

'A book. Actually.'

'Really. How exciting for you.'

Benedict didn't deny it. 'I would, of course, be able to make it worth your while. . . .'

'I see.'

'A person of your . . . experience—'

'What kind of book, Mr Pierce? Tho' I can't see that I could be of any great help.'

Benedict gave her his most reassuring face. 'Well, it's very much about my business – the gossip business: the famous faces, the players in the game, the parties, the glorious incidents . . . the great maze that is Society today, and in the past!'

'I see. And what could I tell you that you didn't know already?'

'I want to go back – if you don't mind me saying – some years . . . say to the time when Anthony Sword started out. . . .'

'Go on.'

'Well, to tell you the truth . . . I need to talk more specifically about Sword, with someone who has . . . an overview . . . of how he fits into the picture. The others are all relatively straightforward, but there's very little on record about him personally.'

'And how would I be able to help you with that, Mr Pierce?'

She was not making it easy for him.

'I do KNOW, Mrs Coutts, he said, taking a well-worn flyer.'

'You do, do you?'

'Absolutely,' said Benedict with as much conviction as he could muster.

Eva Coutts studied him inscrutably. 'I can't say I'm not tempted, Mr Pierce.'

'Well, good . . . good! As I say, I'm sure I can make it

worth your while.' A provisional excitement kindled in his fingers as he lifted his tumbler of neat alcohol in tentative salute.

She inclined her head. Her plump cheeks and make-up reinforced his first impression: the hair might be grey now but she was still a game girl.

'But I'll need to know a bit more, y'know. Have you got a publisher lined up?'

'Mega Books.'

'Ah, yes.'

'You know them?'

'Heard of them, yes. They do Anthony Sword's *Year*, don't they?'

'That's right.'

'Who did you say commissioned it?' asked Eva.

She was more on the ball than he'd given credit.

Benedict had a fleeting feeling of unease. He opted for a modest-but-vague reply. 'Oh – it has, er, come from the top.'

'Not my old mate Sylvester?'

'Do you know him?' he asked cautiously.

'You could say.'

'You'll do it then?'

Eva Coutts tipped back her gin, and closed her eyes. Then she fixed him with a naughty expression and that obscene wink which had lured him so fortuitously across a crowded room. 'We'll see.'

'By the way,' Eva said as he was leaving, 'That Bea whatsername. I wouldn't believe a word she says.'

'Sorry?' Benedict wondered what she was on about.

'Bea Goff. She always was daft as a brush – and getting worse from all I hear.'

'I don't—'

'The *Nair!* party. I saw her all over you. Couldn't believe it at first – I don't get out much these days, as I say, and then who should I see after all these years but her! What a welcome back, eh?'

'Ah. You know her too, then?'

'Bears shit in the woods? 'Scuse my backstage French, dear. I'll tell you one thing for free: she's never had Prince Philip – she's Beattie Gofferty and we shared a dressing room in more provincial pits than I care to remember. I never forget a face, me . . . names perhaps, now and then, but not a face.'

'She does have a reputation for—'

'Making things up. I'll say. Now you can say what you like about Eva Coutts, but I never tell porkies . . . and anyone as does, I can tell a mile off.'

Benedict listened lamely.

'No, take it from me. You want to keep well clear of Bea Goff, or whatever she calls herself these days. Mind you, her memory's not all bad – she knew me all right the other night. Couldn't get out of the door quick enough when she saw me coming, eh?' Eva loosed off a great cackle. 'Must have been a nasty shock for her.'

'I knew she was an actress, briefly,' said Benedict, his jaw stiffening. 'But then she married Lord Malvern. After his first wife died. She was practically a child bride.'

Eva cackled. 'I'd say that was her first credible performance. Up the spout as she was by the ASM at the time.'

'What? I mean . . . really?'

'Oh, yes. The stories I could tell, Mr Pierce.'

He didn't doubt.

Benedict felt dazed as he stepped out into the disturbing normality of Fairlawn Avenue. Evening sunshine slanted through the cherry trees with strange iridescence. But it was not the light that disoriented him. It was the Pandora's Box he had stumbled across. He wondered whether he was up to opening it.

65 | *Rude Society*

By the time Rosy arrived home from seeing the Features woman she had the rest of her evening all worked out: a Lean Cuisine, then the *Travel Show* on television, followed by a documentary on expats who bought farmhouses in Provence. Then, when that was over, she was travelling around Polynesia with Paul Theroux in a dugout – she clutched the book in its crisp bag from Books Etc. Tonight she wanted to be anywhere but London, from the comfort of her own bed.

She slammed the door behind her, kicked her way into the sitting room, coat half off, looking round for Emma.

Jamie Raj was lying on the sofa.

Rosy pulled up short of knocking over two glasses on the floor. The room shrank by a foot each way.

'Oh,' she said, shocked. 'Hello.'

What the hell was he doing here?

Jamie grinned. 'I've come to the ivory tower at last,' he said, indicating the teetering edifices of books on their overladen shelves.

'I wouldn't call this place an ivory tower,' said Emma, bounding into the room. 'More a towering irony.'

She had a larky bow in her red curls and had borrowed Rosy's mock-Versace leggings. She and Jamie were already more than halfway down a bottle of Australian Chardonnay.

From the record player, Julie London was wailing: 'Cry me a river . . . I cried a river over you. . . .'

The two of them were clearly on a roll, giving their preciousness an airing.

'I'd love your job, Jamie. All glitz and no iambic pentameters.'

'I reached the end of the line with iambic pentameters, dearheart.'

'That's the long and the short of it, then?'

And so on. It was like a bad parody of *The Glittering Prizes*, thought Rosy.

Through the window the sky was deep turquoise shot through with blood-orange. The trees in the garden were sinking on to a dark maze. A black jet cut across on the way to Heathrow. Rosy sat by the table and poured herself a drink. Leafing through one of Emma's anotated tomes of Marvell's poems, she listened moodily, not saying a word.

Emma got up to crash bottles around in the kitchen.

'Hey, Rosy!' Jamie moved in on her, picking up a book on literary criticism from the table. A tendril of glossy hair flopped over his forehead as he looked down. His full lips were smiling knowingly.

'I've got this somewhere,' he said. 'Never have got my degree without it. In fact, several pages bring back fond memories of my Finals. Word for word.'

Rosy said nothing, though she knew it was looking more and more as if she was sulking. Those havoc-making amber eyes were far too close for her to be able to make any unincriminating response.

'What's up, darling?'

She tensed at the flip way he called her by his favourite endearment, as if she were just another blonde. She glared at him, then turned back a page and quoted:

'Society is all but rude,
To this delicious solitude.'

The words squelched off the tongue. When you spoke that line out loud, Rosy always thought, it was like licking your lips after chocolate mousse.

'*The Garden*,' said Jamie. 'I love that line, and the bit about stumbling on melons as I pass.'

'You would,' said Rosy.

She left them to it.

Sitting hunched on her bed, hearing gales of laughter from the sitting room, she felt more inadequate than ever. If ever she wanted a hard shell to retire into, it was now. First Brett Trent and now Jamie – people were crowding in on her, even here.

Rosy opened her book and tried to get lost, far away from love's labours, in the South Pacific.

If only Paul Theroux would shut up about his wife and get paddling.

Later, Emma knocked and came right in. 'What's the matter, Rosy?'

'Me? Nothing, I'm fine.'

'Don't give me that.'

Rosy put her book down. 'I got the feeling you two were getting on fine without me, that's all.'

'That bad, eh?'

'Meaning what?'

'Meaning you've got Jamie Raj as bad as any of us, and probably worse.'

'Emma, don't be ridiculous. I work with the guy, okay? It's fine if you like him and want to see him, but I just don't happen to want to see him lying on our sofa when I get home, all right?'

'Oh, really?'

'Yes!'

Emma sat on the edge of the bed. 'It's not what it seems, you know.'

'Nothing ever is,' retorted Rosy.

'He's absolutely gorgeous, and of course I'm attracted to him—'

Here we go, thought Rosy. The old 'I-don't-want-to-do-anything-to-upset-you-but-I-can't-help-myself' routine.

'Not that it's going to do me any good,' said Emma.

'Oh?' said Rosy, suddenly finding the duvet cover fascinating.

'When he called and then we went out last night . . . I had a great time. But all he wanted to talk about was you.'

'Yeah, likely,' sighed Rosy.

'It's true. He's mad keen on you – and going crazier because he says you only think of him as a friend. He went on and on about how he can't make a move because he doesn't want to ruin that, you're the only woman he can really talk to, he's tried making you jealous. . . .'

Rosy snorted. 'Honestly!'

'And tonight when you were so unfriendly . . . he wasn't here because of me – it was to see you, I swear!'

66 | *Moonlight Becomes You*

There was no escape. In the torchlight, her silly face
jutted up at his like a pert little sprite in a woodland
glade. Cornered by his own curiosity, Sword stared
down the ghastly truth: the social writers' whining irri-
tant Bea Goff had tracked him down and was intent on
pressing home her advantage.

'It IS you!' she cried. The brittle spun-sugar hair was
coming adrift with the exertion of following him but
triumph was hers. 'You've been avoiding me, you
naughty man. . . .'

'Merely my prerogative.' Sword was relieved to feel
stirrings of the old bile when it mattered. 'Whatever it
is you want, I'm having none of it. I just don't want to
know.'

'Oh, but you MUST, Mr Sword. I'm having a party
tomorrow – a very select gathering naturally. As of last
week, this is the only place to hold it. . . . Absolutely *le
tout Londres* is trekking up! Of course, it was so clever
of you to find it first!'

He grunted, running through his options. Downright
rudeness was water off a duck's back to the woman. In
the past he had tried everything but brute violence to
rid himself of her persistent publicity-seeking.

'Ever since word leaked out this was where you were, there has been FRANTIC juggling of schedules! The Kents are coming, and the Salcombes, the Bloxfords and all the complicated Crotchet-Blairs ... not to mention the Gloucestershire contingent ... and I have an AN-NOUNCEMENT to make. . . .'

This time however, Sword realised with grim satisfaction, there was one untried solution open to him. He assessed the likelihood that the pristine Grasslands tracksuit she was wearing had ever seen active service – and took off at a brisk trot.

Glancing back, he saw her windmilling after him for a few paces, gasping out his name.

'The trouble I've gone to . . .!' was the last he heard on the wind as he lost her.

He knew now for certain. It was time to leave.

He consulted his watch and hurried across the lawn, pausing for a sentimental second at the sunken garden. Then he pressed on.

Luck was with him. As he'd hoped, he caught her as she crossed his path *en route* for the Social Wing.

'Framboise!'

The singer turned. 'Hey there! You coming in?'

Sword chuckled, indicating his – by now rather sweaty – tracksuit. 'In this old thing . . .?'

She laughed. 'Maybe not. Although. . . .'

'Time for a chat?' he asked.

'Sure.'

They sat in a gazebo at the head of the sunken garden. Appropriate, he thought, remembering the evening she had first sung for him. It was turning out to be a social evening after all. He told her about his unwelcome encounter in the copse.

'Wonder what's going on back in London,' he mused.

'I thought *le tout Londres* was here,' said Framboise.

'Wait for tomorrow.'

They pondered on this for a moment.

Then, without preamble, she took up where they'd left off. 'So why don't you talk about yourself? I don't mean what you've been doing, who you've met, but . . . about why and how? Even here?'

He hesitated. 'I have been.'

'A little. To me, maybe. That wasn't what I meant.'

He knew that.

'Nothing to tell,' said Sword.

'C'mon.'

'Nothing of interest.'

'What you said earlier . . . about being an actor . . .' said Framboise.

Sword turned to face her full on, speaking plainly. 'I'm nobody from nowhere, all right?'

'That old excuse. Gasp, horror!' she said, panto-miming grotesquely. 'Jeez. And everyone else isn't?'

'If you knew anything about Britain . . . London – and how the way you put milk in your fucking tea can give you away . . . one slip puts you in a pigeon-hole for life.'

'That's rich. LOOK who you're talking to.'

'Sorry.'

'Sure. Now you're going to give me the Old Family bullshit. How did the rest of us get here then?'

'You know exactly what it means.'

There was a long pause. She waited expectantly, clearly not going to let him get away with that.

He didn't really want to.

'My family was . . . no. My mother . . .' he began. 'My mother and I have not always seen eye to eye . . . since I discovered that she – God, I need a drink.'

312

'Nah, substitute. You discovered what?'

'That she was involved in –' He couldn't say it. 'That I . . . have to cut the ties with her. Or I go under.'

'What, emotionally?'

'Professionally.'

He felt rather than saw her eyes on him. 'And that's all there is for you?'

That was near the quick. He flinched. 'I made myself what I am. She was never interested in anyone but herself. Oh, she's mellowed now she's older, but I can't forget what she was like. Look . . . let's talk about something else.'

'Okay.'

'Good.'

'Are you gay, or are you one of these new celibate types – don't do it with anyone?' asked Framboise.

He watched the moon's swollen crescent. Whisps of cloud drifted across. Eventually Sword answered.

'There's nothing new about my celibacy.'

'The secret is there are no secrets?' Framboise ushered him along more gently now.

'Something like that.'

'Why?'

He waited for another age then realised he was done for. 'It's like going there,' he said, still focusing on the night sky.

'Where?'

'Up there. Men have gone to the moon. They know they can do it—'

She interrupted the analogy with a calculated chortle. 'It was quite a thrill the first time. . . .'

He silenced her with a look. 'Yes . . . but they don't have to do it all the time.'

'So it's a case of—'

313

'I'm not a textbook case of anything.'

'But you must . . . I mean, do you ever . . . still? And which way?'

'Contrary to what you may imagine, I have never kissed and told.'

67 | *Keeping in Touch*

On their last morning at Grasslands, Sword and Framboise fluttered out together in their kimonos and did it at sunrise. On the cool cloudy pink air, Puccini's duet of parting from *Madame Butterfly* had never been sung so poignantly.

The previous night he had been accepted – *au naturel*, as it were – in the Social Wing. At Framboise's instigation, they had even sung 'For He's a Jolly Good Fellow' in valediction as he had climbed now rather than heaved himself out of the window.

The two of them had talked – really talked – until the first twitterings of the dawn chorus. Sword felt the release like a dam burst. He wondered how much else he had to thank her for.

He gave his red telephone number at the *Dispatch* to the Duchess of York and Mary Hawty.

To Framboise, he gave his home number and a lift down to London.

As the Bentley purred south, windows wound down for the last gusts of country air, Framboise turned to him and smiled. 'It's been kinda interesting, hasn't it.'

'It has been, as they say, enormous.'

'Or rather less enormous in your case,' said Framboise admiringly. 'For the guy who heckled at the back of the class, you turned out a pretty impressive unbeliever.'

For her part, Framboise, attired in a travelling outfit of poncho and slacks, still boasted legs that could kick-start a 747, and proud of them.

Sword grimaced. 'It was a case of having to. Lose weight, I mean. Not believe the tosh and claptrap. I . . . you know, Framboise . . . there are medical problems in store if you get too heavy. . . . What I mean to say is that if I can do it . . . well, begin to tackle it, anyone—'

For once he didn't know what he was trying to say. He was the last person to talk about exercising self-restraint. But he wished she would. He had seen the empty peanut butter jars in her hand luggage.

'Diet or die, hey?' She put it succinctly enough.

'You could try.'

'Who do you think I am – Oprah?'

'Well . . .'

'You know what I can't believe?' she asked, shifting the subject abruptly back to him. 'How different you are to what I imagined. Jeez. The social columnist with the pirate beard and the temper! Lord have mercy . . . what a pussycat!'

'Grr!' obliged Sword, knowing when to let it drop.

'What about the beard? You gonna grow it back?'

'Don't know yet.'

'Are you back to work tomorrow?'

'Who knows?' he cried airily.

'Hey! Call the self-determination therapist!'

They chuckled.

'Don't rush me. I've got some time yet to decide.'

'Let the motley crew run the ship for a while longer, eh?'

Sword hestitated as he negotiated a bend.

'Not so motley. Well, there's an older one who's a bit dog-eared – he's been with me for years but we have, let's say, an understanding of how we operate. The other two are more ritzy. One Beaufort Street maharajah and one Home Counties rose.'

'Younger?'

He sighed. 'Isn't everyone these days?'

'Bet they're missing you.'

'The way I treated them before I went, I very much doubt it.'

Framboise hummed. 'And you said the claptrap was tosh ... I'd say you got something out of Grasslands Hall.'

'Enough with the schmalz!'

'Yeah, but—'

'I may have got more than I bargained for,' said Sword, giving her a teasing sideways glance.

'Whatcha gonna do first when you get back?'

He put his hand over hers as a wordless gesture of thanks. 'I think I am going to call on my mother.'

They purred on smoothly towards the capital.

'Anthony?' She hardly ever used his first name. 'I have something to tell you.'

'Mmm?'

'I'm not sure whether I should, but I think you should know.'

There was an edge to her voice. Sword braced himself. 'You've started now.'

'Okay. You know how Nan Purchase is royal-struck?'

He sighed.

'And you know how she loves to megaphone?'

'Ye-e-s. . . .' The prospect of Nan Purchase giving

317

away his escapades at Grasslands, ridiculing him despite her assurances of confidentiality, was enough to bring back a wave of the old fierce fury.

Framboise rolled her eyes. 'She told me she's having dinner tomorrow night with . . . Benedict Pierce . . .' She watched to see how he was taking it. '. . . And the Queen!'

Sword roared. 'And you've been had.'

'Well, according to Nan, it's all fixed up.'

He was still laughing. 'I find a bit of fun coming on.' And he let out an unseemly Grasslands-type wildman whoop and beat on the substantial steering wheel. A van-driver overtaking them swerved in sudden fright.

'We will keep in touch?' she asked as they drew up outside the flat in one of Islington's sooty Georgian terraces which was Framboise's temporary home.

Sword had just finished telling her more than he had ever told anyone. 'I wouldn't let you go,' he said.

'I think I know that,' she smiled.

'I'll call you then.'

'Bathtimes are good,' said Framboise.

68 | *What to Say?*

At the flower stall outside Temple station Rosy bought a large bunch of champagne roses and struck out along the Embankment.

Another day of not-so-idle chatter was about to begin.

She still hadn't a clue what she was going to say to Jamie.

If she was going to say anything at all.

But she felt the molten gold of sudden optimism beginning to glow inside her.

She got in to find Tina approximating Sword's signature on a stack of photographs. Strictly for the devotees, these showed Sword smiling conspiratorially while apparently cleaning blood off a cutlass.

Pearson was scything through the Court and Social columns of the heavies while scribbling notes with the fever of a man about to crack enemy code. 'It's incredible,' he said.

'What is?' asked Rosy.

'The stories you can get if you know what you're looking for ... the things St Jude gets thanks for ...' said Pearson. His face was ruddier than ever.

'You're very with it for a morning after one of Lord

Diplock's parties, Pearson,' said Tina, arranging the roses in a spare wine cooler.

'It was somewhat restrained.'

'I didn't even know there was a party last night,' said Rosy, knowing full well she wouldn't have gone anyway. 'Was the lovely Emily there?'

'Sadly, no. Stardom has called for my Emily, if you remember.'

'Oh, yes. *Nair!*,' winced Rosy.

'Lottie Landor was there though. I'm afraid I had to rescue her from Diplock's grasp.'

'Yuk,' said Rosy and Tina together.

'He's got some idea he should get some cheap advertising by having a public affair,' explained Pearson. 'Telling me to round up the Beast and get snaps of him mauling her! I should cocoa, compromising a nice lass like that.'

'Urgh. Doing it with Lord Diplock,' said Tina. 'It would be like getting trapped under a heavy old wardrobe which had toppled over with the key still in the door.'

'Thank you, Tina. Very graphic.'

'Was Hawty there?' asked Rosy. She still felt uncomfortable about not trying very hard with the second Nice tip-off she had taken on the phone. Clearly it was too late now to use it.

'For a while. But I hardly spoke to him. No Danielle in sight.'

'She'll have seen sense at last,' said Tina, in her sage of Croydon voice.

Halfway through the morning, Rosy had a call from the assistant features editor.

'How about writing a piece for me,' she said. 'See how it goes before we make any decisions?'

'Okay. Yes, absolutely fine,' said Rosy, glancing round carefully to make sure neither of the others had realised who she was talking to. 'Do you have anything in particular in mind?'

'Iconoclasm. Shoot the PR images, bust the mould, but show that you could bring us your contacts – that's what you wanted, wasn't it?'

'Well, er, yes.' Rosy had forgotten how hyped-up everyone else on the paper got over stories. They screeched along the corridors waving bits of computer print-out, rattling out commands and ideas like express trains, ordering foot soldiers out to cold doorsteps. And they all spoke in Conference-speak, to show they were important enough to have been there.

'I want an exposé of the downside of dynasty, the seediness of seignory, the ache of aristocracy. No glitz, no gloss. Who do you suggest you profile?'

Rosy thought fast. 'There is one person . . . an earl we've been writing about. He was no one until he inherited from a cousin of some kind two years ago. His duties and debts are out of control, the house is crumbling around his ears, none of his ideas to make money are very effective . . . he's pretty low about it.'

'All right then. Do it.'

'Brett? It's Rosy Hope.'

'Hmmmm.'

'Sorry I didn't get back to you sooner after the other night, but . . . you know how it is. How are you?'

No response from the Earl of Trent's end of the line.

'Listen, the reason I'm ringing is that I was wondering if we could meet for lunch.'

321

'Today?' He sounded under the weather.

'Today would be great ... if you could manage it, I know how busy you are,' she added flatteringly.

When he suggested a Mexican restaurant in Covent Garden her heart sank – this was not the time to emerge redolent of its avocado compost and bandit's armpit-scented chilli.

Not if she was likely to see Jamie.

'I don't suppose ...' Rosy crossed her fingers, 'that I could come round to see you at home?'

Didn't serious profile writers always insist on seeing the subject on home territory, surrounded by vital clues as to his true situation?

He told her to come round at 1.15.

She spent the rest of the morning bunkered in the reference library sifting through cuttings on the Earl's disparate – and historically, desperate – family. She was on her way, in all senses.

It was only as her taxi pulled up outside the dark and crumbling facade of the Earl's Pelham Square residence, that she thought to wonder why Jamie had not come into the office that morning.

But then suddenly all thoughts were banished as a blood-curdling howl, almost an animal keening, filled the square.

69 | *Sword Unseen*

'Dear boy!' said Sword. 'The wanderer returns.'

He stood on his terrace with a cordless telephone, trying to acclimatise to the limited green vista of his Highgate garden. It seemed strange and cramped, as if he had not seen it since childhood.

Jamie Raj responded with a cheery sub-Woosterism: 'Sword! Capital fellow! How are you?'

'In fine fettle, thank you.'

'You had a good time, then?'

'A little different from my usual constitutional, but . . . a life-saver. And you? Any problems?'

'Fine. Nothing urgent. A writ from Sir Philip Hawty, which he's sent round to every other paper that has ever carried his name, but apart from that. . . . Are you coming in this morning?'

'I think not. I'd like to see you though.'

'Okay. Where?'

'There's somewhere I'd like to try out.'

They arranged to meet at 12.30.

Once a wooded hunting ground – the cry of 'So-ho!' being an esoteric version of 'Tally-ho!' according to some – the area for which Sword made was now London's most style-conscious square mile. The cappuccino culture thrived again in the bars around the Old Compton Street. Thirty years after Billy Fury made mugs vibrate to the sound of jukeboxes here, it was possible to live or die by your choice of coffee bean.

Sword wandered into the Bar Italia and ordered an espresso. He took it to the far end of the functional narrow room and waited.

He had been coming here since the heyday of Expresso Bongo. The genuine Italians who still shuffled around under the poster of Rocky Marciano all knew him. Admittedly, he was wearing an uncharacteristic dark suit borrowed from his gardener – his own cream linen had hung off him like the skin of a sick and elderly elephant – but surely, he rationalised, that could not be the sole reason for the quiet welcome.

There was not a glimmer of recognition.

Sword gave it a fair chance, then opened his copy of the *Dispatch*.

Jamie was an elegant three minutes later than the appointed time. Sword watched with excitement verging on shock as he realised it had worked.

It was as if he no longer existed.

Jamie stepped inside. Immaculate and poised as a big cat, he looked around. Sword felt the amber eyes flow over him as he sat there determinedly offering no help. Only when it was clear that his colleague had wandered up to the counter to wait, did he cough softly and say, 'Jamie, here!'

If he could only have bottled the look on his face.

'Incredible. Extraordinary!' Jamie was still amazed halfway through his second cappuccino. Sword stuck to plain black shots of caffeine.

'You look so completely different. Even your face – it's as if Brian Blessed has gone and we've got ... I don't know ... Michael Palin in his place ... quite unpiratical in character.'

'I may have to invent a new one.'

'You look ... a lot more relaxed.'

'Oh, I feel it. My return was not nearly as unpleasant as one always dreads. Even the doormat held a pleasant surprise to neutralise the effect of all the brown envelopes addressed with red ink.'

Jamie smiled. 'You know, I heard a rumour that Fergie was at Grasslands a couple of weeks ago.'

Sword turned up his palms in acknowledgement. 'I was two steps ahead of you.'

'Two steps, hops, skips and jumps by the look of you. It really is quite amazing. Did you manage a jog with Fergs, or a steam bath, or whatever it was you did?'

'She kept mainly to the women's side, you know.'

Jamie waited.

'She IS training as a New Life counsellor?' he asked. 'Nan Purchase has been blatantly plugging that line after you went on TV and said so.'

'I very much doubt it, though she was in some of the classes.'

Jamie whistled. 'She didn't say anything—?'

Sword shook his head.

'Anything seems possible.'

'Tell me what's been happening here.'

His deputy reeled off a few of the more amusing episodes, then hesitated.

'Out with it.'

Jamie stirred the dregs in his cup. 'Before you hear it from anyone else ... Benedict's doing a number on

325

you. He's been commissioned to write your biography. Dirty great advance, apparently.'

Sword let the tension grow, then slowly bared his teeth.

'You knew?'

'A large advance, eh? What a shame for him then . . . that the deal's off.'

'It is?'

Sword nodded.

'You're sure?'

'As a grovelling letter from Sylvester at Mega Books can make it. My doormat surprise. It was waiting for me when I arrived home yesterday. Delivered by hand, no less.'

'But—?'

'Don't ask me why. I rang and checked. It's genuine. That's all I want to know.'

Jamie laughed. 'I can't believe you've changed THAT much.'

'So what now?' asked Jamie, setting down his cup. 'Are you coming straight back?'

'I think,' said Sword, with a flash of the old bravado, 'that the game is not up, yet.'

'No-o-o?' Jamie observed him expectantly.

'Ascot. What are we planning this year?'

'I've got all the usual tickets but I was waiting to hear from you.'

'Good man.'

Sword examined his fingernails. 'No point in me coming back this week. I intend to return to the fray at the races – a suitable stage, I feel.'

Jamie nodded. 'We could all go down for a first day column?'

326

'No, no,' said Sword, 'We'll do the usual bunfight, but it has to be Thursday.'

'Whatever.'

'It has to be Ladies' Day.'

70 | *Rosy and the Wildman*

The howling had come from the Earl's house.

Nervously, Rosy paid the cab driver and walked up to the imposing door.

If anything, the rotting stucco of 12 Pelham Square had become crustier in the weeks of sunshine since the Earl of Trent's Green Countdown party.

A smudged retainer opened the door and showed her up the dusty stairs. Without the party hordes, the cavernous house had a creaking, echoing life of its own.

Brett Trent was waiting in the ballroom, where the paint on the *faux* pillars was peeling into Corinthian columns, and the deer and the antelope played peeka-boo through splintered wooden shields. The full-length windows were open.

'Hello, darling, pull up a throne.' He gestured towards a rickety wooden chair. 'As you can see, we have the place to ourselves for once.'

Rosy's polite laugh sounded as hollow as most of the rooms. 'Was that you, a moment ago?' she asked suspiciously. 'Screaming out of the window?'

'I expect so,' he said. 'Although the square's always been a very fashionable place.'

'Er, what was it all about?'

'Wildman therapy. It's the latest thing to release your tension and refocus.'

'I see. Does it work?'

'I'm not sure yet. Someone gave me a book about it and I'm only on the first chapter.'

Rosy stared around.

The Earl followed her gaze. He looked so drawn and pasty, his body gangly and abused as a medical student's skeleton, that she almost felt sorry for him. To put him at ease on the first step to the confessional, she – awkwardly – offered up her own confidence. 'Last time I was here, I made a terrible fool of myself,' she said. 'Worse than normal.'

'Yeah?' he asked vaguely.

'I came with leaves pinned to an old dress and didn't know anyone. I asked Sir Philip Hawty about party politics and he said that his were to find as many young girls as he could before the drink ran out.'

The Earl sniggered.

'So, what did you want to see me about then?' asked the Earl.

They had moved downstairs to the cosier setting of the kitchen table. An elderly retainer clucked around, a pot of PG Tips was stewing and they were making companionable inroads into a packet of Pennywise ginger snaps.

Rosy took a sip of hot, sweet tea, trying to concentrate on the task in hand.

'How would you feel about a piece in the paper that's different from the usual gossip?'

'Different, how?'

'Well . . . a serious feature – along the lines that you were talking about the other evening, in the pub.'

He made no comment, so she went on. 'About how inheriting the earldon hasn't been all riches and glamour, the appalling bills and taxes, the impossible upkeep of the house. . . . I'd present your version of events very sympathetically.'

'My version of events . . .?'

'Your account of what's happened to you over the past two years,' said Rosy hastily.

The Earl gave her a bug-eyed stare, not altogether trusting. She was about to go into greater detail when he said, 'You know Benedict Pierce has been trying to do a piece saying I'm a hopeless drug addict and a cocaine supplier?'

Rosy fiddled with her hair. 'He couldn't do it . . . unless . . . you haven't admitted it to him?'

'What do you think?' he said. She took that to mean that he wouldn't be so stupid.

Neither said anything.

'I have never supplied,' he said.

Rosy felt her back prickle. 'Perhaps . . . we could get a first strike in with this feature. If you think the story is going to come out in a way you wouldn't want . . . then get in first with an account that you are happy with.'

'I don't know—'

'It makes sense,' said Rosy.

The Earl reached for a cigarette. 'And you would write this . . . feature?'

'Yes.'

'Nothing to do with Sword?'

'No.'

'Do I get paid for it?'

'I . . . I could probably arrange for that. I can't promise anything now. I'd have to let you know.'

'Where do we go from here then?' he asked.

'I thought ... I could come over at lunchtimes or in the evening and we can talk, go over papers, documents, whatever. I'm sure to see you at various parties, when I can write a bit about what you feel about them and how other people see you. Then, we ... well, Sword's column always has an Ascot party. Jamie and Pearson were talking about it the other day. Maybe you could come to that and I could work in something in my piece about you being there and how you're always presented in the gossip columns.'

He took a long drag and blew out the smoke.

'What the hell ...' he said. 'Okay.'

71 | *Benedict's Dinner*

The received wisdom that a woman could never be too rich or too thin reached its frightening apotheosis in Nan Purchase, with her sparrow frame and monstrous bank account.

At least that was what Anthony Sword had once said. Benedict Pierce had a very different outlook.

He inspected the table setting and flowers for the twentieth time, and primed the girls in the kitchen for her arrival. He consulted his Rolex: 7.45 and counting.

It was the night Nan was coming to dinner at his flat in Westminster.

The patter of tiny Manolo Blahniks heralded Nan's arrival. Benedict composed his sincerest smile and opened the door.

She was immaculate in Valentino. Her eyes flickered up at him almost as nervously as his were devouring her. This season's Valentino, he noted, as if it might be a good omen. The Manhattan multi-millionairess, he now knew for certain, was perfection among womankind.

'Hello, Benedict.'

'Hello, Nan. You look wonderful.'

He leaned forward to brush his lips on the air above her taut cheeks, and breathed in the rarified expense of her scent. Then he took a step back, paused for a split second, and appraised her with a look of wicked affection. Raffish, but-you've-tamed-me. It usually worked with his women.

'Am I to come in, Benedict?'

'Ah, yes, of course, of course.'

He showed her in, along the pale passage to the sitting room, and began to deal with a frosty bottle of champagne. While he poured it, he could see her eyeballing the silver-framed photograph of his one and only meeting with Her Majesty, at a PR thrash in the Highlands where sponsors had invested thousands in one of her pet projects. The picture was prominently placed on an occasional table, under a lamp.

Benedict smiled modestly as he handed Nan a fluted glass, and offered her the most comfortable seat.

'Smart photograph,' she acknowledged, sitting down so lightly she barely indented the plump damask cushioning.

'Ah, well, you know how it is.'

'She looks a lot happier than she normally does in pictures,' observed Nan.

'Oh, Her Majesty is always happier away from ... official crowds.'

'Sure.'

They sipped in silence for a moment.

'There won't be a crowd here tonight, then?' asked Nan.

'No, um, not at all. In fact.'

'And she's really coming ... here?' Nan cast around with what seemed to Benedict an even tighter smile than usual.

Benedict steeled himself.

'I'm glad you mentioned that,' he said. 'I'm afraid I have rather disappointing news.'

'I know,' said Nan. 'Your column in the *Post* has been just terrible lately.'

'Er, apart from that.'

'Oh?'

'I'm afraid it's most unfortunate. My special guest . . . regrets that she is unable to attend our soirée, after all.' He maintained what he hoped was suitable decorum, underscoring grave disappointment.

'I didn't imagine she would be,' said Nan. 'I read the papers.'

'Ah.' He reached for his glass as a distraction.

'Yes, I believe she's in Windsor, trying to work through the, er . . . intricacies of the family situation,' said Nan, scarcely any more illuminatingly. 'According to your column. And she is, after all, a mother . . . a nurturing person.'

They were edging around each other.

Benedict hardly dared hope whom she imagined he could have invited. This was all very flattering. But he had lured her here now, and there seemed no point in being caught out in too gross a fabrication.

His mind raced. 'I had hoped . . . but she has been having problems with her son, you see. . . .'

'And how!'

'No, no . . . I mean, I think we may have the wrong – I wanted to introduce you to Eva Coutts, a very discreet presence on the London PR scene. I thought it might be interesting for you to meet, but . . . You didn't think I meant – The Queen?' he said, injecting false laughter. 'Coming here?'

'Gimme a break, Benedict.'

He laughed, properly this time, until she said, 'But it sure was good to spread the word around!'

After some amiable enough conversation over the *feuillette* of salmon with miniature vegetables about the state of the West End musical and the claustrophobia induced by Harrods' labyrinthine designer rooms, she said, 'Don't you just love Framboise?'

'Um, who?'

Nan was so surprised she almost took a bite of food. 'You're kidding? E-e-everybody in London is talking about Framboise Duprée!'

He toyed for time with an anorexic carrot.

'Oh, yes, of course! I didn't get the name for a second there. Framby . . .'

'Boise,' said Nan. 'She's this incredible singer – opera, jazz. Big, black and beautiful – and HUGE, my God, in every way. She's with some People of Camden Opera, came over from the States a couple of months back. She turned out to be a lot more than anyone bargained for.'

'She's hot?' asked Benedict, giving up the pretence.

'She's dynamite.'

'You know her well?'

'She's been staying at Grasslands Hall. The stories that have been coming out of there—'

'I'll bet.' It occurred to Benedict that it mightn't be a bad idea to book himself in, or better still, swing a freebie from his guest.

She was staring coyly, almost as if about to take pity on him. 'I maybe shouldn't tell you this . . .'

This was more like the introduction to the Anglo-American trade talks he'd been hoping for.

'. . . but there is someone who has become very friendly with Framboise. . . .'

He encouraged her with a major smoulder.

'Anthony Sword,' said Nan.

Great, just great. Benedict made a dismissive noise.

'Sword's been away.'

'That's right,' she said.

Benedict shook his head.

'All I can say is that Sword and Miss Duprée have become close, very close. So close that other guests had difficulty telling them apart?' Her voice rose at the end, implying he should think about it.

He couldn't take it in at all. 'Couldn't tell them apart . . .? But you said she was black, for a start, and he's shudder-white. . . .'

'True, but not necessarily so.'

Benedict admitted defeat.

He could hardly take in what she proceeded to tell him about Sword and Framboise and their clothes-swapping games. So that was where that rumour had started. Rumour no longer. It was a full-scale copper-bottomed certainty, he realised with glee.

After drinking most of the wine, Benedict was weighing up his chances of making a move on the Valentino'ed divorcee when there was a muffled thump from the direction of the balcony.

This was followed by a sudden crack and tinkle of glass.

'What was that?' cried Nan, arched brows knocking on her hairline.

Benedict shot to his feet.

A burly man in black leather appeared at the shattered window.

It was not the Milk Tray commando.

'Right then, is she 'ere or not? You there, Ma'am? Royal photo-opportunity! Get yer own back on Di!'

shouted Keith 'the Beast' Silver, above the whirr of his motor-drive camera.

72 | *Ascot*

Ascot this year had been billed as 'an oasis of joy in these difficult times for the Royal Family'. That, thought Anthony Sword, was inviting disaster.

He preferred to invite Framboise.

Ladies' Day dawned clear but cool, and by mid-morning when they drove towards Berkshire in the Bentley the clouds were plumping up.

The plan was to meet the others at the racecourse, where – with any luck – they would already have cased the Royal Enclosure and started gathering the day's tittle-tattle.

'You're sure I'm dressed right for the occasion? You did say noticeable,' said Framboise, dubiously fingering a giant cyclamen bowl that seemed to be intended as a hat. Her dress, less a fashion statement than a loud shriek, was strident pink with black dashes.

'You look scrumptious. Like a great watermelon,' chuckled Sword, adjusting his dark glasses.

'Good enough to eat, eh?'

'And very good for one,' he assured her.

Sword's team had established base camp in the car park, as they did every year. It was a focal point where, traditionally, the great and the good passed by – and then went by again if for any reason Sword and his colleagues had not noticed.

Behind his Italian sunglasses, Sword felt secure and defiant.

'The mother of all picnics!' said Jamie Raj, helping to unload the hampers and testing the strength of the trestle table.

'Profiteroles! What's this, Fergie-bait?' asked Pearson, prodding a finger in a vat of chocolate sauce.

The two of them were Dignity and Impudence in their toppers and tails.

Rosy's evident incredulity at his new incarnation had been both gratifying and pitiful to Sword. 'How did you do it? How can I do it?' she'd wailed. Sword thought she looked marvellous as she was – eyes shining and positively peachy in a cream suit – and told her so. She'd looked pleased at the compliment but not, he noted, as radiant as when Jamie added his agreement.

The Beast, manic in ripped tails (it was the one day in the year when he would forgo his black leather), was shooting enough frames to make a silent movie. After the elaborate practical joke of his crashing Benedict Pierce's soirée with Nan Purchase in putative search of the Queen, he was the hit of the week among the gossiping classes.

Framboise, too, was an instant success with the gathering, giving Rosy the inside track on Grasslands, telling Pearson risqué stories from the steam room and complimenting Jamie on his debonair appearance.

They opened the first bottle of Krug.

Sword proposed a toast. 'To . . . health, happiness and plentiful tittle-tattle!'

The others raised their glasses.

'To your return in style!' said Jamie.

'To your return less plentiful,' said Pearson.

They laughed and drank again.

The champagne was barely back on ice before the *Prattler*'s woman on the spot, Honoria Peeke came scampering up. Leaving Sword enveloped in her familiar cloud of gardenia scent, she pushed past and made straight for the heart-throb of the deb circuit. 'Jamie, darling!' she cried.

She proffered a powdered cheek but her nostrils flared like an SOS as she caught sight of the Beast. 'And Pearson! How lovely! What fun this will be. And this must be Framboise! I heard on the vine that you would be here today. Everyone's talking about how divine you are! I must say I can't imagine how you hold a tune when everyone else is singing something different – it's terribly clever of you.'

Sword pulled a face at Framboise, who promptly did her piss-take flummoxed Belle act.

Honoria gushed on. 'Now what are you all up to? Have you seen the Sangsters yet, and is the Aga Khan coming? The Waddington-Clarks, very old friends of mine, are having a bash later if you'd like to pop along.'

'I seem to have a long-standing engagement with a pint of best at the Oxted Arms,' muttered Pearson under his breath.

'Sadly, I must return to London,' said Jamie. 'An unbreakable date.'

From his observation post by the drinks, Sword saw Rosy's expression change. He wondered what that meant.

'Is Sword still away?' asked Honoria, accepting the glass of champagne he handed her, butler-like, without a word.

Rosy caught his eye and smiled.

Jamie cleared his throat.

'Yes, he is, Mrs Peeke,' piped up Sword, attempting a weedy, beardless voice.

Honoria glanced at Jamie, as if for corroboration.

'Sword is always with us in spirit,' said Jamie.

Pearson started to laugh and turned it into a wheeze.

'Er, isn't that Lord Diplock over there by the blue Rolls?' asked Rosy, nodding towards a rival party across the car park.

They all stared.

'Alf Diplock – that dreadful little man with the beautiful cars who was given a peerage?' queried Honoria, taking a delicate sip. 'Frightful waste. I once saw him wearing a frilled dress shirt. I'm sorry, I won't have men like that in my *Prattler* column. Mention one, and you have them all telling one about ladies' nights at Neo-Georgian Homes Association and candlelit suppers for the Rotary Club. It's all magnums and no breeding, don't y'find?'

Sword saw Pearson wiping away a tear. He didn't dare look at Framboise.

He heard her though.

'I love men like that,' said Framboise pleasantly. 'I always find, the frillier the dress shirt, the bigger the dick.'

73 | *Feeling Lucky*

It was always the same at Ascot. On the day every married man was minus £500 before he even got to the racecourse because his wife had complained she had nothing to wear. Worse, the heist was then paraded in joke form on their heads. One infamous matron whose vast hats had long been the benchmark of bad taste, had come as Jodrell Bank.

The brief fashion for real flowers blooming on these hats had been abandoned after too many had been eaten by horses, so Lady – Brenda – Diplock had a vast silk sunflower growing out of her head.

The Diplock party, holding fast to the right side of the VPL – the Visible Pimms Line – in the car park, consisted of Sir Philip Hawty, the actress Lottie Landor and several scions of the motor trade with their wives.

When Benedict sauntered over, there was a gratifying flutter of hands smoothing down Ascot best.

There was already a tipsy line of empty bottles on the grass by the Rolls-Royce.

'Benedict, mate!' boomed Lord Diplock. 'Come and have a shampoo or six.'

Benedict thought he would. After an extremely unpleasant telephone call from Sylvester of Mega Books the previous evening abruptly cancelling the Sword biography, he intended to get drunk, possibly roaring.

Quite apart from the liberating self-parody of Lord (Alf) Diplock's lavish Ascot hospitality, here was the perfect position from which to observe Sword and his mob from the *Dispatch*.

Benedict's breath quickened as he saw the story he had come for being played out before his eyes. Sylvester had cited 'personal reasons' for wimping out of the Sword book. Well Benedict had a few personal reasons for wanting to expose Sword, and if he couldn't do it in print one way, there was always the obvious one.

Over there was the Sword's Secrets team with various guests, and plum in the midst was the familiar roly-poly figure, blacked up just as Nan had described it and ludicrous in a bright pink dress.

Of course.

IT HAD TO BE SWORD. The buffoon was still playing silly buggers.

It all made sense. After all, he reasoned, how else would Jamie Raj have got his hands on Sword's treasured cream Bentley and driven it down here?

'Would you like a quickie?'

Benedict swung round to find a bottle-blonde teenager holding a tray of savoury tarts.

'Quiche, Tracy, it's pronounced quiche. How many times . . .' snarled Brenda Diplock, switching on a thin smile for her guest. 'Can't get the help these days.'

Benedict demurred.

In his experience, these harrowing times were providing all too much good help. Depressingly good help which was lending an entirely new meaning to the term Seasonal Employment. Even here the bars and restaurants were choc-a-bloc with titled meal-makers, washer-Uppers and even a baronet binman.

It was getting to the stage when a social columnist would have to be dragged into the main social event and left begging to be allowed into the kitchens.

Still Benedict clung to the old tenet – the only stories worth doing were the ones they tried to stop you doing. If only it were that simple. It had been quite a while since he'd had the option.

As if on cue with his thoughts, Sir Philip Hawty materialised at Benedict's shoulder. 'Feeling lucky?' he asked.

'So-so,' said Benedict equivocably. 'You?'

'I've got my eye on an interesting filly.'

'We know that,' said Benedict, 'but what about the horses?'

'Oh, very original.' Sir Philip's perma-tan was looking distinctly yellow about the gills, he couldn't help noticing.

Benedict had nothing to lose. 'Still suing me?' he asked conversationally.

The former Home Secretary sighed.

'After much consideration, I have decided . . . No.'

'You're dropping the action?'

'It's the system. Something must be done,' said Sir Philip, but without that smooth matinée-idol determination which had been his political hallmark.

Benedict drank and listened.

'It's enough to make an honourable man turn to the bad – the duplicity of even the most innocent-looking young women these days. The trouble I went to . . . to try to do my best by that lovely young woman . . . and look how I am repaid.'

'But what were you trying to do with her, Sir Philip?'

344

'Let me make matters quite clear. I am speaking God's literal truth when I say that there was never a sexual affair between me and Miss Danielle Kay.'

'That seems to be what she says too. Her exposé in the *Sunday People* was pretty damning of your, ah, performance,' agreed Benedict. 'Bit of smoke and no fire. Just some pretty pictures.'

'Nasty, tacky rubbish,' snapped Sir Philip. 'You of all people should know that appearances are never everything.'

This Benedict acknowledged. 'And what about Mary, you're divorcing again, I gather?'

'If you mean, is the tittle-tattle in the *Dispatch* right, then the answer is yes. Bloody awful business.'

Something in the set of Hawty's mouth made Benedict ask, 'You don't want a divorce now?'

'My politics have always advocated prudent fiscal control,' said Sir Philip pompously. 'And in my wife Mary I had a woman with a fine grasp of the economic principles of housekeeping.'

Benedict had first-hand experience of what they could mean.

Hawty went on. 'The principle of housekeeping which worries me now is which of my residences she is likely to snatch in the settlement.'

For once, the politician had Benedict's full and frank sympathy.

'And you think that her – what did they call him? – "well-respected other man" might strengthen her resolve?'

'He most certainly will,' said Sir Philip bitterly. 'He's her solictor.'

'Ouch.'

It was time to change the subject.

'Look over there, Anthony Sword's lot by the Bentley,' said Benedict, pointing it out.

Sir Philip squinted.

'You wouldn't think that Anthony Sword would come to Ascot in a dress, would you?'

Sir Philip indicated, somewhat wearily, that he would not.

'He's been practising for this day. And you don't happen to recognise the chap in the dark glasses, do you?' asked Benedict.

'No-o. Why?'

They watched fascinated as the man made free with Sword's picnic and then laid a careless arm on the mesmerising figure in pink.

Benedict couldn't resist getting a live audience reaction to his scoop. 'Keep this to yourself, Sir Philip, but THAT, I am now absolutely certain, is . . . what I and others have long suspected. . . . Anthony Sword's Secret Male Lover!'

74 | His Fair Lady

After lunch the crowds gathered ten deep around the unsaddling enclosure waiting for the arrival of the royal party from Windsor Castle. Finally the procession of Landaus rolled down the green course like a line of wooden toy ducklings. The Queen and the Duke of Edinburgh waved from the first carriage, the line escorted by out-riders in scarlet on proud white and grey horses. Temporarily back in the bosom of the Royal Family, Princess Diana – dubbed the the Prisoner of Wales by a wag in the Enclosure – stared out glumly.

The wind was getting up again, tugging at hats and flimsy skirts. 'They call this the Ascot Salute,' said Rosy, hanging on to her straw brim.

Jamie Raj, in all his breathtaking beauty, was standing beside her. A gaggle of nice gals could hardly decide whether to watch him or the Royals.

Rosy's knees turned to water as he smiled at her, then reached out and put his hand on the hat to help hold it on. She swallowed a giggle, suddenly nervous.

Nothing had been said since the evening she'd come home to find him there.

'Rosy, I—'
'Yes?'

'I haven't seen much of you in the last few days – you keep disappearing every lunchtime, charging off every evening before Scribblers-time. . . .'

'Ah . . . I've, er, had a few people to see.'

'Oh. You see, Rosy . . .'

'Yes?'

'What would you say if—'

'What ho, Jamie, Rosy!'

Two glossy blond horns butted in. Naturally Benedict was carrying his topper so as not to diminish his coiffure.

'What ho, Benedict,' said Jamie. Did he look irritated at the interruption?

'How's it going, lovies?'

Rosy tensed, wondering how to react to him. But he treated her no differently to how he had before . . . the Incident.

She and Jamie made non-committal noises.

'You know what I love about Ascot? The fashion-in-the-field. The DRESSES,' said Benedict with strange emphasis.

Blimey, thought Rosy, hardly daring to look at him, maybe the man in a A Star is Worn had misinterpreted Benedict's intentions.

'I didn't know you cared,' said Jamie flippantly.

'Not me, Jamie. I'm very liberal-minded about what goes on IN or OUT of the closet, but I cannot speak for all . . .' said Benedict in a sinister tone.

But Jamie wasn't about to give their rival the edge by asking what he meant. 'How's Lord Diplock – is your column shaping up?'

Benedict nodded back towards the car park. 'Once you let the dogs out of the pound, you have no control over which direction they run,' he said boorishly.

Tosspot, thought Rosy.

And, with an odd leer, he was off in the direction of the paddock.

'What was that about?' asked Rosy, when he had gone.

'God knows,' replied Jamie. 'The weathergirl on TV this morning forecast that "something nasty this way comes" but I had no idea it would be in the form of Benedict Pierce.'

The rumour went round that the Duchess of York had once again watched the Royal Procession with the *hoi polloi* lining the route through Windsor Great Park. The Queen's set face lightened though when one of her horses won the second race. In an uncertain world it was good to know that breeding and money could still bring happiness.

The royal nag won £50 for Jamie too.

By the emerald pool of a parade ring where he and Rosy were studying the form – the Countess of Salcombe was holding hands with the Bunk Bedder, Darlene Trussock was flushed in lilac, Mary Hawty trotted by on the arm of her solicitor beau, as predicted by the Sword's Secrets column – he turned to her: 'It's all about couples, isn't it.'

'Great observations of the world,' said Rosy.

Jamie hesitated, seeming to get to grips with something. 'I'm sorry about Benedict.'

'Don't be.'

'Actually, I'm not.'

She wondered what he meant by that.

'Old news now,' said Rosy.

'Emma told me.'

'Ah.' She felt tense enough after their encounter with

Benedict without dredging up the whole episode again. And what else had Emma told him?

'And you did pay him back by burning down his bedroom . . .!'

Emma had told him quite a bit, it seemed.

Rosy frowned. 'Look, just don't, all right . . . I feel bad enough.'

'You're far too good for Benedict Pierce.'

'What's that got to do with . . .? You're just saying that.'

'Okay, so I am. But if it makes you feel better . . .'

'Do you always lie to me, Jamie?'

He stared for a moment. 'I have done. No, don't look at me like that. The morning after that night with Benedict . . . I said you looked great – you looked awful.'

'Thanks,' said Rosy heavily.

'He was a bastard. It made me realise—'

'Was?'

'IS a bastard,' said Jamie. 'Trying to use you like that.'

Rosy sighed. 'Goes to show, you never can tell.'

'Great clichés of the world,' grinned Jamie.

She smiled.

He turned her gently towards him and bent his head. When he dropped his mouth on to her lips it felt as if she was standing in a sudden warm pool of sunshine.

'As was that,' said Rosy. 'But I don't care.'

'I'll use it again then,' said Jamie.

Forget Ascot, her veins seemed to be hosting some kind of motor-racing Grand Prix. Like Troilus, she was giddy and expectation whirled her round. It could have been the champagne, of course, but Rosy opted for a more heroic explanation.

The sun stopped sulking and came out to stay. The

vivid crowds passed like a merry-go-round while the gleaming racehorses thundered by. She and Jamie wandered around, now and then hand-in-hand, listening, collecting anecdotes.

As they eventually made their way back to the Bentley, Rosy could feel her eyes were not so much dancing as smooching lasciviously to the last record and imploring the DJ for more.

It was only as Sword and the crowd around him came into sight, that she suddenly remembered what Jamie had said to Honoria. His unbreakable date tonight.

She didn't dare ask.

The glorious golden afternoon stuttered and slowed like a film breaking down.

75 | *A Strange Surprise*

Sword's car park party was still in full swing, as Rosy and Jamie approached. Pearson had brought back a giggle of gossip groupies. Even Benedict was there, giving all the indications of being extremely drunk.

'It's all BALLS!' he shouted at Honoria Peeke, and jabbed a fierce finger towards Framboise for good measure. 'This society business. It's theatre, acting, PEOPLE PRETENDING TO BE WHAT THEY ARE NOT! The money buys their tickets and gets them on the top tables – only to find that the people they came to meet – the aristos and well-connected – are doing the catering and playing in the band!'

Sword smiled benignly at Rosy. Still wearing his dark sunglasses, he was watching the performance with an equanimity that would have been unthinkable six weeks previously. She noticed he was sipping mineral water. It was quite extraordinary, she thought.

'Poor Benedict,' concluded Sword drily. 'He has known adversity in this profession but nothing compared to what has happened today. Apparently he has been unable to locate a decent mirror.'

'How horribly inconvenient,' said Honoria, attempting to assuage both sides.

Rosy had to laugh.

Jamie reappeared at her side with another glass of champagne. 'What do you call a well-balanced social columnist?' he whispered in her ear. She shook her head. 'A person with a chip on both shoulders.'

'That's terrible,' said Rosy.

He clinked her glass.

'And talking of chippiness, here's Brett Trent on his way over,' said Jamie.

Rosy swivelled round. 'I wondered where he'd got to,' she said vaguely. 'I said I'd see him here today.'

The Earl shambled up, hands in pockets. His dark tails were as dusty as his tracksuits usually were. Rosy thought he looked appalling.

'Hey! You made it,' she said. 'Drink?'

Jamie produced a glass and filled it with fizz for him. 'Any luck on the nags?'

'Luck? You're joking.'

'I've lost £12,' said Rosy.

'Well, fuck me sideways. And I never took you for a high roller, Rosy,' said the Earl nastily.

She was about to leave them to it, when Benedict's voice rose even higher.

'And YOU – ' He was pointing at Framboise. 'I don't know who you think you're fooling with this ludicrous charade, Sword! What do you think this is – a remake of *Some Like It Hot*?'

Framboise played it cool. She merely smiled and batted her eyelashes.

'The man of mystery is not who he pretends to be,' cried Benedict. 'And let me tell you now – that tomorrow, in the *Daily Post*, all will be revealed!'

Rosy may not have been sure of herself at that moment,

but she was sure that Brett Trent was behaving oddly again. He was in the same state of brooding twitchiness he'd been in that evening when he came looking for her at home.

He was scratching at his filthy clothes, trembling as he lit one cigarette from the last. He alone of all the party was oblivious to Benedict's antics.

They moved a little away from the others, Rosy standing as safe a distance from him as she could – about four inches off an insult. 'So,' she said, thinking of her clandestine feature on him, 'Do you find that you're treated differently at Ascot as an earl?'

He stared silently.

'Has it made any difference to the kind of parties you're invited to, for example?'

A corrosive sneer. Rosy felt her skin peeling, as much from the feebleness of the question as anything.

'Why do you want to do this story?' asked the Earl, eventually. His insect eyes were black buttons, sunk in their puffy sockets.

Why indeed? Because Schadenfreude was the year's in-word? Because it was more than the man's sad story, it was a positive parable of the times? Because it was her ticket back to real journalism?

Rosy took a breath. 'I thought it might help,' she said.

'Help,' said the Earl, slowly.

Rosy felt reassurance was in order. 'Of course.'

An awkward silence.

'I wonder what you know, Rosy.'

'Know? I . . .' On a personal level, she was seriously beginning to wonder that herself, but this was strictly professional confessional. The worst mistake was to be too proud to ask the obvious.

'What are you saying, exactly, Brett?' she asked.

The Earl's laugh ended on a broken note.

'Who knows. . . .?' he said.

Rosy would never be entirely sure what happened next.

She only took her eyes off him for a second due to the commotion in the main party. Squeals and giggles rang out and there were gruff explosions from Sword and Pearson.

Instinctively Rosy span round – to see that Benedict Pierce had launched himself at Framboise and seized on the vast folds of her watermelon dress. Then he paused for effect as if preparing himself to perform a tablecloth trick.

'Anthony Sword, I now unmask you!' he cried victoriously.

'GIT yer clammy hands off me!' roared Framboise, grabbing in turn at his hair.

And then – abruptly – the pantomime stopped. The triumph froze to nausea on the rival columnist's face as he looked up towards Rosy. Stricken, Benedict was left holding on to Framboise's skirt like a tragic friend who is always the bridesmaid.

Rosy saw the same expression spread to the other faces in front of her, a sickening tableau.

She had no idea what was going on.

'Put it down, you fool,' said Sword, authoritatively.

'Don't do this . . . be sensible, Brett,' said Jamie, clearly rattled.

BRETT??

Rosy turned round slowly. Amid the rainbow colours on the bright field, the Earl of Trent was monochrome. His black eyes were sunk in a chalk white death's head; his frizzy black hair fell over the dusty black coat. One bony white hand was on Rosy's shoulder and he pulled her back. In the other trembling hand, the Earl of Trent held an old-fashioned duelling pistol. It was pointing at her.

Muffled gasps from behind. Jamie started towards them, but was stopped by Sword. The others were a frieze of dropped jaws.

'Brett . . .' said Rosy, voice wavering. Her legs were shaking now.

Sword took off his glasses. 'I'm walking towards you, Brett,' he said as if in a film. 'I'm coming towards you and I want you to give me the gun.'

He took the first tentative steps.

There was a sigh as light as a breeze as Honoria Peeke fainted, crumpling on the grass.

'Stop! Don't come any closer . . .!' cried the Earl, grabbing wildly at Rosy's arm. He clawed at her, pulling her round in front of himself as protection.

Then, in the strange silence, came the first sounds of shooting. The Beast, with appalling sang-froid, had begun to take photographs.

Rosy could scarcely breathe.

'Brett, please! Whatever's wrong, we can put it right . . .' she started.

Sword was still moving slowly towards them. He didn't take his eyes off the pistol. 'Give me the gun, Brett,' he commanded.

'I told, I showed you,' ranted the Earl. 'No one takes me seriously! I can't bear it.' He howled a chilling keen.

The Earl raised the pistol and a shot rang out.

Rosy closed her eyes, unable to look, not daring to feel. Then she heard screaming around her.

The 8th Earl of Trent had raised the pistol to his own temple and fired.

For Sword and his rival Benedict Pierce, it was a horrifying simultaneous exclusive.

76 | *Home, James*

Rosy stayed the grim hour it took for the police to arrive, and then take statements, names of witnesses and photographs. She was shaken, but the drama had been mercifully – almost obscenely – short. The others had rushed to comfort her after Jamie had snatched her back from the body of her assailant as the crowds pressed in.

Through the blur of grey coats and Framboise's pink, she could see the Earl's open mouth, howling silently. Although, once more, the Earl of Trent's handling of his heritage had failed him: the antique pistol required both charge and bullet. In his grand attempt to end it all, Trent had merely loaded and triggered the charge – badly singeing his flowing hair and destroying one modish sideburn.

When he came round on the grass, his first dazed words were, 'Do they have Ascot up here too – or is this Hell?'

It took the arrival of the local constabulary to convince him that he was still very much alive – and liable to face yet more charges, this time under the Possession of Firearms Act.

*

When they could wait no longer, Sword drove his reporters and Framboise back to London. Throughout the afternoon, they had been telephoning Ascot copy back to the newspaper but now the Earl would make headlines yet again.

It was almost midnight by the time they were finished at the *Dispatch*. Rosy, who had sat down straight away with her notebooks and tapes, produced at the best possible time her in-depth interview with the near-deceased – his problems, the despair of his last few days and his alarming lack of elementary gunmanship.

The triumph of Hope over Experience, Sword called it.

'Come on,' said Jamie, 'I'll take you home.'

Rosy nodded gratefully.

In the taxi, she remembered. 'Your date – you missed it,' she said, as casually as she could.

'My what?' said Jamie.

'Your unbreakable date. You told Honoria you had to get back for it.'

'Oh, that,' said Jamie, smiling.

That left her dangling.

'I had to say something to Honoria.'

'Did you have a date?' persisted Rosy, unable to stop herself.

'Mmm?'

'That you didn't make?'

Jamie gave her an enigmatic look. 'If you're asking who she was . . .'

Rosy was at that stage of wondering whether she had really kissed him that day or whether it had all been wishful thinking. She said nothing. Outside the cab window, she watched the fairyland pink and gold twinkle of Albert Bridge slide by in the darkness.

He put a warm hand over hers. 'It wasn't only one woman – at least I hoped not. Unless it was the right woman.'

She obviously wasn't expected to make sense of that.

Sure enough, he explained: 'Promise you won't laugh?' He paused for her reaction. 'You know how everyone always talks about how wonderful the small ads are in *Time Out*. . . . I put my own ad in. I was going to collect the replies.'

Rosy smiled, out of sheer relief. Then she realised.

'So now you've got another new selection of eager women,' she sighed.

'I haven't collected them,' he reminded her.

'What if no one replied?' she teased feebly.

'I appealed to the tender-hearted.'

She was not about to admit that even she had intended to add her name to the capital's massed lonely hearts by replying to one of the magazine's ads. What did that say about their differing personalities, that he put one in, while she merely attempted to answer one? Her letter in reply – she shivered as she realised – had been interrupted by the Earl of Trent turning up on her doorstep. It was still half-written, lying on her bedside table.

'How did you bill yourself?' she asked, 'Out of curiosity.'

He laughed. 'It was very Nineties' Angst, unsure and in need of redirection.'

'Oh,' said Rosy.

Oh no. She just knew.

The taxi ticked up outside her flat.

'It's been quite a day,' said Rosy.

'Day off tomorrow,' said Jamie. He returned her gaze steadily.

'What game are you playing with me, Jamie?'

'No game.'

'C'mon. I know all your moves.'

'Only in theory.'

'You'd better come in then,' said Rosy, heart beginning to pound.

He kissed her expertly on the doorstep. Unwilling to break the spell, it was some minutes before she managed to open the door.

Upstairs, it took half an hour to make some coffee.

'It's even better than I ever imagined,' whispered Rosy, sleepily, breaking off from a kiss that could have curled her hair.

Jamie played with a strand. 'So, you imagined, eh?'

Rosy felt herself flushing.

He held her slightly away from him. 'You are so lovely, Rosy. I can't tell you how much I wanted this to happen.'

'Go on, try,' murmured Rosy. 'But not necessarily in words.'

Later, she came back from the kitchen with the milk and cups she'd forgotten, to find him standing by the mess on the table, shoulders shaking with some private joke. He turned, and in his hand, she saw, was a copy of *Time Out*. Her copy, with a biro ring around the ad she had chosen.

'Directionless Oxbridge Graduate,' he read. 'Looks like you might have found me. . . .'

77 | *That Happy Garden State*

'It wasn't a coincidence, was it?' said Rosy the next day over a breakfast the clock said was lunch.

Emma shrugged. 'I may have told Jamie that you'd mentioned the *Time Out* ads,' she replied cagily. 'Ages ago.'

'I didn't only mean that,' said Rosy. 'The page with the ad circled didn't walk out of my room by itself and prop itself up where anyone could see it.'

'Well . . .'

'Well?'

'It worked, didn't it?'

'Worked? So there was a cunning plan, was there?'

Emma didn't make a very good job of looking innocent.

'Did he really put that ad in?' asked Rosy.

'I don't know.'

'Well I do. I'm sure he didn't – you two have just been having a laugh at my expense. And you so conveniently happened to be out when we got back from Ascot,' said Rosy.

'Okay, okay. Jamie might have called me.'

'He what? He tipped you off that he was coming back here. He was so sure . . .!'

361

She was incredulous.

'Calm down. It wasn't like that. The drama at Ascot was on the news. He rang here to find out if I'd seen it and to let me know you were all right so I could tell your parents.'

Rosy was taken aback. 'Really?'

'Yes.'

'I suppose that was kind. I didn't think—'

'Yes,' said Emma firmly. 'He does care.'

They walked to Bishop's Park, buying all the newspapers on the way. Unpractised, pre-Wimbledon tennis lobs plopped over the netting from the public courts. The Friday afternoon roads filled up with cars struggling optimistically from their own overcrowded patch to someone else's.

They sat on the weedy grass reading, glad to be out of doors in the sunshine.

'Your article on the Earl of Trent – it's very good,' said Emma, thoughtfully.

'You don't have to say that.'

'I know. It's very . . . grounded, the way you deal with his decline, and the warning signs. You let him speak for himself. It's all in the details – the mice in the kitchen, the dust, the Pennywise biscuits.'

'I didn't have to do much,' said Rosy sadly. 'I should have done more. It was all there, in his own words. I'd been seeing him nearly every lunchtime this week. I had it all on tape.'

'That's what makes it so powerful.'

'All he ever wanted was for people to like him and take notice of him, and when they did, it was all too much,' said Rosy.

The *Daily Post*'s coverage was far less comprehensive.

Benedict's piece contained an extraordinary flight of imagination which seemed to imply that Sword had taken to dressing up as Framboise and had gone to Ascot to parade a secret male lover.

Rosy couldn't make head or tail of it. Perhaps Benedict had finally flipped.

Strolling back, Emma at last got around to asking.

'Last night,' she said. 'Did you and Jamie . . .?'

Rosy had expected this for hours. 'Did we what?'

'Rosy! I'm dying to know! Ah . . . sorry . . . I didn't mean . . .'

'It's all right.'

'Come on, tell. Did you?'

Rosy shook her head. 'Of course not.'

'No?'

'If I ever do go to bed with Jamie Raj, it's going to be when I decide, not him. Anyway, it may never happen. I'm not going to be another one of his statistics.'

'Quite,' said Emma. 'So has he called you today?'

'No.'

'And you wish he would.'

Rosy said nothing.

Her heart sank further when they reached the flat and there was no message on the answering machine.

It was six o'clock when the doorbell went.

Emma rushed to her bedroom window.

'It's for yo-ho,' she yelled.

'Who is it?'

Emma laughed. 'I think you'll find it's Directionless . . . managed to find his way here again.'

Rosy joined her and looked out.

Jamie stood on the step clutching an A-Z and a com-

363

pass. He looked up when Rosy yanked open the window.

'Where are you going?' she called down.

'Who knows?' he said. 'We'll find out when we get there. So long as you come with me.'

78 | *Flowers for Mama*

On the way to East Sheen, Framboise's sense of occasion prevailed. She insisted on pulling over outside a florist's shop, then dived inside.

She emerged bearing a monstrous forced and potted hibiscus. 'Flowers for Mama,' came her bassoon voice from within the deep pink profusion.

'It reminds me of a midshipman I once met on a cruise,' said Sword, pushing open the car door for her.

'His broiled British sun tan?'

'He wore a shirt like that when we put in at Honolulu.'

Framboise beamed at the voluptuous plant as she settled it on her knees. 'It may not be suitable for your mother after all.'

'She's seen it all, believe me.'

Sword put the Vauxhall into gear and urged it forward. *She wants to meet you*, he'd told Framboise after the mother-and-son reunion two days after his return from Grasslands Hall.

Framboise had agreed immediately. And for once she had known better than to ask for details of the healing process. Some things – even between them – were best left unsaid.

*

The turning into Fairlawn Avenue was punctuated by her enthusiastic cries.

'Will you lookit those little gardens!' rhapsodised Framboise. 'The English roses and the cute trees – it's like in a kids' book, all laid out neat and square! The little paths! Is this it?'

'It is.' Seen through new eyes, it was odd how he noticed the exuberant afternoon flowers and succulent foliage instead of the dingier corners. A weak scent of new-mown grass made him feel both nostalgic and vaguely penitent as he parked outside Number 2 and led the way.

Eva opened the door in her best tea dress and a restrained array of beads. Her plump powdered face registered a second's surprise and then a broad grin as she welcomed them and the plant inside. 'Talk about Birnam Wood, dears.'

Sword hastily relieved Framboise of the hibiscus. 'Mum, this is Framboise; Framboise, my mother Eva Coutts.'

'Delighted to meet you at last, Framboise.' Eva extended a hand. 'I've heard so much – not from Anthony mind, oh no – well not much anyway – but that little girl ... what's her name now? ... was saying only the other day—'

'Mother!'

'I'm delighted to be here, Mrs Coutts.'

'Eva, dear, to you. Now will you take tea, or something stronger?'

'Tea please.'

They followed her into the sitting room where Framboise gurgled with rapture at Eva's mementoes.

It was going to be all right. Not that he'd ever doubted.

'I had an unexpected visitor the other week,' said Eva, casting around to make sure of her audience. 'Benedict Pierce. Asking all sorts of questions about you, Tony.'

'He what? He came here?' Sword choked on a triangle of cucumber sandwich. 'And you let him in?'

'Softly softly catchee monkey,' intoned Eva.

Sword forced himself to remain calm, but his plate shook in his hand. 'You didn't tell me this, the other evening.'

Eva chewed on her lip. 'We had ... more important things to discuss, dear.'

'Hold it – you said catchee monkey?' interjected Framboise.

Eva smiled. 'I let Benedict in for a nice little chat. Told me all about it, he did. How he was writing a book and wanted me to tell all. Help him, was the way he put it.'

'But how?' Sword was perplexed. 'Who told him? How did he know ...?'

Eva looked to Framboise sheepishly. 'That may have been my fault, dear. I decided I ought to get out and about ... and I met him at a party for that show – what's it called? But look, everything's all right now, isn't it? He's not doing his silly book anymore—'

'How do you know about THAT?' groaned Sword.

Framboise chortled in growing appreciation of Eva's powers.

'Well, it was pretty obvious that the danger had passed when you thought you could come and see your ol' mum again. ...'

'I explained all th—'

But Eva stopped him. 'It wasn't that. Benedict told me who was publishing it. And then I had him banged to rights.'

Sword shook his head. 'You did?' he asked wanly.

'Sylvester of Mega Books, that was right, wasn't it? Unpleasant turn of his, after all the pockets you've lined there with *Sword's Year* ... I've never missed an issue ...'

'You know him?'

'You could say.' She paused for dramatic effect. 'He came to my party – the one I gave to get back at you for ignoring me, when I didn't know ... you know, about your TROUBLE, dear. . . .' This was a nod at discretion.

'It's all right, Mum. Framboise knows it all.'

Eva smiled gratefully.

'Sylvester,' prompted Sword.

'Ooh, yes. He came to my party. Made a right spectacle of himself too, with his trousers round his head like a turban, then 'ad two poor girls in my potting shed. Not that he'd want his new young wife to find out what kind of business meeting he was having so late. . . .'

'You mean—' Sword shot a glance at Framboise. She was convulsed with silent laughter, mid-muffin.

'A bit of coercion and blackmail always livens up the empty hours,' admitted Eva, studying her scarlet fingernails disingenuously. 'There's little enough sex, rage and sin around these days, so what there is, you have to make it go a long way, eh?'

'It was you? You blackmailed Sylvester?'

'Ugly word, dear. As they say in the films. There's always a nice way of putting things. . . .'

'You stopped the book.' Sword felt the pieces slip into place.

'I am your mother, dear, after all's said and done.'

'But—'

368

'I don't like to be ignored, dear. I wanted to hurt you. Show you I could still be a force . . . and all the time I didn't know the terrible time you were having. I feel so guilty now . . . I didn't know what to do. . . .'

'And Rosy – she came to the party. I saw her. What does she know?'

Eva shrugged and got up. Her cheeks were flaming pink. 'She's a bright girl. She knows which side her bread's buttered.'

Sword looked to Framboise, who was suddenly serious. 'Go on then,' she said. 'Give your mom a hug.'

The tea was pushed to one side, and the gin cracked open.

'I still can't believe Benedict Pierce had the nerve to come here,' fumed Sword. 'I mean, does HE know?'

'Oh, I don't think so, dear. No. Not apart from me giving you stories, that is. I think – that little girl . . . in the show . . . Emily! . . . Emily told him that.'

'You're sure about that?'

'There's no one knows. Apart from Framboise now, of course.' Eva raised her glass to their new confidante.

'An' she ain't sayin'!' hammed Framboise.

'Anyhow,' continued Eva. 'There's every possibility that Benedict may be equally ashamed of his mother.'

'I'm not!' sighed Sword. 'For the umpteenth time . . . but you must realise how it would look—'

'With mother on the game, I know.' Eva pursed her lips. 'My parties and escorting were always more select than that, as you well know.'

'Or DIDN'T know. Which was how I wanted to KEEP it—'

The long-running battle was about to resume.

'Ehem,' interrupted Framboise. 'Benedict's mother. What were you saying?'

Eva gathered herself. 'The penny dropped when he – Benedict – was standing in my hall. That confused but determined look on his face – it was the spit of her when she used to dry onstage. That and the ASM's beaky nose. And after I saw her pestering him at the show party . . . well it had to be.'

'What on earth are you on about now?'

'Bea Goff,' said Eva. 'I'll stake my reputation – well, make that my suggestive telegram from Orson Welles – on it.'

'On what?' cried Sword and Framboise together.

'That Bea Goff is Benedict's mother.'

79 | First Night

After almost a week without a blonde lunch for Jamie, Rosy was ready to be convinced. Or rather, she was desperate to be convinced.

She had gone out with him every night from work – a first night here, a PR launch there – and she had never enjoyed herself more.

They were having supper at Soho Soho after a film preview, holding hands over the brasserie's bruschetta and roast Mediterranean vegetables.

'This could be the Zanzibar of the Nineties,' observed Jamie, taking in the rough-painted walls, and stylised clientele eating Italian peasant food. There was an outbreak of ad-persons' glasses in one corner and a rash of aubergine velvet jackets on several nearby tables.

'Sorry?' said Rosy.

'The place which sums up an era. In the Seventies, Zanzibar was the seminal meeting place – Zanzibar, London, that is. It was a club in Covent Garden. When you think back to wide lapels and flares as a way of life rather than a fashion statement, Zanzibar is where you picture it.'

'But—' Rosy's brain ticked over. The way Jamie had of declaring utter rubbish so confidently really got to her. He really ought to write more Sunday-paper style pieces. But then again, she realised, perhaps that WAS his attraction. 'You can only have been at prep school in the Travolta years!'

'I was always advanced for my age.'

'I can imagine. So what was the place of the Eighties then?'

Jamie thought for a second.

'Well . . . The Oriel in Sloane Square would cover the early part.'

'The Sloane Ranger mania, you mean.'

'Exactly. Then after that, somewhere in the City, I suppose – one of the champagne bars, Ball Brothers perhaps. Or for power lunches . . . the Savoy, the Connaught. . . .'

Rosy smirked. 'Gets complicated, doesn't it, the more you know about something firsthand. Less easy to pigeon-hole,' she said with a tease in her voice.

'Okay, okay. Maybe I like complicated.'

'Talking of which . . . did *you* know that Eva Coutts was Sword's mother?' she asked. The master gossip had dropped that bombshell over lunch.

'We-ll, to be honest . . . no. Bizarre, the whole business.'

'Hmm.'

'You never had any suspicions about Eva?'

'Not any more than any other daft old bat who phones with stories – why should I?'

'Oh, nothing. I mean, I didn't think you knew. You'd never said, and neither did Pearson.'

'You went to that party of hers,' remembered Jamie. 'You never did say exactly what that was like.'

For whatever reason, a rare burst of discretion found her lips sealed. 'Er, yes. I, um, I can't really recall now ... so many parties under the bridge since, you know.' She felt a surge of what she fervently hoped was sophistication. 'So ... what made him suddenly decide to say now, after all these years?'

Jamie frowned. 'He's been out of character ever since he got back from Grasslands.'

'Out of character?'

'Pleasant. Jolly. Chatty. All on a regular basis.'

'This is true.'

They drank their Pinot Grigio in silence for a moment.

'Going back to complicated ...' began Rosy. 'What about in the personal sense, for you?'

He looked at her questioningly.

'In the blonde sense,' she added.

'I wouldn't call that complicated. Far from it.'

'But that's what you want.'

'Not necessarily,' he replied.

'Oh?'

'Not that you'd believe me if I told you what I really want.'

'Oh, I probably would,' said Rosy. 'That's the trouble.'

Jamie slipped his hand on to her bare forearm. His touch was warm and light as he began lazily to stroke her skin. 'You're different, Rosy.'

She bit back a smart retort. For once, maybe she would try taking a risk without hiding behind the verbal self-defence.

They walked arm-in-arm through the neon-lit streets. High above the blazing signs was the biggest cliché of them all in the shape of a silver moon. When Jamie hailed a cab and ordered it to Beaufort Street she made no murmur of protest. He kissed her thoroughly all the way back to Chelsea.

373

Inside his flat, she was surprised how easy it was to put out of mind all thoughts of the other women he must have brought here. Jamie switched on a couple of dim lamps to reveal a vast brocaded sofa dominating the room and rich red rugs. The walls were covered with dark oil paintings.

Subtle notes she recognised as Fauré filled the tension in the air. For an eternity she stood uncertainly. Then he came over and put his arm tenderly around her waist. 'Are you sure?'

Rosy nodded, not wanting to break the spell.

She was sure he can't have had to ask all his women that.

At close range his eyes were darker and softer than she had ever seen them. His full lips were velvet as he bent to nuzzle her neck. Deftly, he began to undo the buttons on the front of her dress.

'I've wanted this for so long,' he said as he led her gently to the sofa.

'Oh,' said Rosy, 'so I really am different from the others.'

With infinite tenderness he kissed one breast.

Afterwards, when her whole body was liquid gold inside, she closed her eyes with pleasure and sadness. Lying next to her, he looked straight ahead like a beautiful boy king on a tomb.

He doesn't know what to say to me now, she panicked. She lay still, sure he could feel her heart pumping.

'Rosy ...' he said at last, turning to her.

How would he tell her it had been lovely but that's all ...?

'I ... this is going to sound so hack ... but I think I love you, Rosy.'

374

80 | *Party Conversation*

The room was painted snow white. Nan Purchase's idea was for a conceptual salon, a blank stage where the guests would impose their own scenario. For this party – her first – the only concession was a black baby grand at which Framboise Duprée, the toast of the town, was singing.

Conversation rose.

'Benedict, do you know what this party is for?'

'The invitations didn't give a cause. For once, Honoria, we are enjoying the effect without the cause.'

'I'm sorry?'

'No, you don't have to be. This is a party party.'

'How very old-fashioned. Are you sure?'

'As sure as I can be.'

'Only, on the *Prattler*, one absolutely has to get things right.'

'Hmm.'

'This place seems terribly familiar.'

'The Earl of Trent held his Green Countdown party here. He made rather more effort with the decorations.'

'So he did.'

'Poor Brett, having to sell out to Mrs Purchase. Mind you, we saw it coming.'

'How so?'

'What did I tell you . . . the Curse of *Ciao!*'

'There's no need to be vulgar, Benedict. Tell me, who's that over there?'

'Where? The woman, you mean?'

'The one wearing clown's lipstick and all those dreadful beads.'

'Oh, her . . . I don't know.'

'Look, Sword's going over to talk to her now.'

'I wish I could help you, Honoria, but where Sword's concerned, I am, as they say, lying doggo.'

'I was going to ask you about that. After Ascot. Your mention of Sword was rather baffling. . . .'

'What's the matter, darling?'

'It's ludicrous, isn't it, how parties still always make me nervous . . . although tonight maybe I'm trembly for another reason. . . .'

'You look gorgeous in that dress. Very Jean Shrimpton.'

'Thanks. Sandie Shaw, actually. I got it at A Star Is Worn.'

'It makes me want to do unspeakable Sixties' things.'

'What, swimming strokes on the dance floor or swearing you've got high on a joss stick?'

'Come, come . . .'

'I thought I did, last night.'

'I'm sure of it.'

'Did we do the right thing?'

'It was more than all right for me. How was it for you?'

'You know that wasn't what I meant. Working together, and all . . .'

'You have proved the biggest revelation of them all.'

376

'Are you ever serious?'

'About you, I am.'

'I may as well tell you, then. I've been offered a job in Features. They told me this afternoon.'

'Congratulations. Are you going to take it?'

'I might. To get away from you ... for the best possible reasons.'

'Sword would be devastated to lose you.'

'And you?'

'Maybe we could slip away upstairs and I could let you know. . . .'

'Well, it is a party. . . .'

'It is now, Rosy.'

'Ah! Fartly-Abbott!'

'Nearly. It's pronounced Farting-About.'

'Oh. I thought that was a joke.'

'Not for me, it isn't. And you, I recognise your face.'

'Sebastian Hawthorne. Of the *Evening News*. I'm on the Diary.'

'So, what's the gossip?'

'Oh, you know ... in fact you probably do. It's my job to ask you that.'

'So it is. Let's see. The Earl of Trent's dead, shot himself at the races.'

'No!'

'True. I heard it from a girl, who heard it from a chap, whose mother got it from the horse's mouth.'

'Not one of the racehorses? Hang on, let me scribble this down. . . .'

'Sir Philip?'

'Ye-es.'

'Max. Of Maximum Publicity.'

'Indeed?'

'A little bird told me—'

'Not a certain leggy gameshow hostess?'

'The very one, Sir Philip. The lovely Danielle. Ninety-two per cent of *Sunday People* readers polled said you should have done the business, by the way.'

'Hmm.'

'She suggested you might benefit from some professional help in the publicity game.'

'Did she indeed. How much did she make in the end, from our story?'

'Money? Enough. Exposure, inestimable.'

'So ... Max, where does that leave me?'

'Let's see ... the target of an orchestrated dirty tricks campaign, Sir Philip?'

'It has a certain ring to it.'

'It's a classic of our times.'

'And you can see it as a "Let-me-make-the-situation-perfectly-clear situation"?'

'Professionally handled, we could be on to a winner.'

'Tell me more, Max. . . .'

'That was wonderful, Framboise. I love that song, especially the bit that goes, "What a break, for Heaven's sake ..." '

'Ah, one of the lovebirds!'

'Um ... how do you know ...?'

'Don't give me that, Rosy honey. No one keeps anything from Framboise. It's written all over your face – and that Jamie Raj is one devastatin' man.'

'He is, isn't he. I'll never be able to keep him, of course, but you know what? For once, what the hell! I'm living for today.'

'We'll see ... I have a feeling about this.'

'Do, please! Framboise.'

'That's me.'

'I must ask you ... you and Sword?'

'Me? Now, Rosy ...'

'Yes?'

'Let's say, I'm keeping mum on this one. Now git on ... don't keep Jamie waiting too long upstairs.'

'Benedict!'

'Bea ...'

'No – don't go ...! I read your column every day. You're always writing about sons and daughters of the famous. It must mean something. . . .'

'It means you can't get the bloody celebrities themselves to talk to you.'

'Nothing to do with a coded call for a family reunion? Oh, my dear, how you must have suffered!'

'Look, this has all been rather a shock.'

'My poor baby!'

'I'm afraid I'm going to need some time, you know, to think it over. . . .'

'I want you to know I shall always be here for you.'

'Tony, love! Give us a kiss.'

'You look well, Mum – though I wish you'd stop giving Benedict over there those disgusting winks. Red rag to a maddened bullshitter ...'

'Ooh, I couldn't resist. You know me, don't get out much these days, and, well, what a lark it's been! All for the best and that. I haven't had so much fun since ... that film with ... ooh, you know ... the one with the cleft chin, you've written about him ... Sean Connery. It's quite made up for lack of sex, rage and sin lately.'

'You don't do so badly.'

'And you . . . aren't you a sight for sore eyes! And so thin! Are you eating properly again, you were always such a good eater . . .?'

'Mum . . .!'

'I can't help it, a mother worries. . . .'

'Mum, my eating has never been better – and my health has astounded the quacks. No need to worry now.'

'Ooh, that is good to hear. Back to your old self again.'

'Not exactly. But normal service has been resumed.'

'In that case, I might as well mention it now before I toddle off home . . . that little girl . . . mmm, what's her name, the one who used to go out with the MP . . . you know, they went on a lovely holiday . . .'

It was party night, as always.